Weird Tales

Vol. I of II

I0636494

Weird Tales

Vol. I OF *II*

E.T.A. HOFFMANN

Triaslated by J.T. BEALBY

ÆGYPAN PRESS

This text from the 1885 Charles Scribner's Sons (New York)
edition.

Special thanks to Charles Bowen and the Online Distributed
Proofreading Team (which can be found at
http://www.pgdp.net).

Special thanks also to The Internet Archive, which can be
found at http://www.archive.org/details/weirdtales00unkn-
goog

Weird Tales, Vol. I
A publication of
ÆGYPAN PRESS

www.aegypan.com

Table of Contents

The Cremona Violin

Councilor Krespel was one of the strangest, oddest men I ever met with in my life. When I went to live in H—— for a time the whole town was full of talk about him, as he happened to be just then in the midst of one of the very craziest of his schemes. Krespel had the reputation of being both a clever, learn lawyer and a skillful diplomatist. One of the reigning princes of Germany — not, however, one of the most powerful — had appealed to him for assistance in drawing up a memorial, which he was desirous of presenting at the Imperial Court with the view of furthering his legitimate claims upon a certain strip of territory. The project was crowned with the happiest success; and as Krespel had once complained that he could never find a dwelling sufficiently comfortable to suit him, the prince, to reward him for the memorial, undertook to defray the cost of building a house which Krespel might erect just as he pleased. Moreover, the prince was willing to purchase any site that he should fancy. This offer, however, the Councilor would not accept; he insisted that the house should be built in his garden, situated in a very beautiful neighborhood outside the town-walls. So he bought all kinds of materials and had them carted out. Then he might have been seen day after day, attired in his curious garments (which he had made himself according to certain fixed rules of his own), slacking the lime, riddling the sand, packing up the bricks and stones in regular heaps, and so on. All this he did without once consulting an architect or thinking about a plan. One fine day, however, he went to an experienced builder of the town and requested him to be in his garden at daybreak the next morning, with all his journeymen and apprentices, and a large body of laborers, &c., to build him his house. Naturally the builder asked for the architect's plan, and was not a little astonished when Krespel replied that none was needed, and that things would turn out all right in the end, just as he wanted them. Next morning, when the builder and his men came to the place, they found a trench drawn out in the shape of an exact square; and Krespel said, "Here's where you must lay the foundations; then carry up the walls until I say they are high enough." "Without windows and doors, and without partition walls?" broke in the builder, as if alarmed at Krespel's mad folly. "Do what I tell you, my dear sir," replied the Councilor quite calmly; "leave the rest to me; it will be all right." It was only the promise of high pay that could induce the builder to proceed with the ridiculous building; but none has ever been erected under merrier circumstances. As there was an abundant supply of food and drink, the workmen never left their work; and amidst their continuous laughter the four walls were run up with incredible quickness, until one day Krespel cried, "Stop!" Then the workmen, laying down trowel and hammer, came down from the scaffoldings and gathered round Krespel in a circle, whilst every laughing face was asking, "Well, and what now?" "Make way!" cried Krespel; and then running to one end of the garden, he strode slowly towards the square of brick-work. When he came close to the wall he shook his head in a dissatisfied manner, ran to the other end of the garden, again strode slowly towards the brick-work square, and proceeded to act as before. These tactics he pursued several times, until at length, running his sharp nose hard against the wall, he cried, "Come here, come here, men! break me a door in here! Here's where I want a door made!" He gave the exact dimensions in feet and inches, and they did as he bid them. Then he stepped inside the structure, and smiled with satisfaction as the builder remarked that the walls were just the height of a good two-storeyed house. Krespel walked thoughtfully backwards and forwards across the space within, the bricklayers behind him with hammers and picks, and wherever he cried, "Make a window here, six feet high by four feet broad!" "There a little window, three feet by two!" a hole was made in a trice.

It was at this stage of the proceedings that I came to H——; and it was highly amusing to see how hundreds of people stood round about the garden and raised a loud shout whenever the stones flew out and a new window appeared where nobody had for a moment expected it. And in the same manner Krespel proceeded with the buildings and fittings of the rest of the house, and with all the work necessary to that end; everything had to be done on the spot in accordance with the instructions which the Councilor gave from time to time. However, the absurdity of the whole business, the growing conviction that things would in the end turn out better than might have been expected, but above all, Krespel's generosity — which indeed cost him nothing — kept them all in good-humor. Thus were the difficulties overcome which necessarily arose out of this eccentric way of building, and in a short time there was a completely finished house, its outside, indeed, presenting a most extraordinary appearance, no two windows, &c., being alike, but on the other hand the interior arrangements suggested a peculiar feeling of comfort. All who entered the house bore witness to the truth of this; and I too experienced it myself when I was taken in by Krespel after I had become more intimate with him. For hitherto I had not exchanged a word with this eccentric man; his building had occupied him so much that he had not even once been to Professor M——'s to dinner, as he was in the habit of going on Tuesdays. Indeed, in reply to a special invitation, he sent word that he should not set foot over the threshold before the house-warming of his new building took place. All his friends and acquaintances, therefore, confidently looked forward to a great banquet; but Krespel invited nobody except the masters, journeymen, apprentices, and laborers who had built the house. He entertained them with the choicest viands: bricklayer's apprentices devoured partridge pies regardless of consequences; young joiners polished off roast pheasants with the greatest success; whilst hungry laborers helped themselves for once to the choicest morsels of *truffes fricassées*. In the evening their wives and daughters came, and there was a great ball. After waltzing a short while with the wives of the masters, Krespel sat down amongst the town-musicians, took a violin in his hand, and directed the orchestra until daylight.

On the Tuesday after this festival, which exhibited Councilor Krespel in the character of a friend of the people, I at length saw him appear, to my no little joy, at Professor M——'s. Anything more strange and fantastic than Krespel's behavior it would be impossible to find. He was so stiff and awkward in his movements, that he looked every moment as if he would run up against something or do some damage. But he did not; and the lady of the house seemed to be well aware that he would not, for she did not grow a shade paler when he rushed with heavy steps round a table crowded with beautiful cups, or when he manœuvred near a large mirror that reached down to the floor, or even when he seized a flower-pot of beautifully painted porcelain and swung it round in the air as if desirous of making its colors play. Moreover, before dinner he subjected everything in the Professor's room to a most minute examination; he also took down a picture from the wall and hung it up again, standing on one of the cushioned chairs to do so. At the same time he talked a good deal and vehemently; at one time his thoughts kept leaping, as it were, from one subject to another (this was most conspicuous during dinner); at another, he was unable to have done with an idea; seizing upon it again and again, he gave it all sorts of wonderful twists and turns, and couldn't get back into the ordinary track until something else took hold of his fancy. Sometimes his voice was rough and harsh and screeching, and sometimes it was low and drawling and singing; but at no time did it harmonize with what he was talking about. Music was the subject of conversation; the praises of a new composer were being sung, when Krespel, smiling, said in his low singing tones, "I wish the devil with his pitchfork would hurl that atrocious garbler of music millions of fathoms down to the bottomless pit of hell!" Then he burst out passionately and wildly, "She is an angel of heaven, nothing but pure God-given music! — the paragon and queen of song!" — and tears stood in his eyes. To understand this, we had to go back to a celebrated *artiste,* who had been the subject of conversation an hour before.

Just at this time a roast hare was on the table; I noticed that Krespel carefully removed every particle of meat from the bones on his plate, and was most particular in his inquiries after the hare's feet; these the Professor's little five-year-old daughter now brought to him with a very pretty smile. Besides, the children had cast many friendly glances towards Krespel during dinner; now they rose and drew nearer to him, but not without signs of timorous awe. What's the meaning of that? thought I to myself. Dessert was brought in; then the Councilor took a little box from his pocket, in which he had a miniature lathe of steel. This he immediately screwed fast to the table, and turning the bones with incredible skill and rapidity, he made all sorts of little fancy boxes and balls, which the children received with cries of delight. Just as we were rising from table, the Professor's niece asked, "And what is our Antonia doing?" Krespel's face was like that of one who has bitten of a sour orange and wants to look as if it were a sweet one; but this expression soon changed into the likeness of a hideous mask, whilst he laughed behind it with downright bitter, fierce, and as it seemed to me, satanic scorn. "Our Antonia? our dear Antonia?" he asked in his drawling, disagreeable singing way. The Professor hastened to intervene; in the reproving glance which he gave his niece I read that she had touched a point likely to stir up unpleasant memories in Krespel's heart. "How are you getting on with your violins?" interposed the Professor in a jovial manner, taking the Councilor by both hands. Then Krespel's countenance cleared up, and with a firm voice he replied, "Capitally, Professor; you recollect my telling you of the lucky chance which threw that splendid Amati* into my hands. Well, I've only cut it open today — not before today. I hope Antonia has carefully taken the rest of it to pieces." "Antonia is a good child," remarked the Professor. "Yes, indeed, that she is," cried the Councilor, whisking himself round; then, seizing his hat and stick, he hastily rushed out of the room. I saw in the mirror how that tears were standing in his eyes.

* The Amati were a celebrated family of violin-makers of the sixteenth
  and seventeenth centuries, belonging to Cremona in Italy. They form
  the connecting-link between the Brescian school of makers and the
  greatest of all makers, Straduarius and Guanerius.

As soon as the Councilor was gone, I at once urged the
Professor to explain to me what Krespel had to do with
violins, and particularly with Antonia. "Well," replied the
Professor, "not only is the Councilor a remarkably eccentric
fellow altogether, but he practices violin-making in his own
crack-brained way." "Violin-making!" I exclaimed, perfectly
astonished. "Yes," continued the Professor, "according to the
judgment of men who understand the thing, Krespel makes
the very best violins that can be found nowadays; formerly
he would frequently let other people play on those in which
he had been especially successful, but that's been all over and
done with now for a long time. As soon as he has finished a
violin he plays on it himself for one or two hours, with very
remarkable power and with the most exquisite expression,
then he hangs it up beside the rest, and never touches it again
or suffers anybody else to touch it. If a violin by any of the
eminent old masters is hunted up anywhere, the Councilor
buys it immediately, no matter what the price put upon it.
But he plays it as he does his own violins, only once; then he
takes it to pieces in order to examine closely its inner structure, and should he fancy he hasn't found exactly what he
sought for, he in a pet throws the pieces into a big chest,
which is already full of the remains of broken violins." "But
who and what is Antonia?" I inquired, hastily and impetu-
ously. "Well, now, that," continued the Professor, "that is a
thing which might very well make me conceive an unconquerable aversion to the Councilor, were I not convinced that
there is some peculiar secret behind it, for he is such a
good-natured fellow at bottom as to be sometimes guilty of
weakness. When he came to H—— several years ago, he led
the life of an anchorite, along with an old housekeeper, in
—— Street. Soon, by his oddities, he excited the curiosity of
his neighbors; and immediately he became aware of this, he
sought and made acquaintances. Not only in my house but
everywhere we became so accustomed to him that he grew to
be indispensable. In spite of his rude exterior, even the
children liked him, without ever proving a nuisance to him;
for notwithstanding all their friendly passages together, they
always retained a certain timorous awe of him, which secured
him against all overfamiliarity. You have today had an exam-

ple of the way in which he wins their hearts by his ready skill in various things. We all took him at first for a crusty old bachelor, and he never contradicted us. After he had been living here some time, he went away, nobody knew where, and returned at the end of some months. The evening following his return his windows were lit up to an unusual extent! this alone was sufficient to arouse his neighbors' attention, and they soon heard the surpassingly beautiful voice of a female singing to the accompaniment of a piano. Then the music of a violin was heard chiming in and entering upon a keen ardent contest with the voice. They knew at once that the player was the Councilor. I myself mixed in the large crowd which had gathered in front of his house to listen to this extraordinary concert; and I must confess that, beside this voice and the peculiar, deep, soul-stirring impression which the execution made upon me, the singing of the most celebrated *artistes* whom I had ever heard seemed to me feeble and void of expression. Until then I had had no conception of such long-sustained notes, of such nightingale trills, of such undulations of musical sound, of such swelling up to the strength of organ-notes, of such dying away to the faintest whisper. There was not one whom the sweet witchery did not enthral; and when the singer ceased, nothing but soft sighs broke the impressive silence. Somewhere about midnight the Councilor was heard talking violently, and another male voice seemed, to judge from the tones, to be reproaching him, whilst at intervals the broken words of a sobbing girl could be detected.

"The Councilor continued to shout with increasing violence, until he fell into that drawling, singing way that you know. He was interrupted by a loud scream from the girl, and then all was as still as death. Suddenly a loud racket was heard on the stairs; a young man rushed out sobbing, threw himself into a post-chaise which stood below, and drove rapidly away. The next day the Councilor was very cheerful, and nobody had the courage to question him about the events of the previous night. But on inquiring of the housekeeper, we gathered that the Councilor had brought home with him an extraordinarily pretty young lady whom he called Antonia, and she it was who had sung so beautifully. A young man also had come along with them; he had treated Antonia very tenderly, and must evidently have been her betrothed. But he, since the Councilor peremptorily insisted on it, had had to go away again in a hurry. What the relations between Antonia and the Councilor are has remained until now a secret, but this much is certain, that he tyrannises over the poor girl in the most hateful fashion. He watches her as Doctor Bartholo watches his ward in the *Barber of Seville*; she hardly dare show herself at the window; and if, yielding now and again to her earnest entreaties, he takes her into society, he follows her with Argus' eyes, and will on no account suffer a musical note to be sounded, far less let Antonia sing — indeed, she is not permitted to sing in his own house. Antonia's singing on that memorable night, has, therefore, come to be regarded by the townspeople in the light of a tradition of some marvelous wonder that suffices to stir the heart and the fancy; and even those who did not hear it often exclaim, whenever any other singer attempts to display her powers in the place, 'What sort of a wretched squeaking do you call that? Nobody but Antonia knows how to sing.'"

Having a singular weakness for such like fantastic histories, I found it necessary, as may easily be imagined, to make Antonia's acquaintance. I had myself often enough heard the popular sayings about her singing, but had never imagined that that exquisite *artiste* was living in the place, held a captive in the bonds of this eccentric Krespel like the victim of a tyrannous sorcerer. Naturally enough I heard in my dreams on the following night Antonia's marvelous voice, and as she besought me in the most touching manner in a glorious *adagio* movement (very ridiculously it seemed to me, as if I had composed it myself) to save her, I soon resolved, like a second Astolpho,* to penetrate into Krespel's house, as if into another Alcina's magic castle, and deliver the queen of song from her ignominious fetters.

It all came about in a different way from what I had expected; I had seen the Councilor scarcely more than two or

---

* A reference to Ariosto's *Orlando Furioso*. Astolpho, an English cousin of Orlando, was a great boaster, but generous, courteous, gay, and remarkably handsome; he was carried to Alcina's island on the back of a whale.

three times, and eagerly discussed with him the best method of constructing violins, when he invited me to call and see him. I did so; and he showed me his treasures of violins. There were fully thirty of them hanging up in a closet; one amongst them bore conspicuously all the marks of great antiquity (a carved lion's head, &c.), and, hung up higher than the rest and surmounted by a crown of flowers, it seemed to exercise a queenly supremacy over them. "This violin," said Krespel, on my making some inquiry relative to it, "this violin is a very remarkable and curious specimen of the work of some unknown master, probably of Tartini's* age. I am perfectly convinced that there is something especially exceptional in its inner construction, and that, if I took it to pieces, a secret would be revealed to me which I have long been seeking to discover, but — laugh at me if you like — this senseless thing which only gives signs of life and sound as I make it, often speaks to me in a strange way of itself. The first time I played upon it I somehow fancied that I was only the magnetiser who has the power of moving his subject to reveal of his own accord in words the visions of his inner nature. Don't go away with the belief that I am such a fool as to attach even the slightest importance to such fantastic notions, and yet it's certainly strange that I could never prevail upon myself to cut open that dumb lifeless thing there. I am very pleased now that I have not cut it open, for since Antonia has been with me I sometimes play to her upon this violin. For Antonia is fond of it — very fond of it." As the Councilor uttered these words with visible signs of emotion, I felt encouraged to hazard the question, "Will you not play it to me, Councilor." Krespel made a wry face, and falling into his drawling, singing way, said, "No, my good sir!" and that was an end of the matter. Then I had to look at all sorts of rare curiosities, the greater part of them childish trifles; at last thrusting his arm into a chest, he brought out a folded piece

---

* Giuseppe Tartini, born in 1692, died in 1770; was one of the most celebrated violinists of the eighteenth century, and the discoverer (in 1714) of "resultant tones," or "Tartini's tones" as they are frequently called. Most of his life was spent at Padua. He did much to advance the art of the violinist, both by his compositions for that instrument as well as by his treatise on its capabilities.

of paper, which he pressed into my hand, adding solemnly, "You are a lover of art; take this present as a priceless memento, which you must value at all times above everything else." Therewith he took me by the shoulders and gently pushed me towards the door, embracing me on the threshold. That is to say, I was in a symbolical manner virtually kicked out of doors. Unfolding the paper, I found a piece of a first string of a violin about an eighth of an inch in length, with the words, "A piece of the treble string with which the deceased Staraitz* strung his violin for the last concert at which he ever played."

This summary dismissal at mention of Antonia's name led me to infer that I should never see her; but I was mistaken, for on my second visit to the Councilor's I found her in his room, assisting him to put a violin together. At first sight Antonia did not make a strong impression; but soon I found it impossible to tear myself away from her blue eyes, her sweet rosy lips, her uncommonly graceful, lovely form. She was very pale; but a shrewd remark or a merry sally would call up a winning smile on her face and suffuse her cheeks with a deep burning flush, which, however, soon faded away to a faint rosy glow. My conversation with her was quite unconstrained, and yet I saw nothing whatever of the Arguslike watchings on Krespel's part which the Professor had imputed to him; on the contrary, his behavior moved along the customary lines, nay, he even seemed to approve of my conversation with Antonia. So I often stepped in to see the Councilor; and as we became accustomed to each other's society, a singular feeling of homeliness, taking possession of our little circle of three, filled our hearts with inward happiness. I still continued to derive exquisite enjoyment from the Councilor's strange crotchets and oddities; but it was of course Antonia's irresistible charms alone which attracted me, and led me to put up with a good deal which I should otherwise, in the frame of mind in which I then was, have impatiently shunned. For it only too often happened that in the Councilor's characteristic extravagance there was mingled much

* This was the name of a well-known musical family from Bohemia. Karl Stamitz is the one here possibly meant, since he died about eighteen or twenty years previous to the publication of this tale.

that was dull and tiresome; and it was in a special degree irritating to me that, as often as I turned the conversation upon music, and particularly upon singing, he was sure to interrupt me, with that sardonic smile upon his face and those repulsive singing tones of his, by some remark of a quite opposite tendency, very often of a commonplace character. From the great distress which at such times Antonia's glances betrayed, I perceived that he only did it to deprive me of a pretext for calling upon her for a song. But I didn't relinquish my design. The hindrances which the Councilor threw in my way only strengthened my resolution to overcome them; I must hear Antonia sing if I was not to pine away in reveries and dim aspirations for want of hearing her.

One evening Krespel was in an uncommonly good humor; he had been taking an old Cremona violin to pieces, and had discovered that the sound-post was fixed half a line more obliquely than usual — an important discovery! one of incalculable advantage in the practical work of making violins! I succeeded in setting him off at full speed on his hobby of the true art of violin-playing. Mention of the way in which the old masters picked up their dexterity in execution from really great singers (which was what Krespel happened just then to be expatiating upon), naturally paved the way for the remark that now the practice was the exact opposite of this, the vocal score erroneously following the affected and abrupt transitions and rapid scaling of the instrumentalists. "What is more nonsensical," I cried, leaping from my chair, running to the piano, and opening it quickly, "what is more nonsensical than such an execrable style as this, which, far from being music, is much more like the noise of peas rolling across the floor?" At the same time I sang several of the modern *fermatas*, which rush up and down and hum like a well-spun peg-top, striking a few villainous chords by way of accompaniment Krespel laughed outrageously and screamed, "Ha! ha! methinks I hear our German-Italians or our Italian-Germans struggling with an aria from Pucitta,* or Portogallo,† or some

---

* Vincenzo Pucitta (1778-1861) was an Italian opera composer, whose music "shows great facility, but no invention." He also wrote several songs.

† Il Portogallo was the Italian sobriquet of a Portuguese musician named

other *Maestro di capella,* or rather *schiavo d'un primo uomo.*꘎
Now, thought I, now's the time; so turning to Antonia, I
remarked, "Antonia knows nothing of such singing as that,
I believe?" At the same time I struck up one of old Leonardo
Leo's† beautiful soul-stirring songs. Then Antonia's cheeks
glowed; heavenly radiance sparkled in her eyes, which grew
full of reawakened inspiration; she hastened to the piano; she
opened her lips; but at that very moment Krespel pushed her
away, grasped me by the shoulders, and with a shriek that
rose up to a tenor pitch, cried, "My son — my son — my son!"
And then he immediately went on, singing very softly, and
grasping my hand with a bow that was the pink of politeness,
"In very truth, my esteemed and honorable student-friend, in
very truth it would be a violation of the codes of social
intercourse, as well as of all good manners, were I to express
aloud and in a stirring way my wish that here, on this very
spot, the devil from hell would softly break your neck with
his burning claws, and so in a sense make short work of you;
but, setting that aside, you must acknowledge, my dearest
friend, that it is rapidly growing dark, and there are no lamps
burning tonight so that, even though I did not kick you
downstairs at once, your darling limbs might still run a risk
of suffering damage. Go home by all means; and cherish a
kind remembrance of your faithful friend, if it should happen that you never, — pray, understand me, — if you should
never see him in his own house again." Therewith he embraced me, and, still keeping fast hold of me, turned with me
slowly towards the door, so that I could not get another single
look at Antonia.

Of course it is plain enough that in my position I couldn't
thrash the Councilor, though that is what he really deserved.

Mark Anthony Simâo (1763-1829). He lived alternately in Italy and
Portugal, and wrote several operas.

* Literally, "The slave of a *primo uomo,*" *primo uomo* being the masculine
form corresponding to *prima donna,* that is, a singer of hero's parts in
operatic music. At one time also female parts were sung and acted by
men or boys.

† Leonardo Leo, the chief Neapolitan representative of Italian music in
the first part of the eighteenth century, and author of more than forty
operas and nearly one hundred compositions for the Church.

The Professor enjoyed a good laugh at my expense, and assured me that I had ruined forever all hopes of retaining the Councilor's friendship. Antonia was too dear to me, I might say too holy, for me to go and play the part of the languishing lover and stand gazing up at her window, or to fill the *rôle* of the lovesick adventurer. Completely upset, I went away from H——; but, as is usual in such cases, the brilliant colors of the picture of my fancy faded, and the recollection of Antonia, as well as of Antonia's singing (which I had never heard), often fell upon my heart like a soft faint trembling light, comforting me.

Two years afterwards I received an appointment in B——, and set out on a journey to the south of Germany. The towers of M—— rose before me in the red vaporous glow of the evening; the nearer I came the more was I oppressed by an indescribable feeling of the most agonizing distress; it lay upon me like a heavy burden; I could not breathe; I was obliged to get out of my carriage into the open air. But my anguish continued to increase until it became actual physical pain. Soon I seemed to hear the strains of a solemn chorale floating in the air; the sounds continued to grow more distinct; I realized the fact that they were men's voices chanting a church chorale. "What's that? what's that?" I cried, a burning stab darting as it were through my breast "Don't you see?" replied the coachman, who was driving along beside me, "why, don't you see? they're burying somebody up yonder in yon churchyard." And indeed we were near the churchyard; I saw a circle of men clothed in black standing round a grave, which was on the point of being closed. Tears started to my eyes; I somehow fancied they were burying there all the joy and all the happiness of life. Moving on rapidly down the hill, I was no longer able to see into the churchyard; the chorale came to an end, and I perceived not far distant from the gate some of the mourners returning from the funeral. The Professor, with his niece on his arm, both in deep mourning, went close past me without noticing me. The young lady had her handkerchief pressed close to her eyes, and was weeping bitterly. In the frame of mind in which I then was I could not possibly go into the town, so I sent on my servant with the carriage to the hotel where I usually put up, whilst I took a turn in the familiar neighborhood, to get rid of a mood that was possibly only due to physical causes, such as heating on the journey, &c. On arriving at a well-known avenue, which leads to a pleasure resort, I came upon a most extraordinary spectacle. Councilor Krespel was being conducted by two mourners, from whom he appeared to be endeavoring to make his escape by all sorts of strange twists and turns. As usual, he was dressed in his own curious home-made grey coat; but from his little cocked-hat, which he wore perched over one ear in military fashion, a long narrow ribbon of black crape fluttered backwards and forwards in the wind. Around his waist he had buckled a black sword-belt; but instead of a sword he had stuck a long fiddle-bow into it. A creepy shudder ran through my limbs: "He's insane," thought I, as I slowly followed them. The Councilor's companions led him as far as his house, where he embraced them, laughing loudly. They left him; and then his glance fell upon me, for I now stood near him. He stared at me fixedly for some time; then he cried in a hollow voice, "Welcome, my student-friend! you also understand it!" Therewith he took me by the arm and pulled me into the house, up the steps, into the room where the violins hung. They were all draped in black crape; the violin of the old master was missing; in its place was a cypress wreath. I knew what had happened. "Antonia! Antonia!" I cried in inconsolable grief. The Councilor, with his arms crossed on his breast, stood beside me, as if turned into stone. I pointed to the cypress wreath. "When she died," said he in a very hoarse solemn voice, "when she died, the soundpost of that violin broke into pieces with a ringing crack, and the sound-board was split from end to end. The faithful instrument could only live with her and in her; it lies beside her in the coffin, it has been buried with her." Deeply agitated, I sank down upon a chair, whilst the Councilor began to sing a gay song in a husky voice; it was truly horrible to see him hopping about on one foot, and the crape strings (he still had his hat on) flying about the room and up to the violins hanging on the walls.

Indeed, I could not repress a loud cry that rose to my lips when, on the Councilor making an abrupt turn, the crape came all over me; I fancied he wanted to envelop me in it and drag me down into the horrible dark depths of insanity. Suddenly he stood still and addressed me in his singing way, "My son! my son! why do you call out? Have you espied the angel of death? That always precedes the ceremony." Stepping into the middle of the room, he took the violin-bow out of his sword-belt and, holding it over his head with both hands, broke it into a thousand pieces. Then, with a loud laugh, he cried, "Now you imagine my sentence is pronounced, don't you, my son? but it's nothing of the kind – not at all! not at all! Now I'm free – free – free – hurrah! I'm free! Now I shall make no more violins – no more violins – Hurrah! no more violins!" This he sang to a horrible mirthful tune, again spinning round on one foot. Perfectly aghast, I was making the best of my way to the door, when he held me fast, saying quite calmly, "Stay, my student friend, pray don't think from this outbreak of grief, which is torturing me as if with the agonies of death, that I am insane; I only do it because a short time ago I made myself a dressing gown in which I wanted to look like Fate or like God!" The Councilor then went on with a medley of silly and awful rubbish, until he fell down utterly exhausted; I called up the old housekeeper, and was very pleased to find myself in the open air again.

I never doubted for a moment that Krespel had become insane; the Professor, however, asserted the contrary. "There are men," he remarked, "from whom nature or a special destiny has taken away the cover behind which the mad folly of the rest of us runs its course unobserved. They are like thin-skinned insects, which, as we watch the restless play of their muscles, seem to be misshapen, while nevertheless everything soon comes back into its proper form again. All that with us remains thought, passes over with Krespel into action. That bitter scorn which the spirit that is wrapped up in the doings and dealings of the earth often has at hand, Krespel gives vent to in outrageous gestures and agile caprioles. But these are his lightning conductor. What comes up out of the earth he gives again to the earth, but what is divine, that he keeps; and so I believe that his inner consciousness, in spite of the apparent madness which springs from it to the surface, is as right as a trivet. To be sure, Antonia's sudden death grieves him sore, but I warrant that tomorrow will see him going along in his old jog-trot way as usual." And the Professor's prediction was almost literally filled. Next day the Councilor appeared to be just as he formerly was, only he averred that he would never make another violin, nor yet ever play on another. And, as I learned later, he kept his word.

Hints which the Professor let fall confirmed my own private conviction that the so carefully guarded secret of the Councilor's relations to Antonia, nay, that even her death, was a crime which must weigh heavily upon him, a crime that could not be atoned for. I determined that I would not leave H—— without taxing him with the offence which I conceived him to be guilty of; I determined to shake his heart down to its very roots, and so compel him to make open confession of the terrible deed. The more I reflected upon the matter the clearer it grew in my own mind that Krespel must be a villain, and in the same proportion did my intended reproach, which assumed of itself the form of a real rhetorical masterpiece, wax more fiery and more impressive. Thus equipped and mightily incensed, I hurried to his house. I found him with a calm smiling countenance making playthings. "How can peace," I burst out, "how can peace find lodgment even for a single moment in your breast, so long as the memory of your horrible deed preys like a serpent upon you?" He gazed at me in amazement, and laid his chisel aside. "What do you mean, my dear sir?" he asked; "pray take a seat." But my indignation chafing me more and more, I went on to accuse him directly of having murdered Antonia, and to threaten him with the vengeance of the Eternal.

Further, as a newly full-fledged lawyer, full of my profession, I went so far as to give him to understand that I would leave no stone unturned to get a clue to the business, and so deliver him here in this world into the hands of an earthly judge. I must confess that I was considerably disconcerted when, at the conclusion of my violent and pompous harangue, the Councilor, without answering so much as a single word, calmly fixed his eyes upon me as though expecting me to go on again. And this I did indeed attempt to do, but it sounded so ill-founded and so stupid as well that I soon grew silent again. Krespel gloated over my embarrassment, whilst a malicious ironical smile flitted across his face. Then he grew very grave, and addressed me in solemn tones. "Young man, no doubt you think I am foolish, insane; that I can pardon you, since we are both confined in the same madhouse; and you only blame me for deluding myself with the idea that I am God the Father because you imagine yourself to be God the Son. But how do you dare desire to insinuate yourself into the secrets and lay bare the hidden motives of a life that is strange to you and that must continue so? She has gone and the mystery is solved." He ceased speaking, rose, and traversed the room backwards and forwards several times. I ventured to ask for an explanation; he fixed his eyes upon me, grasped me by the hand, and led me to the window, which he threw wide open. Propping himself upon his arms, he leaned out, and, looking down into the garden, told me the history of his life. When he finished I left him, touched and ashamed.

In a few words, his relations with Antonia rose in the following way. Twenty years before, the Councilor had been led into Italy by his favorite engrossing passion of hunting up and buying the best violins of the old masters. At that time he had not yet begun to make them himself, and so of course he had not begun to take to pieces those which he bought. In Venice he heard the celebrated singer Angela ——i, who at that time was playing with splendid success as *prima donna* at St. Benedict's Theatre. His enthusiasm was awakened, not only in her art — which Signora Angela had indeed brought to a high pitch of perfection — but in her angelic beauty as well. He sought her acquaintance; and in spite of all his rugged manners he succeeded in winning her heart, principally through his bold and yet at the same time masterly violin-playing. Close intimacy led in a few weeks to marriage, which, however, was kept a secret, because Angela was unwilling to sever her connection with the theater, neither did she wish to part with her professional name, that by which she was celebrated, nor to add to it the cacophonous "Krespel." With the most extravagant irony he described to me what a strange life of worry and torture Angela led him as soon as she became his wife. Krespel was of opinion that more capriciousness and waywardness were concentrated in

Angela's little person than in all the rest of the *prima donnas* in the world put together. If he now and again presumed to stand up in his own defense, she let loose a whole army of abbots, musical composers, and students upon him, who, ignorant of his true connection with Angela, soundly rated him as a most intolerable, ungallant lover for not submitting to all the Signora's caprices. It was just after one of these stormy scenes that Krespel fled to Angela's country seat to try and forget in playing fantasias on his Cremona, violin the annoyances of the day. But he had not been there long before the Signora, who had followed hard after him, stepped into the room. She was in an affectionate humor; she embraced her husband, overwhelmed him with sweet and languishing glances, and rested her pretty head on his shoulder. But Krespel, carried away into the world of music, continued to play on until the walls echoed again; thus he chanced to touch the Signora somewhat ungently with his arm and the fiddle-bow. She leapt back full of fury, shrieking that he was a "German brute," snatched the violin from his hands, and dashed it on the marble table into a thousand pieces. Krespel stood like a statue of stone before her; but then, as if awakening out of a dream, he seized her with the strength of a giant and threw her out of the window of her own house, and, without troubling himself about anything more, fled back to Venice — to Germany. It was not, however, until some time had elapsed that he had a clear recollection of what he had done; although he knew that the window was scarcely five feet from the ground, and although he was fully cognizant of the necessity, under the above-mentioned circumstances, of throwing the Signora out of the window, he yet felt troubled by a sense of painful uneasiness, and the more so since she had imparted to him in no ambiguous terms an interesting secret as to her condition. He hardly dared to make inquiries; and he was not a little surprised about eight months afterwards at receiving a tender letter from his beloved wife, in which she made not the slightest allusion to what had taken place in her country house, only adding to the intelligence that she had been safely delivered of a sweet little daughter the heartfelt prayer that her dear husband and now a happy father would come at once to Venice. That however

Krespel did not do; rather he appealed to a confidential friend for a more circumstantial account of the details, and learned that the Signora had alighted upon the soft grass as lightly as a bird, and that the sole consequences of the fall or shock had been psychic.

That is to say, after Krespel's heroic deed she had become completely altered; she never showed a trace of caprice, of her former freaks, or of her teasing habits; and the composer who wrote for the next carnival was the happiest fellow under the sun, since the Signora was willing to sing his music without the scores and hundreds of changes which she at other times had insisted upon. "To be sure," added his friend, "there was every reason for preserving the secret of Angela's cure, else every day would see lady singers flying through windows." The Councilor was not a little excited at this news; he engaged horses; he took his seat in the carriage. "Stop!" he cried suddenly. "Why, there's not a shadow of doubt," he murmured to himself, "that as soon as Angela sets eyes upon me again the evil spirit will recover his power and once more take possession of her. And since I have already thrown her out of the window, what could I do if a similar case were to occur again? What would there be left for me to do?" He got out of the carriage, and wrote an affectionate letter to his wife, making graceful allusion to her tenderness in especially dwelling upon the fact that his tiny daughter had like him a little mole behind the ear, and — remained in Germany. Now ensued an active correspondence between them. Assurances of unchanged affection — invitations — laments over the absence of the beloved one — thwarted wishes — hopes, &c. — flew backwards and forwards from Venice to H——, from H—— to Venice. At length Angela came to Germany, and, as is well known, sang with brilliant success as *prima donna* at the great theater in F——. Despite the fact that she was no longer young, she won all hearts by the irresistible charm of her wonderfully splendid singing. At that time she had not lost her voice in the least degree. Meanwhile, Antonia had been growing up; and her mother never tired of writing to tell her father how that a singer of the first rank was developing in her. Krespel's friends in F—— also confirmed this intelligence, and urged him to come for once to F—— to see

and admire this uncommon sight of two such glorious singers. They had not the slightest suspicion of the close relations
in which Krespel stood to the pair. Willingly would he have
seen with his own eyes the daughter who occupied so large a
place in his heart, and who moreover often appeared to him
in his dreams; but as often as he thought upon his wife he
felt very uncomfortable, and so he remained at home
amongst his broken violins. There was a certain promising
young composer, B—— of F——, who was found to have
suddenly disappeared, nobody knew where. This young man
fell so deeply in love with Antonia that, as she returned his
love, he earnestly besought her mother to consent to an
immediate union, sanctified as it would further be by art.
Angela had nothing to urge against his suit; and the Councilor the more readily gave his consent that the young composer's productions had found favor before his rigorous
critical judgment. Krespel was expecting to hear of the con-
summation of the marriage, when he received instead a black-
sealed envelope addressed in a strange hand. Doctor R——
conveyed to the Councilor the sad intelligence that Angela
had fallen seriously ill in consequence of a cold caught at the
theater, and that during the night immediately preceding
what was to have been Antonia's wedding-day, she had died.
To him, the Doctor, Angela had disclosed the fact that she
was Krespel's wife, and that Antonia was his daughter; he,
Krespel, had better hasten therefore to take charge of the
orphan. Notwithstanding that the Councilor was a good deal
upset by this news of Angela's death, he soon began to feel
that an antipathetic, disturbing influence had departed out
of his life, and that now for the first time he could begin to
breathe freely.

The very same day he set out for F——. You could not
credit how heartrending was the Councilor's description of
the moment when he first saw Antonia. Even in the fantastic
oddities of his expression there was such a marvelous power
of description that I am unable to give even so much as a
faint indication of it. Antonia inherited all her mother's
amiability and all her mother's charms, but not the repellent
reverse of the medal. There was no chronic moral ulcer, which
might break out from time to time. Antonia's betrothed put

in an appearance, whilst Antonia herself, fathoming with happy instinct the deeper-lying character of her wonderful father, sang one of old Padre Martini's* motets, which, she knew, Krespel in the heyday of his courtship had never grown tired of hearing her mother sing. The tears ran in streams down Krespel's cheeks; even Angela he had never heard sing like that. Antonia's voice was of a very remarkable and altogether peculiar timbre, at one time it was like the sighing of an Æolian harp, at another like the warbled gush of the nightingale. It seemed as if there was not room for such notes in the human breast. Antonia, blushing with joy and happiness, sang on and on — all her most beautiful songs, B——playing between whiles as only enthusiasm that is intoxicated with delight can play. Krespel was at first transported with rapture, then he grew thoughtful — still — absorbed in reflection. At length he leapt to his feet, pressed Antonia to his heart, and begged her in a low husky voice, "Sing no more if you love me — my heart is bursting — I fear — I fear — don't sing again."

"No!" remarked the Councilor next day to Doctor R——, "when, as she sang, her blushes gathered into two dark red spots on her pale cheeks, I knew it had nothing to do with your nonsensical family likenesses, I knew it was what I dreaded." The Doctor, whose countenance had shown signs of deep distress from the very beginning of the conversation, replied, "Whether it arises from a too early taxing of her powers of song, or whether the fault is Nature's — enough, Antonia labors under an organic failure in the chest, while it is from it too that her voice derives its wonderful power and its singular timbre, which I might almost say transcend the limits of human capabilities of song. But it bears the announcement of her early death; for, if she continues to sing, I wouldn't give her at the most more than six months longer to live." Krespel's heart was lacerated as if by the stabs of

---

* Giambattista Martini, more commonly called Padre Martini, of Bologna, formed an influential school of music there in the latter half of the eighteenth century. He wrote vocal and instrumental pieces both for the church and for the theater. He was also a learned historian of music. He has the merit of having discerned and encouraged the genius of Mozart when, a boy of fourteen, he visited Bologna in 1770.

hundreds of stinging knives. It was as though his life had been for the first time overshadowed by a beautiful tree full of the most magnificent blossoms, and now it was to be sawn to pieces at the roots, so that it could not grow green and blossom anymore. His resolution was taken. He told Antonia all; he put the alternatives before her — whether she would follow her betrothed and yield to his and the world's seductions, but with the certainty of dying early, or whether she would spread round her father in his old days that joy and peace which had hitherto been unknown to him, and so secure a long life. She threw herself sobbing into his arms, and he, knowing the heartrending trial that was before her, did not press for a more explicit declaration. He talked the matter over with her betrothed; but, notwithstanding that the latter averred that no note should ever cross Antonia's lips, the Councilor was only too well aware that even B—— could not resist the temptation of hearing her sing, at any rate arias of his own composition. And the world, the musical public, even though acquainted with the nature of the singer's affliction, would certainly not relinquish its claims to hear her, for in cases where pleasure is concerned people of this class are very selfish and cruel. The Councilor disappeared from F—— along with Antonia, and came to H——. B—— was in despair when he learnt that they had gone. He set out on their track, overtook them, and arrived at H—— at the same time that they did. "Let me see him only once, and then die!" entreated Antonia "Die! die!" cried Krespel, wild with anger, an icy shudder running through him. His daughter, the only creature in the wide world who had awakened in him the springs of unknown joy, who alone had reconciled him to life, tore herself away from his heart, and he — he suffered the terrible trial to take place. B—— sat down to the piano; Antonia sang; Krespel fiddled away merrily, until the two red spots showed themselves on Antonia's cheeks. Then he bade her stop; and as B was taking leave of his betrothed, she suddenly fell to the floor with a loud scream. "I thought," continued Krespel in his narration, "I thought that she was, as I had anticipated, really dead; but as I had prepared myself for the worst, my calmness did not leave me, nor my self-command desert me. I grasped B——, who stood like a silly sheep in his dismay, by the shoulders, and said (here the Councilor fell into his singing tone), 'Now that you, my estimable pianoforte-player, have, as you wished and desired, really murdered your betrothed, you may quietly take your departure; at least have the goodness to make yourself scarce before I run my bright hanger through your heart. My daughter, who, as you see, is rather pale, could very well do with some color from your precious blood. Make haste and run, for I might also hurl a nimble knife or two after you.'

"I must, I suppose, have looked rather formidable as I uttered these words, for, with a cry of the greatest terror, B—— tore himself loose from my grasp, rushed out of the room, and down the steps." Directly after B—— was gone, when the Councilor tried to lift up his daughter, who lay unconscious on the floor, she opened her eyes with a deep sigh, but soon closed them again as if about to die. Then Krespel's grief found vent aloud, and would not be comforted. The Doctor, whom the old housekeeper had called in, pronounced Antonia's case a somewhat serious but by no means dangerous attack; and she did indeed recover more quickly than her father had dared to hope. She now clung to him with the most confiding childlike affection; she entered into his favorite hobbies — into his mad schemes and whims. She helped him take old violins to pieces and glue new ones together. "I won't sing again anymore, but live for you," she often said, sweetly smiling upon him, after she had been asked to sing and had refused. Such appeals however the Councilor was anxious to spare her as much as possible; therefore it was that he was unwilling to take her into society, and solicitously shunned all music. He well understood how painful it must be for her to forego altogether the exercise of that art which she had brought to such a pitch of perfection. When the Councilor bought the wonderful violin that he had buried with Antonia, and was about to take it to pieces, she met him with such sadness in her face and softly breathed the petition, "What! this as well?" By some power, which he could not explain, he felt impelled to leave this particular instrument unbroken, and to play upon it. Scarcely had he drawn the first few notes from it than Antonia cried aloud with joy, "Why, that's me! — now I shall sing again." And, in truth, there was something remarkably striking about the clear, silvery, bell-like tones of the violin; they seemed to have been engendered in the human soul. Krespel's heart was deeply moved; he played, too, better than ever. As he ran up and down the scale, playing bold passages with consummate power and expression, she clapped her hands together and cried with delight, "I did that well! I did that well!"

From this time onwards her life was filled with peace and cheerfulness. She often said to the Councilor, "I should like to sing something, father." Then Krespel would take his violin down from the wall and play her most beautiful songs, and her heart was right glad and happy. Shortly before my arrival in H——, the Councilor fancied one night that he heard somebody playing the piano in the adjoining room, and he soon made out distinctly that B—— was flourishing on the instrument in his usual style. He wished to get up, but felt himself held down as if by a dead weight, and lying as if fettered in iron bonds; he was utterly unable to move an inch. Then Antonia's voice was heard singing low and soft; soon, however, it began to rise and rise in volume until it became an ear-splitting fortissimo; and at length she passed over into a powerfully impressive song which B—— had once composed for her in the devotional style of the old masters. Krespel described his condition as being incomprehensible, for terrible anguish was mingled with a delight he had never experienced before. All at once he was surrounded by a dazzling brightness, in which he beheld B—— and Antonia locked in a close embrace, and gazing at each other in a rapture of ecstasy. The music of the song and of the pianoforte accompanying it went on without any visible signs that Antonia sang or that B—— touched the instrument. Then the Councilor fell into a sort of dead faint, whilst the images vanished away. On awakening he still felt the terrible anguish of his dream. He rushed into Antonia's room. She lay on the sofa, her eyes closed, a sweet angelic smile on her face, her hands devoutly folded, and looking as if asleep and dreaming of the joys and raptures of heaven. But she was — dead.

The Fermata

Hummel's* amusing, vivacious picture, "Company in an Italian Inn," became known by the Art Exhibition at Berlin in the autumn of 1814, where it appeared, to the delight of all who saw and studied it An arbor almost hidden in foliage – a table covered with wine-flasks and fruits – two Italian ladies sitting at it opposite each other, one singing, the other playing a guitar; between them, more in the background, stands an abbot, acting as music-director. With his baton raised, he is awaiting the moment when the Signora shall end, in a long trill, the cadence which, with her eyes directed heavenwards, she is just in the midst of; then down will come his hand, whilst the guitarist gaily dashes off the dominant chord. The abbot is filled with admiration – with exquisite delight – and at the same time his attention is painfully on the stretch. He wouldn't miss the proper downward beat for the world. He hardly dare breathe. He would like to stop the mouth and wings of every buzzing bee and midge. So much the more therefore is he annoyed at the bustling host who must needs come and bring the wine just at this supreme, delicious moment. An outlook upon an avenue, patterned by brilliant strips of light! There a horseman has pulled up, and

---

* Johann Erdmann Hummel, born 1769, died 1852, a German painter, studied in Italy, painted various kinds of pieces, and also wrote treatises on perspective and kindred subjects. The picture here referred to became perhaps almost as much celebrated from the fact of its having suggested this amusing sketch to Hoffmann as for its intrinsic merits as a work of art.

a glass of something refreshing to drink is being handed up to him on horseback.

Before this picture stood the two friends Edward and Theodore. "The more I look at this singer," said Edward, "in her gay attire, who, though rather oldish, is yet full of the true inspiration of her art, and the more I am delighted with the grave but genuine Roman profile and lovely form of the guitarist, and the more my estimable friend the abbot amuses me, the more does the whole picture seem to me instinct with free, strong, vital power. It is plainly a caricature in the higher sense of the term, but rich in grace and vivacity. I should just like to step into that arbor and open one of those dainty little flasks which are ogling me from the table. I tell you what, I fancy I can already smell something of the sweet fragrance of the noble wine. Come, it were a sin for this solicitation to be wasted on the cold senseless atmosphere that is about us here. Let us go and drain a flask of Italian wine in honor of this fine picture, of art, and of merry Italy, where life is exhilarating and given for pleasure."

Whilst Edward was running on thus in disconnected sentences, Theodore stood silent and deeply absorbed in reflection. "Aye, that we will, come along," he said, starting up as if awakening out of a dream; but nevertheless he had some difficulty in tearing himself away from the picture, and as he mechanically followed his friend, he had to stop at the door to cast another longing lingering look back upon the singer and guitarist and abbot. Edward's proposal easily admitted of being carried into execution. They crossed the street diagonally, and very soon a flask exactly like those in the picture stood before them in Sala Tarone's* little blue room. "It seems to me," said Edward, as Theodore still continued very silent and thoughtful, even after several glasses had been drunk, "it seems to me that the picture has made a deeper impression upon you than upon me, and not such an agreeable impression either." "I assure you," replied Theodore, "that I lost nothing of the brightness and grace of that animated composition; yet it is very singular, — it is a faithful representation

---

* The keeper of a well-known tavern in Berlin, at about the time when this tale was written, 1817 to 1820.

of a scene out of my own life, reproducing the portraits of the parties concerned in it in a manner startlingly lifelike. You will, however, agree with me that diverting memories also have the power of strangely moving the mind when they suddenly spring up in this extraordinary and unexpected way, as if awakened by the wave of a magician's wand. That's the case with me just now." "What! a scene out of your own life!" exclaimed Edward, quite astonished. "Do you mean to say the picture represents an episode in your own life? I saw at once that the two ladies and the priest were eminently successful portraits, but I never for a moment dreamed that you had ever come across them in the course of your life. Come now, tell me all about it, how it all came about; we are quite alone, nobody else will come at this time o' day." "Willingly," answered Theodore, "but unfortunately I must go a long way back — to my early youth in fact." "Never mind; fire away," rejoined Edward; "I don't know over much about your early days. If it lasts a good while, nothing worse will happen than that we shall have to empty a bottle more than we at first bargained for; and to that nobody will have any objection, neither we, nor Mr. Tarone."

"That, throwing everything else aside, I at length devoted myself entirely to the noble art of music," began Theodore, "need excite nobody's astonishment, for whilst still a boy I would hardly do anything else but play, and spent hours and hours strumming on my uncle's old creaking, jarring piano. The little town was very badly provided for music; there was nobody who could give me instruction except an old opinionated organist; he, however, was merely a dry arithmetician, and plagued me to death with obscure, unmelodious toccatas and fugues. But I held on bravely, without letting myself be daunted. The old fellow was crabby, and often found a good deal of fault, but he had only to play a good piece in his own powerful style, and I was at once reconciled both with him and with his art. I was then often in a curious state of mind; many pieces particularly of old Sebastian Bach were almost like a fearful ghost-story, and I yielded myself up to that feeling of pleasurable awe to which we are so prone in the days of our fantastic youth. But I entered into a veritable Eden when, as sometimes happened in winter, the bandmaster of the town and his colleagues, supported by a few other moderate dilettante players, gave a concert, and I, owing to the strict time I always kept, was permitted to play the kettledrum in the symphony. It was not until later that I perceived how ridiculous and extravagant these concerts were. My teacher generally played two concertos on the piano by Wolff or Emanuel Bach,* a member of the town band struggled with Stamitz,† while the receiver of excise duties worked away hard at the flute, and took in such an immense supply of breath that he blew out both lights on his music-stand, and always had to have them relighted again. Singing wasn't thought about; my uncle, a great friend and patron of music, always disparaged the local talent in this line. He still dwelt with exuberant delight upon the days gone by, when the four choristers of the four churches of the town agreed together to give *Lottchen am Hofe.*‡ Above all, he was wont to extol the toleration which united the singers in the production of this work of art, for not only the Catholic and the Evangelical but also the Reformed community was split into two bodies – those speaking German and those speaking French. The French chorister was not daunted by the *Lottchen*, but, as my uncle maintained, sang his part, spectacles on nose, in the finest falsetto that ever proceeded forth from a human breast. Now there was amongst us (I mean in the town) a spinster named Meibel, aged about fifty-five, who subsisted upon the scanty pension which she received as a retired court singer of the metropolis, and my uncle was rightly of opinion that Miss Meibel might still do something for her money in the concert hall. She assumed airs of importance, required a good deal of coaxing, but at last consented, so that we came to have *bravuras* in our concerts. She was a singular creature this Miss Meibel. I still retain a lively recollection of her lean little figure. Dressed in a many-colored gown, she was wont to step

---

* The third son of the Sebastian Bach – *the* Bach – just mentioned above. He was sometimes called "the Berlin Bach," or "the Hamburg Bach."

† See note, p. 12 above.

‡ This was one of a species of musical composition called *Singspiele*, a development of the simple song or *Lied*, by Johann Adam Hiller, (properly Hüller), born 1728, died 1804.

forward with her roll of music in her hand, looking very grave and solemn, and to acknowledge the audience with a slight inclination of the upper part of her body. Her headdress was a most remarkable headdress. In front was fastened a nosegay of Italian flowers of porcelain, which kept up a strange trembling and tottering as she sang.

"At the end, after the audience had greeted her with no stinted measure of applause, she proudly handed the music-roll to my uncle, and permitted him to dip his thumb and finger into a little porcelain snuff-box, fashioned in the shape of a pug dog, out of which she took a pinch herself with evident relish. She had a horrible squeaky voice, indulged in all sorts of ludicrous flourishes and roulades, and so you may imagine what an effect all this, combined with her ridiculous manners and style of dress, could not fail to have upon me. My uncle overflowed with panegyrics; that I could not understand, and so turned the more readily to my organist, who, looking with contempt upon vocal efforts in general, delighted me down to the ground as in his hypochondriac malicious way he parodied the ludicrous old spinster.

"The more decidedly I came to share with my master his contempt for singing, the higher did he rate my musical genius. He took a great and zealous interest in instructing me in counterpoint, so that I soon came to write the most ingenious toccatas and fugues. I was once playing one of these ingenious specimens of my skill to my uncle on my birthday (I was nineteen years old), when the waiter of our first hotel stepped into the room to announce the visit of two foreign ladies who had just arrived in the town. Before my uncle could throw off his dressing gown — it was of a large flower pattern — and don his coat and vest, his visitors were already in the room. You know what an electric effect every strange event has upon those who are brought up in the narrow seclusion of a small country town; this in particular, which crossed my path so unexpectedly, was pre-eminently fitted to work a complete revolution within me. Picture to yourself two tall, slender Italian ladies, dressed fantastically and in bright colors, quite up to the latest fashion, meeting my uncle with the freedom of professional *artistes*, and yet with considerable charms of manner, and addressing him in firm and sonorous voices. What the deuce of a strange tongue they speak! Only now and then does it sound at all like German. My uncle doesn't understand a word; embarrassed, mute as a maggot, he steps back and points to the sofa. They sit down, talk together — it sounds like music itself. At length they succeed in making my good uncle comprehend that they are singers on a tour; they would like to give a concert in the place, and have come to him, as he is the man to conduct such musical negotiations.

"Whilst they were talking together I picked up their Christian names, and I fancied that I could now more easily and more distinctly distinguish the one from the other, for their both making their appearance together had at first confused me. Lauretta, apparently the elder of the two, looked about her with sparkling eyes, and talked away at my embarrassed old uncle with gushing vivacity and with demonstrative gestures. She was not too tall, and of a voluptuous build, so that my eyes wandered amid many charms that hitherto had been strangers to them. Teresina, taller, more slender, with a long grave face, spoke but seldom, but what she did say was more intelligible. Now and then a peculiar smile flitted across her features; it almost seemed as if she were highly amused at my good uncle, who had withdrawn into his silken dressing gown like a snail into its shell, and was vainly endeavoring to push out of sight a treacherous yellow string, with which he fastened his night-jacket together, and which would keep tumbling out of his bosom yards and yards long. At length they rose to depart; my uncle promised to arrange everything for the concert for the third day following; then the sisters gave him and me, whom he introduced to them as a young musician, a most polite invitation to take chocolate with them in the afternoon.

"We mounted the steps with a solemn air and awkward gait; we both felt very peculiar, as if we were going to meet some adventure to which we were not equal. In consequence of due previous preparation my uncle had a good many fine things to say about art, which nobody understood, neither he himself nor any of the rest of us. This done, and after I had thrice burned my tongue with the scalding hot chocolate, but with the stoical fortitude of a Scævola had smiled under the fiery infliction, Lauretta at length said that she would sing to us. Teresina took her guitar, tuned it, and struck a few full chords. It was the first time I had heard the instrument, and the characteristic mysterious sounds of the trembling strings made a deep and wonderful impression upon me. Lauretta began very softly and held on, the note rising to *fortissimo*, and then quickly broke into a crisp complicated run through an octave and a half. I can still remember the words of the beginning, *'Sento l'amica speme.'* My heart was oppressed; I had never had an idea of anything of the kind. But as Lauretta continued to soar in bolder and higher flights, and as the musical notes poured upon me like sparkling rays, thicker and thicker, then was the music that had so long lain mute and lifeless within me enkindled, rising up in strong, grand flames. Ah! I had never heard what music was in my life before! Then the sisters sang one of those grand impressive duets of Abbot Steffani* which confine themselves to notes of a low register. My soul was stirred at the sound of Teresina's alto, it was so sonorous, and as pure as silver bells. I couldn't for the life of me restrain my emotion; tears started to my eyes. My uncle coughed warningly, and cast angry glances upon me; it was all of no use, I was really quite beside myself. This seemed to please the sisters; they began to inquire into the nature and extent of my musical studies; I was ashamed of my performances in that line, and with the hardihood born of enthusiastic admiration, I bluntly declared that that day was the first time I had ever heard music. 'The dear good boy!' lisped Lauretta, so sweetly and bewitchingly.

"On reaching home again, I was seized with a sort of fury: I pounced upon all the toccatas and fugues that I had hammered out, as well as a beautiful copy of forty-five variations of a canonical theme that the organist had written and done me the honor of presenting to me, — all these I threw into the fire, and laughed with spiteful glee as the double counterpoint smoked and crackled. Then I sat down at the piano and tried first to imitate the tones of the guitar, then to play the sisters' melodies, and finished by attempting to sing them.

---

* Agostino Steffani, an Italian by birth (1655), spent nearly all his life in Germany at the courts of Munich and Hanover. He wrote several operas, and was renowned for his duets, motets, &c.

At length about midnight my uncle emerged from his bed-room and greeted me with, 'My boy, you'd better just stop that screeching and troop off to bed;' and he put out both candles and went back to his own room. I had no other alternative but to obey. The mysterious power of song came to me in my dreams — at least I thought so — for I sang *'Sento l'amica speme'* in excellent style.

"The next morning my uncle had hunted up everybody who could fiddle and blow for the rehearsal. He was proud to show what good musicians the town possessed; but every-thing seemed to go perversely wrong. Lauretta set to work at a fine scene; but very soon in the recitative the orchestra was all at sixes and sevens, not one of them had any idea of accompaniment Lauretta screamed — raved — wept with im-patience and anger. The organist was presiding at the piano; she attacked him with the bitterest reproaches. He got up and in silent obduracy marched out of the hall. The bandmaster of the town, whom Lauretta had dubbed a 'German ass!' took his violin under his arm, and, banging his hat on his head with an air of defiance, likewise made for the door. The members of his company, sticking their bows under the strings of their violins, and unscrewing the mouthpieces of their brass instruments, followed him. There was nobody but the dilettanti left, and they gazed about them with disconso-late looks, whilst the receiver of excise duties exclaimed, with a tragic air, 'O heaven! how mortified I feel!' All my diffidence was gone, — I threw myself in the bandmaster's way, I begged, I prayed, in my distress I promised him six new minuets with double trios for the annual ball. I succeeded in appeasing him. He went back to his place, his companions followed suit, and soon the orchestra was reconstituted, except that the organist was wanting. He was slowly making his way across the marketplace, no shouting or beckoning could make him turn back. Teresina had looked on at the whole scene with smothered laughter, while Lauretta was now as full of glee as before she had been of anger. She was unstinted in her praise of my efforts; she asked me if I played the piano, and ere I knew what I was about, I sat in the organist's place with the music before me. Never before had I accompanied a singer, still less directed an orchestra. Teresina sat down beside me at the piano and gave me every time; Lauretta encouraged me with repeated 'Bravos!' the orchestra proved manageable, and things continued to improve. Everything was worked out successfully at the second rehearsal; and the effect of the sisters' singing at the concert is not to be described.

"The sovereign's return to his capital was to be celebrated there with several festive demonstrations; the sisters were summoned to sing in the theater and at concerts. Until the time that their presence was required they resolved to remain in our little town, and thus it came to pass that they gave us a few more concerts. The admiration of the public rose to a kind of madness. Old Miss Meibel, however, took with a deliberate air a pinch of snuff out of her porcelain pug and gave her opinion that 'such impudent caterwauling was not singing; singing should be low and melodious.' My friend, the organist, never showed himself again, and, in truth, I did not miss him in the least I was the happiest fellow in the world. The whole day long I spent with the sisters, copying out the vocal scores of what they were to sing in the capital. Lauretta was my ideal; her vile caprices, her terribly passionate violence, the torments she inflicted upon me at the piano — all these I bore with patience. She alone had unsealed for me the springs of true music. I began to study Italian, and try my hand at a few canzonets. In what heavenly rapture was I plunged when Lauretta sang my compositions, or even praised them. Often it seemed to me as if it was not I who had thought out and set what she sang, but that the thought first shone forth in her singing of it. With Teresina I could not somehow get on familiar terms; she sang but seldom, and didn't seem to make much account of all that I was doing, and sometimes I even fancied that she was laughing at me behind my back. At length the time came for them to leave the town. And now I felt for the first time how dear Lauretta had become to me, and how impossible it would be for me to separate from her. Often, when she was in a tender, playful mood, she had caressed me, although always in a perfectly artless fashion; nevertheless, my blood was excited, and it was nothing but the strange coolness with which she was more usually wont to treat me that restrained me from giving reins to my ardor and clasping her in my arms in a delirium of passion. I possessed a tolerably good tenor voice, which, however, I had never practiced, but now I began to cultivate it assiduously. I frequently sang with Lauretta one of those tender Italian duets of which there exists such an endless number. We were just singing one of these pieces, the hour of departure was close at hand — '*Senza di te ben mio, vivere non poss' io*' ('Without thee, my own, I cannot live!') Who could resist that? I threw myself at her feet — I was in despair. She raised me up — 'But, my friend, need we then part?' I pricked up my ears with amazement. She proposed that I should accompany her and Teresina to the capital, for if I intended to devote myself wholly to music I must leave this wretched little town some time or other. Picture to yourself one struggling in the dark depths of boundless despair, who has given up all hopes of life, and who, in the moment in which he expects to receive the blow that is to crush him forever, suddenly finds himself sitting in a glorious bright arbor of roses, where hundreds of unseen but loving voices whisper, 'You are still alive, dear, — still alive' — and you will know how I felt then. Along with them to the capital! that had seized upon my heart as an ineradicable resolution. But I won't tire you with the details of how I set to work to convince my uncle that I ought now by all means to go to the capital, which, moreover, was not very far away. He at length gave his consent, and announced his intention of going with me. Here was a tricksy stroke of fortune! I dare not give utterance to my purpose of traveling in company with the sisters. A violent cold, which my uncle caught, proved my savior.

"I left the town by the stagecoach, but only went as far as the first stopping-station, where I awaited my divinity. A well-lined purse enabled me to make all due and fitting preparations. I was seized with the romantic idea of accompanying the ladies in the character of a protecting paladin — on horseback; I secured a horse, which, though not particularly handsome, was, its owner assured me, quiet, and I rode back at the appointed time to meet the two fair singers. I soon saw the little carriage, which had two seats, coming towards me. Lauretta and Teresina sat on the principal seat, whilst on the other, with her back to the driver, sat their maid, the fat little Gianna, a brown-cheeked Neapolitan. Besides this living freight, the carriage was packed full of boxes, satchels, and baskets of all sizes and shapes, such as invariably accompany ladies when they travel. Two little pug-dogs which Gianna was nursing in her lap began to bark when I gaily saluted the company.

"All was going on very nicely; we were traversing the last stage of the journey, when my steed all at once conceived the idea that it was high time to be returning homewards. Being aware that stern measures were not always blessed with a remarkable degree of success in such cases, I felt advised to have recourse to milder means of persuasion; but the obstinate brute remained insensible to all my well-meant exhortations. I wanted to go forwards, he backwards, and all the advantage that my efforts gave me over him was that instead of taking to his heels for home, he continued to run round in circles. Teresina leaned forward out of the carriage and had a hearty laugh; Lauretta, holding her hands before her face, screamed out as if I were in imminent danger. This gave me the courage of despair, I drove the spurs into the brute's ribs, but that very same moment I was roughly hurled off and found myself sprawling on the ground. The horse stood perfectly still, and, stretching out his long neck, regarded me with what I took to be nothing else than derision. I was not able to rise to my feet; the driver had to come and help me; Lauretta had jumped out and was weeping and lamenting; Teresina did nothing but laugh without ceasing. I had sprained my foot, and couldn't possibly mount again. How was I to get on? My steed was fastened to the carriage, whilst I crept into it. Just picture us all — two rather robust females, a fat servant-girl, two pug-dogs, a dozen boxes, satchels, and baskets, and me as well, all packed into a little carriage. Picture Lauretta's complaints at the uncomfortableness of her seat, the howling of the pups, the chattering of the Neapolitan, Teresina's sulks, the unspeakable pain I felt in my foot, and you will have some idea of my enviable situation! Teresina averred that she could not endure it any longer. We stopped; in a trice she was out of the carriage, had untied my horse, and was up in the saddle, prancing and curvetting around us. I must indeed admit that she cut a fine figure. The dignity

and elegance which marked her carriage and bearing were still
more prominent on horseback. She asked for her guitar, then
dropping the reins on her arm, she began to sing proud
Spanish ballads with a full-toned accompaniment. Her light
silk dress fluttered in the wind, its folds and creases giving
rise to a sheeny play of light, whilst the white feathers of her
hat quivered and shook, like the prattling spirits of the air
which we heard in her voice. Altogether she made such a
romantic figure that I could not keep my eyes off her, notwithstanding that Lauretta reproached her for making herself
such a fantastic simpleton, and predicted that she would
suffer for her audacity. But no accident happened; either the
horse had lost all his stubbornness or he liked the fair singer
better than the paladin; at any rate, Teresina did not creep
back into the carriage again until we had almost reached the
gates of the town.

"If you had seen me then at concerts and operas, if you
had seen me revelling in all sorts of music, and as a diligent
accompanist studying arias, duets, and I don't know what
besides at the piano, you would have perceived, by the complete change in my behavior, that I was filled with a new and
wonderful spirit. I had cast off all my rustic shyness, and sat
at the pianoforte with my score before me like an experienced
professional, directing the performances of my *prima donna.*
All my mind — all my thoughts — were sweet melodies. Utterly
regardless of all the rules of counterpoint, I composed all
sorts of canzonets and arias, which Lauretta sang, though
only in her own room. Why would she never sing any of my
pieces at a concert? I could not understand it. Teresina also
arose before my imagination curvetting on her proud steed
with the lute in her hands, like Art herself disguised in
romance. Without thinking of it consciously, I wrote several
songs of a high and serious nature. Lauretta, it is true, played
with her notes like a capricious fairy queen. There was nothing upon which she ventured in which she had not success.
But never did a roulade cross Teresina's lips; nothing more
than a simple interpolated note, at most a *mordent;* but her
long-sustained tones gleamed like meteors through the darkness of night, awakening strange spirits, who came and gazed

with earnest eyes into the depths of my heart. I know not how I remained ignorant of them so long!

"The sisters were granted a benefit concert; I sang with Lauretta a long scena from Anfossi.* As usual I presided at the piano. We came to the last *fermata.* Lauretta exerted all her skill and art; she warbled trill after trill like a nightingale, executed sustained notes, then long elaborate roulades — a whole *solfeggio.* In fact, I thought she was almost carrying the thing too far this time; I felt a soft breath on my cheek; Teresina stood behind me. At this moment Lauretta took a good start with the intention of swelling up to a 'harmonic shake,' and so passing back into *a tempo.* The devil entered into me; I jammed down the keys with both hands; the orchestra followed suit; and it was all over with Lauretta's trill, just at the supreme moment when she was to excite everybody's astonishment. Almost annihilating me with a look of fury, she crushed her roll of music together, tore it up, and hurled it at my head, so that the pieces flew all over me. Then she rushed like a madwoman through the orchestra into the adjoining room; as soon as we had concluded the piece, I followed her. She wept; she raved. 'Out of my sight, villain,' she screamed as soon as she saw me. 'You devil, you've completely ruined me — my fame, my honor — and oh! my trill. Out of my sight, you devil's own!' She made a rush at me; I escaped through the door. Whilst someone else was performing, Teresina and the music-director at length succeeded in so far pacifying her rage, that she resolved to appear again; but I was not to be allowed to touch the piano. In the last duet that the sisters sang, Lauretta did contrive to introduce the swelling 'harmonic shake,' was rewarded with a storm of applause, and settled down into the best of humors.

"But I could not get over the vile treatment which I had received at her hands in the presence of so many people, and I was firmly resolved to set off home next morning for my native town. I was actually engaged in packing my things together when Teresina came into my room. Observing what I was about, she exclaimed, astonished, 'Are you going to

* Pasquale Anfossi, an Italian operatic composer of the eighteenth century. He was for a time the fashion of the day at Rome, but occupies now only a subordinate rank amongst musicians.

leave us?' I gave her to understand that after the affront which had been put upon me by Lauretta I could not think of remaining any longer in her society. 'And so,' replied Teresina, 'you're going to let yourself be driven away by the extravagant conduct of a little fool, who is now heartily sorry for what she has done and said. Where else can you better live in your art than with us? Let me tell you, it only depends upon yourself and your own behavior to keep her from such pranks as this. You are too compliant, too tender, too gentle. Besides, you rate her powers too highly. Her voice is indeed not bad, and it has a wide compass; but what else are all these fantastic warblings and flourishes, these preposterous runs, these never-ending shakes, but delusive artifices of style, which people admire in the same way that they admire the foolhardy agility of a rope-dancer? Do you imagine that such things can make any deep impression upon us and stir the heart? The 'harmonic shake' which you spoilt I cannot tolerate; I always feel anxious and pained when she attempts it. And then this scaling up into the region of the third line above the stave, what is it but a violent straining of the natural voice, which after all is the only thing that really moves the heart? I like the middle notes and the low notes. A sound that penetrates to the heart, a real quiet, easy transition from note to note, are what I love above all things. No useless ornamentation – a firm, clear, strong note – a definite expression, which carries away the mind and soul – that's real true singing, and that's how I sing. If you can't be reconciled to Lauretta again, then think of Teresina, who indeed likes you so much that you shall in your own way be her musical composer. Don't be cross – but all your elegant canzonets and arias can't be matched with this single ——,' she sang in her sonorous way a simple devotional sort of canzona which I had set a few days before. I had never dreamed that it could sound like that I felt the power of the music going through and through me; tears of joy and rapture stood in my eyes; I seized Teresina's hand, and pressing it to my lips a thousand times, swore I would never leave her.

"Lauretta looked upon my intimacy with her sister with envious but suppressed vexation, and she could not do without me, for, in spite of her skill, she was unable to study a

new piece without help; she read badly, and was rather uncertain in her time. Teresina, on the contrary, sang everything
at sight, and her ear for time was unparalleled. Never did
Lauretta give such free rein to her caprice and violence as
when her accompaniments were being practiced. They were
never right for her; she looked upon them as a necessary evil;
the piano ought not to be heard at all, it should always be
pianissimo; so there was nothing but giving way to her again
and again, and altering the time just as the whim happened
to come into her head at the moment But now I took a firm
stand against her; I combated her impertinences; I taught her
that an accompaniment devoid of energy was not conceivable, and that there was a marked difference between support-
ing and carrying along the song and letting it run to riot,
without form and without time. Teresina faithfully lent me
her assistance. I composed nothing but pieces for the Church,
writing all the solos for a voice of low register. Teresina, too,
tyrannised over me not a little, to which I submitted with a
good grace, since she had more knowledge of, and (so at least
I thought) more appreciation for, German seriousness than
her sister.

"We were touring in South Germany. In a little town we
met an Italian tenor who was making his way from Milan to
Berlin. My fair companions went in ecstasies over their
countryman; he stuck close to them, cultivating in particular
Teresina's acquaintance, so that to my great vexation I soon
came to play rather a secondary part. Once, just as I was about
to enter the room with a roll of music under my arm, the
voices of my companions and the tenor, engaged in an
animated conversation, fell upon my ear. My name was
mentioned; I pricked up my ears; I listened. I now understood
Italian so well that not a word escaped me. Lauretta was
describing the tragical occurrence of the concert when I cut
short her trill by prematurely striking down the concluding
notes of the bar. 'A German ass!' exclaimed the tenor. I felt
as if I must rush in and hurl the flighty hero of the boards
out of the window, but I restrained myself. She then went on
to say that she had been minded to send me about my
business at once, but, moved by my clamorous entreaties, she
had so far had compassion upon me as to tolerate me some

time longer, since I was studying singing under her. This, to my utter amazement, Teresina confirmed. 'Yes, he's a good child,' she added; 'he's in love with me now and sets everything for the alto. He is not without talent, but he must rub off that stiffness and awkwardness which is so characteristic of the Germans. I hope to make a good composer out of him; then he shall write me some good things — for there's very little written as yet for the alto voice — and afterwards I shall let him go his own way. He's very tiresome with his billing and cooing and love-sick sighing, and he worries me too much with his wearisome compositions, which have been but poor stuff up to the present.' 'I at least have now got rid of him,' interrupted Lauretta; 'and Teresina, how the fellow pestered me with his arias and duets you know very well.' And now she began to sing a duet of my composing, which formerly she had praised very highly. The other sister took up the second voice, and they parodied me both in voice and in execution in the most shameful manner. The tenor laughed till the walls rang again. My limbs froze; at once I formed an irrevocable resolve. I quietly slipped away from the door back into my own room, the windows of which looked upon a side street. Opposite was the post office; the post-coach for Bamberg had just driven up to take in the mails and passengers. The latter were all standing ready waiting in the gateway, but I had still an hour to spare. Hastily packing up my things, I generously paid the whole of the bill at the hotel, and hurried across to the post office. As I crossed the broad street I saw the fair sisters and the Italian still standing at the window, and looking out to catch the sound of the post-horn. I leaned back in the corner, and dwelt with a good deal of satisfaction upon the crushing effect of the bitter scathing letter that I had left behind for them in the hotel."

*W*ith evident gratification Theodore tossed off the rest of the fiery Aleatico* that Edward had poured into his glass. The latter, opening a new flask and skillfully shaking off the drops of oil† which swam at the top, remarked, "I should not

---

* A red, aromatic, sweet Italian wine, made chiefly at Florence.

have deemed Teresina capable of such falseness and artfulness. I cannot banish from my mind the recollection of what a charming figure she made as she sat on horseback singing Spanish ballads, whilst the horse pranced along in graceful curvets." "That was her culminating point," interrupted Theodore; "I still remember the strange impression which the scene made upon me. I forgot my pain; she seemed to me like a creature of a higher race. It is indeed very true that such moments are turning-points in one's life, and that in them many images arise which time does not avail to dim. Whenever I have succeeded with any fine *romance*, it has always been when Teresina's image has stepped forth from the treasure-house of my mind in clear bright colors at the moment of writing it."

"But," said Edward, "but let us not forget the artistic Lauretta; and, scattering all rancor to the winds, let us drink to the health of the two sisters." They did so. "Oh," exclaimed Theodore, "how the fragrant breezes of Italy arise out of this wine and fan my cheeks, — my blood rolls with quickened energy in my veins. Oh! why must I so soon leave that glorious land again!" "As yet," interrupted Edward, "as yet in all that you have told me I can see no connection with the beautiful picture, and so I believe that you still have something more to tell me about the sisters. Of course I perceive plainly that the ladies in the picture are none other than Lauretta and Teresina themselves." "You are right, they are," replied Theodore; "and my ejaculations and sighs, and my longings after the glorious land of Italy, will form a fitting introduction to what I still have to say. A short time ago, perhaps about two years since, just before leaving Rome, I made a little excursion on horseback. Before an inn stood a charming girl; the idea struck me how nice it would be to receive a cup of wine at the hands of the pretty child. I pulled up before the door, in a walk so thickly planted on each side with shrubs that the sunlight could only make its way through in patches. In the distance I heard sounds of singing and the tinkling of a guitar. I pricked up my ears and listened,

¶ The wine was presumably in flasks of the usual Italian kind, bottles encased in straw or reed, &c., with oil on the top of the wine instead of a cork in the neck of the bottle.

for the two female voices affected me somehow in a singular fashion; strangely enough dim recollections began to stir within my mind, but they refused to take definite shape. I dismounted and slowly drew near to the vine-clad arbor whence the music seemed to proceed, eagerly catching up every sound in the meantime. The second voice had ceased to sing. The first sang a canzonet alone. As I came nearer and nearer that which had at first seemed familiar to me, and which had at first attracted my attention, gradually faded away. The singer was now in the midst of a florid, elaborate *fermata*. Up and down she warbled, up and down; at length she stopped, holding a note on for some time. But all at once a female voice began to let off a torrent of abuse, maledictions, curses, vituperations! A man protested; a second laughed. The other female voice took part in the altercation. The quarrel continued to wax louder and more violent, with true Italian fury. At length I stood immediately in front of the arbor; an abbot rushes out and almost runs over me; he turns his head to look at me; I recognize my good friend Signor Lodovico, my musical news-monger from Rome. 'What in the name of wonder' — I exclaim. 'Oh, sir! sir!' he screams, 'save me, protect me from this mad fury, from this crocodile, this tiger, this hyæna, this devil of a woman. Yes, I did, I did; I was beating time to Anfossi's canzonet, and brought down my baton too soon whilst she was in the midst of the *fermata*; I cut short her trill; but why did I meet her eyes, the devilish divinity! The deuce take all *fermatas*, I say!' In a most curious state of mind I hastened into the arbor along with the priest, and recognized at the first glance the sisters Lauretta and Teresina. The former was still shrieking and raging, and her sister still seriously remonstrating with her. Mine host, his bare arms crossed over his chest, was looking on laughing, whilst a girl was placing fresh flasks on the table. No sooner did the sisters catch sight of me than they threw themselves upon me exclaiming, 'Ah! Signor Teodoro!' and covered me with caresses. The quarrel was forgotten. 'Here you have a composer,' said Lauretta to the abbot, 'as charming as an Italian and as strong as a German.' Both sisters, continually interrupting each other, began to recount the happy days we had spent together, to speak of my musical abilities whilst still a youth, of our practicings together, of the excellence of my compositions; never did they like singing anything else but what I had set.

"Teresina at length informed me that a manager had engaged her as his first singer in tragic casts for the next carnival; but she would give him to understand that she would only sing on condition that the composition of at least one tragic opera was intrusted to me. The tragic was above all others my special department, and so on, and so on. Lauretta on her part maintained that it would be a pity if I did not follow my bent for the light and the graceful, in a word, for *opera buffa.* She had been engaged as first lady singer for this species of composition; and that nobody but I should write the piece in which she was to appear was simply a matter of course. You may fancy what my feelings were as I stood between the two. In a word, you perceive that the company which I had joined was the same as that which Hummel painted, and that just at the moment when the priest is on the point of cutting short Lauretta's *fermata.*" "But did they not make any allusion," asked Edward, "to your departure from them, or to the scathing letter?" "Not with a single syllable," answered Theodore, "and you may be sure I didn't, for I had long before banished all animosity from my heart, and come to look back upon my adventure with the sisters as a merry prank. I did, however, so far revert to the subject that I related to the priest how that, several years before, exactly the same sort of mischance befell me in one of Anfossi's arias as had just befallen him. I painted the period of my connection with the sisters in tragi-comical colors, and, distributing many a keen sideblow, I let them feel the superiority, which the ripe experiences, both of life and of art, of the years that had elapsed in the interval had given me over them. 'And a good thing it was,' I concluded, 'that I did cut short that *fermata,* for it was evidently meant to last through eternity, and I am firmly of opinion that if I had left the singer alone, I should be sitting at the piano now.' 'But, signor,' replied the priest, 'what director is there who would dare to prescribe laws to the *prima donna?* Your offence was much more heinous than mine, you in the concert hall, and I here in the leafy arbor. Besides, I was only director in imagination; nobody need attach any importance to that, and if the sweet fiery glances of these heavenly eyes had not fascinated me, I should not have made an ass of myself.' The priest's last words proved tranquilising, for, although Lauretta's eyes had begun to flash with anger as the priest spoke, before he had finished she was quite appeased.

"We spent the evening together. Many changes take place in fourteen years, which was the interval that had passed since I had seen my fair friends. Lauretta, although looking some-what older, was still not devoid of charms. Teresina had worn better, without losing her graceful form. Both were dressed in rather gay colors, and their manners were just the same as before, that is, fourteen years younger than the ladies them-selves. At my request Teresina sang some of the serious songs that had once so deeply affected me, but I fancied that they sounded differently from what they did when I first heard them; and Lauretta's singing too, although her voice had not appreciably lost anything, either in power or in compass, seemed to me to be quite different from my recollection of it of former times The sisters' behavior towards me, their feigned ecstasies, their rude admiration, which, however, took the shape of gracious patronage, had done much to put me in a bad humor, and now the obtrusiveness of this compari-son between the images in my mind and the not over and above pleasing reality, tended to put me in a still worse. The droll priest, who in all the sweetest words you can imagine was playing the *amoroso* to both sisters at once, as well as frequent applications to the good wine, at length restored me to good humor, so that we spent a very pleasant evening in perfect concord and gaiety. The sisters were most pressing in their invitations to me to go home with them, that we might at once talk over the parts which I was to set for them and so concert measures accordingly. I left Rome without taking any further steps to find out their place of abode."

"And yet, after all," said Edward, "it is to them that you owe the awakening of your genius for music." "That I admit," replied Theodore, "I owed them that and a host of good melodies besides, and that is just the reason why I did not want to see them again. Every composer can recall certain impressions which time does not obliterate. The spirit of music spake, and his voice was the creative word which suddenly awakened the kindred spirit slumbering in the breast of the artist; then the latter rose like a sun which can nevermore set. Thus it is unquestionably true that all melodies which, stirred up in this way, proceed from the depths of the composer's being, seem to us to belong to the singer alone who fanned the first spark within us. We hear her voice and record only what she has sung. It is, however, the inheritance of us weak mortals that, clinging to the clods, we are only too fain to draw down what is above the earth into the miserable narrowness characteristic of things of the earth. Thus it comes to pass that the singer becomes our lover — or even our wife. The spell is broken, and the melody of her nature, which formerly revealed glorious things, is now prostituted to complaints about broken soup-plates or ink-stains in new linen. Happy is the composer who never again so long as he lives sets eyes upon the woman who by virtue of some mysterious power enkindled in him the flame of music. Even though the young artist's heart may be rent by pain and despair when the moment comes for parting from his lovely enchantress, nevertheless her form will continue to exist as a divinely beautiful strain which lives on and on in the pride of youth and beauty, engendering melodies in which time after time he perceives the lady of his love. But what is she else if not the Highest Ideal which, working its way from within outwards, is at length reflected in the external independent form?"

"A strange theory, but yet plausible," was Edward's comment, as the two friends, arm in arm, passed out from Sala Tarone's into the street.

Signor Formica*

I

The celebrated painter Salvator Rosa comes to Rome, and is attacked by a dangerous illness. What befalls him in this illness.

Celebrated people commonly have many ill things said of them, whether well-founded or not And no exception was made in the case of that admirable painter Salvator Rosa, whose living pictures cannot fail to impart a keen and characteristic delight to those who look upon them.

At the time that Salvator's fame was ringing through Naples, Rome, and Tuscany — nay, through all Italy, and painters who were desirous of gaining applause were striving to imitate his peculiar and unique style, his malicious and envious rivals were laboring to spread abroad all sorts of evil reports intended to sully with ugly black stains the glorious splendor of his artistic fame. They affirmed that he had at a former period of his life belonged to a company of banditti,†

---

* This tale was written for the Leipsic *Taschenbuch zum geselligen Vergnügen* for the year 1820.

† Respecting the facts of Salvator Rosa's life there exists more than one disputed statement; and of these perhaps the most disputed is his share of complicity (if any) in the evil doings of Calabrian banditti. Poor, and of a wild and self-willed disposition, but with a strong and independent character, he was unable to find a suitable master in Naples, so, at the age of eighteen, he set out to study the lineaments of nature face to face, and spent some time amidst the grand and savage scenery of Calabria. Here it is certain that he came into contact with the banditti who haunted those wild regions. He is alleged to have been taken prisoner by a band, and to have become a member of the troop. Accepting this as true, we may perhaps charitably believe that he was prompted not so much by a regard for his own safety, as by the wish to secure a rare opportunity for studying his art unhin-

and that it was to his experiences during this lawless time that he owed all the wild, fierce, fantastically-attired figures which he introduced into his pictures, just as the gloomy fearful wildernesses of his landscapes — the *selve selvagge* (savage woods) — to use Dante's expression, were faithful representations of the haunts where they lay hidden. What was worse still, they openly charged him with having been concerned in the atrocious and bloody revolt which had been set on foot by the notorious Masaniello* in Naples. They even described the share he had taken in it, down to the minutest details.

The rumor ran that Aniello Falcone,† the painter of battle-pieces, one of the best of Salvator's masters, had been stung into fury and filled with bloodthirsty vengeance because the Spanish soldiers had slain one of his relatives in a hand-to-hand encounter. Without delay he leagued together a band of daring spirits, mostly young painters, put arms into their hands, and gave them the name of the "Company of Death." And in truth this band inspired all the fear and consternation suggested by its terrible name. At all hours of the day they traversed the streets of Naples in little companies, and cut down without mercy every Spaniard whom they met. They did more — they forced their way into the holy sanctuaries, and relentlessly murdered their unfortunate foes whom terror had driven to seek refuge there. At night they gathered round their chief, the bloody-minded madman Masaniello,‡ and

---

dered, and also charitably hope that the accusations of his enemies, that he actively participated in the deeds of his companions, are unfounded, or, at any rate, exaggerations. It may be remarked that the "Life and Times of Salvator Rosa" by Lady Morgan (1824) is admittedly a romance rather than an accurate and faithful biography.

* Masaniello, a poor fisherman of Naples, was for a week in July, 1647, absolute king of his native city. At that time Naples was subject to the crown of Spain. The people, provoked by the exasperating rapacity and extortion of the Viceroy of the King of Spain, rose in rebellion, choosing Masaniello as their captain and leader.

† Aniello Falcone (1600–65), teacher of Salvator Rosa and founder of the *Compagnia della Morte*, painted battle-pieces which bear a high reputation. His works are said to be scarce and much sought after.

‡ At first the young fisherman administered stern but impartial justice; but afterwards his mind seems to have reeled under the intense

painted him by torchlight, so that in a short time there were
hundreds of these little pictures* circulating in Naples and
the neighborhood.

This is the ferocious band of which Salvator Rosa was
alleged to have been a member, working hard at butchering
his fellow-men by day, and by night working just as hard at
painting. The truth about him has however been stated by a
celebrated art-critic, Taillasson,† I believe. His works are characterized by defiant originality, and by fantastic energy both
of conception and of execution. He delighted to study Nature, not in the lovely attractiveness of green meadows, flourishing fields, sweet-smelling groves, murmuring springs, but
in the sublime as seen in towering masses of rock, in the wild
seashore, in savage inhospitable forests; and the voices that
he loved to hear were not the whisperings of the evening
breeze or the musical rustle of leaves, but the roaring of the
hurricane and the thunder of the cataract. To one viewing his
desolate landscapes, with the strange savage figures stealthily
moving about in them, here singly, there in troops, the
uncomfortable thoughts arise unbidden, "Here's where a
fearful murder took place, there's where the bloody corpse
was hurled into the ravine," etc.

Admitting all this, and even that Taillasson is further right
when he maintains that Salvator's "Plato," nay, that even his
"Holy St. John proclaiming the Advent of the Saviour in the
Wilderness," look just a little like highway robbers — admitting this, I say, it is nevertheless unjust to argue from the
character of the works to the character of the artist himself,
and to assume that he, who represents with lifelike fidelity
what is savage and terrible, must himself have been a savage,
terrible man. He who prates most about the sword is often
he who wields it the worst; he who feels in the depths of his
soul all the horrors of a bloody deed, so that, taking the

---

excitement and strain of his position, and he began to act the part of
an arbitrary and cruel tyrant. Several hundreds of persons are said to
have been put to death by his order during the few days he held power.

* Amongst them more than one by Salvator himself.

† A French painter and writer on painting; was born near Bordeaux in
1746, and died at Paris in 1809. Besides other works he wrote *Observations sur quelques grands peintres* (1807).

palette or the pencil or the pen in his hand, he is able to give living form to his feelings, is often the one least capable of practicing similar deeds. Enough! I don't believe a single word of all those evil reports, by which men sought to brand the excellent Salvator an abandoned murderer and robber, and I hope that you, kindly reader, will share my opinion. Otherwise, I see grounds for fearing that you might perhaps entertain some doubts respecting what I am about to tell you of this artist; the Salvator I wish to put before you in this tale — that is, according to my conception of him — is a man bubbling over with the exuberance of life and fiery energy, but at the same time a man endowed with the noblest and most loyal character — a character, which, like that of all men who think and feel deeply, is able even to control that bitter irony which arises from a clear view of the significance of life. I need scarcely add that Salvator was no less renowned as a poet and musician than as a painter. His genius was revealed in magnificent refractions. I repeat again, I do not believe that Salvator had any share in Masaniello's bloody deeds; on the contrary, I think it was the horrors of that fearful time which drove him from Naples to Rome, where he arrived a poor poverty-stricken fugitive, just at the time that Masaniello fell.

Not over well dressed, and with a scanty purse containing not more than a few bright sequins* in his pocket, he crept through the gate just after nightfall. Somehow or other, he didn't exactly know how, he wandered as far as the Piazza Navona. In better times he had once lived there in a large house near the Pamfili Palace. With an ill-tempered growl, he gazed up at the large plate-glass windows glistening and glimmering in the moonlight "Hm!" he exclaimed peevishly, "it'll cost me dozens of yards of colored canvas before I can open my studio up there again." But all at once he felt as if paralyzed in every limb, and at the same moment more weak and feeble than he had ever felt in his life before. "But shall I," he murmured between his teeth as he sank down upon the stone steps leading up to the house door, "shall I really be

---

* The sequin was a gold coin of Venice and Tuscany, worth about 9s. 3d. It is sometimes used as equivalent to ducat (see note p. 98).

able to finish canvas enough in the way the fools want it done? Hm! I have a notion that that will be the end of it!"

A cold cutting night wind blew down the street. Salvator recognized the necessity of seeking a shelter. Rising with difficulty, he staggered on into the Corso,* and then turned into the Via Bergognona. At length he stopped before a little house with only a couple of windows, inhabited by a poor widow and her two daughters. This women had taken him in for little pay the first time he came to Rome, an unknown stranger noticed of nobody; and so he hoped again to find a lodging with her, such as would be best suited to the sad condition in which he then was.

He knocked confidently at the door, and several times called out his name aloud. At last he heard the old woman slowly and reluctantly wakening up out of her sleep. She shuffled to the window in her slippers, and began to rain down a shower of abuse upon the knave who was come to worry her in this way in the middle of the night; her house was not a wine-shop, &c., &c. Then there ensued a good deal of cross-questioning before she recognized her former lodger's voice; but on Salvator's complaining that he had fled from Naples and was unable to find a shelter in Rome, the old dame cried, "By all the blessed saints of Heaven! Is that you, Signor Salvator? Well now, your little room up above, that looks on to the court, is still standing empty, and the old fig tree has pushed its branches right through the window and into the room, so that you can sit and work like as if you was in a beautiful cool arbor. Aye, and how pleased my girls will be that you have come back again, Signor Salvator. But, d'ye know, my Margarita's grown a big girl and fine-looking? You won't give her anymore rides on your knee now. And — and your little pussy, just fancy, three months ago she choked herself with a fish-bone. Ah well, we all shall come to the grave at last. But, d'ye know, my fat neighbor, who you so often laughed at and so often painted in such funny ways — d'ye know, she *did* marry that young fellow, Signor Luigi,

---

* The Corso is a wide thoroughfare running almost north and south from the Piazza del Popolo, a square on the north side of Rome, to the center of the city. It is in the Corso that the horse-races used to take place during the Carnival.

after all. Ah well! *nozze e magistrati sono da dio destinati* (marriages and magistrates are made in heaven) they say."

"But," cried Salvator, interrupting the old woman, "but, Signora Caterina, I entreat you by the blessed saints, do, pray, let me in, and then tell me all about your fig tree and your daughters, your cat and your fat neighbor — I am perishing of weariness and cold."

"Bless me, how impatient we are," rejoined the old dame; *"Chi va piano va sano, chi va presto more lesto* (more haste less speed, take things cool and live longer), I tell you. But you are tired, you are cold; where are the keys? quick with the keys!"

But the old woman still had to wake up her daughters and kindle a fire — but oh! she was such a long time about it — such a long, long time. At last she opened the door and let poor Salvator in; but scarcely had he crossed the threshold than, overcome by fatigue and illness, he dropped on the floor as if dead. Happily the widow's son, who generally lived at Tivoli, chanced to be at his mother's that night He was at once turned out of his bed to make room for the sick guest, which he willingly submitted to.

The old woman was very fond of Salvator, putting him, as far as his artistic powers went, above all the painters in the world; and in everything that he did she also took the greatest pleasure. She was therefore quite beside herself to see him in this lamentable condition, and wanted to run off to the neighboring monastery to fetch her father confessor, that he might come and fight against the adverse power of the disease with consecrated candles or some powerful amulet or other. On the other hand, her son thought it would be almost better to see about getting an experienced physician at once, and off he ran there and then to the Spanish Square, where he knew the distinguished Doctor Splendiano Accoramboni dwelt. No sooner did the doctor learn that the painter Salvator Rosa lay ill in the Via Bergognona than he at once declared himself ready to call early and see the patient.

Salvator lay unconscious, struck down by a most severe attack of fever. The old dame had hung up two or three pictures of saints above his bed, and was praying fervently. The girls, though bathed in tears, exerted themselves from time to time to get the sick man to swallow a few drops of the cooling lemonade which they had made, whilst their brother, who had taken his place at the head of the bed, wiped the cold sweat from his brow. And so morning found them, when with a loud creak the door opened, and the distinguished Doctor Splendiano Accoramboni entered the room.

If Salvator had not been so seriously ill that the two girls' hearts were melted in grief, they would, I think, for they were in general frolicsome and saucy, have enjoyed a hearty laugh at the Doctor's extraordinary appearance, instead of retiring shyly, as they did, into the corner, greatly alarmed. It will indeed be worth while to describe the outward appearance of the little man who presented himself at Dame Caterina's in the Via Bergognona in the grey of the morning. In spite of all his excellent capabilities for growth, Doctor Splendiano Accoramboni had not been able to advance beyond the respectable stature of four feet Moreover, in the days of his youth, he had been distinguished for his elegant figure, so that, before his head, always indeed somewhat ill-shaped, and his big cheeks, and his stately double chin had put on too much fat, before his nose had grown bulky and spread owing to overmuch indulgence in Spanish snuff, and before his little belly had assumed the shape of a wine-tub from too much fattening on macaroni, the priestly cut of garments, which he at that time had affected, had suited him down to the ground. He was then in truth a pretty little man, and accordingly the Roman ladies had styled him their *caro puppazetto* (sweet little pet).

That however was now a thing of the past. A German painter, seeing Doctor Splendiano walking across the Spanish Square, said — and he was perhaps not far wrong — that it looked as if some strapping fellow of six feet or so had walked away from his own head, which had fallen on the shoulders of a little marionette clown, who now had to carry it about as his own. This curious little figure walked about in patchwork — an immense quantity of pieces of Venetian damask of a large flower pattern that had been cut up in making a dressing gown; high up round his waist he had buckled a broad leather belt, from which an excessively long rapier hung; whilst his snow-white wig was surmounted by a high conical cap, not unlike the obelisk in St. Peter's Square. Since the said wig, like a piece of texture all tumbled and tangled, spread out thick and wide all over his back, it might very well be taken for the cocoon out of which the fine silkworm had crept.

The worthy Splendiano Accoramboni stared through his big, bright spectacles, with his eyes wide open, first at his patient, then at Dame Caterina. Calling her aside, he croaked with bated breath, "There lies our talented painter Salvator Rosa, and he's lost if my skill doesn't save him, Dame Caterina. Pray tell me when he came to lodge with you? Did he bring many beautiful large pictures with him?"

"Ah! my dear Doctor," replied Dame Caterina, "the poor fellow only came last night. And as for pictures — why, I don't know nothing about them; but there's a big box below, and Salvator begged me to take very good care of it, before he became senseless like what he now is. I daresay there's a fine picture packed in it, as he painted in Naples."

What Dame Caterina said was, however, a falsehood; but we shall soon see that she had good reasons for imposing upon the Doctor in this way.

"Good! Very good!" said the Doctor, simpering and stroking his beard; then, with as much solemnity as his long rapier, which kept catching in all the chairs and tables he came near, would allow, he approached the sick man and felt his pulse, snorting and wheezing, so that it had a most curious effect in the midst of the reverential silence which had fallen upon all the rest. Then he ran over in Greek and Latin the names of a hundred and twenty diseases that Salvator had not, then almost as many which he might have had, and concluded by saying that on the spur of the moment he didn't recollect the name of his disease, but that he would within a short time find a suitable one for it, and along therewith, the proper remedies as well. Then he took his departure with the same solemnity with which he had entered, leaving them all full of trouble and anxiety.

At the bottom of the steps the Doctor requested to see Salvator's box; Dame Caterina showed him one — in which were two or three of her deceased husband's cloaks now laid aside, and some old worn-out shoes. The Doctor smilingly tapped the box, on this side and on that, and remarked in a tone of satisfaction "We shall see! we shall see!" Some hours later he returned with a very beautiful name for his patient's disease, and brought with him some big bottles of an evil-smelling potion, which he directed to be given to the patient constantly. This was a work of no little trouble, for Salvator showed the greatest aversion for — utter loathing of the stuff, which looked, and smelt, and tasted, as if it had been con-cocted from Acheron itself. Whether it was that the disease, since it had now received a name, and in consequence really signified something, had only just begun to put forth its virulence, or whether it was that Splendiano's potion made too much of a disturbance inside the patient — it is at any rate certain that the poor painter grew weaker and weaker from day to day, from hour to hour. And notwithstanding Doctor Splendiano Accoramboni's assurance that, after the vital process had reached a state of perfect equilibrium, he would give it a new start like the pendulum of a clock, they were all very doubtful as to Salvator's recovery, and thought that the Doctor had perhaps already given the pendulum such a violent start that the mechanism was quite impaired.

Now it happened one day that when Salvator seemed scarcely able to move a finger he was suddenly seized with the paroxysm of fever; in a momentary accession of fictitious strength he leapt out of bed, seized the full medicine bottles, and hurled them fiercely out of the window. Just at this moment Doctor Splendiano Accoramboni was entering the house, when two or three bottles came bang upon his head, smashing all to pieces, whilst the brown liquid ran in streams all down his face, and wig, and ruff. Hastily rushing into the house, he screamed like a madman, "Signer Salvator has gone out of his mind, he's become insane; no skill can save him now, he'll be dead in ten minutes. Give me the picture, Dame Caterina, give me the picture — it's mine, the scanty reward of all my trouble. Give me the picture, I say."

But when Dame Caterina opened the box, and Doctor Splendiano saw nothing but the old cloaks and torn shoes, his eyes spun round in his head like a pair of fire-wheels; he gnashed his teeth; he stamped; he consigned poor Salvator, the widow, and all the family to the devil; then he rushed out of the house like an arrow from a bow, or as if he had been shot from a cannon.

After the violence of the paroxysm had spent itself, Salvator again relapsed into a deathlike condition. Dame Caterina was fully persuaded that his end was really come, and away she sped as fast as she could to the monastery, to fetch Father Boniface, that he might come and administer the sacrament to the dying man. Father Boniface came and looked at the sick man; he said he was well acquainted with the peculiar signs which approaching death is wont to stamp upon the human countenance, but that for the present there were no indications of them on the face of the insensible Salvator. Something might still be done, and he would procure help at once, only Doctor Splendiano Accoramboni with his Greek names and infernal medicines was not to be allowed to cross the threshold again. The good Father set out at once, and we shall see later that he kept his word about sending the promised help.

Salvator recovered consciousness again; he fancied he was lying in a beautiful flower-scented arbor, for green boughs and leaves were interlacing above his head. He felt a salutary warmth glowing in his veins, but it seemed to him as if somehow his left arm was bound fast "Where am I?" he asked in a faint voice. Then a handsome young man, who had stood at his bedside, but whom he had not noticed until just now, threw himself upon his knees, and grasping Salvator's right hand, kissed it and bathed it with tears, as he cried again and again, "Oh! my dear sir! my noble master! now it's all right; you are saved, you'll get better."

"But do tell me" — began Salvator, when the young man begged him not to exert himself, for he was too weak to talk; he would tell him all that had happened. "You see, my esteemed and excellent sir," began the young man, "you see, you were very ill when you came from Naples, but your condition was not, I warrant, by any means so dangerous but that a few simple remedies would soon have set you, with your strong constitution, on your legs again, had you not through Carlos's well-intentioned blunder in running off for the nearest physician fallen into the hands of the redoubtable

Pyramid Doctor, who was making all preparations for bringing you to your grave."

"What do you say?" exclaimed Salvator, laughing heartily,
notwithstanding the feeble state he was in. "What do you say?
— the Pyramid Doctor? Aye, aye, although I was very ill, I saw
that the little knave in damask patchwork, who condemned
me to drink his horrid, loathsome devil's brew, wore on his
head the obelisk from St. Peter's Square — and so that's why
you call him the Pyramid Doctor?"

"Why, good heavens!" said the young man, likewise laughing, "why, Doctor Splendiano Accoramboni must have come
to see you in his ominous conical nightcap; and, do you
know, you may see it flashing every morning from his window
in the Spanish Square like a portentous meteor. But it's not
by any means owing to this cap that he's called the Pyramid
Doctor; for that there's quite another reason. Doctor Splendiano is a great lover of pictures, and possesses in truth quite
a choice collection, which he has gained by a practice of a
peculiar nature. With eager cunning he lies in wait for painters and their illnesses. More especially he loves to get foreign
artists into his toils; let them but eat an ounce or two of
macaroni too much, or drink a glass more Syracuse than is
altogether good for them, he will afflict them with first one
and then the other disease, designating it by a formidable
name, and proceeding at once to cure them of it. He generally
bargains for a picture as the price of his attendance; and as
it is only specially obstinate constitutions which are able to
withstand his powerful remedies, it generally happens that he
gets his picture out of the chattels left by the poor foreigner,
who meanwhile has been carried to the Pyramid of Cestius,
and buried there. It need hardly be said that Signor Splendiano always picks out the best of the pictures the painter has
finished, and also does not forget to bid the men take several
others along with it. The cemetery near the Pyramid of
Cestius is Doctor Splendiano Accoramboni's corn-field,
which he diligently cultivates, and for that reason he is called
the Pyramid Doctor. Dame Caterina had taken great pains,
of course with the best intentions, to make the Doctor believe
that you had brought a fine picture with you; you may
imagine therefore with what eagerness he concocted his po-

tions for you. It was a fortunate thing that in the paroxysm of fever you threw the Doctor's bottles at his head, it was also a fortunate thing that he left you in anger, and no less fortunate was it that Dame Caterina, who believed you were in the agonies of death, fetched Father Boniface to come and administer to you the sacrament. Father Boniface understands something of the art of healing; he formed a correct diagnosis of your condition and fetched me" —

"Then you also are a doctor?" asked Salvator in a faint whining tone.

"No," replied the young man, a deep blush mantling his cheeks, "no, my estimable and worthy sir, I am not in the least a doctor like Signor Splendiano Accoramboni; I am however a chirurgeon. I felt as if I should sink into the earth with fear — with joy — when Father Boniface came and told me that Salvator Rosa lay sick unto death in the Via Bergognona, and required my help. I hastened here, opened a vein in your left arm, and you were saved. Then we brought you up into this cool airy room that you formerly occupied. Look, there's the easel which you left behind you; yonder are a few sketches which Dame Caterina has treasured up as if they were relics. The virulence of your disease is subdued; simple remedies such as Father Boniface can prepare is all that you want, except good nursing, to bring back your strength again. And now permit me once more to kiss this hand — this creative hand that charms from Nature her deepest secrets and clothes them in living form. Permit poor Antonio Scacciati to pour out all the gratitude and immeasurable joy of his heart that Heaven has granted him to save the life of our great and noble painter, Salvator Rosa." Therewith the young surgeon threw himself on his knees again, and, seizing Salvator's hand, kissed it and bathed it in tears as before.

"I don't understand," said the artist, raising himself up a little, though with considerable difficulty, "I don't understand, my dear Antonio, what it is that is so especially urging you to show me all this respect. You are, you say, a chirurgeon, and we don't in a general way find this trade going hand in hand with art —"

"As soon," replied the young man, casting down his eyes, "as soon as you have picked up your strength again, my dear sir, I have a good deal to tell you that now lies heavy on my heart."

"Do so," said Salvator; "you may have every confidence in me — that you may, for I don't know that any man's face has made a more direct appeal to my heart than yours. The more I look at you the more plainly I seem to trace in your features a resemblance to that incomparable young painter — I mean Sanzio."* Antonio's eyes were lit up with a proud, radiant light — he vainly struggled for words with which to express his feelings.

At this moment Dame Caterina appeared, followed by Father Boniface, who brought Salvator a medicine which he had mixed scientifically according to prescription, and which the patient swallowed with more relish and felt to have a more beneficial effect upon him than the Acheronian waters of the Pyramid Doctor Splendiano Accoramboni.

II

*B*y Salvator Rosa's intervention Antonio Scacciati attains to a high honor. Antonio discloses the cause of his persistent trouble to Salvator, who consoles him and promises to help him.

And Antonio's words proved true. The simple but salutary remedies of Father Boniface, the careful nursing of good Dame Caterina and her daughters, the warmer weather which now came — all co-operated so well together with Salvator's naturally robust constitution that he soon felt sufficiently well to think about work again; first of all he designed a few sketches which he thought of working out afterwards.

Antonio scarcely ever left Salvator's room; he was all eyes when the painter drew out his sketches; whilst his judgment in respect to many points showed that he must have been initiated into the secrets of art.

---

* The great painter Sanzio Raphael.

"See here," said Salvator to him one day, "see here, Antonio, you understand art matters so well that I believe you have not merely cultivated your excellent judgment as a critic, but must have wielded the brush as well."

"You will remember," rejoined Antonio, "how I told you, my dear sir, when you were just about coming to yourself again after your long unconsciousness, that I had several things to tell you which lay heavy on my mind. Now is the time for me to unfold all my heart to you. You must know then, that though I am called Antonio Scacciati, the chirurgeon, who opened the vein in your arm for you, I belong also entirely to art – to the art which, after bidding eternal farewell to my hateful trade, I intend to devote myself for once and for all."

"Ho! ho!" exclaimed Salvator, "Ho! ho! Antonio, weigh well what you are about to do. You are a clever chirurgeon, and perhaps will never be anything more than a bungling painter all your life long; for, with your permission, as young as you are, you are decidedly too old to begin to use the charcoal now. Believe me, a man's whole lifetime is scarce long enough to acquire a knowledge of the True – still less the practical ability to represent it."

"Ah! but, my dear sir," replied Antonio, smiling blandly, "don't imagine that I should now have come to entertain the foolish idea of taking up the difficult art of painting had I not practiced it already on every possible occasion from my very childhood. In spite of the fact that my father obstinately kept me away from everything connected with art, yet Heaven was graciously pleased to throw me in the way of some celebrated artists. I must tell you that the great Annibal*

---

* Annabale Caracci, a painter of Bologna of the latter half of the sixteenth century. His most celebrated work is a series of frescoes on mythological subjects in the Farnese Palace at Rome. Along with his cousin Lodovico and his brother Agostino he founded the so-called Eclectic School of Painting; their maxim was that "accurate observation of Nature should be combined with judicious imitation of the best masters." The Caracci enjoyed the highest reputation amongst their contemporaries as teachers of their art. Annibale died in 1609; Masaniello's revolt occurred, as already mentioned, in 1647; Antonio must therefore have been at least fifty years of age. This however is not the only anachronism that Hoffmann is guilty of.

interested himself in the orphan boy, and also that I may with justice call myself Guido Reni's* pupil."

"Well then," said Salvator somewhat sharply, a way of speaking he sometimes had, "well then, my good Antonio, you have indeed had great masters, and so it cannot fail but that, without detriment to your surgical practice, you must have been a great pupil. Only I don't understand how you, a faithful disciple of the gentle, elegant Guido, whom you perhaps outdo in elegance in your own pictures — for pupils do do those sort of things in their enthusiasm — how you can find any pleasure in my productions, and can really regard me as a master in the Art."

At these words, which indeed sounded a good deal like derisive mockery, the hot blood rushed into the young man's face.

"Oh, let me lay aside all the diffidence which generally keeps my lips closed," he said, "and let me frankly lay bare the thoughts I have in my mind. I tell you, Salvator, I have never honored any master from the depths of my soul as I do you. What I am amazed at in your works is the sublime greatness of conception which is often revealed You grasp the deepest secrets of Nature: you comprehend the mysterious hieroglyphics of her rocks, of her trees, and of her waterfalls, you hear her sacred voice, you understand her language, and possess the power to write down what she has said to you. Verily I can call your bold free style of painting nothing else than writing down. Man alone and his doings does not suffice you; you behold him only in the midst of Nature, and in so far as his essential character is conditioned by natural phenomena; and in these facts I see the reason why you are only truly great in landscapes, Salvator, with their wonderful figures. Historical painting confines you within limits which clog your imagination to the detriment of your genius for reproducing your higher intuitions of Nature."

"That's talk you've picked up from envious historical painters," said Salvator, interrupting his young companion; "like them, Antonio, you throw me the choice bone of

---

* The well-known painter Guido, born in 1575 and died in 1642. He early excited the envy of Annibale Caracci.

landscape-painting that I may gnaw away at it, and so spare their own good flesh. Perhaps I do understand the human figure and all that is dependent upon it. But this senseless repetition of others' words" —

"Don't be angry," continued Antonio, "don't be angry, my good sir; I am not blindly repeating anybody's words, and I should not for a moment think of trusting to the judgment of our painters here in Rome at any rate. Who can help greatly admiring the bold draftsmanship, the powerful expression, but above all the living movement of your fingers? It's plain to see that you don't work from a stiff, inflexible model, or even from a dead skeleton form; it is evident that you yourself are your own breathing, living model, and that when you sketch or paint, you have the figure you want to put on your canvas reflected in a great mirror opposite to you."

"The devil! Antonio," exclaimed Salvator, laughing, "I believe you must often have had a peep into my studio when I was not aware of it, since you have such an accurate knowledge of what goes on within."

"Perhaps I may," replied Antonio; "but let me go on. I am not by a long way so anxious to classify, the pictures which your powerful mind suggests to you as are those pedantic critics who take such great pains in this line. In fact, I think that the word 'landscape,' as generally employed, has but an indifferent application to your productions; I should prefer to call them historical representations in the highest sense of the word. If we fancy that this or the other rock or this or the other tree is gazing at us like a gigantic being with thoughtful earnest eyes, so again, on the other hand, this or the other group of fantastically attired men resembles some remarkable stone which has been endowed with life; all Nature, breathing and moving in harmonious unity, lends accents to the sublime thought which leapt into existence in your mind. This is the spirit in which I have studied your pictures, and so in this way it is, my grand and noble master, that I owe to you my truer perceptions in matters of art. But pray don't imagine that I have fallen into childish imitation. However much I would like to possess the free bold pencil that you possess, I do not attempt to conceal the fact that Nature's colors appear to me different from what I see them in your pictures. Although it is useful, I think, for the sake of acquiring technique, for the pupil to imitate the style of this or that master, yet, so soon as he comes to stand in any sense on his own feet, he ought to aim at representing Nature as he himself sees her. Nothing but this true method of perception, this unity with oneself, can give rise to character and truth. Guido shared these sentiments; and that fiery man Preti,* who, as you are aware, is called *Il Calabrese* — a painter who certainly, more than any other man, has reflected upon his art — also warned me against all imitation. Now you know, Salvator, why I so much respect you, without imitating you."

Whilst the young man had been speaking, Salvator had kept his eyes fixed unchangeably upon him; he now clasped him tumultuously to his heart.

"Antonio," he then said, "what you have just now said are wise and thoughtful words. Young as you are, you are nevertheless, so far as the true perception of art is concerned, a long way ahead of many of our old and much vaunted masters, who have a good deal of stupid foolish twaddle about their painting, but never get at the true root of the matter. Body alive, man! When you were talking about my pictures, I then began to understand myself for the first time, I believe; and because you do not imitate my style, — do not, like a good many others, take a tube of black paint in your hand, or dab on a few glaring colors, or even make two or three crippled figures with repulsive faces look up from the midst of filth and dirt, and then say, 'There's a Salvator for you!' — just for these very reasons I think a good deal of you. I tell you, my lad, you'll not find a more faithful friend than I am — that I can promise you with all my heart and soul."

Antonio was beside himself with joy at the kind way in which the great painter thus testified to his interest in him. Salvator expressed an earnest desire to see his pictures. Antonio took him there and then to his studio.

---

* Mattia Preti, known as *Il Cavaliere Calabrese*, from his having been born in Calabria. He was a painter of the Neapolitan school and a pupil of Lanfranco, and lived during the greater part of the seventeenth century. Owing to his many disputes and quarrels he was more than once compelled to flee for his life.

Salvator had in truth expected to find something fairly good from the young man who spoke so intelligently about art, and who, it appeared, had a good deal in him; but nevertheless he was greatly surprised at the sight of Antonio's fine pictures. Everywhere he found boldness in conception, and correctness in drawing; and the freshness of the coloring, the good taste in the arrangement of the drapery, the uncommon delicacy of the extremities, the exquisite grace of the heads, were all so many evidences that he was no unworthy pupil of the great Reni. But Antonio had avoided this master's besetting sin of an endeavor, only too conspicuous, to sacrifice expression to beauty. It was plain that Antonio was aiming to reach Annibal's strength, without having as yet succeeded.

Salvator spent some considerable time of thoughtful silence in the examination of each of the pictures. Then he said, "Listen, Antonio: it is indeed undeniable that you were born to follow the noble art of painting. For not only has Nature endowed you with the creative spirit from which the finest thoughts pour forth in an inexhaustible stream, but she has also granted you the rare ability to surmount in a short space of time the difficulties of technique. It would only be false flattery if I were to tell you that you had yet advanced to the level of your masters, that you are yet equal to Guido's exquisite grace or to Annibal's strength; but certain I am that you excel by a long way all the painters who hold up their heads so proudly in the Academy of St. Luke* here — Tiarini,† Gessi,‡ Sementa,¶ and all the rest of them, not even excepting Lanfranco§ himself, for he only understands fresco-painting. And yet, Antonio, and yet, if I were in your place, I should deliberate awhile before throwing away the lancet altogether,

---

* The Accademia di San Luca, a school of art, founded at Rome about 1595, Federigo Zuccaro being its first director.

† Alessandro Tiarini (1577-1668) of Bologna, was a pupil of the Caracci.

‡ Giovanni Francesco Gessi (1588-1649), sometimes called "The second Guido," was a pupil of Guido.

¶ Sementi or Semenza (1580-1638), also a pupil of Guido.

§ Giovanni Lanfranco (1581-1647), studied first under Agostino Caracci. He was the first to encourage the early genius of Salvator Rosa.

and confining myself entirely to the pencil That sounds rather strange, but listen to me. Art seems to be having a bad time of it just now, or rather the devil seems to be very busy amongst our painters nowadays, bravely setting them together by the ears. If you cannot make up your mind to put up with all sorts of annoyances, to endure more and more scorn and contumely in proportion as you advance in art, and as your fame spreads to meet with malicious scoundrels everywhere, who with a friendly face will force themselves upon you in order to ruin you the more surely afterwards, — if you cannot, I say, make up your mind to endure all this — let painting alone. Think of the fate of your teacher, the great Annibal, whom a rascally band of rivals malignantly persecuted in Naples, so that he did not receive one single commission for a great work, being everywhere rejected with contempt; and this is said to have been instrumental in bringing about his early death. Think of what happened to Domenichino*

The atmosphere of the age they lived in was highly charged with vigor of thought and an irrepressible vitality for artistic production. Under the conditions which these things sup-

---

* Zampieri Domenichino (1581–1641) was a pupil of the Caracci. The work here referred to is a series of frescoes, which he did not live to quite finish, representing the events of the life of St. Januarius, in the chapel of the Tesoro of the cathedral at Naples, which he began in 1630.

The malicious spite which the text attributes to the rivals of Domenichino is not at all exaggerated. There did really exist a so-called "Cabal of Naples," consisting chiefly of the painters Corenzio, Ribera, and Caracciolo, who leagued together to shut out all competition from other artists; and their persecution of the Bolognese Domenichino is well known. Often on returning to his work in the morning he found that someone had obliterated what he had done on the previous day.

Not only have we a faithful picture of the Italian artist's life in the middle of the seventeenth century depicted in this tale, but the actual facts of the lives of Salvator Rosa, of Preti, of the Caracci, as well as the existence of Falcone's *Compagnia della Morte*, furnish ample materials and illustrations of the wild lives they did lead, of their jealousies and heartburnings, of their quarrelsomeness and revengefulness. They seem to have been ready on all occasions to exchange the brush for the sword. They were filled to overflowing with restless energy.

pose the artists of that age could not well have been otherwise than what they were. when he was painting the dome of the chapel of St. Januarius. Didn't the villains of painters — I won't mention a single name, not even the rascals Belisario* and Ribera† — didn't they bribe Domenichino's servant to strew ashes in the lime? So the plaster wouldn't stick fast on the walls, and the painting had no stability. Think of all that, and examine yourself well whether your spirit is strong enough to endure things like that, for if not, your artistic power will be broken, and along with the resolute courage for work you will also lose your ability."

"But, Salvator," replied Antonio, "it would hardly be possible for me to have more scorn and contumely to endure, supposing I took up painting entirely and exclusively, then I have already endured whilst merely a chirurgeon. You have been pleased with my pictures, you have indeed! and at the same time declared from inner conviction that I am capable of doing better things than several of our painters of the Academy. But these are just the men who turn up their noses at all that I have industriously produced, and say contemptuously, 'Do look, here's our chirurgeon wants to be a painter!' And for this very reason my resolve is only the more unshaken; I will sever myself from a trade that grows with every day more hateful. Upon you, my honored master, I now stake all my hopes. Your word is powerful; if you would speak a good word for me, you might overthrow my envious persecutors at a single blow, and put me in the place where I ought to be."

"You repose great confidence in me," rejoined Salvator. "But now that we thoroughly understand each other's views on painting, and I have seen your works, I don't really know that there is anybody for whom I would rather take up the cudgels than for you."

---

*   Belisario Corenzio, a Greek (1558-1643). "Envious, jealous, cunning, treacherous, quarrelsome, he looked upon all other painters as his enemies."

†   Giuseppe Ribera, called *Il Spagnoletto*, a Spaniard by birth (1589), was a painter of the Neapolitan school, and delighted in horrible and gloomy subjects. He died in 1656.

Salvator once more inspected Antonio's pictures, and stopped before one representing a "Magdalene at the Saviour's feet," which he especially praised.

"In this Magdalene," he said, "you have deviated from the usual mode of representation. Your Magdalene is not a thoughtful virgin, but a lovely artless child rather, and yet she is such a marvelous child that hardly anybody else but Guido could have painted her. There is a unique charm in her dainty figure; you must have painted with inspiration; and, if I mistake not, the original of this Magdalene is alive and to be found in Rome. Come, confess, Antonio, you are in love!"

Antonio's eyes sought the ground, whilst he said in a low shy voice, "Nothing escapes your penetration, my dear sir; perhaps it is as you say, but do not blame me for it. That picture I set the highest store by, and hitherto I have guarded it as a holy secret from all men's eyes."

"What do you say?" interrupted Salvator. "None of the painters here have seen your picture?"

"No, not one," was Antonio's reply.

"All right then, Antonio," continued Salvator, his eyes sparkling with delight "Very well then, you may rely upon it, I will overwhelm your envious overweening persecutors, and get you the honor you deserve. Intrust your picture to me; bring it to my studio secretly by night, and then leave all the rest to me. Will you do so?"

"Gladly, with all my heart," replied Antonio. "And now I should very much like to talk to you about my love-troubles as well; but I feel as if I ought not to do so today, after we have opened our minds to each other on the subject of art. I also entreat you to grant me your assistance both in word and deed later on in this matter of my love."

"I am at your service," said Salvator, "for both, both when and where you require me." Then as he was going away, he once more turned round and said, smiling, "See here, Antonio, when you disclosed to me the fact that you were a painter, I was very sorry that I had spoken about your resemblance to Sanzio. I took it for granted that you were as silly as most of our young folk, who, if they bear but the slightest resemblance in the face to any great master, at once trim their beard or hair as he does, and from this cause fancy it is their business to imitate the style of the master in their art achievements, even though it is a manifest violation of their natural talents to do so. Neither of us has mentioned Raphael's name, but I assure you that I have discerned in your pictures clear indications that you have grasped the full significance of the inimitable thoughts which are reflected in the works of this the greatest of the painters of the age. You understand Raphael, and would give me a different answer from what Velasquez* did when I asked him not long ago what he thought of Sanzio. 'Titian,' he replied, 'is the greatest painter; Raphael knows nothing about carnation.' This Spaniard, methinks, understands flesh but not criticism; and yet these men in St. Luke elevate him to the clouds because he once painted cherries which the sparrows picked at."†

It happened not many days afterwards that the Academicians of St. Luke met together in their church to prove the works which had been announced for exhibition. There too Salvator had sent Scacciati's fine picture. In spite of themselves the painters were greatly struck with its grace and power; and from all lips there was heard nothing but the most extravagant praise when Salvator informed them that he had brought the picture with him from Naples, as the legacy of a young painter who had been cut off in the pride of his days.

It was not long before all Rome was crowding to see and admire the picture of the young unknown painter who had died so young; it was unanimously agreed that no such work had been done since Guido Reni's time; some even went so far in their just enthusiasm as to place this exquisitely lovely Magdalene before Guido's creations of a similar kind. Amongst the crowd of people who were always gathered round Scacciati's picture, Salvator one day observed a man who, besides presenting a most extraordinary appearance,

---

* Don Diego Velazquez de Silva, the great Spanish painter, born in 1599, died in 1660. He twice visited Italy and Naples, in 1629–31 and in 1648–51, and was for a time intimate with Ribera.

† This suggests the legend of Quentin Massys of Antwerp and the fly, or the still older, but perhaps not more historical story of the Greek painters, Zeuxis and the bunch of grapes, which the birds came to peck at, and Parrhasius, whose curtain deceived even Zeuxis himself.

behaved as if he were crazy. Well advanced in years, he was tall, thin as a spindle, with a pale face, a long sharp nose, a chin equally as long, ending moreover in a little pointed beard, and with grey, gleaming eyes. On the top of his light sand-colored wig he had set a high hat with a magnificent feather; he wore a short dark red mantle or cape with many bright buttons, a sky-blue doublet slashed in the Spanish style, immense leather gauntlets with silver fringes, a long rapier at his side, light grey stockings drawn up above his bony knees and gartered with yellow ribbons, whilst he had bows of the same sort of yellow ribbon on his shoes.

This remarkable figure was standing before the picture like one enraptured: he raised himself on tiptoe; he stooped down till he became quite small; then he jumped up with both feet at once, heaved deep sighs, groaned, nipped his eyes so close together that the tears began to trickle down his cheeks, opened them wide again, fixed his gaze immovably upon the charming Magdalene, sighed again, lisped in a thin, querulous, mutilated voice, *"Ah! carissima – benedettissima! Ah! Marianna – Mariannina – bellissima,"* &c. ("Oh! dearest – most adored! Ah! Marianna – sweet Marianna! my most beautiful!") Salvator, who had a mad fancy for such oddities, drew near to the old fellow, intending to engage him in conversation about Scacciati's work, which seemed to afford him so much exquisite delight Without paying any particular heed to Salvator, the old gentleman stood cursing his poverty, because he could not give a million sequins for the picture, and place it under lock and key where nobody could set their infernal eyes upon it. Then, hopping up and down again, he blessed the Virgin and all the holy saints that the reprobate artist who had painted the heavenly picture which was driving him to despair and madness was dead.

Salvator concluded that the man either was out of his mind, or was an Academician of St. Luke with whom he was unacquainted.

All Rome was full of Scacciati's wonderful picture; people could scarcely talk about anything else, and this of course was convincing proof of the excellence of the work. And when the painters were again assembled in the church of St. Luke, to decide about the admission of certain other pictures which had been announced for exhibition, Salvator Rosa all at once asked, whether the painter of the "Magdalene at the Saviour's Feet" was not worthy of being admitted a member of the Academy. They all with one accord, including even that hairsplitter in criticism, Baron Josépin,* declared that such a great artist would have been an ornament to the Academy, and expressed their sorrow at his death in the choicest phrases, although, like the crazy old man, they were praising Heaven in their hearts that he was dead. Still more, they were so far carried away by their enthusiasm that they passed a resolution to the effect that the admirable young painter whom death had snatched away from art so early should be nominated a member of the Academy in his grave, and that masses should be read for the benefit of his soul in the church of St. Luke. They therefore begged Salvator to inform them what was the full name of the deceased, the date of his birth, the place where he was born, &c.

Then Salvator rose and said in a loud voice, "Signors, the honor you are anxious to render to a dead man you can more easily bestow upon a living man who walks in your midst. Learn that the 'Magdalene at the Saviour's Feet' — the picture which you so justly exalt above all other artistic productions that the last few years have given us, is not the work of a dead Neapolitan painter as I pretended (this I did simply to get an unbiassed judgment from you); that painting, that master-piece, which all Rome is admiring, is from the hand of Signor Antonio Scacciati, the chirurgeon."

The painters sat staring at Salvator as if suddenly thunder-struck, incapable of either moving or uttering a single sound. He, however, after quietly exulting over their embarrassment for some minutes, continued, "Well now, signors, you would not tolerate the worthy Antonio amongst you because he is a chirurgeon; but I think that the illustrious Academy of St. Luke has great need of a surgeon to set the limbs of the many crippled figures which emerge from the studios of a good

---

*   Giuseppe Cesari, colled Josépin or the Chevalier d'Arpin, a painter of the Roman school, born in 1560 or 1568, died in 1640. He posed as an artistic critic in Rome during the later years of his life, and his judgment was claimed by his friends to be authoritative and final in all matters connected with art.

many amongst your number. But of course you will no longer scruple to do what you ought to have done long ago, namely, elect that excellent painter Antonio Scacciati a member of the Academy."

The Academicians, swallowing Salvator's bitter pill, feigned to be highly delighted that Antonio had in this way given such incontestable proofs of his talent, and with all due ceremony nominated him a member of the Academy.

As soon as it became known in Rome that Antonio was the author of the wonderful picture he was overwhelmed with congratulations, and even with commissions for great works, which poured in upon him from all sides. Thus by Salvator's shrewd and cunning stratagem the young man emerged all at once out of his obscurity, and with the first real step he took on his artistic career rose to great honor.

Antonio revelled in ecstasies of delight. So much the more therefore did Salvator wonder to see him, some days later, appear with his face pale and distorted, utterly miserable and woebegone. "Ah! Salvator!" said Antonio, "what advantage has it been to me that you have helped me to rise to a level far beyond my expectations, that I am now overwhelmed with praise and honor, that the prospect of a most successful artistic career is opening out before me? Oh! I am utterly miserable, for the picture to which, next to you, my dear sir, I owe my great triumph, has proved the source of my lasting misfortune."

"Stop!" replied Salvator, "don't sin against either your art or your picture. I don't believe a word about the terrible misfortune which, you say, has befallen you. You are in love, and I presume you can't get all your wishes gratified at once, on the spur of the moment; that's all it is. Lovers are like children; they scream and cry if anybody only just touches their doll. Have done, I pray you, with that lamentation, for I tell you I can't do with it. Come now, sit yourself down there and quietly tell me all about your fair Magdalene, and give me the history of your love affair, and let me know what are the stones of offence that we have to remove, for I promise you my help beforehand. The more adventurous the schemes are which we shall have to undertake, the more I shall like them. In fact, my blood is coursing hotly in my veins again, and my regimen requires that I engage in a few wild pranks. But go on with your story, Antonio, and as I said, let's have it quietly without any sighs and lamentations, without any Ohs! and Ahs!"

Antonio took his seat on the stool which Salvator had pushed up to the easel at which he was working, and began as follows: —

"There is a high house in the Via Ripetta,* with a balcony which projects far over the street so as at once to strike the eye of anyone entering through the Porta del Popolo, and there dwells perhaps the most whimsical oddity in all Rome, — an old bachelor with every fault that belongs to that class of persons — avaricious, vain, anxious to appear young, amorous, foppish. He is tall, as thin as a switch, wears a gay Spanish costume, a sandy wig, a conical hat, leather gauntlets, a rapier at his side" —

"Stop, stop!" cried Salvator, interrupting him, "excuse me a minute or two, Antonio." Then, turning about the picture at which he was painting, he seized his charcoal and in a few free bold strokes sketched on the back side of the canvas the eccentric old gentleman whom he had seen behaving like a crazed man in front of Antonio's picture.

"By all the saints!" cried Antonio, as he leapt to his feet, and, forgetful of his unhappiness, burst out into a loud laugh, "by all the saints! that's he! That's Signor Pasquale Capuzzi, whom I was just describing, that's he to the very T."

"So you see," said Salvator calmly, "that I am already acquainted with the worthy gentleman who most probably is your bitter enemy. But go on."

"Signor Pasquale Capuzzi," continued Antonio, "is as rich as Crœsus, but at the same time, as I just told you, a sordid miser and an incurable coxcomb. The best thing about him

---

* In a previous note it was stated that the Via del Corse ran from the Piazza del Popolo southwards to the center of the city of Rome. Besides this street there are two others which run from the same square in almost the same direction, the Via di Ripetta and the Via del Babuino, the former being to the west of the Via del Corso and the latter to the east, and each gradually gets more distant from the Via del Corso the farther it recedes from the Square. On the opposite side of the Piazza del Popolo is the Porta del Popolo.

is that he loves art, particularly music and painting; but he mixes up so much folly with it all that even in these things there's no getting on with him. He considers himself the greatest musical composer in the world, and that there's not a singer in the Papal choir who can at all approach him. Accordingly he looks down upon our old Frescobaldi* with contempt; and when the Romans talk about the wonderful charm of Ceccarelli's voice, he informs them that Ceccarelli knows as much about singing as a pair of top-boots, and that he, Capuzzi, knows which is the right way to fascinate the public. But as the first singer of the Pope bears the proud name of Signor Odoardo Ceccarelli di Merania, so our Capuzzi is greatly delighted when anybody calls him Signor Pasquale Capuzzi di Senigaglia; for it was in Senigaglia† that he was born, and the popular rumor goes that his mother, being startled at sight of a sea-dog (seal) suddenly rising to the surface, gave birth to him in a fisherman's boat, and that accounts, it is said, for a good deal of the sea-cur in his nature. Several years ago he brought out an opera on the stage, which was fearfully hissed; but that hasn't cured him of his mania for writing execrable music. Indeed, when he heard Francesco Cavalli's‡ opera *Le Nozze di Feti e di Peleo,* he swore that the composer had filched the sublimest of the thoughts from his own immortal works, for which he was near being thrashed and even stabbed. He still has a craze for singing arias, and accompanies his hideous squalling on a wretched jarring, jangling guitar, all out of tune. His faithful Pylades is an ill-bred dwarfish eunuch, whom the Romans call Pitichinaccio. There is a third member of the company — guess who it is? — Why, none other than the Pyramid Doctor, who kicks up a noise like a melancholy ass and yet fancies he's singing an excellent bass, quite as good as Martinelli of the Papal

---

* Girolamo Frescobaldi, the most distinguished organist of the seventeenth century, born about 1587 or 1588. He early won a reputation both as a singer and as an organist.

† Senigaglia or Senigallia, a town on the Adriatic, in the province of Ancona.

‡ Pietro Francesco Cavalli, whose real name was Caletti-Bruni. He was organist at St. Mark's at Venice for about thirty-six years (1640–1676). He composed both for the Church and for the stage.

choir. Now these three estimable people are in the habit of meeting in the evening on the balcony of Capuzzi's house, where they sing Carissimi's* motets, until all the dogs and cats in the neighborhood round break out into dirges of miawing and howling, and all their neighbors heartily wish the devil would run away with all the blessed three.

"With this whimsical old fellow, Signor Pasquale Capuzzi, of whom my description will have enabled you to form a tolerably adequate idea, my father lived on terms of intimacy, since he trimmed his wig and beard. When my father died, I undertook this business; and Capuzzi was in the highest degree satisfied with me, because, as he once affirmed, I knew better than anybody else how to give his moustaches a bold upward twirl; but the real reason was because I was satisfied with the few pence with which he rewarded me for my pains. But he firmly believed that he more than richly indemnified me, since, whilst I was trimming his beard, he always closed his eyes and croaked through an aria from his own compositions, which, however, almost split my ears; and yet the old fellow's crazy gestures afforded me a good deal of amusement, so that I continued to attend him. One day when I went, I quietly ascended the stairs, knocked at the door, and opened it, when lo, there was a girl — an angel of light, who came to meet me. You know my Magdalene; it was she. I stood stock still, rooted to the spot. No, Salvator, you shall have no Ohs! and Ahs! Well, the first sight of this, the most lovely maiden of her sex, enkindled in me the most ardent passionate love. The old man informed me with a smirk that the young lady was the daughter of his brother Pietro, who had died at Senigaglia, that her name was Marianna, and that she was quite an orphan; being her uncle and guardian, he had taken her into his house. You can easily imagine that henceforward Capuzzi's house was my Paradise. But no matter what devices I had recourse to, I could never succeed in getting a *téte-à-téte* with Marianna, even for a single moment. Her glances, how-

---

* Giacomo Carissimi, attached during the greater part of his life to the church of San Apollinaris at Rome. He died in 1674. He did much for musical art, perfecting recitative and advancing the development of the sacred cantata. His accompaniments are generally distinguished for "lightness and variety."

ever, and many a stolen sigh, and many a soft pressure of the hand, resolved all doubts as to my good fortune. The old man divined what I was after, — which was not a very difficult thing for him to do. He informed me that my behavior towards his niece was not such as to please him altogether, and he asked me what was the real purport of my attentions. Then I frankly confessed that I loved Marianna with all my heart, and that the greatest earthly happiness I could conceive was a union with her. Whereupon Capuzzi, after measuring me from top to toe, burst out in a guffaw of contempt, and declared that he never had any idea that such lofty thoughts could haunt the brain of a paltry barber. I was almost boiling with rage; I said he knew very well that I was no paltry barber but rather a good surgeon, and, moreover, in so far as concerned the noble art of painting, a faithful pupil of the great Annibal Caracci and of the unrivalled Guido Reni. But the infamous Capuzzi only replied by a still louder guffaw of laughter, and in his horrible falsetto squeaked, 'See here, my sweet Signor barber, my excellent Signor surgeon, my honored Annibal Caracci, my beloved Guido Reni, be off to the devil, and don't ever show yourself here again, if you don't want your legs broken.' Therewith the cranky, knock-kneed old fool laid hold of me with no less an intention than to kick me out of the room, and hurl me down the stairs. But that, you know, was past everything. With ungovernable fury I seized the old fellow and tripped him up, so that his legs stuck uppermost in the air; and there I left him screaming aloud, whilst I ran down the stairs and out of the house-door; which, I need hardly say, has been closed to me ever since.

"And that's how matters stood when you came to Rome and when Heaven inspired Father Boniface with the happy idea of bringing me to you. Then so soon as your clever trick had brought me the success for which I had so long been vainly striving, that is, when I was accepted by the Academy of St. Luke, and all Rome was heaping up praise and honor upon me to a lavish extent, I went straightway to the old gentleman and suddenly presented myself before him in his own room, like a threatening apparition. Such at least he must have thought me, for he grew as pale as a corpse, and retreated behind a great table, trembling in every limb. And in a firm and earnest way I represented to him that it was not now a paltry barber or a surgeon, but a celebrated painter and Academician of St. Luke, Antonio Scacciati, to whom he would not, I hoped, refuse the hand of his niece Marianna. You should have seen into what a passion the old fellow flew. He screamed; he flourished his arms about like one possessed of devils; he yelled that I, a ruffianly murderer, was seeking his life, that I had stolen his Marianna from him since I had portrayed her in my picture, and it was driving him mad, driving him to despair, for all the world, all the world, were fixing their covetous, lustful eyes upon his Marianna, his life, his hope, his all; but I had better take care, he would burn my house over my head, and me and my picture in it. And therewith he kicked up such a din, shouting, 'Fire! Murder! Thieves! Help!' that I was perfectly confounded, and only thought of making the best of my way out of the house.

"The crackbrained old fool is over head and ears in love with his niece; he keeps her under lock and key; and as soon as he succeeds in getting dispensation from the Pope, he will compel her to a shameful alliance with himself. All hope for me is lost!"

"Nay, nay, not quite," said Salvator, laughing, "I am of opinion that things could not be in a better form for you, Marianna loves you, of that you are convinced; and all we have to do is to get her out of the power of that fantastic old gentleman, Signor Pasquale Capuzzi. I should like to know what there is to hinder a couple of stout enterprising fellows like you and me from accomplishing this. Pluck up your courage, Antonio. Instead of bewailing, and sighing, and fainting like a lovesick swain, it would be better to set to work to think out some plan for rescuing your Marianna. You just wait and see, Antonio, how finely we'll circumvent the old dotard; in such like emprises, the wildest extravagance hardly seems to me wild enough. I'll set about it at once, and learn what I can about the old man, and about his usual habits of life. But you must not be seen in this affair, Antonio. Go away quietly home, and come back to me early tomorrow morning, then we'll consider our first plan of attack."

Herewith Salvator shook the paint out of his brush, threw on his mantle, and hurried to the Corso, whilst Antonio betook himself home as Salvator had bidden him — his heart comforted and full of lusty hope again.

III

Signor Pasquale Capuzzi turns up at Salvator Rosa's studio. What takes place there. The cunning scheme which Rosa and Scacciati carry out, and the consequences of the same.

Next morning Salvator, having in the meantime inquired into Capuzzi's habits of life, very greatly surprised Antonio by a description of them, even down to the minutest details.

"Poor Marianna," said Salvator, "leads a sad life of it with the crazy old fellow. There he sits sighing and ogling the whole day long, and, what is worse still, in order to soften her heart towards him, he sings her all and sundry love ditties that he has ever composed or intends to compose. At the same time he is so monstrously jealous that he will not even permit the poor young girl to have the usual female attendance, for fear of intrigues and amours, which the maid might be induced to engage in. Instead, a hideous little apparition with hollow eyes and pale flabby cheeks appears every morning and evening to perform for sweet Marianna the services of a tiring-maid. And this little apparition is nobody else but that tiny Tomb Thumb of a Pitichinaccio, who has to don female attire. Capuzzi, whenever he leaves home, carefully locks and bolts every door; besides which there is always a confounded fellow keeping watch below, who was formerly a bravo, and then a gendarme, and now lives under Capuzzi's rooms. It seems, therefore, a matter almost impossible to effect an entrance into his house, but nevertheless I promise you, Antonio, that this very night you shall be in Capuzzi's own room and shall see your Marianna, though this time it will only be in Capuzzi's presence."

"What do you say?" cried Antonio, quite excited; "what do you say? We shall manage it tonight? I thought it was impossible."

"There, there," continued Salvator, "keep still, Antonio, and let us quietly consider how we may with safety carry out the plan which I have conceived. But in the first place I must tell you that I have already scraped an acquaintance with Signor Pasquale Capuzzi without knowing it. That wretched spinet, which stands in the comer there, belongs to the old fellow, and he wants me to pay him the preposterous sum of ten ducats* for it. When I was convalescent I longed for some music, which always comforts me and does me a deal of good, so I begged my landlady to get me some such an instrument as that Dame Caterina soon ascertained that there was an old gentleman living in the Via Ripetta who had a fine spinet to sell I got the instrument brought here. I did not trouble myself either about the price or about the owner. It was only yesterday evening that I learned quite by chance that the gentleman who intended to cheat me with this rickety old thing was Signor Pasquale Capuzzi. Dame Caterina had enlisted the services of an acquaintance living in the same house, and indeed on the same floor as Capuzzi, — and now you can easily guess whence I have got all my budget of news."

"Yes," replied Antonio, "then the way to get in is found; your landlady" —

"I know very well, Antonio," said Salvator, cutting him short, "I know what you're going to say. You think you can find a way to your Marianna through Dame Caterina. But you'll find that we can't do anything of that sort; the good dame is far too talkative; she can't keep the least secret, and

---

* The first silver ducat is believed to have been struck in 1140 by Roger II., Norman king of Sicily; and ducats have been struck constantly since the twelfth century, especially at Venice (see *Merchant of Venice*). They have varied considerably both in weight and fineness, and consequently in value, at different times and places. Ducats have been struck in both gold and silver. The early Venetian silver ducat was worth about five shillings. The name is said, according to one account, to have been derived from the last word of the Latin legend found on the earliest Venetian gold coins: — *Sit tibi, Christe, datus, quem tu regis, ducatus* (duchy); according to another account it is taken from *"il ducato,"* the name generally applied to the duchy of Apulia.

so we can't for a single moment think of employing her in this business. Now just quietly listen to me. Every evening when it's dark Signor Pasquale, although it's very hard work for him owing to his being knock-kneed, carries his little friend the eunuch home in his arms, as soon as he has finished his duties as maid. Nothing in the world could induce the timid Pitichinaccio to set foot on the pavement at that time of night. So that when" —

At this moment somebody knocked at Salvator's door, and to the consternation of both, Signor Pasquale stepped in in all the splendor of his gala attire. On catching sight of Scacciati he stood stock still as if paralyzed, and then, opening his eyes wide, he gasped for air as though he had some difficulty in breathing. But Salvator hastily ran to meet him, and took him by both hands, saying, "My dear Signor Pasquale, your presence in my humble dwelling is, I feel, a very great honor. May I presume that it is your love for art which brings you to me? You wish to see the newest things I have done, perchance to give me a commission for some work. Pray in what, my dear Signor Pasquale, can I serve you?"

"I have a word or two to say to you, my dear Signor Salvator," stammered Capuzzi painfully, "but — alone — when you are alone. With your leave I will withdraw and come again at a more seasonable time."

"By no means," said Salvator, holding the old gentleman fast, "by no means, my dear sir. You need not stir a step; you could not have come at a more seasonable time, for, since you are a great admirer of the noble art of painting, and the patron of all good painters, I am sure you will be greatly pleased for me to introduce to you Antonio Scacciati here, the first painter of our time, whose glorious work — the wonderful 'Magdalene at the Saviour's Feet' — has excited throughout all Rome the most enthusiastic admiration. You too, I need hardly say, have also formed a high opinion of the work, and must be very anxious to know the great artist himself."

The old man was seized with a violent trembling; he shook as if he had a shivering fit of the ague, and shot fiery wrathful looks at poor Antonio. He however approached the old gentleman, and, bowing with polished courtesy, assured him that he esteemed himself happy at meeting in such an unexpected way with Signor Pasquale Capuzzi, whose great learning in music as well as in painting was a theme for wonder not only in Rome but throughout all Italy, and he concluded by requesting the honor of his patronage.

This behavior of Antonio, in pretending to meet the old gentleman for the first time in his life, and in addressing him in such flattering phrases, soon brought him round again. He forced his features into a simpering smile, and, as Salvator now let his hands loose, gave his moustache an elegant upward curl, at the same time stammering out a few unintelligible words. Then, turning to Salvator, he requested payment of the ten ducats for the spinet he had sold him.

"Oh! that trifling little matter we can settle afterwards, my good sir," was Salvator's answer. "First have the goodness to look at this sketch of a picture which I have drawn, and drink a glass of good Syracuse whilst you do so." Salvator meanwhile placed his sketch on the easel and moved up a chair for the old gentleman, and then, when he had taken his seat, he presented him with a large and handsome wine-cup full of good Syracuse — the little pearllike bubbles rising gaily to the top.

Signor Pasquale was very fond of a glass of good wine — when he had nothing to pay for it; and now he ought to have been in an especially happy frame of mind, for, besides nourishing his heart with the hope of getting ten ducats for a rotten, worn-out spinet, he was sitting before a splendid, boldly-designed picture, the rare beauty of which he was quite capable of estimating at its full worth. And that he was in this happy frame of mind he evidenced in divers way; he simpered most charmingly; he half closed his little eyes; he assiduously stroked his chin and moustache; and lisped time after time, "Splendid! delicious!" but they did not know to which he was referring, the picture or the wine.

When he had thus worked himself round into a quiet cheerful humor, Salvator suddenly began — "They tell me, my dear sir, that you have a most beautiful and amiable niece, named Marianna — is it so? All the young men of the city are so smitten with love that they stupidly do nothing but run up and down the Via Ripetta, almost dislocating their necks in their efforts to look up at your balcony for a sight of your sweet Marianna, to snatch a single glance from her heavenly eyes."

Suddenly all the charming simpers, all the good humor which had been called up into the old gentleman's face by the good wine, were gone. Looking gloomily before him, he said sharply, "Ah! that's an instance of the corruption of our abandoned young men. They fix their infernal eyes, there probate seducers, upon mere children. For I tell you, my good sir, that my niece Marianna is quite a child, quite a child, only just outgrown her nurse's care."

Salvator turned the conversation upon something else; the old gentleman recovered himself. But just as he, his face again radiant with sunshine, was on the point of putting the full wine-cup to his lips, Salvator began anew. "But pray tell me, my dear sir, if it is indeed true that your niece, with her sixteen summers, really has such beautiful auburn hair, and eyes so full of heaven's own loveliness and joy, as has Antonio's 'Magdalene?' It is generally maintained that she has."

"I don't know," replied the old gentleman, still more sharply than before, "I don't know. But let us leave my niece in peace; rather let us exchange a few instructive words on the noble subject of art, as your fine picture here of itself invites me to do."

Always when Capuzzi raised the wine-cup to his lips to take a good draft, Salvator began anew to talk about the beautiful Marianna, so that at last the old gentleman leapt from his chair in a perfect passion, banged the cup down upon the table and almost broke it, screaming in a high shrill voice, "By the infernal pit of Pluto! by all the furies! you will turn my wine into poison — into poison I tell you. But I see through you, you and your fine friend Signor Antonio, you think to make sport of me. But you'll find yourselves deceived Pay me the ten ducats you owe me immediately, and then I will leave you and your associate, that barber-fellow Antonio, to make your way to the devil."

Salvator shouted, as if mastered by the most violent rage, "What! you have the audacity to treat me in this way in my own house! Do you think I'm going to pay you ten ducats for that rotten box; the woodworms have long ago eaten all the goodness and all the music out of it? Not ten — not five — not three — not one ducat shall you have for it, it's scarcely worth a farthing. Away with the tumbledown thing!" and he kicked over the little instrument again and again, till the strings were all jarring and jangling together.

"Ha!" screeched Capuzzi, "justice is still to be had in Rome; I will have you arrested, sir, — arrested and cast into the deepest dungeon there is," and off he was rushing out of the room, blustering like a hailstorm. But Salvator took fast hold of him with both hands, and drew him down into the chair again, softly murmuring in his ear, "My dear Signor Pasquale, don't you perceive that I was only jesting with you? You shall have for your spinet, not ten, but *thirty* ducats cash down." And he went on repeating, "thirty bright ducats in ready money," until Capuzzi said in a faint and feeble voice, "What do you say, my dear sir? Thirty ducats for the spinet without its being repaired?" Then Salvator released his hold of the old gentleman, and asserted on his honor that within an hour the instrument should be worth thirty — nay, forty ducats, and that Signor Pasquale should receive as much for it.

Taking in a fresh supply of breath, and sighing deeply, the old gentleman murmured, "Thirty — forty ducats!" Then he began, "But you have greatly offended me, Signor Salvator" — "Thirty ducats," repeated Salvator. Capuzzi simpered, but then began again, "But you have grossly wounded my feelings, Signor Salvator" — "Thirty ducats," exclaimed Salvator, cutting him short; and he continued to repeat, "Thirty ducats! thirty ducats!" as long as the old gentleman continued to sulk — till at length Capuzzi said, radiant with delight, "If you will give me thirty, — I mean forty ducats for the spinet, all shall be forgiven and forgotten, my dear sir."

"But," began Salvator, "before I can fulfil my promise, I still have one little condition to make, which you, my honored Signor Pasquale Capuzzi di Senigaglia, can easily grant. You are the first musical composer in all Italy, besides being the foremost singer of the day. When I heard in the opera *Le Nozze di Teti e Peleo* the great scene which that shameless Francesco Cavalli has thievishly taken from your works, I was enraptured. If you would only sing me that aria whilst I put the spinet to rights you would confer upon me a pleasure than which I can conceive of none more enjoyable."

Puckering up his mouth into the most winning of smiles, and blinking his little grey eyes, the old gentleman replied, "I perceive, my good sir, that you are yourself a clever musician, for you possess taste and know how to value the deserving better than these ungrateful Romans. Listen — listen — to the aria of all arias."

Therewith he rose to his feet, and, stretching himself up to his full height, spread out his arms and closed both eyes, so that he looked like a cock preparing to crow; and he at once began to screech in such a way that the walls rang again, and Dame Caterina and her two daughters soon came running in, fully under the impression that such lamentable sounds must betoken some accident or other. At sight of the crowing old gentleman they stopped on the threshold utterly astonished; and thus they formed the audience of the incomparable musician Capuzzi.

Meanwhile Salvator, having picked up the spinet and thrown back the lid, had taken his palette in hand, and in bold firm strokes had begun on the lid of the instrument the most remarkable piece of painting that ever was seen. The central idea was a scene from Cavalli's opera *Le Nozze di Teti*, but there was a multitude of other personages mixed up with it in the most fantastic way. Amongst them were the recognizable features of Capuzzi, Antonio, Marianna (faithfully reproduced from Antonio's picture), Salvator himself, Dame Caterina and her two daughters, — and even the Pyramid Doctor was not wanting, — and all grouped so intelligently, judiciously, and ingeniously, that Antonio could not conceal his astonishment, both at the artist's intellectual power as well as at his technique.

Meanwhile old Capuzzi had not been content with the aria which Salvator had requested him to give, but, carried away by his musical madness, he went on singing or rather screeching without intermission, working his way through the most awful recitatives from one execrable scene to another. He must have been going on for nearly two hours when he sank back in his chair, breathless, and with his face as red as a cherry. And just at this same time also Salvator had so far worked out his sketch that the figures began to wear a look of vitality, and the whole, viewed at a little distance, had the appearance of a finished work.

"I have kept my word with respect to the spinet, my dear Signer Pasquale," breathed Salvator in the old man's ear. He started up as if awakening out of a deep sleep. Immediately his glance fell upon the painted instrument, which stood directly opposite him. Then, opening his eyes wide as if he saw a miracle, and jauntily throwing his conical hat on the top of his wig, he took his crutch-stick under his arm, made one bound to the spinet, tore the lid off the hinges, and holding it above his head, ran like a madman out of the room, down the stairs, and away, away out of the house altogether, followed by the hearty laughter of Dame Caterina and both her daughters.

"The old miser," said Salvator, "knows very well that he has only to take yon painted lid to Count Colonna or to my friend Rossi and he will at once get forty ducats for it, or even more."

Salvator and Antonio then both deliberated how they should carry out the plan of attack which was to be made when night came. We shall soon see what the two adventurers resolved upon, and what success they had in their adventure.

As soon as it was dark, Signer Pasquale, after locking and bolting the door of his house, carried the little monster of an eunuch home as usual. The whole way the little wretch was whining and growling, complaining that not only did he sing Capuzzi's arias till he got catarrh in the throat and burn his fingers cooking the macaroni, but he had now to lend himself to duties which brought him nothing but sharp boxes of the ear and rough kicks, which Marianna lavishly distrib- uted to him as soon as ever he came near her. Old Capuzzi consoled him as well as he could, promising to provide him an ampler supply of sweetmeats than he had hitherto done; indeed, as the little man would nohow cease his growling and querulous complaining, Pasquale even laid himself under the obligation to get a natty abbot's coat made for the little torment out of an old black plush waistcoat which he (the dwarf) had often set covetous eyes upon. He demanded a wig and a sword as well. Parleying upon these points they arrived at the Via Bergognona, for that was where Pitichinaccio dwelt, only four doors from Salvator.

The old man set the dwarf cautiously down and opened the street door; and then, the dwarf on in front, they both began to climb up the narrow stairs, which were more like a rickety ladder for hens and chickens than steps for respectable people. But they had hardly mounted halfway up when a terrible racket began up above, and the coarse voice of some wild drunken fellow was heard cursing and swearing, and demanding to be shown the way out of the damned house. Pitichinaccio squeezed himself close to the wall, and entreated Capuzzi, in the name of all the saints, to go on first. But before Capuzzi had ascended two steps, the fellow who was up above came tumbling headlong downstairs, caught hold of the old man, and whisked him away like a whirlwind out through the open door below into the middle of the street. There they both lay, — Capuzzi at bottom and the drunken brute like a heavy sack on top of him. The old gentleman screamed piteously for help; two men came up at once and with considerable difficulty freed him from the heavy weight lying upon him; the other fellow, as soon as he was lifted up, reeled away cursing.

"Good God! what's happened to you, Signor Pasquale? What are you doing here at this time of night? What big quarrel have you been getting mixed up in in that house there?" thus asked Salvator and Antonio, for that is who the two men were.

"Oh, I shall die!" groaned Capuzzi; "that son of the devil has crushed all my limbs; I can't move."

"Let me look," said Antonio, feeling all over the old gentleman's body, and suddenly he pinched his right leg so sharply that Capuzzi screamed out aloud.

"By all the saints!" cried Antonio in consternation, "by all the saints! my dear Signer Pasquale, you've broken your right leg in the most dangerous place. If you don't get speedy help you will within a short time be a dead man, or at any rate be lame all your life long."

A terrible scream escaped the old man's breast. "Calm yourself, my dear sir," continued Antonio, "although I'm now a painter, I haven't altogether forgotten my surgical practice. We will carry you to Salvator's house and I will at once bind up" —

"My dear Signor Antonio," whined Capuzzi, "you nourish hostile feelings towards me, I know." "But," broke in Salvator, "this is now no longer the time to talk about enmity; you are in danger, and that is enough for honest Antonio to exert all his skill on your behalf. Lay hold, friend Antonio."

Gently and cautiously they lifted up the old man between them, him screaming with the unspeakable pain caused by his broken leg, and carried him to Salvator's dwelling.

Dame Caterina said that she had had a foreboding that something was going to happen, and so she had not gone to bed. As soon as she caught sight of the old gentleman and heard what had befallen him, she began to heap reproaches upon him for his bad conduct. "I know," she said, "I know very well, Signor Pasquale, who you've been taking home again. Now that you've got your beautiful niece Marianna in the house with you, you think you've no further call to have womenfolk about you, and you treat that poor Pitichinaccio most shameful and infamous, putting him in petticoats. But look to it. *Ogni carne ha il suo osso* (Every house has its skeleton). Why if you have a girl about you, don't you need womenfolk? *Fate il passo secondo la gamba* (Cut your clothes according to your cloth), and don't you require anything either more or less from your Marianna than what is right. Don't lock her up as if she were a prisoner, nor make your house a dungeon. *Asino punto convien che trotti* (If you are in the stream, you had better swim with it); you have a beautiful niece and you must alter your ways to suit her, that is, you must only do what she wants you to do. But you are an ungallant and hard-hearted man, aye, and even in love, and jealous as well, they say, which I hope at your years is not true. Your pardon for telling you it all straight out, but *chi ha nel petto fiele non puo sputar miele* (when there's bile in the heart there can't be honey in the mouth). So now, if you don't die of your broken leg, which at your great age is not at all unlikely, let this be a warning to you; and leave your niece free to do what she likes, and let her marry the fine young gentleman as I know very well."

And so the stream went on uninterruptedly, whilst Salvator and Antonio cautiously undressed the old gentleman and put him to bed. Dame Caterina's words were like knives cutting deeply into his breast; but whenever he attempted to intervene, Antonio signed to him that all speaking was dangerous, and so he had to swallow his bitter gall. At length Salvator sent Dame Caterina away, to fetch some ice-cold water that Antonio wanted.

Salvator and Antonio satisfied themselves that the fellow who had been sent to Pitichinaccio's house had done his duty well. Notwithstanding the apparently terrible fall, Capuzzi had not received the slightest damage beyond a slight bruise or two. Antonio put the old gentleman's right foot in splints and bandaged it up so tight that he could not move. Then they wrapped him up in cloths that had been soaked in ice-cold water, as a precaution, they alleged, against inflammation, so that the old gentleman shook as if with the ague.

"My good Signor Antonio," he groaned feebly, "tell me if it is all over with me. Must I die?"

"Compose yourself," replied Antonio. "If you will only compose yourself, Signor Pasquale! As you have come through the first dressing with so much nerve and without fainting, I think we may say that the danger is past; but you will require the most attentive nursing. At present we mustn't let you out of the doctor's sight."

"Oh! Antonio," whined the old gentleman, "you know how I like you, how highly I esteem your talents. Don't leave me. Give me your dear hand — so! You won't leave me, will you, my dear good Antonio?"

"Although I am now no longer a surgeon," said Antonio, "although I've quite given up that hated trade, yet I will in your case, Signor Pasquale, make an exception, and will undertake to attend you, for which I shall ask nothing except that you give me your friendship, your confidence again. You were a little hard upon me" —

"Say no more," lisped the old gentleman, "not another word, my dear Antonio" —

"Your niece will be half dead with anxiety," said Antonio again, "at your not returning home. You are, considering your condition, brisk and strong enough, and so as soon as day dawns we'll carry you home to your own house. There I will again look at your bandage, and arrange your bed as it ought to be, and give your niece her instructions, so that you may soon get well again."

The old gentleman heaved a deep sigh and closed his eyes, remaining some minutes without speaking. Then, stretching out his hand towards Antonio, he drew him down close beside him, and whispered, "It was only a jest that you had with Marianna, was it not, my dear sir? — one of those merry conceits that young folks have" —

"Think no more about that, Signor Pasquale," replied Antonio. "Your niece did, it is true, strike my fancy; but I have now quite different things in my head, and — to confess honestly to it — I am very pleased that you did return a sharp answer to my foolish suit. I thought I was in love with your Marianna, but what I really saw in her was only a fine model for my 'Magdalene.' And this probably explains how it is that, now that my picture is finished, I feel quite indifferent towards her."

"Antonio," cried the old man, in a strong voice, "Antonio, you glorious fellow! What comfort you give me — what help — what consolation! Now that you don't love Marianna I feel as if all my pain had gone."

"Why, I declare, Signor Pasquale," said Salvator, "if we didn't know you to be a grave and sensible man, with a true perception of what is becoming to your years, we might easily believe that you were yourself by some infatuation in love with your niece of sixteen summers."

Again the old gentleman closed his eyes, and groaned and moaned at the horrible pain, which now returned with redoubled violence.

The first red streaks of morning came shining in through the window. Antonio announced to the old gentleman that it was now time to take him to his own house in the Via Ripetta. Signor Pasquale's reply was a deep and piteous sigh. Salvator and Antonio lifted him out of bed and wrapped him in a wide mantle which had belonged to Dame Caterina's husband, and which she lent them for this purpose. The old gentleman implored them by all the saints to take off the villainous cold bandages in which his bald head was swathed, and to give him his wig and plumed hat. And also, if it were possible, Antonio was to put his moustache a little in order, that Marianna might not be too much frightened at sight of him.

Two porters with a litter were standing all ready before the door. Dame Caterina, still storming at the old man, and mixing a great many proverbs in her abuse, carried down the bed, in which they then carefully packed him; and so, accompanied by Salvator and Antonio, he was taken home to his own house.

No sooner did Marianna see her uncle in this wretched plight than she began to scream, whilst a torrent of tears gushed from her eyes; without noticing her lover, who had come along with him, she grasped the old man's hands and pressed them to her lips, bewailing the terrible accident that had befallen him — so much pity had the good child for the old man who plagued and tormented her with his amorous folly. Yet at this same moment the inherent nature of woman asserted itself in her; for it only required a few significant glances from Salvator to put her in full possession of all the facts of the case. Now, for the first time, she stole a glance at the happy Antonio, blushing hotly as she did so; and a pretty sight it was to see how a roguish smile gradually routed and broke through her tears. Salvator, at any rate, despite the "Magdalene," had not expected to find the little maiden half so charming, or so sweetly pretty as he now really discovered her to be; and, whilst almost feeling inclined to envy Antonio his good fortune, he felt that it was all the more necessary to get poor Marianna away from her hateful uncle, let the cost be what it might.

Signor Pasquale forgot his trouble in being received so affectionately by his lovely niece, which was indeed more than he deserved. He simpered and pursed up his lips so that his moustache was all of a totter, and groaned and whined, not with pain, but simply and solely with amorous longing.

Antonio arranged his bed professionally, and, after Capuzzi had been laid on it, tightened the bandage still more, at the same time so muffling up his left leg as well that he had to lay there motionless like a log of wood. Salvator withdrew and left the lovers alone with their happiness.

The old gentleman lay buried in cushions; moreover, as an extra precaution, Antonio had bound a thick piece of cloth well steeped in water round his head, so that he might not hear the lovers whispering together. This was the first time they unburdened all their hearts to each other, swearing eternal fidelity in the midst of tears and rapturous kisses. The old gentleman could have no idea of what was going on, for Marianna ceased not, frequently from time to time, to ask him how he felt, and even permitted him to press her little white hand to his lips.

When the morning began to be well advanced, Antonio hastened away to procure, as he said, all the things that the old gentleman required, but in reality to invent some means for putting him, at any rate for some hours, in a still more helpless condition, as well as to consult with Salvator what further steps were then to be taken.

IV

*O*f the new attack made by Salvator Rosa and Antonio Scacciati upon Signer Pasquale Capuzzi and upon his company, and of what further happens in consequence.

Next morning Antonio came to Salvator, melancholy and dejected.

"Well, what's the matter?" cried Salvator when he saw him coming, "what are you hanging your head about? What's happened to you now, you happy dog? can you not see your mistress every day, and kiss her and press her to your heart?"

"Oh! Salvator, it's all over with my happiness, it's gone forever," cried Antonio. "The devil is making sport of me. Our stratagem has failed, and we now stand on a footing of open enmity with that cursed Capuzzi."

"So much the better," said Salvator; "so much the better. But come, Antonio, tell me what's happened."

"Just imagine, Salvator," began Antonio, "yesterday when I went back to the Via Ripetta after an absence of at the most two hours, with all sorts of medicines, whom should I see but the old gentleman standing in his own doorway fully dressed. Behind him was the Pyramid Doctor and the deuced ex-gendarme, whilst a confused something was bobbing about round their legs. It was, I believe, that little monster Pitichinaccio. No sooner did the old man get sight of me than he shook his fist at me, and began to heap the most fearful curses and imprecations upon me, swearing that if I did but approach his door he would have all my bones broken. 'Be off to the devil, you infamous barber-fellow,' he shrieked; 'you think to outwit me with your lying and knavery. Like the very devil himself, you lie in wait for my poor innocent Marianna, and fancy you are going to get her into your toils — but stop a moment! I will spend my last ducat to have the vital spark stamped out of you, ere you're aware of it. And your fine patron, Signor Salvator, the murderer — bandit — who's escaped the halter — he shall be sent to join his captain Masaniello in hell — I'll have him out of Rome; that won't cost me much trouble.'

"Thus the old fellow raged, and as the damned ex-gendarme, incited by the Pyramid Doctor, was making preparations to bear down upon me, and a crowd of curious onlookers began to assemble, what could I do but quit the field with all speed? I didn't like to come to you in my great trouble, for I know you would only have laughed at me and my inconsolable complaints. Why, you can hardly keep back your laughter now."

As Antonio ceased speaking, Salvator did indeed burst out laughing heartily.

"Now," he cried, "now the thing is beginning to be rather interesting. And now, my worthy Antonio, I will tell you in detail all that took place at Capuzzi's after you had gone. You had hardly left the house when Signor Splendiano Accoramboni, who had learned — God knows in what way — that his bosom-friend, Capuzzi, had broken his right leg in the night, drew near in all solemnity, with a surgeon. Your bandage and the entire method of treatment you have adopted with Signor Pasquale could not fail to excite suspicion. The surgeon removed the splints and bandages, and they discovered, what we both very well know, that there was not even so much as an ossicle of the worthy Capuzzi's right foot dislocated, still less broken. It didn't require any uncommon sagacity to understand all the rest."

"But," said Antonio, utterly astonished, "but my dear, good sir, do tell me how you have learned all that; tell me how you get into Capuzzi's house and know everything that takes place there."

"I have already told you," replied Salvator, "that an acquaintance of Dame Caterina lives in the same house, and moreover, on the same floor as Capuzzi. This acquaintance, the widow of a wine-dealer, has a daughter whom my little Margaret often goes to see. Now girls have a special instinct for finding out their fellows, and so it came about that Rose — that's the name of the wine-dealer's daughter — and Margaret soon discovered in the living room a small vent-hole, leading into a dark closet that adjoins Marianna's apartment. Marianna had been by no means inattentive to the whispering and murmuring of the two girls, nor had she failed to notice the vent-hole, and so the way to a mutual exchange of communications was soon opened and made use of. Whenever old Capuzzi takes his afternoon nap the girls gossip away to their heart's content. You will have observed that little Margaret, Dame Caterina's and my favorite, is not so serious and reserved as her elder sister, Anna, but is an arch, frolicsome, droll little thing. Without expressly making mention of your love-affair I have instructed her to get Marianna to tell her everything that takes place in Capuzzi's house. She has proved a very apt pupil in the matter; and if I laughed at your pain and despondency just now it was because I knew what would comfort you, knew I could prove to you that the affair has now taken a most favorable turn. I have quite a big budget full of excellent news for you."

"Salvator!" cried Antonio, his eyes sparkling with joy, "how you cause my hopes to rise! Heaven be praised for the vent-hole. I will write to Marianna; Margaret shall take the letter with her" —

"Nay, nay, we can have none of that, Antonio," replied Salvator. "Margaret can be useful to us without being your love-messenger exactly. Besides, accident, which often plays many fine tricks, might carry your amorous confessions into old Capuzzi's hands, and so bring an endless amount of fresh trouble upon Marianna, just at the very moment when she is on the point of getting the lovesick old fool under her thumb. For listen to what then happened. The way in which Marianna received the old fellow when we took him home has quite reformed him. He is fully convinced that she no longer loves you, but that she has given him at least one half of her heart, and that all he has to do is to win the other half. And Marianna, since she imbibed the poison of your kisses, has advanced three years in shrewdness, artfulness, and experience. She has convinced the old man, not only that she had no share in our trick, but that she hates our goings-on, and will meet with scorn every device on your part to approach her. In his excessive delight the old man was too hasty, and swore that if he could do anything to please his adored Marianna he would do it immediately, she had only to give utterance to her wish. Whereupon Marianna modestly asked for nothing except that her *zio carissimo* (dearest uncle) would take her to see Signor Formica in the theater outside the Porta del Popolo. This rather posed Capuzzi; there were consultations with the Pyramid Doctor and with Pitichinaccio; at last Signor Pasquale and Signor Splendiano came to the resolution that they really would take Marianna to this theater tomorrow. Pitichinaccio, it was resolved, should accompany them in the disguise of a handmaiden, to which he only gave his consent on condition that Signor Pasquale would make him a present, not only of the plush waistcoat, but also of a wig, and at night would, alternately with the Pyramid Doctor, carry him home. That bargain they finally made; and so the curious leash will certainly go along with pretty Marianna to see Signor Formica tomorrow, in the theater outside the Porta del Popolo."

It is now necessary to say who Signor Formica was, and what he had to do with the theater outside the Porta del Popolo.

At the time of the Carnival in Rome, nothing is more sad than when the theater-managers have been unlucky in their choice of a musical composer, or when the first tenor at the

Argentina theater has lost his voice on the way, or when the male prima donna* of the Valle theater is laid up with a cold, — in brief, when the chief source of recreation which the Romans were hoping to find proves abortive, and then comes Holy Thursday and all at once cuts off all the hopes which might perhaps have been realized It was just after one of these unlucky Carnivals — almost before the strict fast-days were past, when a certain Nicolo Musso opened a theater outside the Porta del Popolo, where he stated his intention of putting nothing but light impromptu comic sketches on the boards. The advertisement was drawn up in an ingenious and witty style, and consequently the Romans formed a favorable preconception of Musso's enterprise; but independently of this they would in their longing to still their dramatic hunger have greedily snatched at any the poorest pabulum of this description. The interior arrangements of the theater, or rather of the small booth, did not say much for the pecuniary resources of the enterprising manager. There was no orchestra, nor were there boxes. Instead, a gallery was put up at the back, where the arms of the house of Colonna were conspicuous — a sign that Count Colonna had taken Musso and his theater under his especial protection. A platform of slight elevation, covered with carpets and hung round with curtains, which, according to the requirements of the piece, had to represent a wood or a room or a street — this was the stage. Add to this that the spectators had to content themselves with hard uncomfortable wooden benches, and it was no wonder that Signor Musso's patrons on first entering were pretty loud in their grumblings at him for calling a paltry wooden booth a theater. But no sooner had the first two actors who appeared exchanged a few words together than the attention of the audience was arrested; as the piece proceeded their interest took the form of applause, their applause grew to admiration, their admiration to the wildest pitch of enthusiastic excitement, which found vent in loud and continuous laughter, clapping of hands, and screams of "Bravo! Bravo!"

---

* Female parts continued to be played by boys in England down to the Restoration (1660). The practice of women playing in female parts was introduced somewhat earlier in Italy, but only in certain kinds of performances.

And indeed it would not have been very easy to find anything more perfect than these extemporised representations of Nicolo Musso; they overflowed with wit, humor, and genius, and lashed the follies of the day with an unsparing scourge. The audience were quite carried away by the incomparable characterization which distinguished all the actors, but particularly by the inimitable mimicry of Pasquarello,* by his marvelously natural imitations of the voice, gait, and postures of well-known personages. By his inexhaustible humor, and the point and appositeness of his impromptus, he quite carried his audience away. The man who played the *rôle* of Pasquarello, and who called himself Signor Formica, seemed to be animated by a spirit of singular originality; often there was something so strange in either tone or gesture, that the audience, even in the midst of the most unrestrained burst of laughter, felt a cold shiver run through them. He was excellently supported by Dr. Gratiano,† who in pantomimic action, in voice, and in his talent for saying the most delightful things mixed up with apparently the most extravagant nonsense, had perhaps no equal in the world. This *rôle* was played by an old Bolognese named Maria Agli. Thus in a short time all educated Rome was seen hastening in a continuous stream to Nicolo Musso's little theater outside the Porta del Popolo, whilst Formica's name was on everybody's lips, and people shouted with wild enthusiasm, *"Oh! Formica! Formica benedetto! Oh! Formicissimo!"* — not only in the theater but also in the streets. They regarded him as a supernatural visitant, and many an old lady who had

---

* This word is undoubtedly connected with *Pasquillo* (a satire), or with *Pasquino,* a Roman cobbler of the fifteenth century, whose shop stood near the Braschi Palace, near the Piazza Navona. He lashed the follies of his day, particularly the vices of the clergy, with caustic satire, scathing wit, and bitter stinging irony. After his death his name was transferred to a mutilated statue, upon which such satiric effusions continued to be fastened.

Pasquarello would thus combine the characteristics of the English clown with those of the Roman Pasquino.

† Doctor Gratiano, a character in the popular Italian theater called *Commedia dell' Arte,* was represented as a Bolognese doctor, and wore a mask with black nose and forehead and red cheeks. His *rôle* was that of a "pedantic and tedious poser."

split her sides with laughing in the theater, would suddenly look grave and say solemnly, *"Scherza coi fanti e lascia star santi"* (Jest with children but let the saints alone), if anybody ventured to say the least thing in disparagement of Formica's acting. This arose from the fact that outside the theater Signor Formica was an inscrutable mystery. Never was he seen anywhere, and all efforts to discover traces of him were vain, whilst Nicolo Musso on his part maintained an inexorable silence respecting his retreat.

And this was the theater that Marianna was anxious to go to.

"Let us make a decisive onslaught upon our foes," said Salvator; "we couldn't have a finer opportunity than when they're returning home from the theater." Then he imparted to Antonio the details of a plan, which, though appearing adventurous and daring, Antonio nevertheless embraced with joy, since it held out to him a prospect that he should be able to carry off his Marianna from the hated old Capuzzi. He also heard with approbation that Salvator was especially concerned to chastise the Pyramid Doctor.

When night came, Salvator and Antonio each took a guitar and went to the Via Ripetta, where, with the express view of causing old Capuzzi annoyance, they complimented lovely Marianna with the finest serenade that ever was heard. For Salvator played and sang in masterly style, whilst Antonio, as far as the capabilities of his fine tenor would allow him, almost rivalled Odoardo Ceccarelli. Although Signor Pasquale appeared on the balcony and tried to silence the singers with abuse, his neighbors, attracted to their windows by the good singing, shouted to him that he and his companions howled and screamed like so many cats and dogs, and yet he wouldn't listen to good music when it did come into the street; he might just go inside and stop up his ears if he didn't want to listen to good singing. And so Signor Pasquale had to bear nearly all night long the torture of hearing Salvator and Antonio sing songs which at one time were the sweetest of love songs and at another mocked at the folly of amorous old fools. They plainly saw Marianna standing at the window, notwithstanding that Signor Pasquale besought her in the sweetest phrases and protestations not to expose herself to the noxious night air.

Next evening the most remarkable company that ever was seen proceeded down the Via Ripetta towards the Porta del Popolo. All eyes were turned upon them, and people asked each other if these were maskers left from the Carnival. Signor Pasquale Capuzzi, spruce and smug, all elegance and politeness, wearing his gay Spanish suit well brushed, parading a new yellow feather in his conical hat, and stepping along in shoes too little for him, as if he were walking amongst eggs, was leading pretty Marianna on his arm; her slender figure could not be seen, still less her face, since she was smothered up to an unusual extent in her veil and wraps. On the other side marched Doctor Splendiano Accoramboni in his great wig, which covered the whole of his back, so that to look at him from behind there appeared to be a huge head walking along on two little legs. Close behind Marianna, and almost clinging to her, waddled the little monster Pitichinaccio, dressed in fiery red petticoats, and having his head covered all over in hideous fashion with bright-colored flowers.

This evening Signor Formica outdid himself even, and, what he had never done before, introduced short songs into his performance, burlesquing the style of certain well-known singers. Old Capuzzi's passion for the stage, which in his youth had almost amounted to infatuation, was now stirred up in him anew. In a rapture of delight he kissed Marianna's hand time after time, and protested that he would not miss an evening visiting Nicolo Musso's theater with her. Signor Formica he extolled to the very skies, and joined hand and foot in the boisterous applause of the rest of the spectators. Signor Splendiano was less satisfied, and kept continually admonishing Signor Capuzzi and lovely Marianna not to laugh so immoderately. In a single breath he ran over the names of twenty or more diseases which might arise from splitting the sides with laughing. But neither Marianna nor Capuzzi heeded him in the least. As for Pitichinaccio, he felt very uncomfortable. He had been obliged to sit behind the Pyramid Doctor, whose great wig completely overshadowed him. Not a single thing could he see on the stage, nor any of the actors, and was, moreover, repeatedly bothered and annoyed by two forward women who had placed themselves near him. They called him a dear, comely little lady, and asked him if he was married, though to be sure, he was very young, and whether he had any children, who they dare be bound were sweet little creatures, and so forth. The cold sweat stood in beads on poor Pitichinaccio's brow; he whined and whimpered, and cursed the day he was born.

After the conclusion of the performance, Signor Pasquale waited until the spectators had withdrawn from the theater. The last light was extinguished just as Signor Splendiano had lit a small piece of a wax torch at it; and then Capuzzi, with his worthy friends and Marianna, slowly and circumspectly set out on their return journey.

Pitichinaccio wept and screamed; Capuzzi, greatly to his vexation, had to take him on his left arm, whilst with the right he led Marianna. Doctor Splendiano showed the way with his miserable little bit of torch, which only burned with difficulty, and even then in a feeble sort of a way, so that the wretched light it cast merely served to reveal to them the thick darkness of the night.

Whilst they were still a good distance from the Porta del Popolo they all at once saw themselves surrounded by several tall figures closely enveloped in mantles. At this moment the torch was knocked out of the Doctor's hand, and went out on the ground. Capuzzi, as well as the Doctor, stood still without uttering a sound. Then, without their knowing where it came from, a pale reddish light fell upon the muffled figures, and four grisly skulls riveted their hollow ghastly eyes upon the Pyramid Doctor. "Woe — woe — woe betide thee, Splendiano Accoramboni!" thus the terrible specters shrieked in deep, sepulchral tones. Then one of them wailed, "Do you know me? do you know me, Splendiano? I am Cordier, the French painter, who was buried last week, and whom your medicaments brought to his grave." Then the second, "Do you know me, Splendiano? I am Küfner, the German painter, whom you poisoned with your infernal electuary." Then the third, "Do you know me, Splendiano? I am Liers, the Fleming, whom you killed with your pills, and whose brother you defrauded of a picture." Then the fourth, "Do you know me, Splendiano? I am Ghigi, the Neapolitan painter, whom you dispatched with your powders." And lastly all four together, "Woe — woe — woe upon thee, Splendiano Accoramboni, cursed Pyramid Doctor! We bid you come — come down to us beneath the earth. Away — away — away with you! Hallo! hallo!" and so saying they threw themselves upon the unfortunate Doctor, and, raising him in their arms, whisked him away like a whirlwind.

Now, although Signor Pasquale was a good deal overcome by terror, yet it is surprising with what remarkable promptitude he recovered courage so soon as he saw that it was only his friend Accoramboni with whom the specters were concerned. Pitichinaccio had stuck his head, with the flower-bed that was on it, under Capuzzi's mantle, and clung so fast round his neck that all efforts to shake him off proved futile.

"Pluck up your spirits," Capuzzi exhorted Marianna, when nothing more was to be seen of the specters or of the Pyramid Doctor; "pluck up your spirits, and come to me, my sweet little ducky bird! As for my worthy friend Splendiano, it's all over with him. May St. Bernard, who also was an able physician and gave many a man a lift on the road to happiness, may he help him, if the revengeful painters whom he hastened to get to his Pyramid break his neck! But who'll sing the bass of my canzonas now? And this booby, Pitichinaccio, is squeezing my throat so, that, adding in the fright caused by Splendiano's abduction, I fear I shall not be able to produce a pure note for perhaps six weeks to come. Don't be alarmed, my Marianna, my darling! It's all over now."

She assured him that she had quite recovered from her alarm, and begged him to let her walk alone without support, so that he could free himself from his troublesome pet. But Signor Pasquale only took faster hold of her, saying that he wouldn't suffer her to leave his side a yard in that pitch darkness for anything in the world.

In the very same moment as Signor Pasquale, now at his ease again, was about to proceed on his road, four frightful fiendlike figures rose up just in front of him as if out of the earth; they wore short flaring red mantles and fixed their keen glittering eyes upon him, at the same time making horrible noises — yelling and whistling. "Ugh! ugh! Pasquale Capuzzi! You cursed fool! You amorous old devil! We belong to your fraternity; we are the evil spirits of love, and have come to carry you off to hell — to hell-fire — you and your crony Pitichinaccio." Thus screaming, the Satanic figures fell upon the old man. Capuzzi fell heavily to the ground and Pitichinaccio along with him, both raising a shrill piercing cry of distress and fear, like that of a whole troop of cudgelled asses.

Marianna had meanwhile torn herself away from the old man and leapt aside. Then one of the devils clasped her softly in his arms, whispering the sweet glad words, "O Marianna! my Marianna! At last we've managed it! My friends will carry the old man a long, long way from here, whilst we seek a better place of safety."

"O my Antonio!" whispered Marianna softly.

But suddenly the scene was illuminated by the light of several torches, and Antonio felt a stab in his shoulder. Quick as lightning he turned round, drew his sword, and attacked the fellow, who with his stiletto upraised was just preparing to aim a second blow. He perceived that his three companions were defending themselves against a superior number of gendarmes. He managed to beat off the fellow who had attacked him, and joined his friends. Although they were maintaining their ground bravely, the contest was yet too unequal; the gendarmes would infallibly have proved victorious had not two others suddenly ranged themselves with a shout on the side of the young men, one of them immediately cutting down the fellow who was pressing Antonio the hardest.

In a few minutes more the contest was decided against the police. Several lay stretched on the ground seriously wounded; the rest fled with loud shouts towards the Porta del Popolo.

Salvator Rosa (for he it was who had hastened to Antonio's assistance and cut down his opponent) wanted to take Antonio and the young painters who were disguised in the devils' masks and there and then pursue the gendarmes into the city.

Maria Agli, however, who had come along with him, and, notwithstanding his advanced age, had tackled the police as stoutly as any of the rest, urged that this would be imprudent, for the guard at the Porta del Popolo would be certain to have intelligence of the affair and would arrest them. So they all betook themselves to Nicolo Musso, who gladly received them into his narrow little house not far from the theater. The artists took off their devils' masks and laid aside their mantles, which had been rubbed over with phosphorus, whilst Antonio, who, beyond the insignificant scratch on his shoulder, was not wounded at all, exercised his surgical skill in binding up the wounds of the rest — Salvator, Agli, and his young comrades — for they had none of them got off without being wounded, though none of them in the least degree dangerously.

The adventure, notwithstanding its wildness and audacity, would undoubtedly have been successful, had not Salvator and Antonio overlooked one person, who upset everything. The *ci-devant* bravo and gendarme Michele, who dwelt below in Capuzzi's house, and was in a certain sort his general servant, had, in accordance with Capuzzi's directions, followed them to the theater, but at some distance off, for the old gentleman was ashamed of the tattered reprobate. In the same way Michele was following them homewards. And when the specters appeared, Michele who, be it remarked, feared neither death nor devil, suspecting that something was wrong, hurried back as fast as he could run in the darkness to the Porta del Popolo, raised an alarm, and returned with all the gendarmes he could find, just at the moment when, as we know, the devils fell upon Signor Pasquale, and were about to carry him off as the dead men had the Pyramid Doctor.

In the very hottest moment of the fight, one of the young painters observed distinctly how one of the fellows, taking Marianna in his arms (for she had fainted), made off to the gate, whilst Signor Pasquale ran after him with incredible swiftness, as if he had got quicksilver in his legs. At the same time, by the light of the torches, he caught a glimpse of something gleaming, clinging to his mantle and whimpering; no doubt it was Pitichinaccio.

Next morning Doctor Splendiano was found near the Pyramid of Cestius, fast asleep, doubled up like a ball and squeezed into his wig, as if into a warm soft nest. When he was awakened, he rambled in his talk, and there was some difficulty in convincing him that he was still on the surface of the earth, and in Rome to boot. And when at length he reached his own house, he returned thanks to the Virgin and all the saints for his rescue, threw all his tinctures, essences, electuaries, and powders out of the window, burnt his prescriptions, and vowed to heal his patients in the future by no other means than by anointing and laying on of hands, as some celebrated physician of former ages, who was at the same time a saint (his name I cannot recall just at this moment), had with great success done before him. For his patients died as well as the patients of other people, and then they already saw the gates of heaven open before them ere they died, and in fact everything else that the saint wanted them to see.

"I can't tell you," said Antonio next day to Salvator, "how my heart boils with rage since my blood has been spilled. Death and destruction overtake that villain Capuzzi! I tell you, Salvator, that I am determined to *force* my way into his house. I will cut him down if he opposes me and carry off Marianna."

"An excellent plan!" replied Salvator, laughing. "An excellent plan! Splendidly contrived! Of course I presume you have also found some means for transporting Marianna through the air to the Spanish Square, so that they shall not seize you and hang you before you can reach that place of refuge. No, my dear Antonio, violence can do nothing for you this time. You may lay your life on it too that Signor Pasquale will now take steps to guard against any open attack. Moreover, our adventure has made a good deal of noise, and the irrepressible laughter of the people at the absurd way in which we have read a lesson to Splendiano and Capuzzi has roused the police out of their light slumber, and they, you may be sure, will now exert all their feeble efforts to entrap us. No, Antonio, let us have recourse to craft. *Con arte e con inganno si vive mezzo l'anno, con inganno e con arte si vive l'altra parte* (If cunning and scheming will help us six months through, scheming and cunning will help us the other six too), says Dame Caterina, nor is she far wrong. Besides, I can't help laughing to see how we've gone and acted for all the world like thoughtless boys, and I shall have to bear most of the blame, for I am a good bit older than you. Tell me now, Antonio, supposing our scheme had been successful, and you had actually carried off

Marianna from the old man, where would you have fled to, where would you have hidden her, and how would you have managed to get united to her by the priest before the old man could interfere to prevent it? You shall, however, in a few days, really and truly run away with your Marianna. I have let Nicolo Musso as well as Signor Formica into all the secret, and in common with them devised a plan which can scarcely fail. So cheer up, Antonio; Signor Formica will help you."

"Signor Formica?" replied Antonio in a tone of indifference which almost amounted to contempt. "Signor Formica! In what way can that buffoon help me?"

"Ho! ho!" laughed Salvator. "Please to bear in mind, I beg you, that Signor Formica is worthy of your respect. Don't you know that he is a sort of magician who in secret is master of the most mysterious arts? I tell you, Signor Formica will help you. Old Maria Agli, the clever Bolognese Doctor Gratiano, is also a sharer in the plot, and will, moreover, have an important part to play in it. You shall abduct your Marianna, Antonio, from Musso's theater."

"You are flattering me with false hopes, Salvator," said Antonio. "You have just now said yourself that Signor Pasquale will take care to avoid all open attacks. How can you suppose then, after his recent unpleasant experience, that he can possibly make up his mind to visit Musso's theater again?"

"It will not be such a difficult thing as you imagine to entice the old man there," replied Salvator. "What will be more difficult to effect, will be, to get him in the theater without his satellites. But, be that as it may, what you have now got to do, Antonio, is to have everything prepared and arranged with Marianna, so as to flee from Rome the moment the favorable opportunity comes. You must go to Florence; your skill as a painter will, after your arrival, in itself recommend you there; and you shall have no lack of acquaintances, nor of honorable patronage and assistance — that you may leave to me to provide for. After we have had a few days' rest, we will then see what is to be done further. Once more, Antonio — live in hope; Formica will help you."

V

*O*f the new mishap which befalls Signor Pasquale Capussi. *Antonio Scacciati successfully carries out his plan in Nicolo Musso's theater, and flees to Florence.*

Signor Pasquale was only too well aware who had been at the bottom of the mischief that had happened to him and the poor Pyramid Doctor near the Porta del Popolo, and so it may be imagined how enraged he was against Antonio, and against Salvator Rosa, whom he rightly judged to be the ringleader in it all. He was untiring in his efforts to comfort poor Marianna, who was quite ill from fear, — so she said; but in reality she was mortified that the scoundrel Michele with his gendarmes had come up, and torn her from her Antonio's arms. Meanwhile Margaret was very active in bringing her tidings of her lover; and she based all her hopes upon the enterprising mind of Salvator. With impatience she waited from day to day for something fresh to happen, and by a thousand petty tormenting ways let the old gentleman feel the effects of this impatience; but though she thus tamed his amorous folly and made him humble enough, she failed to reach the evil spirit of love that haunted his heart. After she had made him experience to the full all the tricksy humors of the most wayward girl, and then suffered him just once to press his withered lips upon her tiny hand, he would swear in his excessive delight that he would never cease fervently kissing the Pope's toe until he had obtained dispensation to wed his niece, the paragon of beauty and amiability. Marianna was particularly careful not to interrupt him in these outbreaks of passion, for by encouraging these gleams of hope in the old man's breast she fanned the flame of hope in her own, for the more he could be lulled into the belief that he held her fast in the indissoluble chains of love, the more easy it would be for her to escape him.

Some time passed, when one day at noon Michele came stamping upstairs, and, after he had had to knock a good many times to induce Signor Pasquale to open the door, announced with considerable prolixity that there was a gentleman below who urgently requested to see Signor Pasquale Capuzzi, who he knew lived there.

"By all the blessed saints of Heaven!" cried the old gentleman, exasperated; "doesn't the knave know that on no account do I receive strangers in my own house?"

But the gentleman was of very respectable appearance, reported Michele, rather oldish, talked well, and called himself Nicolo Musso.

"Nicolo Musso," murmured Capuzzi reflectively; "Nicolo Musso, who owns the theater beyond the Porta del Popolo; what can he want with me?" Whereupon, carefully locking and bolting the door, he went downstairs with Michele, in order to converse with Nicolo in the street before the house.

"My dear Signor Pasquale," began Nicolo, approaching to meet him, and bowing with polished ease, "that you deign to honor me with your acquaintance affords me great pleasure. You lay me under a very great obligation. Since the Romans saw you in my theater — you, a man of the most approved taste, of the soundest knowledge, and a master in art, not only has my fame increased, but my receipts have doubled. I am therefore all the more deeply pained to learn that certain wicked wanton boys made a murderous attack upon you and your friends as you were returning from my theater at night. But I pray you, Signor Pasquale, by all the saints, don't cherish any grudge against me or my theater on account of this outrage, which shall be severely punished. Don't deprive me of the honor of your company at my performances!"

"My dear Signor Nicolo," replied the old man, simpering, "be assured that I never enjoyed myself more than I did when I visited your theater. Your Formica and your Agli — why, they are actors who cannot be matched anywhere. But the fright almost killed my friend Signor Splendiano Accoramboni, nay, it almost proved the death of me — no, it was too great; and though it has not made me averse from your theater, it certainly has from the road there. If you will put up your theater in the Piazza del Popolo, or in the Via Babuina, or in the Via Ripetta, I certainly will not fail to visit you a single evening; but there's no power on earth shall ever get me outside the Porta del Popolo at night-time again."

Nicolo sighed deeply, as if greatly troubled. "That is very hard upon me," said he then, "harder perhaps than you will believe, Signor Pasquale. For unfortunately — I had based all my hopes upon you. I came to solicit your assistance."

"My assistance?" asked the old gentleman in astonishment "My assistance, Signor Nicolo? In what way could it profit you?"

"My dear Signor Pasquale," replied Nicolo, drawing his handkerchief across his eyes, as if brushing away the trickling tears, "my most excellent Signor Pasquale, you will remember that my actors are in the habit of interspersing songs through their performances. This practice I was thinking of extending imperceptibly more and more, then to get together an orchestra, and, in a word, at last, eluding all prohibitions to the contrary, to establish an opera-house. You, Signor Capuzzi, are the first composer in all Italy; and we can attribute it to nothing but the inconceivable frivolity of the Romans and the malicious envy of your rivals that we hear anything else but your pieces exclusively at all the theaters. Signor Pasquale, I came to request you on my bended knees to allow me to put your immortal works, as far as circumstances will admit, on my humble stage."

"My dear Signor Nicolo," said the old gentleman, his face all sunshine, "what are we about to be talking here in the public street? Pray deign to have the goodness to climb up one or two rather steep flights of stairs. Come along with me up to my poor dwelling."

Almost before Nicolo got into the room, the old gentleman brought forward a great pile of dusty music manuscript, opened it, and, taking his guitar in his hands, began to deliver himself of a series of frightful high-pitched screams which he denominated singing.

Nicolo behaved like one in raptures. He sighed; he uttered extravagant expressions of approval; he exclaimed at intervals, *"Bravo! Bravissimo! Benedettissimo Capuzzi!"* until at last he threw himself at the old man's feet as if utterly beside himself with ecstatic delight, and grasped his knees. But he nipped them so hard that the old gentleman jumped off his seat, calling out with pain, and saying to Nicolo, "By the saints! Let me go, Signor Nicolo; you'll kill me."

"Nay," replied Nicolo, "nay, Signor Pasquale, I will not rise until you have promised that Formica may sing in my theater the day after tomorrow the divine arias which you have just executed."

"You are a man of taste," groaned Pasquale, — "a man of deep insight. To whom could I better intrust my compositions than to you? You shall take all my arias with you. Only let me go. But, good God! I shall not hear them — my divine masterpieces! Oh! let me go, Signor Nicolo."

"No," cried Nicolo, still on his knees, and tightly pressing the old gentleman's thin spindle-shanks together, "no, Signor Pasquale, I will not let you go until you give me your word that you will be present in my theater the night after tomorrow. You need not fear any new attack! Why, don't you think that the Romans, once they have heard your work, will bring you home in triumph by the light of hundreds of torches? But in case that does not happen, I myself and my faithful comrades will take our arms and accompany you home ourselves."

"You yourself will accompany me home, with your comrades?" asked Pasquale; "and how many may that be?"

"Eight or ten persons will be at your command, Signor Pasquale. Do yield to my intercession and resolve to come."

"Formica has a fine voice," lisped Pasquale. "How finely he will execute my arias."

"Do come, oh! do come!" exhorted Nicolo again, giving the old gentleman's knees an extra grip.

"You will pledge yourself that I shall reach my own house without being molested?" asked the old gentleman.

"I pledge my honor and my life," was Nicolo's reply, as he gave the knees a still sharper grip.

"Agreed!" cried the old gentleman; "I will be in your theater the day after tomorrow."

Then Nicolo leapt to his feet and pressed Pasquale in so close an embrace that he gasped and panted quite out of breath.

At this moment Marianna entered the room. Signor Pasquale tried to frighten her away again by the look of resentment which he hurled at her; she, however, took not the slightest notice of it, but going straight up to Musso, addressed him as if in anger, — "It is in vain for you, Signor Nicolo, to attempt to entice my dear uncle to go to your theater. You are forgetting that the infamous trick lately played by some reprobate seducers, who were lying in wait for me, almost cost the life of my dearly beloved uncle, and of his worthy friend Splendiano; nay, that it almost cost my life too. Never will I give my consent to my uncle's again exposing himself to such danger. Desist from your entreaties, Nicolo. And you, my dearest uncle, you will stay quietly at home, will you not, and not venture out beyond the Porta del Popolo again at night-time, which is a friend to nobody?"

Signor Pasquale was thunderstruck. He opened his eyes wide and stared at his niece. Then he rewarded her with the sweetest endearments, and set forth at considerable length how that Signor Nicolo had pledged himself so to arrange matters as to avoid every danger on the return home.

"None the less," said Marianna, "I stick to my word, and beg you most earnestly, my dearest uncle, not to go to the theater outside the Porta del Popolo. I ask your pardon, Signor Nicolo, for speaking out frankly in your presence the dark suspicion that lurks in my mind. You are, I know, acquainted with Salvator Rosa and also with Antonio Scacciati. What if you are acting in concert with our enemies? What if you are only trying with evil intent to entice my dear uncle into your theater in order that they may the more safely carry out some fresh villainous scheme, for I know that my uncle will not go without me?"

"What a suspicion!" cried Nicolo, quite alarmed. "What a terrible suspicion, Signora! Have you such a bad opinion of me? Have I such an ill reputation that you conceive I could be guilty of this the basest treachery? But if you think so unfavorably of me, if you mistrust the assistance I have promised you, why then let Michele, who I know rescued you out of the hands of the robbers — let Michele accompany you, and let him take a large body of gendarmes with him, who can wait for you outside the theater, for you cannot of course expect me to fill my auditorium with police."

Marianna fixed her eyes steadily upon Nicolo's, and then said, earnestly and gravely, "What do you say? That Michele and gendarmes shall accompany us? Now I see plainly, Signor Nicolo, that you mean honestly by us, and that my nasty suspicion is unfounded. Pray forgive me my thoughtless words. And yet I cannot banish my nervousness and anxiety about my dear uncle; I must still beg him not to take this dangerous step."

Signor Pasquale had listened to all this conversation with such curious looks as plainly served to indicate the nature of the struggle that was going on within him. But now he could no longer contain himself; he threw himself on his knees before his beautiful niece, seized her hands, kissed them, bathed them with the tears which ran down his cheeks, exclaiming as if beside himself, "My adored, my angelic Marianna! Fierce and devouring are the flames of the passion which burns at my heart Oh! this nervousness, this anxiety — it is indeed the sweetest confession that you love me." And then he besought her not to give way to fear, but to go and listen in the theater to the finest arias which the most divine of composers had ever written.

Nicolo too abated not in his entreaties, plainly showing his disappointment, until Marianna permitted her scruples to be overcome; and she promised to lay all fear aside and accompany the best and dearest of uncles to the theater outside the Porta del Popolo. Signor Pasquale was in ectasies, was in the seventh heaven of delight. He was convinced that Marianna loved him; and he now might hope to hear his music on the stage, and win the laurel wreath which had so long been the vain object of his desires; he was on the point of seeing his dearest dreams fulfilled. Now he would let his light shine in perfect glory before his true and faithful friends, for he never thought for a moment but that Signor Splendiano and little Pitichinaccio would go with him as on the first occasion.

The night that Signor Splendiano had slept in his wig near the Pyramid of Cestius he had had, besides the specters who ran away with him, all sorts of sinister apparitions to visit him. The whole cemetery was alive, and hundreds of corpses had stretched out their skeleton arms towards him, moaning and wailing that even in their graves they could not get over the torture caused by his essences and electuaries. Accordingly the Pyramid Doctor, although he could not contradict Signor Pasquale that it was only a wild freakish trick played upon him by a parcel of godless boys, grew melancholy; and, albeit not ordinarily superstitiously inclined, he yet now saw specters everywhere, and was tormented by forebodings and bad dreams.

As for Pitichinaccio, he could not be convinced that they were not real devils come straight from the flames of hell who had fallen upon Signor Pasquale and upon himself, and the bare mention of that dreadful night was enough to make him scream. All the asseverations of Signor Pasquale that there had been nobody behind the masks but Antonio Scacciati and Salvator Rosa were of none effect, for Pitichinaccio wept and swore that in spite of his terror and apprehension he had clearly recognized both the voice and the behavior of the devil Fanfarelli in the one who had pinched his belly black and blue.

It may therefore be imagined what an almost endless amount of trouble it cost Signor Pasquale to persuade the two to go with him once more to Nicolo Musso's theater. Splendiano was the first to make the resolve to go, — after he had procured from a monk of St. Bernard's order a small consecrated bag of musk, the perfume of which neither dead man nor devil could endure; with this he intended to arm himself against all assaults. Pitichinaccio could not resist the temptation of a promised box of candied grapes, but Signor Pasquale had besides expressly to give his consent that he might wear his new abbot's coat, instead of his petticoats, which he affirmed had proved an immediate source of attraction to the devil.

What Salvator feared seemed therefore as if it would really take place; and yet his plan depended entirely, he continued to repeat, upon Signor Pasquale's being in Nicolo's theater alone with Marianna, without his faithful satellites. Both Antonio and Salvator greatly racked their brains how they should prevent Splendiano and Pitichinaccio from going along with Signor Pasquale. Every scheme that occurred to them for the accomplishment of this desideratum had to be given up owing to want of time, for the principal plan in Nicolo's theater had to be carried out on the evening of the following day.

But Providence, which often employs the most unlikely instruments for the chastisement of fools, interposed on behalf of the distressed lovers, and put it into Michele's head to practice some of his blundering, thus accomplishing what Salvator and Antonio's craft was unable to accomplish.

That same night there was heard in the Via Ripetta before Signor Pasquale's house such a chorus of fearful screams and of cursing and raving and abuse that all the neighbors were startled up out of their sleep, and a body of gendarmes, who had been pursuing a murderer as far as the Spanish Square, hastened up with torches, supposing that some fresh deed of violence was being committed. But when they, and a crowd of other people whom the noise had attracted, came upon the anticipated scene of murder, they found poor little Pitichinaccio lying as if dead on the ground, whilst Michele was thrashing the Pyramid Doctor with a formidable bludgeon. And they saw the Doctor reel to the floor just at the moment when Signor Pasquale painfully scrambled to his feet, drew his rapier, and furiously attacked Michele. Round about were lying pieces of broken guitars. Had not several people grasped the old man's arm he would assuredly have run Michele right through the heart. The ex-bravo, on now becoming aware by the light of the torches whom he had been molesting, stood as if petrified, his eyes almost starting out of his head, "a painted desperado, on the balance between will and power," as it is said somewhere. Then, uttering a fearful scream, he tore his hair and begged for pardon and mercy. Neither the Pyramid Doctor nor Pitichinaccio was seriously injured, but they had been so soundly cudgelled that they could neither move nor stir, and had to be carried home.

Signor Pasquale had himself brought this mishap upon his own shoulders.

We know that Salvator and Antonio complimented Marianna with the finest serenade that could be heard; but I have forgotten to say that to the old gentleman's very exceeding indignation they repeated it during several successive nights. At length Signor Pasquale whose rage was kept in check by his neighbors, was foolish enough to have recourse to the authorities of the city, urging them to forbid the two painters to sing in the Via Ripetta. The authorities, however, replied that it would be a thing unheard of in Rome to prevent anybody from singing and playing the guitar where he pleased, and it was irrational to ask such a thing. So Signor Pasquale determined to put an end to the nuisance himself, and promised Michele a large reward if he seized the first opportunity to fall upon the singers and give them a good sound drubbing. Michele at once procured a stout bludgeon, and lay in wait every night behind the door. But it happened that Salvator and Antonio judged it prudent to omit their serenading in the Via Ripetta for some nights preceding the carrying into execution of their plan, so as not to remind the old gentleman of his adversaries. Marianna remarked quite innocently that though she hated Antonio and Salvator, yet she liked their singing, for nothing was so nice as to hear music floating upwards in the night air.

This Signor Pasquale made a mental note of, and as the essence of gallantry purposed to surprise his love with a serenade on his part, which he had himself composed and carefully practiced up with his faithful friends. On the very night preceding that in which he was hoping to celebrate his greatest triumph in Nicolo Musso's theater, he stealthily slipped out of the house and went and fetched his associates, with whom he had previously arranged matters. But no sooner had they sounded the first few notes on their guitars than Michele, whom Signor Pasquale had thoughtlessly forgotten to apprise of his design, burst forth from behind the door, highly delighted at finding that the opportunity which was to bring him in the promised reward had at last come, and began to cudgel the musicians most unmercifully, with the results of which we are already acquainted. Of course there was no further mention made of either Splendiano or Pitichinaccio's accompanying Signor Pasquale to Nicolo's theater, for they were both confined to their bed beplastered all over. Signor Pasquale, however, was unable to stay away, although his back and shoulders were smarting not a little from the drubbing he had himself received; every note in his arias was a cord which drew him thither with irresistible power.

"Well now," said Salvator to Antonio, "since the obstacle which we took to be insurmountable has been removed out of our way of itself, it all depends now entirely upon your address not to let the favorable moment slip for carrying off your Marianna from Nicolo's theater. But I needn't talk, you'll not fail; I will greet you now as the betrothed of Capuzzi's lovely niece, who in a few days will be your wife. I wish you happiness, Antonio, and yet I feel a shiver run through me when I think upon your marriage."

"What do you mean, Salvator?" asked Antonio, utterly astounded.

"Call it a crotchet, call it a foolish fancy, or what you will, Antonio," rejoined Salvator, — "at any rate I love the fair sex; but there is not one, not even she on whom I foolishly dote, for whom I would gladly die, but what excites in my heart, so soon as I think of a union with her such as marriage is, a suspicion that makes me tremble with a most unpleasant feeling of awe. That which is inscrutable in the nature of woman mocks all the weapons of man. She whom we believe to have surrendered herself to us entirely, heart and soul, whom we believe to have unfolded all her character to us, is the first to deceive us, and along with the sweetest of her kisses we imbibe the most pernicious of poisons."

"And my Marianna?" asked Antonio, amazed.

"Pardon me, Antonio," continued Salvator, "even your Marianna, who is loveliness and grace personified, has given me a fresh proof of how dangerous the mysterious nature of woman is to us. Just call to mind what was the behavior of that innocent, inexperienced child when we carried her uncle home, how at a single glance from me she divined everything — everything, I tell you, and, as you yourself admitted, proceeded to play her part with the utmost sagacity. But that is not to be at all compared with what took place on the occasion of Musso's visit to the old gentleman. The most practiced address, the most impenetrable cunning, — in short, all the inventive arts of the most experienced woman of the world could not have done more than little Marianna did, in order to deceive the old gentleman with perfect success. She could not have acted in any better way to prepare the road for us for any kind of enterprise. Our feud with the cranky old fool — any sort of cunning scheme seems justified, but — come, my dear Antonio, never mind my fanciful crotchets, but be happy with your Marianna; as happy as you can."

If a monk had taken his place beside Signor Pasquale when he set out along with his niece to go to Nicolo Musso's theater, everybody would have thought that the strange pair were being led to execution. First went valiant Michele, repulsive in appearance, and armed to the teeth; then came Signor Pasquale and Marianna, followed by fully twenty gendarmes.

Nicolo received the old gentleman and his lady with every mark of respect at the entrance to the theater, and conducted them to the seats which had been reserved for them, immediately in front of the stage. Signor Pasquale felt highly flattered by this mark of honor, and gazed about him with proud and sparkling eyes, whilst his pleasure, his joy, was greatly enhanced to find that all the seats near and behind Marianna were occupied by women alone. A couple of violins and a bass-fiddle were being tuned behind the curtains of the stage; the old gentleman's heart beat with expectation; and when all at once the orchestra struck up the *ritornello* of his work, he felt an electric thrill tingling in every nerve.

Formica came forward in the character of Pasquarello, and sang — sang in Capuzzi's own voice, and with all his characteristic gestures, the most hopeless aria that ever was heard. The theater shook with the loud and boisterous laughter of the audience. They shouted; they screamed wildly, "O Pasquale Capuzzi! Our most illustrious composer and artist! Bravo! Bravissimo!" The old gentleman, not perceiving the ridicule and irony of the laughter, was in raptures of delight. The aria came to an end, and the people cried "Sh! sh!" for Doctor Gratiano, played on this occasion by Nicolo Musso himself, appeared on the stage, holding his hands over his ears and shouting to Pasquarello for goodness' sake to stop his ridiculous screeching.

Then the Doctor asked Pasquarello how long he had taken to the confounded habit of singing, and where he had got that execrable piece from.

Whereupon Pasquarello replied, that he didn't know what the Doctor would have; he was like the Romans, and had no taste for real music, since he failed to recognize the most talented of musicians. The aria had been written by the greatest of living composers, in whose service he had the good fortune to be, receiving instruction in both music and singing from the master himself.

Gratiano then began guessing, and mentioned the names of a great number of well-known composers and musicians, but at every distinguished name Pasquarello only shook his head contemptuously.

At length Pasquarello said that the Doctor was only exposing gross ignorance, since he did not know the name of the greatest composer of the time. It was no other than Signor Pasquale Capuzzi, who had done him the honor of taking him into his service. Could he not see that he was the friend and servant of Signor Pasquale?

Then the Doctor broke out into a loud long roar of laughter, and cried. What! Had he (Pasquarello) after running away from him (the Doctor), with whom, besides getting his wages and food, he had had his palm tickled with many a copper, had he gone and taken service with the biggest and most inveterate old coxcomb who ever stuffed himself with macaroni, to the patched Carnival fool who strutted about like a satisfied old hen after a shower of rain, to the snarling skinflint, the love-sick old poltroon, who infected the air of the Via Ripetta with the disgusting bleating which he called singing? &c., &c.

To which Pasquarello, quite incensed, made reply that it was nothing but envy which spoke in the Doctor's words; he (Pasquarello) was of course speaking with his heart in his mouth (*parla col cuore in mano*); the Doctor was not at all the man to pass an opinion upon Signor Pasquale Capuzzi di Senigaglia; he was speaking with his heart in his mouth. The Doctor himself had a strong tang of all that he blamed in the excellent Signor Pasquale; but he was speaking with his heart in his mouth; he (Pasquarello) had himself often heard fully six hundred people at once laugh most heartily at Doctor Gratiano, and so forth. Then Pasquarello spoke a long panegyric upon his new master, Signor Pasquale, attributing to him all the virtues under the sun; and he concluded with a description of his character, which he portrayed as being the very essence of amiability and grace.

"Heaven bless you, Formica!" lisped Signor Capuzzi to himself; "Heaven bless you, Formica! I perceive you have designed to make my triumph perfect, since you are upbraiding the Romans for all their envious and ungrateful persecution of me, and are letting them know *who* I really am."

"Ha! here comes my master himself," cried Pasquarello at this moment, and there entered on the stage — Signor Pasquale Capuzzi himself, just as he breathed and walked, his very clothes, face, gestures, gait, postures, in fact so perfectly like Signor Capuzzi in the auditorium, that the latter, quite aghast, let go Marianna's hand, which hitherto he had held fast in his own, and tapped himself, his nose, his wig, in order to discover whether he was not dreaming, or seeing double, whether he was really sitting in Nicolo Musso's theater and dare credit the miracle.

Capuzzi on the stage embraced Doctor Gratiano with great kindness, and asked how he was. The Doctor replied that he had a good appetite, and slept soundly, at his service (*per servirlo*); and as for his purse — well, it was suffering from a galloping consumption. Only yesterday he had spent his last ducat for a pair of rosemary-colored stockings for his sweetheart, and was just going to walk round to one or two bankers to see if he could borrow thirty ducats" —

"But how can you pass over your best friends?" said Capuzzi. "Here, my dear sir, here are fifty ducats, come take them."

"Pasquale, what are you about?" said the real Capuzzi in an undertone.

Dr. Gratiano began to talk about a bond and about interest; but Signor Capuzzi declared that he could not think of asking for either from such a friend as the Doctor was.

"Pasquale, have you gone out of your senses?" exclaimed the real Capuzzi a little louder.

After many grateful embraces Doctor Gratiano took his leave. Now Pasquarello drew near with a good many bows, and extolled Signor Capuzzi to the skies, adding, however, that his purse was suffering from the same complaint as Gratiano's, and he begged for some of the same excellent medicine that had cured his. Capuzzi on the stage laughed, and said he was pleased to find that Pasquarello knew how to turn his good humor to advantage, and threw him several glittering ducats.

"Pasquale, you must be mad, possessed of the devil," cried the real Capuzzi aloud. He was bidden be still.

Pasquarello went still further in his eulogy of Capuzzi, and came at last to speak, of the aria which he (Capuzzi) had composed, and with which he (Pasquarello) hoped to enchant everybody. The fictitious Capuzzi clapped Pasquarello heartily on the back, and went on to say that he might venture to tell him (Pasquarello), his faithful servant, in confidence, that in reality he knew nothing whatever of the science of music, and in respect to the aria of which he had just spoken, as well as all pieces that he had ever composed, why, he had stolen them out of Frescobaldi's canzonas and Carissimi's motets.

"I tell you you're lying in your throat, you knave," shouted the Capuzzi off the stage, rising from his seat. Again he was bidden keep still, and the woman who sat next him drew him down on the bench.

"It's now time to think about other and more important matters," continued Capuzzi on the stage. He was going to give a grand banquet the next day, and Pasquarello must look alive and have everything that was necessary prepared. Then he produced and read over a list of all the rarest and most expensive dishes, making Pasquarello tell him how much each would cost, and at the same time giving him the money for them.

"Pasquale! You're insane! You've gone mad! You good-for-nothing scamp! You spendthrift!" shouted the real Capuzzi at intervals, growing more and more enraged the higher the cost of this the most nonsensical of dinners rose.

At length, when the list was finished, Pasquarello asked what had induced him to give such a splendid banquet.

"Tomorrow will be the happiest and most joyous day of my life," replied the fictitious Capuzzi. "For know, my good Pasquarello, that I am going to celebrate tomorrow the auspicious marriage of my dear niece Marianna. I am going to give her hand to that brave young fellow, the best of all artists, Scacciati."

Hardly had the words fallen from his lips when the real Capuzzi leapt to his feet, utterly beside himself, quite out of his mind, his face all aflame with the most fiendish rage, and doubling his fists and shaking them at his counterpart on the stage, he yelled at the top of his voice, "No, you won't, no, you won't, you rascal! you scoundrel, you, — Pasquale! Do you mean to cheat yourself out of your Marianna, you hound? Are you going to throw her in the arms of that scoundrel, — sweet Marianna, thy life, thy hope, thy all? Ah! look to it! Look to it! you infatuated fool. Just remember what sort of a reception you will meet with from yourself. You shall beat yourself black and blue with your own hands, so that you will have no relish to think about banquets and weddings!"

But the Capuzzi on the stage doubled his fists like the Capuzzi below, and shouted in exactly the same furious way, and in the same high-pitched voice, "May all the spirits of hell sit at your heart, you abominable nonsensical Pasquale, you atrocious skinflint — you love-sick old fool — you gaudy tricked-out ass with the cap and bells dangling about your ears. Take care lest I snuff out the candle of your life, and so at length put an end to the infamous tricks which you try to foist upon the good, honest, modest Pasquale Capuzzi."

Amidst the most fearful cursing and swearing of the real Capuzzi, the one on the stage dished up one fine anecdote after the other about him.

"You'd better attempt," shouted at last the fictitious Capuzzi, "you only dare, Pasquale, you amorous old ape, to interfere with the happiness of these two young people, whom Heaven has destined for each other."

At this moment there appeared at the back of the stage Antonio Scacciati and Marianna locked in each other's arms. Albeit the old gentleman was at other times somewhat feeble on his legs, yet now fury gave him strength and agility. With a single bound he was on the stage, had drawn his sword, and was charging upon the pretended Antonio. He found, how-ever, that he was held fast behind. An officer of the Papal guard had stopped him, and said in a serious voice, "Recollect where you are, Signor Pasquale; you are in Nicolo Musso's theater. Without intending it, you have today played a most ridiculous *rôle*. You will not find either Antonio or Marianna here." The two persons whom Capuzzi had taken for his niece and her lover now drew near, along with the rest of the actors. The faces were all completely strange to him. His rapier escaped from his trembling hand; he took a deep breath as if awakening out of a bad dream; he grasped his brow with both hands; he opened his eyes wide. The presentiment of what had happened suddenly struck him, and he shouted, "Marianna!" in such a stentorian voice that the walls rang again.

But she was beyond reach of his shouts. Antonio had taken advantage of the opportunity whilst Pasquale, oblivious of all about him and even of himself, was quarreling with his double, to make his way to Marianna, and back with her through the audience, and out at a side door, where a carriage stood ready waiting; and away they went as fast as their horses could gallop towards Florence.

"Marianna!" screamed the old man again, "Marianna! she is gone. She has fled. That knave Antonio has stolen her from me. Away! after them! Have pity on me, good people, and take torches and help me to look for my little darling. Oh! you serpent!"

And he tried to make for the door. But the officer held him fast, saying, "Do you mean that pretty young lady who sat beside you? I believe I saw her slip out with a young man — I think Antonio Scacciati — a long time ago, when you began your idle quarrel with one of the actors who wore a mask like your face. You needn't make a trouble of it; every inquiry shall at once be set on foot, and Marianna shall be brought back to you as soon as she is found. But as for yourself, Signor Pasquale, your behavior here and your murderous attempt upon the life of that actor compel me to arrest you."

Signor Pasquale, his face as pale as death, incapable of uttering a single word or even a sound, was led away by the very same gendarmes who were to have protected him against masked devils and specters. Thus it came to pass that on the selfsame night on which he had hoped to celebrate his triumph, he was plunged into the midst of trouble and of all the frantic despondency which amorous old fools feel when they are deceived.

VI

Salvator Rosa leaves Rome and goes to Florence. Conclusion of the history.

Everything here below beneath the sun is subject to continual change; and perhaps there is nothing which can be called more inconstant than human opinion, which turns round in an everlasting circle like the wheel of fortune. He who reaps great praise today is overwhelmed with biting censure tomorrow; today we trample under foot the man who tomorrow will be raised far above us.

Of all those who in Rome had ridiculed and mocked at old Pasquale Capuzzi, with his sordid avarice, his foolish amorousness, his insane jealousy, who did not wish poor tormented Marianna her liberty? But now that Antonio had successfully carried off his mistress, all their ridicule and mockery was suddenly changed into pity for the old fool, whom they saw wandering about the streets of Rome with his head hanging on his breast, utterly disconsolate. Misfortunes seldom come singly; and so it happened that Signor Pasquale, soon after Marianna had been taken from him, lost his best bosom-friends also. Little Pitichinaccio choked himself in foolishly trying to swallow an almond-kernel in the middle of a cadenza; but a sudden stop was put to the life of the illustrious Pyramid Doctor Signor Splendiano Accoramboni by a slip of the pen, for which he had only himself to blame. Michele's drubbing made such work with him that he fell into a fever. He determined to make use of a remedy which he claimed to have discovered, so, calling for pen and ink, he wrote down a prescription in which, by employing a wrong sign, he increased the quantity of a powerful substance to a dangerous extent. But scarcely had he swallowed the medicine than he sank back on the pillows and died, establishing, however, by his own death in the most splendid and satisfactory manner the efficacy of the last tincture which he ever prescribed.

As already remarked, all those whose laughter had been the loudest, and who had repeatedly wished Antonio success in his schemes, had now nothing but pity for the old gentleman; and the bitterest blame was heaped, not so much upon Antonio, as upon Salvator Rosa, whom, to be sure, they regarded as the instigator of the whole plan.

Salvator's enemies, of whom he had a goodly number, exerted all their efforts to fan the flame. "See you," they said, "he was one of Masaniello's doughty partisans, and is ready to turn his hand to any deed of mischief, to any disreputable enterprise; we shall be the next to suffer from his presence in the city; he is a dangerous man."

And the jealous faction who had leagued together against Salvator did actually succeed in stemming the tide of his prosperous career. He sent forth from his studio one picture after the other, all bold in conception, and splendidly executed; but the so-called critics shrugged their shoulders, now pointing out that the hills were too blue, the trees too green, the figures now too long, now too broad, finding fault everywhere where there was no fault to be found, and seeking to detract from his hard-earned reputation in all the ways they could think of. Especially bitter in their persecution of him were the Academicians of St. Luke, who could not forget how he took them in about the surgeon; they even went beyond the limits of their own profession, and decried the clever stanzas which Salvator at that time wrote, hinting very plainly that he did not cultivate his fruit on his own garden soil, but plundered that of his neighbors. For these reasons, therefore, Salvator could not manage to surround himself with the splendor which he had lived amidst formerly in Rome. Instead of being visited by the most eminent of the Romans in a large studio, he had to remain with Dame Caterina and his green fig tree; but amid these poor surroundings he frequently found both consolation and tranquility of mind.

Salvator took the malicious machinations of his enemies to heart more than he ought to have done; he even began to feel that an insidious disease, resulting from chagrin and dejection, was gnawing at his vitals. In this unhappy frame of mind he designed and executed two large pictures which excited quite an uproar in Rome. Of these one represented the transitoriness of all earthly things, and in the principal figure, that of a wanton female bearing all the indications of her degrading calling about her, was recognized the mistress of one of the cardinals; the other portrayed the Goddess of Fortune dispensing her rich gifts. But cardinals' hats, bishops' mitres, gold medals, decorations of orders, were falling upon bleating sheep, braying asses, and other such like contemptible animals, whilst well-made men in ragged clothes were vainly straining their eyes upwards to get even the smallest gift. Salvator had given free rein to his embittered mood, and the animals' heads bore the closest resemblance to the features of various eminent persons. It is easy to imagine, therefore, how the tide of hatred against him rose, and that he was more bitterly persecuted than ever.

Dame Caterina warned him, with tears in her eyes, that as soon as it began to be dark she had observed suspicious characters lurking about the house and apparently dogging his every footstep. Salvator saw that it was time to leave Rome; and Dame Caterina and her beloved daughters were the only people whom it caused him pain to part from. In response to the repeated invitations of the Duke of Tuscany,* he went to Florence; and here at length he was richly indemnified for all the mortification and worry which he had had to struggle against in Rome, and here all the honor and all the fame which he so truly deserved were freely conferred upon him. The Duke's presents and the high prices which he received for his pictures soon enabled him to remove into a large house and to furnish it in the most magnificent style. There he was wont to gather round him the most illustrious authors and scholars of the day, amongst whom it will be sufficient to mention Evangelista Toricelli,† Valerio Chimentelli, Bat-

---

* This was Ferdinand II., a member of the illustrious Florentine family of the Medici. He upheld the family tradition by his liberal patronage of science and letters.

† Evangelista Torricelli, the successor of the great Galileo in the chair of philosophy and mathematics at Florence, is inseparably associated with the discovery that water in a suction-pump will only rise to the height of about thirty-two feet. This paved the way to his invention of the barometer in 1643.

Other members of the Accademia de' Percossi were Dati, Lippi, tista Ricciardi, Andrea Cavalcanti, Pietro Salvati, Filippo Apolloni, Volumnio Bandelli, Francesco Rovai. They formed an association for the prosecution of artistic and scientific pursuits, whilst Salvator was able to contribute an element of whimsicality to the meetings, which had a singular effect in animating and enlivening the mind. The banqueting-hall was like a beautiful grove with fragrant bushes and flowers and splashing fountains; and the dishes even, which were served up by pages in eccentric costumes, were very wonderful to look at, as if they came from some distant land of magic. These meetings of writers and savans in Salvator Rosa's house were called at that time the Accademia de' Percossi.

Though Salvator's mind was in this way devoted to science and art, yet his real true nature came to life again when he was with his friend Antonio Scacciati, who, along with his lovely Marianna, led the pleasant *sans souci* life of an artist. They often recalled poor old Signor Pasquale whom they had deceived, and all that had taken place in Nicolo Musso's theater. Antonio asked Salvator how he had contrived to enlist in his cause the active interest not only of Musso but of the excellent Formica, and of Agli too. Salvator replied that it had been very easy, for Formica was his most intimate friend in Rome, so that it had been a work of both pleasure and love to him to arrange everything on the stage in accordance with the instructions Salvator gave him. Antonio protested that, though still he could not help laughing over the scene which had paved the way to his happiness, he yet wished with all his heart to be reconciled to the old gentleman, even if he should never touch a penny of Marianna's fortune, which the old gentleman had confiscated; the practice of his art brought him in a sufficient income. Marianna too was often unable to restrain her tears when she thought that her father's brother might go down to his grave without having forgiven her the trick which she had played upon him; and so Pasquale's hatred overshadowed like a dark cloud the brightness of their happiness. Salvator comforted them both – Antonio and Marianna – by saying that time had adjusted still worse difficulties, and that chance would perhaps bring

---

Viviani, Bandinelli, &c.

the old gentleman near them in some less dangerous way than if they had remained in Rome, or were to return there now.

We shall see that a prophetic spirit spoke in Salvator.

A considerable time elapsed, when one day Antonio burst into Salvator's studio breathless and pale as death. "Salvator!" he cried, "Salvator, my friend, my protector! I am lost if you do not help me. Pasquale Capuzzi is here; he has procured a warrant for my arrest for the seduction of his niece."

"But what can Signor Pasquale do against you now?" asked Salvator. "Have you not been united to Marianna by the Church?"

"Oh!" replied Antonio, giving way completely to despair, "the blessing of the Church herself cannot save me from ruin. Heaven knows by what means the old man has been able to approach the Pope's nephew.* At any rate the Pope's nephew has taken the old man under his protection, and has infused into him the hope that the Holy Father will declare my marriage with Marianna to be null and void; nay, yet further, that he will grant him (the old man) dispensation to marry his niece."

"Stop!" cried Salvator, "now I see it all; now I see it all. What threatens to be your ruin, Antonio, is this man's hatred against me. For I must tell you that this nephew of the Pope's, a proud, coarse, boorish clown, was amongst the animals in my picture to whom the Goddess of Fortune is dispensing her gifts. That it was I who helped you to win your Marianna, though indirectly, is well known, not only to this man, but to all Rome, — which is quite reason enough to persecute you since they cannot do anything to me. And so, Antonio, having brought this misfortune upon you, I must make every effort to assist you, and all the more that you are my dearest and most intimate friend. But, by the saints! I don't see in what way I can frustrate your enemies' little game" —

Therewith Salvator, who had continued to paint at a picture all the time, laid aside brush, palette, and maulstick, and, rising up from his easel, began to pace the room backwards and forwards, his arms crossed over his breast, Antonio

---

* An allusion to the well-known nepotism of the Popes. The man here mentioned is one of the Barberini, nephew of Pope Urban VIII.

meanwhile being quite wrapt up in his own thoughts, and with his eyes fixed unchangeably upon the floor.

At length Salvator paused before him and said with a smile, "See here, Antonio, I cannot do anything myself against your powerful enemies, but I know one who can help you, and who will help you, and that is — Signor Formica."

"Oh!" said Antonio, "don't jest with an unhappy man, whom nothing can save."

"What! you are despairing again?" exclaimed Salvator, who was now all at once in the merriest humor, and he laughed aloud. "I tell you, Antonio, my friend Formica shall help you in Florence as he helped you in Rome. Go away quietly home and comfort your Marianna, and calmly wait and see how things will turn out. I trust you will be ready at the shortest notice to do what Signor Formica, who is really here in Florence at the present time, shall require of you." This Antonio promised most faithfully, and hope revived in him again, and confidence.

Signor Pasquale Capuzzi was not a little astonished at receiving a formal invitation from the Accademia de' Percossi. "Ah!" he exclaimed, "Florence is the place then where a man's merits are recognized, where Pasquale Capuzzi di Senigaglia, a man gifted with the most excellent talents, is known and valued." Thus the thought of his knowledge and his art, and the honor that was shown him on their account, overcame the repugnance which he would otherwise have felt against a society at the head of which stood Salvator Rosa. His Spanish gala-dress was more carefully brushed than ever; his conical hat was equipped with a new feather; his shoes were provided with new ribbons; and so Signor Pasquale appeared at Salvator's as brilliant as a rose-chafer,* and his face all sunshine. The magnificence which he saw on all sides of him, even Salvator himself, who had received him dressed in the richest apparel, inspired him with deep respect, and, after the manner of little souls, who, though at first proud and puffed up, at once grovel in the dust whenever they come into contact with what they feel to be superior to themselves,

---

* *Cetonia aurata,* L., called also the gold-chafer; it is colored green and gold.

Pasquale's behavior towards Salvator, whom he would gladly have done a mischief to in Rome, was nothing but humility and submissive deference.

So much attention was paid to Signor Pasquale from all sides, his judgment was appealed to so unconditionally, and so much was said about his services to art, that he felt new life infused into his veins; and an unusual spirit was awakened within him, so that his utterances on many points were more sensible than might have been expected. If it be added that never in his life before had he been so splendidly entertained, and never had he drunk such inspiriting wine, it will readily be conceived that his pleasure was intensified from moment to moment, and that he forgot all the wrong which had been done him at Rome as well as the unpleasant business which had brought him to Florence. Often after their banquets the Academicians were wont to amuse themselves with short impromptu dramatic representations, and so this evening the distinguished playwright and poet Filippo Apolloni called upon those who generally took part in them to bring the festivities to a fitting conclusion with one of their usual performances. Salvator at once withdrew to make all the necessary preparations.

Not long afterwards the bushes at the farther end of the banqueting-hall began to move, the branches with their foliage were parted, and a little theater provided with seats for the spectators became visible.

"By the saints!" exclaimed Pasquale Capuzzi, terrified, "where am I? Surely that's Nicolo Musso's theater."

Without heeding his exclamation, Evangelista Toricelli and Andrea Cavalcanti — both of them grave, respectable, venerable men — took him by the arm and led him to a seat immediately in front of the stage, taking their places on each side of him.

This was no sooner done than there appeared on the boards — Formica in the character of Pasquarello.

"You reprobate, Formica!" shouted Pasquale, leaping to his feet and shaking his doubled fist at the stage. Toricelli and Cavalcanti's stern, reproving glances bade him sit still and keep quiet.

Pasquarello wept and sobbed, and cursed his destiny, which brought him nothing but grief and heart-breaking, declared he didn't know how he should ever set about it if he wanted to laugh again, and concluded by saying that if he could look upon blood without fainting, he should certainly cut his throat, or should throw himself in the Tiber if he could only let that cursed swimming alone when he got into the water.

Doctor Gratiano now joined him, and inquired what was the cause of his trouble.

Whereupon Pasquarello asked him whether he did not know anything about what had taken place in the house of his master, Signor Pasquale Capuzzi di Senigaglia, whether he did not know that an infamous scoundrel had carried off pretty Marianna, his master's niece?

"Ah!" murmured Capuzzi, "I see you want to make your excuses to me, Formica; you wish for my pardon — well, we shall see."

Doctor Gratiano expressed his sympathy, and observed that the scoundrel must have gone to work very cunningly to have eluded all the inquiries which had been instituted by Capuzzi.

"Ho! ho!" rejoined Pasquarello. "The Doctor need not imagine that the scoundrel, Antonio Scacciati, had succeeded in escaping the sharpness of Signor Pasquale Capuzzi, supported as he was, moreover, by powerful friends. Antonio had been arrested, his marriage with Marianna annulled, and Marianna herself had again come into Capuzzi's power.

"Has he got her again?" shouted Capuzzi, beside himself; "has he got her again, good Pasquale? Has he got his little darling, his Marianna? Is the knave Antonio arrested? Heaven bless you, Formica!"

"You take a too keen interest in the play, Signor Pasquale," said Cavalcanti, quite seriously. "Pray permit the actors to proceed with their parts without interrupting them in this disturbing fashion."

Ashamed of himself, Signor Pasquale resumed his seat, for he had again risen to his feet.

Doctor Gratiano asked what had taken place then.

A wedding, continued Pasquarello, a wedding had taken place. Marianna had repented of what she had done; Signor

Pasquale had obtained the desired dispensation from the Holy Father, and had married his niece.

"Yes, yes," murmured Pasquale Capuzzi to himself, whilst his eyes sparkled with delight, "yes, yes, my dear, good Formica; he will marry his sweet Marianna, the happy Pasquale. He knew that the dear little darling had always loved him, and that it was only Satan who had led her astray."

"Why then, everything is all right," said Doctor Gratiano, "and there's no cause for lamentation."

Pasquarello began, however, to weep and sob more violently than before, till at length, as if overcome by the terrible nature of his pain, he fainted away. Doctor Gratiano ran backwards and forwards in great distress, was so sorry he had no smelling-bottle with him, felt in all his pockets, and at last produced a roasted chestnut, and put it under the insensible Pasquarello's nose. He at once recovered, sneezing violently, and begging him to attribute his faintness to his weak nerves, he related how that, immediately after the marriage, Marianna had been afflicted with the saddest melancholy, continually calling upon Antonio, and treating the old gentleman with contempt and aversion. But the old fellow, quite infatuated by his passion and jealousy, had not ceased to torment the poor girl with his folly in the most abominable way. And here Pasquarello mentioned a host of mad tricks which Pasquale had done, and which were really current in Rome about him. Signor Capuzzi sat on thorns; he murmured at intervals, "Curse you, Formica! You are lying! What evil spirit is in you?" He was only prevented from bursting out into a violent passion by Toricelli and Cavalcanti, who sat watching him with an earnest gaze.

Pasquarello concluded his narration by telling that Marianna had at length succumbed to her unsatisfied longing for her lover, her great distress of mind, and the innumerable tortures which were inflicted upon her by the execrable old fellow, and had died in the flower of her youth.

At this moment was heard a mournful *De profundis* sung by hollow, husky voices, and men clad in long black robes appeared on the stage, bearing an open coffin, within which was seen the corpse of lovely Marianna wrapped in white shrouds. Behind it came Signor Pasquale Capuzzi in the deepest mourning, feebly staggering along and wailing aloud, beating his breast, and crying in a voice of despair, "O Marianna! Marianna!"

So soon as the real Capuzzi caught sight of his niece's corpse he broke out into loud lamentations, and both Capuzzis, the one on the stage and the one off, gave vent to their grief in the most heartrending wails and groans, "O Marianna! O Marianna! O unhappy me! Alas! Alas for me!"

Let the reader picture to himself the open coffin with the corpse of the lovely child, surrounded by the hired mourners singing their dismal *De profundis* in hoarse voices, and then the comical masks of Pasquarello and Dr. Gratiano, who were expressing their grief in the most ridiculous gestures, and lastly the two Capuzzis, wailing and screeching in despair. Indeed, all who were witnesses of the extraordinary spectacle could not help feeling, even in the midst of the unrestrained laughter they had burst out into at sight of the wonderful old gentleman, that their hearts were chilled by a most uncomfortable feeling of awe.

Now the stage grew dark, and it thundered and lightened, and there rose up from below a pale ghostly figure, which bore most unmistakably the features of Capuzzi's dead brother, Pietro of Senigaglia, Marianna's father.

"O you infamous brother, Pasquale! what have you done with my daughter? what have you done with my daughter?" wailed the figure, in a dreadful and hollow voice. "Despair, you atrocious murderer of my child. You shall find your reward in hell."

Capuzzi on the stage dropped on the floor as if struck by lightning, and at the same moment the real Capuzzi reeled from his seat unconscious. The bushes rustled together again, and the stage was gone, and also Marianna and Capuzzi and the ghastly specter Pietro. Signor Pasquale Capuzzi lay in such a dead faint that it cost a good deal of trouble to revive him.

At length he came to himself with a deep sigh, and, stretching out both hands before him as if to ward off the horror that had seized him, he cried in a husky voice, "Leave me alone, Pietro." Then a torrent of tears ran down his cheeks, and he sobbed and cried, "Oh! Marianna, my darling child — my — my Marianna." "But recollect yourself," said now

Cavalcanti, "recollect yourself, Signor Pasquale, it was only on the stage that you saw your niece dead. She is alive; she is here to crave pardon for the thoughtless step which love and also your own inconsiderate conduct drove her to take."

And Marianna, and behind her Antonio Scacciati, now ran forward from the back part of the hall and threw themselves at the old gentleman's feet, — for he had meanwhile been placed in an easy chair. Marianna, looking most charming and beautiful, kissed his hands and bathed them with scalding tears, beseeching him to pardon both her and Antonio, to whom she had been united by the blessing of the Church.

Suddenly the hot blood surged into the old man's pallid face, fury flashed from his eyes, and he cried in a half-choked voice, "Oh! you abominable scoundrel! You poisonous serpent whom I nourished in my bosom!" Then old Toricelli, with grave and thoughtful dignity, put himself in front of Capuzzi, and told him that he (Capuzzi) had seen a representation of the fate that would inevitably and irremediably overtake him if he had the hardihood to carry out his wicked purpose against Antonio and Marianna's peace and happiness. He depicted in startling colors the folly and madness of amorous old men, who call down upon their own heads the most ruinous mischief which Heaven can inflict upon a man, since all the love which might have fallen to their share is lost, and instead hatred and contempt shoot their fatal darts at them from every side.

At intervals lovely Marianna cried in a tone that went to everybody's heart, "O my uncle, I will love and honor you as my own father; you will kill me by a cruel death if you rob me of my Antonio." And all the eminent men by whom the old gentleman was surrounded cried with one accord that it would not be possible for a man like Signor Pasquale Capuzzi di Senigaglia, a patron of art and himself an artist, not to forgive the young people, and assume the part of father to the most lovely of ladies, not possible that he could refuse to accept with joy as his son-in-law such an artist as Antonio Scacciati, who was highly esteemed throughout all Italy and richly crowned with fame and honor.

Then it was patent to see that a violent struggle went on within the old gentleman. He sighed, moaned, clasped his hands before his face, and, whilst Toricelli was continuing to speak in a most impressive manner, and Marianna was appealing to him in the most touching accents, and the rest were extolling Antonio all they knew how, he kept looking down — now upon his niece, now upon Antonio, whose splendid clothes and rich chains of honor bore testimony to the truth of what was said about the artistic fame he had earned.

Gone was all rage out of Capuzzi's countenance; he sprang up with radiant eyes, and pressed Marianna to his heart, saying, "Yes, I forgive you, my dear child; I forgive you, Antonio. Far be it from me to disturb your happiness. You are right, my worthy Signor Toricelli; Formica has shown me in the tableau on the stage all the mischief and ruin that would have befallen me had I carried out my insane design. I am cured, quite cured of my folly. But where is Signor Formica, where is my good physician? let me thank him a thousand times for my cure; it is he alone who has accomplished it. The terror that he has caused me to feel has brought about a complete revolution within me."

Pasquarello stepped forward. Antonio threw himself upon his neck, crying, "O Signor Formica, you to whom I owe my life, my all — oh! take off this disfiguring mask, that I may see your face, that Formica may not be any longer a mystery to me."

Pasquarello took off his cap and his artificial mask, which looked like a natural face, since it offered not the slightest hindrance to the play of countenance, and this Formica, this Pasquarello, was transformed into — Salvator Rosa.*

---

* The painter Salvator Rosa did really play at Rome the *rôle* of Pasquarello here attributed to him; but it was on the occasion of his second visit to the Eternal City about 1639. On the other hand, it was after 1647 (the year of Masaniello's revolt at Naples) that Salvator again came to Rome (the third visit), where he stayed until he was obliged to flee farther, namely, to Florence, in consequence of the two pictures already mentioned. It seems evident therefore that Hoffmann has not troubled himself about his dates, or strict historical fidelity, but seems rather to have combined the incidents of the painter's two visits to Rome — *i.e.,* his second and his third visit.

"Salvator!" exclaimed Marianna, Antonio, and Capuzzi, utterly astounded.

"Yes," said that wonderful man, "it is Salvator Rosa, whom the Romans would not recognize as painter and poet, but who in the character of Formica drew from them, without their being aware of it, almost every evening for more than a year, in Nicolo Musso's wretched little theater, the most noisy and most demonstrative storms of applause, from whose mouth they willingly took all the scorn, and all the satiric mockery of what is bad, which they would on no account listen to and see in Salvator's poems and pictures. It is Salvator Formica who has helped you, dear Antonio."

"Salvator," began old Capuzzi, "Salvator Rosa, albeit I have always regarded you as my worst enemy, yet I have always prized your artistic skill very highly, and now I love you as the worthiest friend I have, and beg you to accept my friendship in return."

"Tell me," replied Salvator, "tell me, my worthy Signor Pasquale, what service I can render you, and accept my assurances beforehand, that I will leave no stone unturned to accomplish whatever you may ask of me."

And now the genial smile which had not been seen upon Capuzzi's face since Marianna had been carried off, began to steal back again. Taking Salvator's hand he lisped in a low voice, "My dear Signor Salvator, you possess an unlimited influence over good Antonio; beseech him in my name to permit me to spend the short rest of my days with him, and my dear daughter Marianna, and to accept at my hands the inheritance left her by her mother, as well as the good dowry which I was thinking of adding to it. And he must not look jealous if I occasionally kiss the dear sweet child's little white hand; and ask him — every Sunday at least when I go to Mass, to trim up my rough moustache, for there's nobody in all the wide world understands it so well as he does."

It cost Salvator an effort to repress his laughter at the strange old man; but before he could make any reply, Antonio and Marianna, embracing the old gentleman, assured him that they should not believe he was fully reconciled to them, and should not be really happy, until he came to live with them as their dear father, never to leave them again. Antonio added that not only on Sunday, but every other day, he would trim Capuzzi's moustache as elegantly as he knew how, and accordingly the old gentleman was perfectly radiant with delight. Meanwhile a splendid supper had been prepared, to which the entire company now turned in the best of spirits.

In taking my leave of you, beloved reader, I wish with all my heart that, whilst you have been reading the story of the wonderful Signor Formica, you have derived as much pure pleasure from it as Salvator and all his friends felt on sitting down to their supper.

*The Sandman**

NATHANAEL TO LOTHAIR

I know you are all very uneasy because I have not written for such a long, long time. Mother, to be sure, is angry, and Clara, I dare say, believes I am living here in riot and revelry, and quite forgetting my sweet angel, whose image is so deeply engraved upon my heart and mind. But that is not so; daily and hourly do I think of you all, and my lovely Clara's form comes to gladden me in my dreams, and smiles upon me with her bright eyes, as graciously as she used to do in the days when I went in and out amongst you. Oh! how could I write to you in the distracted state of mind in which I have been, and which, until now, has quite bewildered me! A terrible thing has happened to me. Dark forebodings of some awful fate threatening me are spreading themselves out over my head like black clouds, impenetrable to every friendly ray of sunlight. I must now tell you what has taken place; I must, that I see well enough, but only to think upon it makes the wild laughter burst from my lips. Oh! my dear, dear Lothair, what shall I say to make you feel, if only in an inadequate way, that that which happened to me a few days ago could thus really exercise such a hostile and disturbing influence upon my life? Oh that you were here to see for yourself! but now you will, I suppose, take me for a superstitious ghost-seer. In a word, the terrible thing which I have experienced, the fatal effect of which I in vain exert every effort to shake off,

* "The Sandman" forms the first of a series of tales called "The Night-pieces," and was published in 1817.

is simply that some days ago, namely, on the 30th October, at twelve o'clock at noon, a dealer in weather-glasses came into my room and wanted to sell me one of his wares. I bought nothing, and threatened to kick him downstairs, whereupon he went away of his own accord.

You will conclude that it can only be very peculiar relations — relations intimately intertwined with my life — that can give significance to this event, and that it must be the person of this unfortunate hawker which has had such a very inimical effect upon me. And so it really is. I will summon up all my faculties in order to narrate to you calmly and patiently as much of the early days of my youth as will suffice to put matters before you in such a way that your keen sharp intellect may grasp everything clearly and distinctly, in bright and living pictures. Just as I am beginning, I hear you laugh and Clara say, "What's all this childish nonsense about!" Well, laugh at me, laugh heartily at me, pray do. But, good God! my hair is standing on end, and I seem to be entreating you to laugh at me in the same sort of frantic despair in which Franz Moor entreated Daniel to laugh him to scorn.* But to my story.

Except at dinner we, *i.e.*, I and my brothers and sisters, saw but little of our father all day long. His business no doubt took up most of his time. After our evening meal, which, in accordance with an old custom, was served at seven o'clock, we all went, mother with us, into father's room, and took our places around a round table. My father smoked his pipe, drinking a large glass of beer to it. Often he told us many wonderful stories, and got so excited over them that his pipe always went out; I used then to light it for him with a spill, and this formed my chief amusement. Often, again, he would give us picture books to look at, whilst he sat silent and motionless in his easy chair, puffing out such dense clouds of smoke that we were all as it were enveloped in mist. On such evenings mother was very sad; and directly it struck nine

---

* See Schiller's *Räuber* Act V., Scene 1. Franz Moor, seeing that the failure of all his villainous schemes is inevitable, and that his own ruin is close upon him, is at length overwhelmed with the madness of despair, and unburdens the terrors of his conscience to the old servant Daniel, bidding him laugh him to scorn.

she said, "Come, children! off to bed! Come! The 'Sandman' is come I see." And I always did seem to hear something trampling upstairs with slow heavy steps; that must be the Sandman. Once in particular I was very much frightened at this dull trampling and knocking; as mother was leading us out of the room I asked her, "O mamma! but who is this nasty Sandman who always sends us away from papa? What does he look like?" "There is no Sandman, my dear child," mother answered; "when I say the Sandman is come, I only mean that you are sleepy and can't keep your eyes open, as if somebody had put sand in them." This answer of mother's did not satisfy me; nay, in my childish mind the thought clearly unfolded itself that mother denied there was a Sandman only to prevent us being afraid, — why, I always heard him come upstairs. Full of curiosity to learn something more about this Sandman and what he had to do with us children, I at length asked the old woman who acted as my youngest sister's attendant, what sort of a man he was — the Sandman? "Why, 'thanael, darling, don't you know?" she replied. "Oh! he's a wicked man, who comes to little children when they won't go to bed and throws handfuls of sand in their eyes, so that they jump out of their heads all bloody; and he puts them into a bag and takes them to the half-moon as food for his little ones; and they sit there in the nest and have hooked beaks like owls, and they pick naughty little boys' and girls' eyes out with them." After this I formed in my own mind a horrible picture of the cruel Sandman. When anything came blundering upstairs at night I trembled with fear and dismay; and all that my mother could get out of me were the stammered words "The Sandman! the Sandman!" whilst the tears coursed down my cheeks. Then I ran into my bedroom, and the whole night through tormented myself with the terrible apparition of the Sandman. I was quite old enough to perceive that the old woman's tale about the Sandman and his little ones' nest in the half-moon couldn't be altogether true; nevertheless the Sandman continued to be for me a fearful incubus, and I was always seized with terror — my blood always ran cold, not only when I heard anybody come up the stairs, but when I heard anybody noisily open my father's room door and go in. Often he stayed away for a long season altogether; then he would come several times in close succession.

This went on for years, without my being able to accustom myself to this fearful apparition, without the image of the horrible Sandman growing any fainter in my imagination. His intercourse with my father began to occupy my fancy ever more and more; I was restrained from asking my father about him by an unconquerable shyness; but as the years went on the desire waxed stronger and stronger within me to fathom the mystery myself and to see the fabulous Sandman. He had been the means of disclosing to me the path of the wonderful and the adventurous, which so easily find lodgment in the mind of the child. I liked nothing better than to hear or read horrible stories of goblins, witches, Tom Thumbs, and so on; but always at the head of them all stood the Sandman, whose picture I scribbled in the most extraordinary and repulsive forms with both chalk and coal everywhere, on the tables, and cupboard doors, and walls. When I was ten years old my mother removed me from the nursery into a little chamber off the corridor not far from my father's room. We still had to withdraw hastily whenever, on the stroke of nine, the mysterious unknown was heard in the house. As I lay in my little chamber I could hear him go into father's room, and soon afterwards I fancied there was a fine and peculiar smelling steam spreading itself through the house. As my curiosity waxed stronger, my resolve to make somehow or other the Sandman's acquaintance took deeper root. Often when my mother had gone past, I slipped quickly out of my room into the corridor, but I could never see anything, for always before I could reach the place where I could get sight of him, the Sandman was well inside the door. At last, unable to resist the impulse any longer, I determined to conceal myself in father's room and there wait for the Sandman.

One evening I perceived from my father's silence and mother's sadness that the Sandman would come; accordingly, pleading that I was excessively tired, I left the room before nine o'clock and concealed myself in a hiding place close beside the door. The street door creaked, and slow, heavy, echoing steps crossed the passage towards the stairs. Mother hurried past me with my brothers and sisters. Softly — softly — I opened father's room door. He sat as usual, silent and motionless, with his back towards it; he did not hear me; and in a moment I was in and behind a curtain drawn before my father's open wardrobe, which stood just inside the room. Nearer and nearer and nearer came the echoing footsteps. There was a strange coughing and shuffling and mumbling outside. My heart beat with expectation and fear. A quick step now close, close beside the door, a noisy rattle of the handle, and the door flies open with a bang. Recovering my courage with an effort, I take a cautious peep out. In the middle of the room in front of my father stands the Sandman, the bright light of the lamp falling full upon his face. The Sandman, the terrible Sandman, is the old advocate *Coppelius* who often comes to dine with us.

But the most hideous figure could not have awakened greater trepidation in my heart than this Coppelius did. Picture to yourself a large broad-shouldered man, with an immensely big head, a face the color of yellow-ochre, grey bushy eyebrows, from beneath which two piercing, greenish, catlike eyes glittered, and a prominent Roman nose hanging over his upper lip. His distorted mouth was often screwed up into a malicious smile; then two dark-red spots appeared on his cheeks, and a strange hissing noise proceeded from between his tightly clenched teeth. He always wore an ash-grey coat of an old-fashioned cut, a waistcoat of the same, and nether extremities to match, but black stockings and buckles set with stones on his shoes. His little wig scarcely extended beyond the crown of his head, his hair was curled round high up above his big red ears, and plastered to his temples with cosmetic, and a broad closed hair-bag stood out prominently from his neck, so that you could see the silver buckle that fastened his folded neck-cloth. Altogether he was a most disagreeable and horribly ugly figure; but what we children detested most of all was his big coarse hairy hands; we could never fancy anything that he had once touched. This he had noticed; and so, whenever our good mother quietly placed a piece of cake or sweet fruit on our plates, he delighted to touch it under some pretext or other, until the bright tears stood in our eyes, and from disgust and loathing we lost the enjoyment of the tit-bit that was intended to please us. And he did just the same thing when father gave us a glass of sweet wine on holidays. Then he would quickly pass his hand over it, or even sometimes raise the glass to his blue lips, and he laughed quite sardonically when all we dared do was to express our vexation in stifled sobs. He habitually called us the "little brutes;" and when he was present we might not utter a sound; and we cursed the ugly spiteful man who deliberately and intentionally spoilt all our little pleasures. Mother seemed to dislike this hateful Coppelius as much as we did; for as soon as he appeared her cheerfulness and bright and natural manner were transformed into sad, gloomy seriousness. Father treated him as if he were a being of some higher race, whose ill-manners were to be tolerated, whilst no efforts ought to be spared to keep him in good-humor. He had only to give a slight hint, and his favorite dishes were cooked for him and rare wine uncorked.

As soon as I saw this Coppelius, therefore, the fearful and hideous thought arose in my mind that he, and he alone, must be the Sandman; but I no longer conceived of the Sandman as the bugbear in the old nurse's fable, who fetched children's eyes and took them to the half-moon as food for his little ones — no! but as an ugly specterlike fiend bringing trouble and misery and ruin, both temporal and everlasting, everywhere wherever he appeared.

I was spellbound on the spot. At the risk of being discovered, and, as I well enough knew, of being severely punished, I remained as I was, with my head thrust through the curtains listening. My father received Coppelius in a ceremonious manner. "Come, to work!" cried the latter, in a hoarse snarling voice, throwing off his coat. Gloomily and silently my father took off his dressing gown, and both put on long black smock-frocks. Where they took them from I forgot to notice. Father opened the folding-doors of a cupboard in the wall; but I saw that what I had so long taken to be a cupboard was really a dark recess, in which was a little hearth. Coppelius approached it, and a blue flame crackled upwards from it. Round about were all kinds of strange utensils. Good God! as my old father bent down over the fire how different he looked! His gentle and venerable features seemed to be drawn up by some dreadful convulsive pain into an ugly, repulsive Satanic mask. He looked like Coppelius. Coppelius plied the red-hot tongs and drew bright glowing masses out of the thick smoke and began assiduously to hammer them. I fancied that there were men's faces visible round about, but without eyes, having ghastly deep black holes where the eyes should have been. "Eyes here! Eyes here!" cried Coppelius, in a hollow sepulchral voice. My blood ran cold with horror; I screamed and tumbled out of my hiding place into the floor. Coppelius immediately seized upon me. "You little brute! You little brute!" he bleated, grinding his teeth. Then, snatching me up, he threw me on the hearth, so that the flames began to singe my hair. "Now we've got eyes — eyes — a beautiful pair of children's eyes," he whispered, and, thrusting his hands into the flames he took out some red-hot grains and was about to strew them into my eyes. Then my father clasped his hands and entreated him, saying, "Master, master, let my Nathanael keep his eyes — oh! do let him keep them." Coppelius laughed shrilly and replied, "Well then, the boy may keep his eyes and whine and pule his way through the world; but we will now at any rate observe the mechanism of the hand and the foot." And therewith he roughly laid hold upon me, so that my joints cracked, and twisted my hands and my feet, pulling them now this way, and now that, "That's not quite right altogether! It's better as it was! — the old fellow knew what he was about." Thus lisped and hissed Coppelius; but all around me grew black and dark; a sudden convulsive pain shot through all my nerves and bones; I knew nothing more.

I felt a soft warm breath fanning my cheek; I awakened as if out of the sleep of death; my mother was bending over me. "Is the Sandman still there?" I stammered. "No, my dear child; he's been gone a long, long time; he'll not hurt you." Thus spoke my mother, as she kissed her recovered darling and pressed him to her heart. But why should I tire you, my dear Lothair? why do I dwell at such length on these details, when there's so much remains to be said? Enough — I was detected in my eavesdropping, and roughly handled by Coppelius. Fear and terror had brought on a violent fever, of which I lay ill several weeks. "Is the Sandman still there?" these were the first words I uttered on coming to myself again, the first sign of my recovery, of my safety. Thus, you see, I have only to relate to you the most terrible moment of my youth for you to thoroughly understand that it must not be ascribed to the weakness of my eyesight if all that I see is colorless, but to the fact that a mysterious destiny has hung a dark veil of clouds about my life, which I shall perhaps only break through when I die.

Coppelius did not show himself again; it was reported he had left the town.

It was about a year later when, in pursuance of the old unchanged custom, we sat around the round table in the evening. Father was in very good spirits, and was telling us amusing tales about his youthful travels. As it was striking nine we all at once heard the street door creak on its hinges, and slow ponderous steps echoed across the passage and up the stairs. "That is Coppelius," said my mother, turning pale. "Yes, it is Coppelius," replied my father in a faint broken voice. The tears started from my mother's eyes. "But, father, father," she cried, "must it be so?" "This is the last time," he replied; "this is the last time he will come to me, I promise you. Go now, go and take the children. Go, go to bed — good-night."

As for me, I felt as if I were converted into cold, heavy stone; I could not get my breath. As I stood there immovable my mother seized me by the arm. "Come, Nathanael! do come along!" I suffered myself to be led away; I went into my room. "Be a good boy and keep quiet," mother called after me; "get into bed and go to sleep." But, tortured by indescribable fear and uneasiness, I could not close my eyes. That hateful, hideous Coppelius stood before me with his glittering eyes, smiling maliciously down upon me; in vain did I strive to banish the image. Somewhere about midnight there was a terrific crack, as if a cannon were being fired off. The whole house shook; something went rustling and clattering past my door; the house-door was pulled to with a bang. "That is Coppelius," I cried, terror-struck, and leapt out of bed. Then I heard a wild heartrending scream; I rushed into my father's room; the door stood open, and clouds of suffocating smoke came rolling towards me. The servant-maid shouted, "Oh! my master! my master!" On the floor in front of the smoking hearth lay my father, dead, his face burned black and fearfully distorted, my sisters weeping and moaning around him, and my mother lying near them in a swoon. "Coppelius, you atrocious fiend, you've killed my father," I shouted. My senses left me. Two days later, when my father was placed in his coffin, his features were mild and gentle again as they had been when he was alive. I found great consolation in the thought that his association with the diabolical Coppelius could not have ended in his everlasting ruin.

Our neighbors had been awakened by the explosion; the affair got talked about, and came before the magisterial authorities, who wished to cite Coppelius to clear himself. But he had disappeared from the place, leaving no traces behind him.

Now when I tell you, my dear friend, that the weather-glass hawker I spoke of was the villain Coppelius, you will not blame me for seeing impending mischief in his inauspicious reappearance. He was differently dressed; but Coppelius's figure and features are too deeply impressed upon my mind for me to be capable of making a mistake in the matter. Moreover, he has not even changed his name. He proclaims himself here, I learn, to be a Piedmontese mechanician, and styles himself Giuseppe Coppola.

I am resolved to enter the lists against him and revenge my father's death, let the consequences be what they may.

Don't say a word to mother about the reappearance of this odious monster. Give my love to my darling Clara; I will write to her when I am in a somewhat calmer frame of mind. Adieu, &c.

CLARA TO NATHANAEL

*Y*ou are right, you have not written to me for a very long time, but nevertheless I believe that I still retain a place in your mind and thoughts. It is a proof that you were thinking a good deal about me when you were sending off your last letter to brother Lothair, for instead of directing it to him you directed it to me. With joy I tore open the envelope, and did not perceive the mistake until I read the words, "Oh! my dear, dear Lothair." Now I know I ought not to have read anymore of the letter, but ought to have given it to my brother. But as you have so often in innocent raillery made it a sort of reproach against me that I possessed such a calm, and, for a woman, cool-headed temperament that I should be like the woman we read of — if the house was threatening to tumble down, I should, before hastily fleeing, stop to smooth down a crumple in the window-curtains — I need hardly tell you that the beginning of your letter quite upset me. I could scarcely breathe; there was a bright mist before my eyes. Oh! my darling Nathanael! what could this terrible thing be that had happened? Separation from you — never to see you again, the thought was like a sharp knife in my heart. I read on and on. Your description of that horrid Coppelius made my flesh creep. I now learnt for the first time what a terrible and violent death your good old father died. Brother Lothair, to whom I handed over his property, sought to comfort me, but with little success. That horrid weather-glass hawker Giuseppe Coppola followed me everywhere; and I am almost ashamed to confess it, but he was able to disturb my sound and in general calm sleep with all sorts of wonderful dream-shapes. But soon — the next day — I saw everything in a different light. Oh! do not be angry with me, my best-beloved, if, despite your strange presentiment that Coppelius will do you some mischief, Lothair tells you I am in quite as good spirits, and just the same as ever.

I will frankly confess, it seems to me that all that was fearsome and terrible of which you speak, existed only in your own self, and that the real true outer world had but little to do with it. I can quite admit that old Coppelius may have been highly obnoxious to you children, but your real detestation of him arose from the fact that he hated children.

Naturally enough the gruesome Sandman of the old nurse's story was associated in your childish mind with old

Coppelius, who, even though you had not believed in the Sandman, would have been to you a ghostly bugbear, especially dangerous to children. His mysterious labors along with your father at night-time were, I daresay, nothing more than secret experiments in alchemy, with which your mother could not be over well pleased, owing to the large sums of money that most likely were thrown away upon them; and besides, your father, his mind full of the deceptive striving after higher knowledge, may probably have become rather indifferent to his family, as so often happens in the case of such experimentalists. So also it is equally probable that your father brought about his death by his own imprudence, and that Coppelius is not to blame for it. I must tell you that yesterday I asked our experienced neighbor, the chemist, whether in experiments of this kind an explosion could take place which would have a momentarily fatal effect. He said, "Oh, certainly!" and described to me in his prolix and circumstantial way how it could be occasioned, mentioning at the same time so many strange and funny words that I could not remember them at all. Now I know you will be angry at your Clara, and will say, "Of the Mysterious which often clasps man in its invisible arms there's not a ray can find its way into this cold heart. She sees only the varied surface of the things of the world, and, like the little child, is pleased with the golden glittering fruit; at the kernel of which lies the fatal poison."

Oh! my beloved Nathanael, do you believe then that the intuitive prescience of a dark power working within us to our own ruin cannot exist also in minds which are cheerful, natural, free from care? But please forgive me that I, a simple girl, presume in any way to indicate to you what I really think of such an inward strife. After all, I should not find the proper words, and you would only laugh at me, not because my thoughts were stupid, but because I was so foolish as to attempt to tell them to you.

If there is a dark and hostile power which traitorously fixes a thread in our hearts in order that, laying hold of it and drawing us by means of it along a dangerous road to ruin, which otherwise we should not have trod — if, I say, there is such a power, it must assume within us a form like ourselves, nay, it must be ourselves; for only in that way can we believe in it, and only so understood do we yield to it so far that it is able to accomplish its secret purpose. So long as we have sufficient firmness, fortified by cheerfulness, to always acknowledge foreign hostile influences for what they really are, whilst we quietly pursue the path pointed out to us by both inclination and calling, then this mysterious power perishes in its futile struggles to attain the form which is to be the reflected image of ourselves. It is also certain, Lothair adds, that if we have once voluntarily given ourselves up to this dark physical power, it often reproduces within us the strange forms which the outer world throws in our way, so that thus it is we ourselves who engender within ourselves the spirit which by some remarkable delusion we imagine to speak in that outer form. It is the phantom of our own self whose intimate relationship with, and whose powerful influence upon our soul either plunges us into hell or elevates us to heaven. Thus you will see, my beloved Nathanael, that I and brother Lothair have well talked over the subject of dark powers and forces; and now, after I have with some difficulty written down the principal results of our discussion, they seem to me to contain many really profound thoughts. Lothair's last words, however, I don't quite understand altogether; I only dimly guess what he means; and yet I cannot help thinking it is all very true, I beg you, dear, strive to forget the ugly advocate Coppelius as well as the weather-glass hawker Giuseppe Coppola. Try and convince yourself that these foreign influences can have no power over you, that it is only the belief in their hostile power which can in reality make them dangerous to you. If every line of your letter did not betray the violent excitement of your mind, and if I did not sympathize with your condition from the bottom of my heart, I could in truth jest about the advocate Sandman and weather-glass hawker Coppelius. Pluck up your spirits! Be cheerful! I have resolved to appear to you as your guardian-angel if that ugly man Coppola should dare take it into his head to bother you in your dreams, and drive him away with a good hearty laugh. I'm not afraid of him and his nasty hands, not the least little bit; I won't let him either as advocate spoil any dainty tit-bit I've taken, or as Sandman rob me of my eyes.

My darling, darling Nathanael,
Eternally your, &c. &c.

NATHANAEL TO LOTHAIR

I am very sorry that Clara opened and read my last letter to you; of course the mistake is to be attributed to my own absence of mind. She has written me a very deep philosophical letter, proving conclusively that Coppelius and Coppola only exist in my own mind and are phantoms of my own self, which will at once be dissipated, as soon as I look upon them in that light. In very truth one can hardly believe that the mind which so often sparkles in those bright, beautifully smiling, childlike eyes of hers like a sweet lovely dream could draw such subtle and scholastic distinctions. She also mentions your name. You have been talking about me. I suppose you have been giving her lectures, since she sifts and refines everything so acutely. But enough of this! I must now tell you it is most certain that the weather-glass hawker Giuseppe Coppola is not the advocate Coppelius. I am attending the lectures of our recently appointed Professor of Physics, who, like the distinguished naturalist,* is called Spalanzani, and is of Italian origin. He has known Coppola for many years; and it is also easy to tell from his accent that he really is a Piedmontese. Coppelius was a German, though no honest German, I fancy. Nevertheless I am not quite satisfied. You and Clara will perhaps take me for a gloomy dreamer, but nohow can I get rid of the impression which Coppelius's cursed face made upon me. I am glad to learn from Spalan-

---

* Lazaro Spallanzani, a celebrated anatomist and naturalist (1729-1799), filled for several years the chair of Natural History at Pavia, and traveled extensively for scientific purposes in Italy, Turkey, Sicily, Switzerland, &c.

zani that he has left the town. This Professor Spalanzani is a very queer fish. He is a little fat man, with prominent cheek-bones, thin nose, projecting lips, and small piercing eyes. You cannot get a better picture of him than by turning over one of the Berlin pocket-almanacs* and looking at Cagliostro's† portrait engraved by Chodowiecki;‡ Spalanzani looks just like him.

Once lately, as I went up the steps to his house, I perceived that beside the curtain which generally covered a glass door there was a small chink. What it was that excited my curiosity I cannot explain; but I looked through. In the room I saw a female, tall, very slender, but of perfect proportions, and splendidly dressed, sitting at a little table, on which she had placed both her arms, her hands being folded together. She sat opposite the door, so that I could easily see her angelically beautiful face. She did not appear to notice me, and there was moreover a strangely fixed look about her eyes, I might almost say they appeared as if they had no power of vision; I thought she was sleeping with her eyes open. I felt quite uncomfort-able, and so I slipped away quietly into the Professor's lec-ture-room, which was close at hand. Afterwards I learnt that the figure which I had seen was Spalanzani's daughter, Olim-pia, whom he keeps locked in a most wicked and unaccount-able way, and no man is ever allowed to come near her. Perhaps, however, there is after all, something peculiar about her; perhaps she's an idiot or something of that sort. But why am I telling you all this? I could have told you it all better

---

* Or Almanacs of the Muses, as they were also sometimes called, were periodical, mostly yearly publications, containing all kinds of literary effusions; mostly, however, lyrical. They originated in the eighteenth century. Schiller, A.W. and F. Schlegel, Tieck, and Chamisso, amongst others, conducted undertakings of this nature.

† Joseph Balsamo, a Sicilian by birth, calling himself Count Cagliostro, one of the greatest impostors of modern times, lived during the latter part of the eighteenth century. See Carlyle's "Miscellanies" for an account of his life and character.

‡ Daniel Nikolas Chodowiecki, painter and engraver, of Polish descent, was born at Dantzic in 1726. For some years he was so popular an artist that few books were published in Prussia without plates or vignettes by him. The catalogue of his works is said to include 3000 items.

and more in detail when I see you. For in a fortnight I shall be amongst you. I must see my dear sweet angel, my Clara, again. Then the little bit of ill-temper, which, I must confess, took possession of me after her fearfully sensible letter, will be blown away. And that is the reason why I am not writing to her as well today. With all best wishes, &c.

*N*othing more strange and extraordinary can be imagined, gracious reader, than what happened to my poor friend, the young student Nathanael, and which I have undertaken to relate to you. Have you ever lived to experience anything that completely took possession of your heart and mind and thoughts to the utter exclusion of everything else? All was seething and boiling within you; your blood, heated to fever pitch, leapt through your veins and inflamed your cheeks. Your gaze was so peculiar, as if seeking to grasp in empty space forms not seen of any other eye, and all your words ended in sighs betokening some mystery. Then your friends asked you, "What is the matter with you, my dear friend? What do you see?" And, wishing to describe the inner pictures in all their vivid colors, with their lights and their shades, you in vain struggled to find words with which to express yourself. But you felt as if you must gather up all the events that had happened, wonderful, splendid, terrible, jocose, and awful, in the very first word, so that the whole might be revealed by a single electric discharge, so to speak. Yet every word and all that partook of the nature of communication by intelligible sounds seemed to be colorless, cold, and dead. Then you try and try again, and stutter and stammer, whilst your friends' prosy questions strike like icy winds upon your heart's hot fire until they extinguish it. But if, like a bold painter, you had first sketched in a few audacious strokes the outline of the picture you had in your soul, you would then easily have been able to deepen and intensify the colors one after the other, until the varied throng of living figures carried your friends away, and they, like you, saw themselves in the midst of the scene that had proceeded out of your own soul.

Strictly speaking, indulgent reader, I must indeed confess to you, nobody has asked me for the history of young Nathanael; but you are very well aware that I belong to that remarkable class of authors who, when they are bearing anything about in their minds in the manner I have just described, feel as if everybody who comes near them, and also the whole world to boot, were asking, "Oh! what is it? Oh! do tell us, my good sir?" Hence I was most powerfully impelled to narrate to you Nathanael's ominous life. My soul was full of the elements of wonder and extraordinary peculiarity in it; but, for this very reason, and because it was necessary in the very beginning to dispose you, indulgent reader, to bear with what is fantastic — and that is not a little thing — I racked my brain to find a way of commencing the story in a significant and original manner, calculated to arrest your attention. To begin with "Once upon a time," the best beginning for a story, seemed to me too tame; with "In the small country town S—— lived," rather better, at any rate allowing plenty of room to work up to the climax; or to plunge at once *in medias res,* "'Go to the devil!' cried the student Nathanael, his eyes blazing wildly with rage and fear, when the weather-glass hawker Giuseppe Coppola" — well, that is what I really had written, when I thought I detected something of the ridiculous in Nathanael's wild glance; and the history is anything but laughable. I could not find any words which seemed fitted to reflect in even the feeblest degree the brightness of the colors of my mental vision. I determined not to begin at all. So I pray you, gracious reader, accept the three letters which my friend Lothair has been so kind as to communicate to me as the outline of the picture, into which I will endeavor to introduce more and more color as I proceed with my narrative. Perhaps, like a good portrait-painter, I may succeed in depicting more than one figure in such wise that you will recognize it as a good likeness without being acquainted with the original, and feel as if you had very often seen the original with your own bodily eyes. Perhaps, too, you will then believe that nothing is more wonderful, nothing more fantastic than real life, and that all that a writer can do is to present it as a dark reflection from a dim cut mirror.

In order to make the very commencement more intelligible, it is necessary to add to the letters that, soon after the death of Nathanael's father, Clara and Lothair, the children of a distant relative, who had likewise died, leaving them orphans, were taken by Nathanael's mother into her own house. Clara and Nathanael conceived a warm affection for each other, against which not the slightest objection in the world could be urged. When therefore Nathanael left home to prosecute his studies in G——, they were betrothed. It is from G—— that his last letter is written, where he is attending the lectures of Spalanzani, the distinguished Professor of Physics.

I might now proceed comfortably with my narration, did not at this moment Clara's image rise up so vividly before my eyes that I cannot turn them away from it, just as I never could when she looked upon me and smiled so sweetly. Nowhere would she have passed for beautiful; that was the unanimous opinion of all who professed to have any technical knowledge of beauty. But whilst architects praised the pure proportions of her figure and form, painters averred that her neck, shoulders, and bosom were almost too chastely modeled, and yet, on the other hand, one and all were in love with her glorious Magdalene hair, and talked a good deal of nonsense about Battonilike* coloring. One of them, a veritable romanticist, strangely enough likened her eyes to a lake by Ruisdael,† in which is reflected the pure azure of the cloudless sky, the beauty of woods and flowers, and all the bright and varied life of a living landscape. Poets and musicians went still further and said, "What's all this talk about seas and reflections? How can we look upon the girl without feeling that wonderful heavenly songs and melodies beam upon us from her eyes, penetrating deep down into our hearts, till all becomes awake and throbbing with emotion? And if we cannot sing anything at all passable then, why, we

---

* Pompeo Girolamo Batoni, an Italian painter of the eighteenth century, whose works were at one time greatly overestimated.

† Jakob Ruysdael (c. 1625-1682), a painter of Haarlem, in Holland. His favorite subjects were remote farms, lonely stagnant water, deep-shaded woods with marshy paths, the seacoast — subjects of a dark melancholy kind. His sea-pieces are greatly admired.

are not worth much; and this we can also plainly read in the rare smile which flits around her lips when we have the hardihood to squeak out something in her presence which we pretend to call singing, in spite of the fact that it is nothing more than a few single notes confusedly linked together." And it really was so. Clara had the powerful fancy of a bright, innocent, unaffected child, a woman's deep and sympathetic heart, and an understanding clear, sharp, and discriminating. Dreamers and visionaries had but a bad time of it with her; for without saying very much — she was not by nature of a talkative disposition — she plainly asked, by her calm steady look, and rare ironical smile, "How can you imagine, my dear friends, that I can take these fleeting shadowy images for true living and breathing forms?" For this reason many found fault with her as being cold, prosaic, and devoid of feeling; others, however, who had reached a clearer and deeper conception of life, were extremely fond of the intelligent, child-like, large-hearted girl But none had such an affection for her as Nathanael, who was a zealous and cheerful cultivator of the fields of science and art. Clara clung to her lover with all her heart; the first clouds she encountered in life were when he had to separate from her. With what delight did she fly into his arms when, as he had promised in his last letter to Lothair, he really came back to his native town and entered his mother's room! And as Nathanael had foreseen, the moment he saw Clara again he no longer thought about either the advocate Coppelius or her sensible letter; his ill-humor had quite disappeared.

Nevertheless Nathanael was right when he told his friend Lothair that the repulsive vendor of weather-glasses, Coppola, had exercised a fatal and disturbing influence upon his life. It was quite patent to all; for even during the first few days he showed that he was completely and entirely changed. He gave himself up to gloomy reveries, and moreover acted so strangely; they had never observed anything at all like it in him before. Everything, even his own life, was to him but dreams and presentiments. His constant theme was that every man who delusively imagined himself to be free was merely the plaything of the cruel sport of mysterious powers, and it was vain for man to resist them; he must humbly submit to whatever destiny had decreed for him. He went so far as to maintain that it was foolish to believe that a man could do anything in art or science of his own accord; for the inspiration in which alone any true artistic work could be done did not proceed from the spirit within outwards, but was the result of the operation directed inwards of some Higher Principle existing without and beyond ourselves.

This mystic extravagance was in the highest degree repugnant to Clara's clear intelligent mind, but it seemed vain to enter upon any attempt at refutation. Yet when Nathanael went on to prove that Coppelius was the Evil Principle which had entered into him and taken possession of him at the time he was listening behind the curtain, and that this hateful demon would in some terrible way ruin their happiness, then Clara grew grave and said, "Yes, Nathanael. You are right; Coppelius is an Evil Principle; he can do dreadful things, as bad as could a Satanic power which should assume a living physical form, but only — only if you do not banish him from your mind and thoughts. So long as you believe in him he exists and is at work; your belief in him is his only power." Whereupon Nathanael, quite angry because Clara would only grant the existence of the demon in his own mind, began to dilate at large upon the whole mystic doctrine of devils and awful powers, but Clara abruptly broke off the theme by making, to Nathanael's very great disgust, some quite commonplace remark. Such deep mysteries are sealed books to cold, unsusceptible characters, he thought, without being clearly conscious to himself that he counted Clara amongst these inferior natures, and accordingly he did not remit his efforts to initiate her into these mysteries. In the morning, when she was helping to prepare breakfast, he would take his stand beside her, and read all sorts of mystic books to her, until she begged him — "But, my dear Nathanael, I shall have to scold you as the Evil Principle which exercises a fatal influence upon my coffee. For if I do as you wish, and let things go their own way, and look into your eyes whilst you read, the coffee will all boil over into the fire, and you will none of you get any breakfast." Then Nathanael hastily banged the book to and ran away in great displeasure to his own room.

Formerly he had possessed a peculiar talent for writing pleasing, sparkling tales, which Clara took the greatest delight in listening to; but now his productions were gloomy, unintelligible, and wanting in form, so that, although Clara out of forbearance towards him did not say so, he nevertheless felt how very little interest she took in them. There was nothing that Clara disliked so much as what was tedious; at such times her intellectual sleepiness was not to be overcome; it was betrayed both in her glances and in her words. Nathanael's effusions were, in truth, exceedingly tedious. His ill-humor at Clara's cold prosaic temperament continued to increase; Clara could not conceal her distaste of his dark, gloomy, wearying mysticism; and thus both began to be more and more estranged from each other without exactly being aware of it themselves. The image of the ugly Coppelius had, as Nathanael was obliged to confess to himself, faded considerably in his fancy, and it often cost him great pains to present him in vivid colors in his literary efforts, in which he played the part of the ghoul of Destiny. At length it entered into his head to make his dismal presentiment that Coppelius would ruin his happiness the subject of a poem. He made himself and Clara, united by true love, the central figures, but represented a black hand as being from time to time thrust into their life and plucking out a joy that had blossomed for them. At length, as they were standing at the altar, the terrible Coppelius appeared and touched Clara's lovely eyes, which leapt into Nathanael's own bosom, burning and hissing like bloody sparks. Then Coppelius laid hold upon him, and hurled him into a blazing circle of fire, which spun round with the speed of a whirlwind, and, storming and blustering, dashed away with him. The fearful noise it made was like a furious hurricane lashing the foaming sea-waves until they rise up like black, white-headed giants in the midst of the raging struggle. But through the midst of the savage fury of the tempest he heard Clara's voice calling, "Can you not see me, dear? Coppelius has deceived you; they were not my eyes which burned so in your bosom; they were fiery drops of your own heart's blood. Look at me, I have got my own eyes still." Nathanael thought, "Yes, that is Clara, and I am hers forever." Then this thought laid a powerful grasp upon the fiery circle so that it stood still, and the riotous turmoil died away rumbling down a dark abyss. Nathanael looked into Clara's eyes; but it was death whose gaze rested so kindly upon him.

Whilst Nathanael was writing this work he was very quiet and sober-minded; he filed and polished every line, and as he had chosen to submit himself to the limitations of metre, he did not rest until all was pure and musical. When, however, he had at length finished it and read it aloud to himself he was seized with horror and awful dread, and he screamed, "Whose hideous voice is this?" But he soon came to see in it again nothing beyond a very successful poem, and he confidently believed it would enkindle Clara's cold temperament, though to what end she should be thus aroused was not quite clear to his own mind, nor yet what would be the real purpose served by tormenting her with these dreadful pictures, which prophesied a terrible and ruinous end to her affection.

Nathanael and Clara sat in his mother's little garden. Clara was bright and cheerful, since for three entire days her lover, who had been busy writing his poem, had not teased her with his dreams or forebodings. Nathanael, too, spoke in a gay and vivacious way of things of merry import, as he formerly used to do, so that Clara said, "Ah! now I have you again. We have driven away that ugly Coppelius, you see." Then it suddenly occurred to him that he had got the poem in his pocket which he wished to read to her. He at once took out the manuscript and began to read. Clara, anticipating something tedious as usual, prepared to submit to the infliction, and calmly resumed her knitting. But as the somber clouds rose up darker and darker she let her knitting fall on her lap and sat with her eyes fixed in a set stare upon Nathanael's face. He was quite carried away by his own work, the fire of enthusiasm colored his cheeks a deep red, and tears started from his eyes. At length he concluded, groaning and showing great lassitude; grasping Clara's hand, he sighed as if he were being utterly melted in inconsolable grief, "Oh! Clara! Clara!" She drew him softly to her heart and said in a low but very grave and impressive tone, "Nathanael, my darling Nathanael, throw that foolish, senseless, stupid thing into the fire." Then Nathanael leapt indignantly to his feet, crying, as he pushed Clara from him, "You damned lifeless automaton!" and rushed away. Clara was cut to the heart, and wept bitterly. "Oh! he has never loved me, for he does not understand me," she sobbed.

Lothair entered the arbor. Clara was obliged to tell him all that had taken place. He was passionately fond of his sister; and every word of her complaint fell like a spark upon his heart, so that the displeasure which he had long entertained against his dreamy friend Nathanael was kindled into furious anger. He hastened to find Nathanael, and upbraided him in harsh words for his irrational behavior towards his beloved sister. The fiery Nathanael answered him in the same style. "A fantastic, crack-brained fool," was retaliated with, "A miserable, common, everyday sort of fellow." A meeting was the inevitable consequence. They agreed to meet on the following morning behind the garden-wall, and fight, according to the custom of the students of the place, with sharp rapiers. They went about silent and gloomy; Clara had both heard and seen the violent quarrel, and also observed the fencing-master bring the rapiers in the dusk of the evening. She had a presentiment of what was to happen. They both appeared at the appointed place wrapped up in the same gloomy silence, and threw off their coats. Their eyes flaming with the bloodthirsty light of pugnacity, they were about to begin their contest when Clara burst through the garden door. Sobbing, she screamed, "You savage, terrible men! Cut me down before you attack each other; for how can I live when my lover has slain my brother, or my brother slain my lover?" Lothair let his weapon fall and gazed silently upon the ground, whilst Nathanael's heart was rent with sorrow, and all the affection which he had felt for his lovely Clara in the happiest days of her golden youth was awakened within him. His murderous weapon, too, fell from his hand; he threw himself at Clara's feet. "Oh! can you ever forgive me, my only, my dearly loved Clara? Can you, my dear brother Lothair, also forgive me?" Lothair was touched by his friend's great distress; the three young people embraced each other amidst endless tears, and swore never again to break their bond of love and fidelity.

Nathanael felt as if a heavy burden that had been weighing him down to the earth was now rolled from off him, nay, as if by offering resistance to the dark power which had possessed him, he had rescued his own self from the ruin which had threatened him. Three happy days he now spent amidst the loved ones, and then returned to G——, where he had still a year to stay before settling down in his native town for life.

Everything having reference to Coppelius had been concealed from the mother, for they knew she could not think of him without horror, since she as well as Nathanael believed him to be guilty of causing her husband's death.

*W*hen Nathanael came to the house where he lived he was greatly astonished to find it burned down to the ground, so that nothing but the bare outer walls were left standing amidst a heap of ruins. Although the fire had broken out in the laboratory of the chemist who lived on the ground-floor, and had therefore spread upwards, some of Nathanael's bold, active friends had succeeded in time in forcing a way into his room in the upper storey and saving his books and manuscripts and instruments. They had carried them all uninjured into another house, where they engaged a room for him; this he now at once took possession of. That he lived opposite Professor Spalanzani did not strike him particularly, nor did it occur to him as anything more singular that he could, as he observed, by looking out of his window, see straight into the room where Olimpia often sat alone. Her figure he could plainly distinguish, although her features were uncertain and confused. It did at length occur to him, however, that she remained for hours together in the same position in which he had first discovered her through the glass door, sitting at a little table without any occupation whatever, and it was evident that she was constantly gazing across in his direction. He could not but confess to himself that he had never seen a finer figure. However, with Clara mistress of his heart, he remained perfectly unaffected by Olimpia's stiffness and apathy; and it was only occasionally that he sent a fugitive glance over his compendium across to her — that was all.

He was writing to Clara; a light tap came at the door. At his summons to "Come in," Coppola's repulsive face appeared peeping in. Nathanael felt his heart beat with trepidation; but, recollecting what Spalanzani had told him about his fellow-countryman Coppola, and what he had himself so faithfully promised his beloved in respect to the Sandman Coppelius, he was ashamed at himself for this childish fear of specters. Accordingly, he controlled himself with an effort, and said, as quietly and as calmly as he possibly could, "I don't want to buy any weather-glasses, my good friend; you had better go elsewhere." Then Coppola came right into the room, and said in a hoarse voice, screwing up his wide mouth into a hideous smile, whilst his little eyes flashed keenly from beneath his long grey eyelashes, "What! Nee weather-gless? Nee weather-gless? 've got foine oyes as well — foine oyes!" Affrighted, Nathanael cried, "You stupid man, how can you have eyes? — eyes — eyes?" But Coppola, laying aside his weather-glasses, thrust his hands into his big coat-pockets and brought out several spy-glasses and spectacles, and put them on the table. "Theer! Theer! Spect'cles! Spect'cles to put 'n nose! Them's my oyes — foine oyes." And he continued to produce more and more spectacles from his pockets until the table began to gleam and flash all over. Thousands of eyes were looking and blinking convulsively, and staring up at Nathanael; he could not avert his gaze from the table. Coppola went on heaping up his spectacles, whilst wilder and ever wilder burning flashes crossed through and through each other and darted their blood-red rays into Nathanael's breast. Quite overcome, and frantic with terror, he shouted, "Stop! stop! you terrible man!" and he seized Coppola by the arm, which he had again thrust into his pocket in order to bring out still more spectacles, although the whole table was covered all over with them. With a harsh disagreeable laugh Coppola gently freed himself; and with the words "So! went none! Well, here foine gless!" he swept all his spectacles together, and put them back into his coat-pockets, whilst from a breast-pocket he produced a great number of larger and smaller perspectives. As soon as the spectacles were gone Nathanael recovered his equanimity again; and, bending his thoughts upon Clara, he clearly discerned that the gruesome incubus had proceeded only from himself, as also that Coppola was a right honest mechanician and optician, and far from being Coppelius's dreaded double and ghost And then, besides, none of the glasses which Coppola now placed on the table had anything at all singular about them, at least nothing so weird as the spectacles; so, in order to square accounts with himself, Nathanael now really determined to buy something of the man. He took up a small, very beautifully cut pocket perspective, and by way of proving it looked through the window. Never before in his life had he had a glass in his hands that brought out things so clearly and sharply and distinctly. Involuntarily he directed the glass upon Spalanzani's room; Olimpia sat at the little table as usual, her arms laid upon it and her hands folded. Now he saw for the first time the regular and exquisite beauty of her features. The eyes, however, seemed to him to have a singular look of fixity and lifelessness. But as he continued to look closer and more carefully through the glass he fancied a light like humid moonbeams came into them. It seemed as if their power of vision was now being enkindled; their glances shone with ever-increasing vivacity. Nathanael remained standing at the window as if glued to the spot by a wizard's spell, his gaze rivetted unchangeably upon the divinely beautiful Olimpia. A coughing and shuffling of the feet awakened him out of his enchaining dream, as it were. Coppola stood behind him, "Tre zechini" (three ducats). Nathanael had completely forgotten the optician; he hastily paid the sum demanded.

"Ain't 't? Foine gless? foine gless?" asked Coppola in his harsh unpleasant voice, smiling sardonically. "Yes, yes, yes," rejoined Nathanael impatiently; "adieu, my good friend." But Coppola did not leave the room without casting many peculiar side-glances upon Nathanael; and the young student heard him laughing loudly on the stairs. "Ah well!" thought he, "he's laughing at me because I've paid him too much for this little perspective — because I've given him too much money — that's it" As he softly murmured these words he fancied he detected a gasping sigh as of a dying man stealing awfully through the room; his heart stopped beating with fear. But to be sure he had heaved a deep sigh himself; it was quite plain. "Clara is quite right," said he to himself, "in holding me to be an incurable ghost-seer; and yet it's very ridiculous — aye, more than ridiculous, that the stupid thought of having paid Coppola too much for his glass should cause me this strange anxiety; I can't see any reason for it."

Now he sat down to finish his letter to Clara; but a glance through the window showed him Olimpia still in her former posture. Urged by an irresistible impulse he jumped up and seized Coppola's perspective; nor could he tear himself away from the fascinating Olimpia until his friend and brother Siegmund called for him to go to Professor Spalanzani's lecture. The curtains before the door of the all-important room were closely drawn, so that he could not see Olimpia. Nor could he even see her from his own room during the two following days, notwithstanding that he scarcely ever left his window, and maintained a scarce interrupted watch through Coppola's perspective upon her room. On the third day curtains even were drawn across the window. Plunged into the depths of despair, — goaded by longing and ardent desire, he hurried outside the walls of the town. Olimpia's image hovered about his path in the air and stepped forth out of the bushes, and peeped up at him with large and lustrous eyes from the bright surface of the brook. Clara's image was completely faded from his mind; he had no thoughts except for Olimpia. He uttered his love-plaints aloud and in a lachrymose tone, "Oh! my glorious, noble star of love, have you only risen to vanish again, and leave me in the darkness and hopelessness of night?"

Returning home, he became aware that there was a good deal of noisy bustle going on in Spalanzani's house. All the doors stood wide open; men were taking in all kinds of gear and furniture; the windows of the first floor were all lifted off their hinges; busy maid-servants with immense hair-brooms were driving backwards and forwards dusting and sweeping, whilst within could be heard the knocking and hammering of carpenters and upholsterers. Utterly astonished, Nathanael stood still in the street; then Siegmund joined him, laughing, and said, "Well, what do you say to our old Spalanzani?" Nathanael assured him that he could not say anything, since he knew not what it all meant; to his great astonishment, he could hear, however, that they were turning the quiet gloomy house almost inside out with their dusting

and cleaning and making of alterations. Then he learned from
Siegmund that Spalanzani intended giving a great concert
and ball on the following day, and that half the university
was invited. It was generally reported that Spalanzani was
going to let his daughter Olimpia, whom he had so long so
jealously guarded from every eye, make her first appearance.

Nathanael received an invitation. At the appointed hour,
when the carriages were rolling up and the lights were gleaming brightly in the decorated halls, he went across to the
Professor's, his heart beating high with expectation. The
company was both numerous and brilliant. Olimpia was
richly and tastefully dressed. One could not but admire her
figure and the regular beauty of her features. The striking
inward curve of her back, as well as the wasplike smallness of
her waist, appeared to be the result of too-tight lacing. There
was something stiff and measured in her gait and bearing that
made an unfavorable impression upon many; it was ascribed
to the constraint imposed upon her by the company. The
concert began. Olimpia played on the piano with great skill;
and sang as skillfully an *aria di bravura*, in a voice which was,
if anything, almost too sharp, but clear as glass bells.
Nathanael was transported with delight; he stood in the
background farthest from her, and owing to the blinding
lights could not quite distinguish her features. So, without
being observed, he took Coppola's glass out of his pocket,
and directed it upon the beautiful Olimpia. Oh! then he
perceived how her yearning eyes sought him, how every note
only reached its full purity in the loving glance which penetrated to and inflamed his heart. Her artificial *roulades* seemed
to him to be the exultant cry towards heaven of the soul
refined by love; and when at last, after the *cadenza*, the long
trill rang shrilly and loudly through the hall, he felt as if he
were suddenly grasped by burning arms and could no longer
control himself, — he could not help shouting aloud in his
mingled pain and delight, "Olimpia!" All eyes were turned
upon him; many people laughed. The face of the cathedral
organist wore a still more gloomy look than it had done
before, but all he said was, "Very well!"

The concert came to an end, and the ball began. Oh! to
dance with her — with her — that was now the aim of all

Nathanael's wishes, of all his desires. But how should he have
courage to request her, the queen of the ball, to grant him
the honor of a dance? And yet he couldn't tell how it came
about, just as the dance began, he found himself standing
close beside her, nobody having as yet asked her to be his
partner; so, with some difficulty stammering out a few words,
he grasped her hand. It was cold as ice; he shook with an
awful, frosty shiver. But, fixing his eyes upon her face, he saw
that her glance was beaming upon him with love and longing,
and at the same moment he thought that the pulse began to
beat in her cold hand, and the warm life-blood to course
through her veins. And passion burned more intensely in his
own heart also; he threw his arm round her beautiful waist
and whirled her round the hall. He had always thought that
he kept good and accurate time in dancing, but from the
perfectly rhythmical evenness with which Olimpia danced,
and which frequently put him quite out, he perceived how
very faulty his own time really was. Notwithstanding, he
would not dance with any other lady; and everybody else who
approached Olimpia to call upon her for a dance, he would
have liked to kill on the spot. This, however, only happened
twice; to his astonishment Olimpia remained after this without a partner, and he failed not on each occasion to take her
out again. If Nathanael had been able to see anything else
except the beautiful Olimpia, there would inevitably have
been a good deal of unpleasant quarreling and strife; for it
was evident that Olimpia was the object of the smothered
laughter only with difficulty suppressed, which was heard in
various corners amongst the young people; and they followed
her with very curious looks, but nobody knew for what
reason. Nathanael, excited by dancing and the plentiful supply of wine he had consumed, had laid aside the shyness
which at other times characterized him. He sat beside Olimpia, her hand in his own, and declared his love enthusiasti-
cally and passionately in words which neither of them understood, neither he nor Olimpia. And yet she perhaps did, for
she sat with her eyes fixed unchangeably upon his, sighing
repeatedly, "Ach! Ach! Ach!" Upon this Nathanael would
answer, "Oh, you glorious heavenly lady! You ray from the
promised paradise of love! Oh! what a profound soul you

have! my whole being is mirrored in it!" and a good deal more in the same strain. But Olimpia only continued to sigh "Ach! Ach!" again and again.

Professor Spalanzani passed by the two happy lovers once or twice, and smiled with a look of peculiar satisfaction. All at once it seemed to Nathanael, albeit he was far away in a different world, as if it were growing perceptibly darker down below at Professor Spalanzani's. He looked about him, and to his very great alarm became aware that there were only two lights left burning in the hall, and they were on the point of going out. The music and dancing had long ago ceased. "We must part — part!" he cried, wildly and despairingly; he kissed Olimpia's hand; he bent down to her mouth, but ice-cold lips met his burning ones. As he touched her cold hand, he felt his heart thrilled with awe; the legend of "The Dead Bride"* shot suddenly through his mind. But Olimpia had drawn him closer to her, and the kiss appeared to warm her lips into vitality. Professor Spalanzani strode slowly through the empty apartment, his footsteps giving a hollow echo; and his figure had, as the flickering shadows played about him, a ghostly, awful appearance. "Do you love me? Do you love me, Olimpia? Only one little word — Do you love me?" whispered Nathanael, but she only sighed, "Ach! Ach!" as she rose to her feet. "Yes, you are my lovely, glorious star of love," said Nathanael, "and will shine forever, purifying and enno-bling my heart" "Ach! Ach!" replied Olimpia, as she moved along. Nathanael followed her; they stood before the Profes-sor. "You have had an extraordinarily animated conversation with my daughter," said he, smiling; "well, well, my dear Mr.

---

* Phlegon, the freedman of Hadrian, relates that a young maiden, Philemium, the daughter of Philostratus and Charitas, became deeply enamored of a young man, named Machates, a guest in the house of her father. This did not meet with the approbation of her parents, and they turned Machates away. The young maiden took this so much to heart that she pined away and died. Some time afterwards Machates returned to his old lodgings, when he was visited at night by his beloved, who came from the grave to see him again. The story may be read in Heywood's (Thos.) "Hierarchie of Blessed Angels," Book vii., p. 479 (London, 1637). Goethe has made this story the foundation of his beautiful poem *Die Braut von Korinth*, with which form of it Hoffmann was most likely familiar.

Nathanael, if you find pleasure in talking to the stupid girl, I am sure I shall be glad for you to come and do so." Nathanael took his leave, his heart singing and leaping in a perfect delirium of happiness.

During the next few days Spalanzani's ball was the general topic of conversation. Although the Professor had done everything to make the thing a splendid success, yet certain gay spirits related more than one thing that had occurred which was quite irregular and out of order. They were especially keen in pulling Olimpia to pieces for her taciturnity and rigid stiffness; in spite of her beautiful form they alleged that she was hopelessly stupid, and in this fact they discerned the reason why Spalanzani had so long kept her concealed from publicity. Nathanael heard all this with inward wrath, but nevertheless he held his tongue; for, thought he, would it indeed be worth while to prove to these fellows that it is their own stupidity which prevents them from appreciating Olimpia's profound and brilliant parts? One day Siegmund said to him, "Pray, brother, have the kindness to tell me how you, a sensible fellow, came to lose your head over that Miss Wax-face — that wooden doll across there?" Nathanael was about to fly into a rage, but he recollected himself and replied, "Tell me, Siegmund, how came it that Olimpia's divine charms could escape your eye, so keenly alive as it always is to beauty, and your acute perception as well? But Heaven be thanked for it, otherwise I should have had you for a rival, and then the blood of one of us would have had to be spilled." Siegmund, perceiving how matters stood with his friend, skillfully interposed and said, after remarking that all argument with one in love about the object of his affections was out of place, "Yet it's very strange that several of us have formed pretty much the same opinion about Olimpia. We think she is — you won't take it ill, brother? — that she is singularly statuesque and soulless. Her figure is regular, and so are her features, that can't be gainsaid; and if her eyes were not so utterly devoid of life, I may say, of the power of vision, she might pass for a beauty. She is strangely measured in her movements, they all seem as if they were dependent upon some wound-up clock-work. Her playing and singing has the disagreeably perfect, but insensitive time of a singing machine, and her dancing is the same. We felt quite afraid of this Olimpia, and did not like to have anything to do with her; she seemed to us to be only acting *like* a living creature, and as if there was some secret at the bottom of it all." Nathanael did not give way to the bitter feelings which threatened to master him at these words of Siegmund's; he fought down and got the better of his displeasure, and merely said, very earnestly, "You cold prosaic fellows may very well be afraid of her. It is only to its like that the poetically organized spirit unfolds itself. Upon me alone did her loving glances fall, and through my mind and thoughts alone did they radiate; and only in her love can I find my own self again. Perhaps, however, she doesn't do quite right not to jabber a lot of nonsense and stupid talk like other shallow people. It is true, she speaks but few words; but the few words she docs speak are genuine hieroglyphs of the inner world of Love and of the higher cognition of the intellectual life revealed in the intuition of the Eternal beyond the grave. But you have no understanding for all these things, and I am only wasting words." "God be with you, brother," said Siegmund very gently, almost sadly, "but it seems to me that you are in a very bad way. You may rely upon me, if all — No, I can't say anymore." It all at once dawned upon Nathanael that his cold prosaic friend Siegmund really and sincerely wished him well, and so he warmly shook his proffered hand.

Nathanael had completely forgotten that there was a Clara in the world, whom he had once loved — and his mother and Lothair. They had all vanished from his mind; he lived for Olimpia alone. He sat beside her every day for hours together, rhapsodising about his love and sympathy enkindled into life, and about psychic elective affinity* — all of which Olimpia listened to with great reverence. He fished up from the very bottom of his desk all the things that he had ever written — poems, fancy sketches, visions, romances, tales, and the heap was increased daily with all kinds of aimless sonnets, stanzas, canzonets. All these he read to Olimpia hour after hour without growing tired; but then he had never had such

---

* This phrase (*Die Wahlverwandschaft* in German) has been celebrated as the title of one of Goethe's works.

an exemplary listener. She neither embroidered, nor knitted; she did not look out of the window, or feed a bird, or play with a little pet dog or a favorite cat, neither did she twist a piece of paper or anything of that kind round her finger; she did not forcibly convert a yawn into a low affected cough — in short, she sat hour after hour with her eyes bent unchangeably upon her lover's face, without moving or altering her position, and her gaze grew more ardent and more ardent still. And it was only when at last Nathanael rose and kissed her lips or her hand that she said, "Ach! Ach!" and then "Good-night, dear." Arrived in his own room, Nathanael would break out with, "Oh! what a brilliant — what a profound mind! Only you — you alone understand me." And his heart trembled with rapture when he reflected upon the wondrous harmony which daily revealed itself between his own and his Olimpia's character; for he fancied that she had expressed in respect to his works and his poetic genius the identical sentiments which he himself cherished deep down in his own heart in respect to the same, and even as if it was his own heart's voice speaking to him. And it must indeed have been so; for Olimpia never uttered any other words than those already mentioned. And when Nathanael himself in his clear and sober moments, as, for instance, directly after waking in a morning, thought about her utter passivity and taciturnity, he only said, "What are words — but words? The glance of her heavenly eyes says more than any tongue of earth. And how can, anyway, a child of heaven accustom herself to the narrow circle which the exigencies of a wretched mundane life demand?"

Professor Spalanzani appeared to be greatly pleased at the intimacy that had sprung up between his daughter Olimpia and Nathanael, and showed the young man many unmistakable proofs of his good feeling towards him; and when Nathanael ventured at length to hint very delicately at an alliance with Olimpia, the Professor smiled all over his face at once, and said he should allow his daughter to make a perfectly free choice. Encouraged by these words, and with the fire of desire burning in his heart, Nathanael resolved the very next day to implore Olimpia to tell him frankly, in plain words, what he had long read in her sweet loving glances, —

that she would be his forever. He looked for the ring which his mother had given him at parting; he would present it to Olimpia as a symbol of his devotion, and of the happy life he was to lead with her from that time onwards. Whilst looking for it he came across his letters from Clara and Lothair; he threw them carelessly aside, found the ring, put it in his pocket, and ran across to Olimpia. Whilst still on the stairs, in the entrance-passage, he heard an extraordinary hubbub; the noise seemed to proceed from Spalanzani's study. There was a stamping — a rattling — pushing — knocking against the door, with curses and oaths intermingled. "Leave hold — leave hold — you monster — you rascal — staked your life and honor upon it? — Ha! ha! ha! ha! — That was not our wager — I, I made the eyes — I the clock-work. — Go to the devil with your clock-work — you damned dog of a watch-maker — be off — Satan — stop — you paltry turner — you infernal beast! — stop — begone — let me go." The voices which were thus making all this racket and rumpus were those of Spalanzani and the fearsome Coppelius. Nathanael rushed in, impelled by some nameless dread. The Professor was grasping a female figure by the shoulders, the Italian Coppola held her by the feet; and they were pulling and dragging each other backwards and forwards, fighting furiously to get possession of her. Nathanael recoiled with horror on recognizing that the figure was Olimpia. Boiling with rage, he was about to tear his beloved from the grasp of the madmen, when Coppola by an extraordinary exertion of strength twisted the figure out of the Professor's hands and gave him such a terrible blow with her, that he reeled backwards and fell over the table all amongst the phials and retorts, the bottles and glass cylinders, which covered it: all these things were smashed into a thousand pieces. But Coppola threw the figure across his shoulder, and, laughing shrilly and horribly, ran hastily down the stairs, the figure's ugly feet hanging down and banging and rattling like wood against the steps. Nathanael was stupefied; — he had seen only too distinctly that in Olimpia's pallid waxed face there were no eyes, merely black holes in their stead; she was an inanimate puppet. Spalanzani was rolling on the floor; the pieces of glass had cut his head and breast and arm; the blood was escaping from him in streams. But he gathered his strength together by an effort.

"After him — after him! What do you stand staring there for? Coppelius — Coppelius — he's stolen my best automaton — at which I've worked for twenty years — staked my life upon it — the clock-work — speech — movement — mine — your eyes — stolen your eyes — damn him — curse him — after him — fetch me back Olimpia — there are the eyes." And now Nathanael saw a pair of bloody eyes lying on the floor staring at him; Spalanzani seized them with his uninjured hand and threw them at him, so that they hit his breast Then madness dug her burning talons into him and swept down into his heart, rending his mind and thoughts to shreds. "Aha! aha! aha! Fire-wheel — fire-wheel! Spin round, fire-wheel! merrily, merrily! Aha! wooden doll! spin round, pretty wooden doll!" and he threw himself upon the Professor, clutching him fast by the throat. He would certainly have strangled him had not several people, attracted by the noise, rushed in and torn away the madman; and so they saved the Professor, whose wounds were immediately dressed. Siegmund, with all his strength, was not able to subdue the frantic lunatic, who continued to scream in a dreadful way, "Spin round, wooden doll!" and to strike out right and left with his doubled fists. At length the united strength of several succeeded in overpowering him by throwing him on the floor and binding him. His cries passed into a brutish bellow that was awful to hear; and thus raging with the harrowing violence of madness, he was taken away to the madhouse.

Before continuing my narration of what happened further to the unfortunate Nathanael, I will tell you, indulgent reader, in case you take any interest in that skillful mechanician and fabricator of automata, Spalanzani, that he recovered completely from his wounds. He had, however, to leave the university, for Nathanael's fate had created a great sensation; and the opinion was pretty generally expressed that it was an imposture altogether unpardonable to have smuggled a wooden puppet instead of a living person into intelligent tea-circles, — for Olimpia had been present at several with success. Lawyers called it a cunning piece of knavery, and all the harder to punish since it was directed against the public;

and it had been so craftily contrived that it had escaped unobserved by all except a few preternaturally acute students, although everybody was very wise now and remembered to have thought of several facts which occurred to them as suspicious. But these latter could not succeed in making out any sort of a consistent tale. For was it, for instance, a thing likely to occur to anyone as suspicious that, according to the declaration of an elegant beau of these tea-parties, Olimpia had, contrary to all good manners, sneezed oftener than she had yawned? The former must have been, in the opinion of this elegant gentleman, the winding up of the concealed clock-work; it had always been accompanied by an observable creaking, and so on. The Professor of Poetry and Eloquence took a pinch of snuff, and, slapping the lid to and clearing his throat, said solemnly, "My most honorable ladies and gentlemen, don't you see then where the rub is? The whole thing is an allegory, a continuous metaphor. You understand me? *Sapienti sat.*" But several most honorable gentlemen did not rest satisfied with this explanation; the history of this automaton had sunk deeply into their souls, and an absurd mistrust of human figures began to prevail. Several lovers, in order to be fully convinced that they were not paying court to a wooden puppet, required that their mistress should sing and dance a little out of time, should embroider or knit or play with her little pug, &c., when being read to, but above all things else that she should do something more than merely listen — that she should frequently speak in such a way as to really show that her words presupposed as a condition some thinking and feeling. The bonds of love were in many cases drawn closer in consequence, and so of course became more engaging; in other instances they gradually relaxed and fell away. "I cannot really be made responsible for it," was the remark of more than one young gallant. At the tea-gatherings everybody, in order to ward off suspicion, yawned to an incredible extent and never sneezed. Spalanzani was obliged, as has been said, to leave the place in order to escape a criminal charge of having fraudulently imposed an automaton upon human society. Coppola, too, had also disappeared.

When Nathanael awoke he felt as if he had been oppressed by a terrible nightmare; he opened his eyes and experienced an indescribable sensation of mental comfort, whilst a soft and most beautiful sensation of warmth pervaded his body. He lay on his own bed in his own room at home; Clara was bending over him, and at a little distance stood his mother and Lothair. "At last, at last, O my darling Nathanael; now we have you again; now you are cured of your grievous illness, now you are mine again." And Clara's words came from the depths of her heart; and she clasped him in her arms. The bright scalding tears streamed from his eyes, he was so over-come with mingled feelings of sorrow and delight; and he gasped forth, "My Clara, my Clara!" Siegmund, who had staunchly stood by his friend in his hour of need, now came into the room. Nathanael gave him his hand — "My faithful brother, you have not deserted me." Every trace of insanity had left him, and in the tender hands of his mother and his beloved, and his friends, he quickly recovered his strength again. Good fortune had in the meantime visited the house; a niggardly old uncle, from whom they had never expected to get anything, had died, and left Nathanael's mother not only a considerable fortune, but also a small estate, pleasantly situated not far from the town. There they resolved to go and live, Nathanael and his mother, and Clara, to whom he was now to be married, and Lothair. Nathanael was become gentler and more childlike than he had ever been before, and now began really to understand Clara's supremely pure and noble character. None of them ever reminded him, even in the remotest degree, of the past. But when Siegmund took leave of him, he said, "By heaven, brother! I was in a bad way, but an angel came just at the right moment and led me back upon the path of light. Yes, it was Clara." Siegmund would not let him speak further, fearing lest the painful recollections of the past might arise too vividly and too intensely in his mind.

The time came for the four happy people to move to their little property. At noon they were going through the streets. After making several purchases they found that the lofty tower of the town-house was throwing its giant shadows across the marketplace. "Come," said Clara, "let us go up to the top once more and have a look at the distant hills." No sooner said than done. Both of them, Nathanael and Clara, went up the tower; their mother, however, went on with the servant-girl to her new home, and Lothair, not feeling inclined to climb up all the many steps, waited below. There the two lovers stood arm-in-arm on the topmost gallery of the tower, and gazed out into the sweet-scented wooded landscape, beyond which the blue hills rose up like a giant's city.

"Oh! do look at that strange little grey bush, it looks as if it were actually walking towards us," said Clara. Mechanically he put his hand into his sidepocket; he found Coppola's perspective and looked for the bush; Clara stood in front of the glass. Then a convulsive thrill shot through his pulse and veins; pale as a corpse, he fixed his staring eyes upon her; but soon they began to roll, and a fiery current flashed and sparkled in them, and he yelled fearfully, like a hunted animal. Leaping up high in the air and laughing horribly at the same time, he began to shout, in a piercing voice, "Spin round, wooden doll! Spin round, wooden doll!" With the strength of a giant he laid hold upon Clara and tried to hurl her over, but in an agony of despair she clutched fast hold of the railing that went round the gallery. Lothair heard the madman raging and Clara's scream of terror: a fearful presentiment flashed across his mind. He ran up the steps; the door of the second flight was locked. Clara's scream for help rang out more loudly. Mad with rage and fear, he threw himself against the door, which at length gave way. Clara's cries were growing fainter and fainter, — "Help! save me! save me!" and her voice died away in the air. "She is killed — murdered by that madman," shouted Lothair. The door to the gallery was also locked. Despair gave him the strength of a giant; he burst the door off its hinges. Good God! there was Clara in the grasp of the madman Nathanael, hanging over the gallery in the air; she only held to the iron bar with one hand. Quick as lightning, Lothair seized his sister and pulled her back, at the same time dealing the madman a blow in the face with his doubled fist, which sent him reeling backwards, forcing him to let go his victim.

Lothair ran down with his insensible sister in his arms. She was saved. But Nathanael ran round and round the gallery, leaping up in the air and shouting, "Spin round, fire-wheel!

Spin round, fire-wheel!" The people heard the wild shouting, and a crowd began to gather. In the midst of them towered the advocate Coppelius, like a giant; he had only just arrived in the town, and had gone straight to the marketplace. Some were going up to overpower and take charge of the madman, but Coppelius laughed and said, "Ha! ha! wait a bit; he'll come down of his own accord;" and he stood gazing upwards along with the rest. All at once Nathanael stopped as if spellbound; he bent down over the railing, and perceived Coppelius. With a piercing scream, "Ha! foine oyes! foine oyes!" he leapt over.

When Nathanael lay on the stone pavement with a broken head, Coppelius had disappeared in the crush and confusion.

Several years afterwards it was reported that, outside the door of a pretty country house in a remote district, Clara had been seen sitting hand in hand with a pleasant gentleman, whilst two bright boys were playing at her feet. From this it may be concluded that she eventually found that quiet domestic happiness which her cheerful, blithesome character required, and which Nathanael, with his tempest-tossed soul, could never have been able to give her.

The Entail

*N*ot far from the shore of the Baltic Sea is situated the ancestral castle of the noble family Von R——, called R–sitten. It is a wild and desolate neighborhood, hardly anything more than a single blade of grass shooting up here and there from the bottomless drift-sand; and instead of the garden that generally ornaments a baronial residence, the bare walls are approached on the landward side by a thin forest of firs, that with their never-changing vesture of gloom despise the bright garniture of Spring, and where, instead of the joyous carolling of little birds awakened anew to gladness, nothing is heard but the ominous croak of the raven and the whirring scream of the storm-boding sea-gull. A quarter of a mile distant Nature suddenly changes. As if by the wave of a magician's wand you are transported into the midst of thriving fields, fertile arable land, and meadows. You see, too, the large and prosperous village, with the land-steward's spacious dwelling-house; and at the angle of a pleasant thicket of alders you may observe the foundations of a large castle, which one of the former proprietors had intended to erect. His successors, however, living on their property in Courland, left the building in its unfinished state; nor would Freiherr* Roderick von R—— proceed with the structure when he again took up his

---

* Freiherr = Baron, though not exactly in the present significance of the term in Germany. A Freiherr belongs to the "superior nobility," and is a Baron of the older nobility of the Middle Ages; and he ranks immediately after a Count (Graf). The title Baron is now restricted to comparatively newer creations, and its bearer belongs to the "lower nobility." In this tale "Freiherr" and "Baron" are used indifferently.

residence on the ancestral estate, since the lonely old castle was more suitable to his temperament, which was morose and averse to human society. He had its ruinous walls repaired as well as circumstances would admit, and then shut himself up within them along with a cross-grained house-steward and a slender establishment of servants.

He was seldom seen in the village, but on the other hand he often walked and rode along the sea-beach; and people claimed to have heard him from a distance, talking to the waves and listening to the rolling and hissing of the surf, as though he could hear the answering voice of the spirit of the sea. Upon the topmost summit of the watchtower he had a sort of study fitted up and supplied with telescopes — with a complete set of astronomical apparatus, in fact. Thence during the daytime he frequently watched the ships sailing past on the distant horizon like white-winged sea-gulls; and there he spent the starlight nights engaged in astronomical, or, as some professed to know, with astrological labors, in which the old house-steward assisted him. At any rate the rumor was current during his own lifetime that he was devoted to the occult sciences or the so-called Black Art, and that he had been driven out of Courland in consequence of the failure of an experiment by which an august princely house had been most seriously offended. The slightest allusion to his residence in Courland filled him with horror; but for all the troubles which had there unhinged the tenor of his life he held his predecessors entirely to blame, in that they had wickedly deserted the home of their ancestors. In order to fetter, for the future, at least the head of the family to the ancestral castle, he converted it into a property of entail. The sovereign was the more willing to ratify this arrangement since by its means he would secure for his country a family distinguished for all chivalrous virtues, and which had already begun to ramify into foreign countries.

Neither Roderick's son Hubert, nor the next Roderick, who was so called after his grandfather, would live in their ancestral castle; both preferred Courland. It is conceivable, too, that, being more cheerful and fond of life than the gloomy astrologer, they were repelled by the grim loneliness of the place. Freiherr Roderick had granted shelter and subsistence on the property to two old maids, sisters of his father, who were living in indigence, having been but niggardly provided for. They, together with an aged serving-woman, occupied the small warm rooms of one of the wings; besides them and the cook, who had a large apartment on the ground floor adjoining the kitchen, the only other person was a worn-out *chasseur,* who tottered about through the lofty rooms and halls of the main building, and discharged the duties of castellan. The rest of the servants lived in the village with the land-steward. The only time at which the desolated and deserted castle became the scene of life and activity was late in autumn, when the snow first began to fall and the season for wolf-hunting and boar-hunting arrived. Then came Freiherr Roderick with his wife, attended by relatives and friends and a numerous retinue, from Courland. The neighboring nobility, and even amateur lovers of the chase who lived in the town hard by, came down in such numbers that the main building, together with the wings, barely sufficed to hold the crowd of guests. Well-served fires roared in all the stoves and fireplaces, while the spits were creaking from early dawn until late at night, and hundreds of light-hearted people, masters and servants, were running up and downstairs; here was heard the jingling and rattling of drinking glasses and jovial hunting choruses, there the footsteps of those dancing to the sound of the shrill music, — everywhere loud mirth and jollity; so that for four or five weeks together the castle was more like a first-rate hostelry situated on a main highroad than the abode of a country gentleman. This time Freiherr Roderick devoted, as well as he was able, to serious business, for, withdrawing from the revelry of his guests, he discharged the duties attached to his position as lord of the entail. He not only had a complete statement of the revenues laid before him, but he listened to every proposal for improvement and to every the least complaint of his tenants, endeavoring to establish order in everything, and check all wrongdoing and injustice as far as lay in his power.

In these matters of business he was honestly assisted by the old advocate V——, who had been law agent of the R—— family and Justitiarius* of their estates in P—— from father to son for many years; accordingly, V—— was wont to set out for the estate at least a week before the day fixed for the arrival of the Freiherr. In the year 179- the time came round again when old V—— was to start on his journey for R-sitten. However strong and healthy the old man, now seventy years of age, might feel, he was yet quite assured that a helping hand would prove beneficial to him in his business. So he said to me one day as if in jest, "Cousin!" (I was his great-nephew, but he called me "cousin," owing to the fact that his own Christian name and mine were both the same) — "Cousin, I was thinking it would not be amiss if you went along with me to R-sitten and felt the sea-breezes blow about your ears a bit. Besides giving me good help in my often laborious work, you may for once in a while see how you like the rollicking life of a hunter, and how, after drawing up a neatly-written protocol one morning, you will frame the next when you come to look in the glaring eyes of such a sturdy brute as a grim shaggy wolf or a wild boar gnashing his teeth, and whether you know how to bring him down with a well-aimed shot." Of course I could not have heard such strange accounts of the merry hunting parties at R-sitten, or entertain such a true heartfelt affection for my excellent old great-uncle as I did, without being highly delighted that he wanted to take me with him this time. As I was already pretty well skilled in the sort of business he had to transact, I promised to work with unwearied industry, so as to relieve him of all care and trouble.

Next day we sat in the carriage on our way to R-sitten, well wrapped up in good fur coats, driving through a thick snow-storm, the first harbinger of the coming winter. On the journey the old gentleman told me many remarkable stories about the Freiherr Roderick, who had established the estate-tail and appointed him (V——), in spite of his youth, to be his Justitiarius and executor. He spoke of the harsh and violent character of the old nobleman, which seemed to be inherited by all the family, since even the present master of the estate, whom he had known as a mild-tempered and

---

** The Justitiarius acted as justiciary in the seignorial courts of justice, which were amongst the privileges accorded to the nobility of certain ranks, in certain cases, by the feudal institutions of the Middle Ages. This privilege the R—— family is represented as exercising.

almost effeminate youth, acquired more and more as the years went by the same disposition. He therefore recommended me strongly to behave with as much resolute self-reliance and as little embarrassment as possible, if I desired to possess any consideration in the Freiherr's eyes; and at length he began to describe the apartments in the castle which he had selected to be his own once for all, since they were warm and comfortable, and so conveniently retired that we could withdraw from the noisy convivialities of the hilarious company whenever we pleased. The rooms, namely, which were on every visit reserved for him, were two small ones, hung with warm tapestry, close beside the large hall of justice, in the wing opposite that in which the two old maids resided.

At last, after a rapid but wearying journey, we arrived at R–sitten, late at night. We drove through the village; it was Sunday, and from the alehouse proceeded the sounds of music, and dancing, and merrymaking; the steward's house was lit up from basement to garret, and music and song were there too. All the more striking therefore was the inhospitable desolation into which we now drove. The sea-wind howled in sharp cutting dirges as it were about us, whilst the somber firs, as if they had been roused by the wind from a deep magic trance, groaned hoarsely in a responsive chorus. The bare black walls of the castle towered above the snow-covered ground; we drew up at the gates, which were fast locked. But no shouting or cracking of whips, no knocking or hammering, was of any avail; the whole castle seemed to be dead; not a single light was visible at any of the windows. The old gentleman shouted in his strong stentorian voice, "Francis, Francis, where the deuce are you? In the devil's name rouse yourself; we are all freezing here outside the gates. The snow is cutting our faces till they bleed. Why the devil don't you stir yourself?" Then the watchdog began to whine, and a wandering light was visible on the ground floor. There was a rattling of keys, and soon the ponderous wings of the gate creaked back on their hinges. "Ha! a hearty welcome, a hearty welcome, Herr Justitiarius. Ugh! it's rough weather!" cried old Francis, holding the lantern above his head, so that the light fell full upon his withered face, which was drawn up into a curious grimace, that was meant for a friendly smile.

The carriage drove into the court, and we got out; then I obtained a full view of the old servant's extraordinary figure, almost hidden in his wide old-fashioned chasseur livery, with its many extraordinary lace decorations. Whilst there were only a few grey locks on his broad white forehead, the lower part of his face wore the ruddy hue of health; and, notwithstanding that the cramped muscles of his face gave it something of the appearance of a whimsical mask, yet the rather stupid good nature which beamed from his eyes and played about his mouth compensated for all the rest.

"Now, old Francis," began my great-uncle, knocking the snow from his fur coat in the entrance hall, "now, old man, is everything prepared? Have you had the hangings in my room well dusted, and the beds carried in? and have you had a big roaring fire both yesterday and today?" "No," replied Francis, quite calmly, "no, my worshipful Herr Justitiarius, we've got none of that done." "Good Heavens!" burst out my great-uncle, "I wrote to you in proper time; you know that I always come at the time I fix. Here's a fine piece of stupid carelessness! I shall have to sleep in rooms as cold as ice." "But you see, worshipful Herr Justitiarius," continued Francis, most carefully clipping a burning thief from the wick of the candle with the snuffers and stamping it out with his foot, "but, you see, sir, all that would not have been of much good, especially the fires, for the wind and the snow have taken up their quarters too much in the rooms, driving in through the broken windows, and then" — "What!" cried my uncle, interrupting him as he spread out his fur coat and placing his arms akimbo, "do you mean to tell me the windows are broken, and you, the castellan of the house, have done nothing to get them mended?" "But, worshipful Herr Justitiarius," resumed the old servant calmly and composedly, "but we can't very well get at them owing to the great masses of stones and rubbish lying all over the room." "Damn it all, how come there to be stones and rubbish in my room?" cried my uncle. "Your lasting health and good luck, young gentleman!" said the old man, bowing politely to me, as I happened to sneeze;*

---

* At the present time the Germans say *Prosit!* under like circumstances. This of course reminds one of the Greek custom of regarding sneezing as an auspicious omen.

but he immediately added, "They are the stones and plaster of the partition wall which fell in at the great shock." "Have you had an earthquake?" blazed up my uncle, now fairly in a rage. "No, not an earthquake, worshipful Herr Justitiarius," replied the old man, grinning all over his face, "but three days ago the heavy wainscot ceiling of the justice-hall fell in with a tremendous crash." "Then may the" — My uncle was about to rip out a terrific oath in his violent passionate manner, but jerking up his right arm above his head and taking off his fox-skin cap with his left, he suddenly checked himself; and turning to me, he said with a hearty laugh, "By my troth, cousin, we must hold our tongues; we mustn't ask anymore questions, or else we shall hear of some still worse misfortune, or have the whole castle tumbling to pieces about our ears." "But," he continued, wheeling round again to the old servant, "but, bless me, Francis, could you not have had the common sense to get me another room cleaned and warmed? Could you not have quickly fitted up a room in the main building for the court-day?" "All that has been already done," said the old man, pointing to the staircase with a gesture that invited us to follow him, and at once beginning to ascend them. "Now there's a most curious noodle for you!" exclaimed my uncle as we followed old Francis. The way led through long lofty vaulted corridors, in the dense darkness of which Francis's flickering light threw a strange reflection. The pillars, capitals, and vari-colored arches seemed as if they were floating before us in the air; our own shadows stalked along beside us in gigantic shape, and the grotesque paintings on the walls over which they glided seemed all of a tremble and shake; whilst their voices, we could imagine, were whispering in the sound of our echoing footsteps, "Wake us not, oh! wake us not — us whimsical spirits who sleep here in these old stones." At last, after we had traversed a long suite of cold and gloomy apartments, Francis opened the door of a hall in which a fire blazing brightly in the grate offered us as it were a homelike welcome with its pleasant crackling.

"I felt quite comfortable the moment I entered, but my uncle, standing still in the middle of the hall, looked round him and said in a tone which was so very grave as to be almost solemn, "And so this is to be the justice-hall!" Francis held his candle above his head, so that my eye fell upon a light spot in the wide dark wall about the size of a door; then he said in a pained and muffled voice, "Justice has been already dealt out here." "What possesses you, old man?" asked my uncle, quickly throwing aside his fur coat and drawing near to the fire. "It slipped over my lips, I couldn't help it," said Francis; then he lit the great candles and opened the door of the adjoining room, which was very snugly fitted up for our reception. In a short time a table was spread for us before the fire, and the old man served us with several well-dressed dishes, which were followed by a brimming bowl of punch, prepared in true Northern style, — a very acceptable sight to two weary travelers like my uncle and myself. My uncle then, tired with his journey, went to bed as soon as he had finished supper; but my spirits were too much excited by the novelty and strangeness of the place, as well as by the punch, for me to think of sleep. Meanwhile, Francis cleared the table, stirred up the fire, and bowing and scraping politely, left me to myself.

Now I sat alone in the lofty spacious *Rittersaal* or Knight's Hall. The snowflakes had ceased to beat against the lattice, and the storm had ceased to whistle; the sky was clear, and the bright full moon shone in through the wide oriel-windows, illuminating with magical effect all the dark corners of the curious room into which the dim light of my candles and the fire could not penetrate. As one often finds in old castles, the walls and ceiling of the hall were ornamented in a peculiar antique fashion, the former with fantastic paintings and carvings, gilded and colored in gorgeous tints, the latter with heavy wainscoting. Standing out conspicuously from the great pictures, which represented for the most part wild bloody scenes in bear-hunts and wolf-hunts, were the heads of men and animals carved in wood and joined on to the painted bodies, so that the whole, especially in the flickering light of the fire and the soft beams of the moon, had an effect as if all were alive and instinct with terrible reality. Between these pictures reliefs of knights had been inserted, of life size, walking along in hunting costume; probably they were the ancestors of the family who had delighted in the chase. Everything, both in the paintings and in the carved work, bore the dingy hue of extreme old age; so much the more conspicuous therefore was the bright bare place on that one of the walls through which were two doors leading into adjoining apartments. I soon concluded that there too there must have been a door, that had been bricked up later; and hence it was that this new part of the wall, which had neither been painted like the rest, nor yet ornamented with carvings, formed such a striking contrast with the others. Who does not know with what mysterious power the mind is enthralled in the midst of unusual and singularly strange circumstances? Even the dullest imagination is aroused when it comes into a valley girt around by fantastic rocks, or within the gloomy walls of a church or an abbey, and it begins to have glimpses of things it has never yet experienced. When I add that I was twenty years of age, and had drunk several glasses of strong punch, it will easily be conceived that as I sat thus in the *Rittersaal* I was in a more exceptional frame of mind than I had ever been before. Let the reader picture to himself the stillness of the night within, and without the rumbling roar of the sea — the peculiar piping of the wind, which rang upon my ears like the tones of a mighty organ played upon by spectral hands — the passing scudding clouds which, shining bright and white, often seemed to peep in through the rattling oriel-windows like giants sailings past — in very truth, I felt, from the slight shudder which shook me, that possibly a new sphere of existences might now be revealed to me visibly and perceptibly. But this feeling was like the shivery sensations that one has on hearing a graphically narrated ghost story, such as we all like. At this moment it occurred to me that I should never be in a more seasonable mood for reading the book which, in common with everyone who had the least leaning towards the romantic, I at that time carried about in my pocket, — I mean Schiller's "Ghost-seer." I read and read, and my imagination grew ever more and more excited. I came to the marvelously enthralling description of the wedding feast at Count Von V——'s.

Just as I was reading of the entrance of Jeronimo's bloody figure,* the door leading from the gallery into the antecham-

---

* This refers to an episode in Schiller's work, related by a Sicilian. The

ber flew open with a tremendous bang. I started to my feet
in terror; the book fell from my hands. In the very same
moment, however, all was still again, and I began to be
ashamed of my childish fears. The door must have been burst
open by a strong gust of wind or in some other natural
manner. It is nothing; my overstrained fancy converts every
ordinary occurrence into the supernatural. Having thus
calmed my fears, I picked up my book from the ground, and
again threw myself in the armchair; but there came a sound
of soft, slow, measured footsteps moving diagonally across
the hall, whilst there was a sighing and moaning at intervals,
and in this sighing and moaning there was expressed the
deepest trouble, the most hopeless grief, that a human being
can know. "Ha! it must be some sick animal locked up
somewhere in the basement storey. Such acoustic deceptions
at night time, making distant sounds appear close at hand,
are well known to everybody. Who will suffer himself to be
terrified at such a thing as that?" Thus I calmed my fears
again. But now there was a scratching at the new portion of
the wall, whilst louder and deeper sighs were audible, as if
gasped out by someone in the last throes of mortal anguish.
"Yes, yes; it is some poor animal locked up somewhere; I will
shout as loudly as I can, I will stamp violently on the floor,
then all will be still, or else the animal below will make itself
heard more distinctly, and in its natural cries," I thought. But
the blood ran cold in my veins; the cold sweat, too, stood
upon my forehead, and I remained sitting in my chair as if
transfixed, quite unable to rise, still less to cry out. At length
the abominable scratching ceased, and I again heard the
footsteps. Life and motion seemed to be awakened in me; I
leapt to my feet, and went two or three steps forward. But
then there came an ice-cold draft of wind through the hall,
whilst at the same moment the moon cast her bright light
upon the statue of a grave if not almost terrible-looking man;
and then, as though his warning voice rang through the

---

story is of a familiar type. Two brothers, Jeronymo and Lorenzo, fall
in love with the same Lady Antonia; the elder brother is secretly killed
by the younger. But on the marriage day of the murderer the murdered
man appears in the disguise of a monk, and proceeds to reveal himself
in his bloody habiliments and show his ghastly wounds.

louder thunders of the waves and the shriller piping of the wind, I heard distinctly, "No further, no further! or you will sink beneath all the fearful horrors of the world of specters." Then the door was slammed too with the same violent bang as before, and I plainly heard the footsteps in the anteroom, then going down the stairs. The main door of the castle was opened with a creaking noise, and afterwards closed again. Then it seemed as if a horse were brought out of the stable, and after a while taken back again, and finally all was still.

At that same moment my attention was attracted to my old uncle in the adjoining room; he was groaning and moaning painfully. This brought me fully to consciousness again; I seized the candles and hurried into the room to him. He appeared to be struggling with an ugly, unpleasant dream. "Wake up, wake up!" I cried loudly, taking him gently by the hand, and letting the full glare of the light fall upon his face. He started up with a stifled shout, and then, looking kindly at me, said, "Aye, you have done quite right — that you have, cousin, to wake me. I have had a very ugly dream, and it's all solely owing to this room and that hall, for they made me think of past times and many wonderful things that have happened here. But now let us turn to and have a good sound sleep." Therewith the old gentleman rolled himself in the bed-covering and appeared to fall asleep at once. But when I had extinguished the candles and likewise crept into bed, I heard him praying in a low tone to himself.

Next morning we began work in earnest; the land-steward brought his account-books, and various other people came, some to get a dispute settled, some to get arrangements made about other matters. At noon my uncle took me with him to the wing where the two old Baronesses lived, that we might pay our respects to them with all due form. Francis having announced us, we had to wait some time before a little old dame, bent with the weight of her sixty years, and attired in gay-colored silks, who styled herself the noble ladies' lady-in-waiting, appeared and led us into the sanctuary. There we were received with comical ceremony by the old ladies, whose curious style of dress had gone out of fashion years and years before. I especially was an object of astonishment to them when my uncle, with considerable humor, introduced me as a young lawyer who had come to assist him in his business. Their countenances plainly indicated their belief that, owing to my youth, the welfare of the tenants of R–sitten was placed in jeopardy. Although there was a good deal that was truly ridiculous during the whole of this interview with the old ladies, I was nevertheless still shivering from the terror of the preceding night; I felt as if I had come in contact with an unknown power, or rather as if I had grazed against the outer edge of a circle, one step across which would be enough to plunge me irretrievably into destruction, as though it were only by the exertion of all the power of my will that I should be able to guard myself against *that* awful dread which never slackens its hold upon you until it ends in incurable insanity. Hence it was that the old Baronesses, with their remarkable towering headdresses, and their peculiar stuff gowns, tricked off with gay flowers and ribbons, instead of striking me as merely ridiculous, had an appearance that was both ghostly and awe-inspiring. My fancy seemed to glean from their yellow withered faces and blinking eyes, ocular proof of the fact that they had succeeded in establishing themselves on at least a good footing with the ghosts who haunted the castle, as it derived auricular confirmation of the same fact from the wretched French which they croaked, partly between their tightly-closed blue lips and partly through their long thin noses, and also that they themselves possessed the power of setting trouble and dire mischief at work. My uncle, who always had a keen eye for a bit of fun, entangled the old dames in his ironical way in such a mish-mash of nonsensical rubbish that, had I been in any other mood, I should not have known how to swallow down my immoderate laughter; but, as I have just said, the Baronesses and their twaddle were, and continued to be, in my regard, ghostly, so that my old uncle, who was aiming at affording me an especial diversion, glanced across at me time after time utterly astonished. So after dinner, when we were alone together in our room, he burst out, "But in Heaven's name, cousin, tell me what is the matter with you? You don't laugh; you don't talk; you don't eat; and you don't drink. Are you ill, or is anything else the matter with you?" I now hesitated not a moment to tell him circumstantially all my terrible, awful experiences of the previous night I did not conceal anything, and above all I did not conceal that I had drunk a good deal of punch, and had been reading Schiller's "Ghostseer." "This I must confess to," I add, "for only so can I credibly explain how it was that my overstrained and active imagination could create all those ghostly spirits, which only exist within the sphere of my own brain."

I fully expected that my uncle would now pepper me well with the stinging pellets of his wit for this my fanciful ghost-seeing; but, on the contrary, he grew very grave, and his eyes became riveted in a set stare upon the floor, until he jerked up his head and said, fixing me with his keen fiery eyes, "Your book I am not acquainted with, cousin; but your ghostly visitants were due neither to it nor to the fumes of the punch. I must tell you that I dreamt exactly the same things that you saw and heard. Like you, I sat in the easy chair beside the fire (at least I dreamt so); but what was only revealed to you as slight noises I saw and distinctly comprehended with the eye of my mind. Yes, I beheld that foul fiend come in, stealthily and feebly step across to the bricked-up door, and scratch at the wall in hopeless despair until the blood gushed out from beneath his torn fingernails; then he went downstairs, took a horse out of the stable, and finally put him back again. Did you also hear the cock crowing in a distant farmyard up at the village? You came and awoke me, and I soon resisted the baneful ghost of that terrible man, who is still able to disturb in this fearful way the quiet lives of the living." The old gentleman stopped; and I did not like to ask him further questions, being well aware that he would explain everything to me when he deemed that the proper time was come for doing so. After sitting for a while, deeply absorbed in his own thoughts, he went on, "Cousin, do you think you have courage enough to encounter the ghost again now that you know all that happens, — that is to say, along with me?" Of course I declared that I now felt quite strong enough, and ready for what he wished. "Then let us watch together during the coming night," the old gentleman went on to say. "There is a voice within me telling me that this evil spirit must fly, not so much before the power of my will as before my courage, which rests upon a basis of firm conviction. I feel that it is not at all presumption in me, but rather a good and pious deed, if I venture life and limb to exorcise this foul fiend that is banishing the sons from the old castle of their ancestors. But what am I thinking about? There can be no risk in the case at all, for with such a firm, honest mind and pious trust that I feel I possess, I and everybody cannot fail to be, now and always, victorious over such ghostly antagonists. And yet if, after all, it should be God's will that this evil power be enabled to work me mischief, then you must bear witness, cousin, that I fell in honest Christian fight against the spirit of hell which was here busy about its fiendish work. As for yourself, keep at a distance; no harm will happen to you then."

Our attention was busily engaged with divers kinds of business until evening came. As on the day before, Francis had cleared away the remains of the supper, and brought us our punch. The full moon shone brightly through the gleaming clouds, the sea-waves roared, and the night-wind howled and shook the oriel window till the panes rattled. Although inwardly excited, we forced ourselves to converse on indifferent topics. The old gentleman had placed his striking watch on the table; it struck twelve. Then the door flew open with a terrific bang, and, just as on the preceding night, soft slow footsteps moved stealthily across the hall in a diagonal direction, whilst there were the same sounds of sighing and moaning. My uncle turned pale, but his eyes shone with an unusual brilliance. He rose from his armchair, stretching his tall figure up to its full height, so that as he stood there with his left arm propped against his side and with his right stretched out towards the middle of the hall, he had the appearance of a hero issuing his commands. But the sighing and moaning were growing every moment louder and more perceptible, and then the scratching at the wall began more horribly even than on the previous night. My uncle strode forwards straight towards the walled-up door, and his steps were so firm that they echoed along the floor. He stopped immediately in front of the place, where the scratching noise continued to grow worse and worse, and said in a strong solemn voice, such as I had never before heard from his lips, "Daniel, Daniel! what are you doing here at this hour?" Then there was a horrible unearthly scream, followed by a dull thud as if a heavy weight had fallen to the ground. "Seek for pardon and mercy at the throne of the Almighty; that is your place. Away with you from the scenes of this life, in which you can nevermore have part." And as the old gentleman uttered these words in a tone still stronger than before, a feeble wail seemed to pass through the air and die away in the blustering of the storm, which was just beginning to rage. Crossing over to the door, the old gentleman slammed it to, so that the echo rang loudly through the empty anteroom. There was something so supernatural almost in both his language and his gestures that I was deeply struck with awe. On resuming his seat in his armchair his face was as if transfigured; he folded his hands and prayed inwardly. In this way several minutes passed, when he asked me in that gentle tone which always went right to my heart, and which he always had so completely at his command, "Well, cousin?" Agitated and shaken by awe, terror, fear, and pious respect and love, I threw myself upon my knees and rained down my warm tears upon the hand he offered me. He clasped me in his arms, and pressing me fervently to his heart said very tenderly, "Now we will go and have a good quiet sleep, good cousin;" and we did so. And as nothing of an unusual nature occurred on the following night, we soon recovered our former cheerfulness, to the prejudice of the old Baronesses; for though there did still continue to be something ghostly about them and their odd manners, yet it emanated from a diverting ghost which the old gentleman knew how to call up in a droll fashion.

At length, after the lapse of several days, the Baron put in his appearance, along with his wife and a numerous train of servants for the hunting; the guests who had been invited also arrived, and the castle, now suddenly awakened to animation, became the scene of the noisy life and revelry which have been before described. When the Baron came into our hall soon after his arrival, he seemed to be disagreeably surprised at the change in our quarters. Casting an ill-tempered glance towards the bricked-up door, he turned abruptly round and passed his hand across his forehead, as if desirous of banishing some disagreeable recollection. My great-uncle mentioned the damage done to the justice-hall and the adjoining apartments; but the Baron found fault with Francis for not accommodating us with better lodgings, and he good-naturedly requested the old gentleman to order anything he might want to make his new room comfortable; for it was much less satisfactory in this respect than that which he had usually occupied. On the whole, the Baron's bearing towards my old uncle was not merely cordial, but largely colored by a certain deferential respect, as if the relation in which he stood towards him was that of a younger relative. But this was the sole trait that could in any way reconcile me to his harsh, imperious character, which was now developed more and more every day. As for me, he seemed to notice me but little; if he did notice me at all, he saw in me nothing more than the usual secretary or clerk. On the occasion of the very first important memorandum that I drew up, he began to point out mistakes, as he conceived, in the wording. My blood boiled, and I was about to make a caustic reply, when my uncle interposed, informing him briefly that I did my work exactly in the way he wished, and that in legal matters of this kind he alone was responsible. When we were left alone, I complained bitterly of the Baron, who would, I said, always inspire me with growing aversion. "I assure you, cousin," replied the old gentleman, "that the Baron, notwithstanding his unpleasant manner, is really one of the most excellent and kind-hearted men in the world. As I have already told you, he did not assume these manners until the time he became lord of the entail; previous to then he was a modest, gentle youth. Besides, he is not, after all, so bad as you make him out to be; and further, I should like to know why you are so averse to him." As my uncle said these words he smiled mockingly, and the blood rushed hotly and furiously into my face. I could not pretend to hide from myself — I saw it only too clearly, and felt it too unmistakably — that my peculiar antipathy to the Baron sprang out of the fact that I loved, even to madness, a being who appeared to me to be the loveliest and most fascinating of her sex who had ever trod the earth. This lady was none other than the Baroness herself. Her appearance exercised a powerful and irresistible charm upon me at the very moment of her arrival, when I saw her traversing the apartments in her Russian sable cloak, which fitted close to the exquisite symmetry of her shape, and with a rich veil wrapped about her head. Moreover, the circumstance that the two old aunts, with still more extraordinary gowns and be-ribboned headdresses than I had yet seen them wear, were sweeping along one on each side of her and cackling their welcomes in French, whilst the Baroness was looking about her in a way so gentle as to baffle all description, nodding graciously first to one and then to another, and then adding in her flutelike voice a few German words in the pure sonorous dialect of Courland — all this formed a truly remarkable and unusual picture, and my imagination involuntarily connected it with the ghostly midnight visitant, — the Baroness being the angel of light who was to break the ban of the spectral powers of evil. This wondrously lovely lady stood forth in startling reality before my mind's eye.

At that time she could hardly be nineteen years of age, and her face, as delicately beautiful as her form, bore the impression of the most angelic good nature; but what I especially noticed was the indescribable fascination of her dark eyes, for a soft melancholy gleam of aspiration shone in them like dewy moonshine, whilst a perfect elysium of rapture and delight was revealed in her sweet and beautiful smile. She often seemed completely lost in her own thoughts, and at such moments her lovely face was swept by dark and fleeting shadows. Many observers would have concluded that she was affected by some distressing pain; but it rather seemed to me that she was struggling with gloomy apprehensions of a future pregnant with dark misfortunes; and with these, strangely enough, I connected the apparition of the castle, though I could not give the least explanation of why I did so.

On the morning following the Baron's arrival, when the company assembled to breakfast, my old uncle introduced me to the Baroness; and, as usually happens with people in the frame of mind in which I then was, I behaved with indescribable absurdity. In answer to the beautiful lady's simple inquiries how I liked the castle, &c., I entangled myself in the most extraordinary and nonsensical phrases, so that the old aunts ascribed my embarrassment simply and solely to my profound respect for the noble lady, and thought they were called upon condescendingly to take my part, which they did by praising me in French as a very nice and clever young man, as a *garçon très joli* (handsome lad). This vexed me; so suddenly recovering my self-possession, I threw out a *bonmot* in better French than the old dames were mistresses of; whereupon they opened their eyes wide in astonishment, and pampered their long thin noses with a liberal supply of snuff. From the Baroness's turning from me with a more serious air to talk to some other lady, I perceived that my *bonmot* bordered closely upon folly; this vexed me still more, and I wished the two old ladies to the devil. My old uncle's irony had long before brought me through the stage of the languishing love-sick swain, who in childish infatuation coddles his love-troubles; but I knew very well that the Baroness had made a deeper and more powerful impression upon my heart than any other woman had hitherto done. I saw and heard nothing but her; nevertheless I had a most explicit and unequivocal consciousness that it would be not only absurd, but even utter madness to dream of an amour, albeit I perceived no less clearly the impossibility of gazing and adoring at a distance like a love-lorn boy. Of such conduct I should have been perfectly ashamed. But what I could do, and what I resolved to do, was to become more intimate with this beautiful girl without allowing her to get any glimpse of my real feelings, to drink the sweet poison of her looks and words, and then, when far away from her, to bear her image in my heart for many, many days, perhaps forever. I was excited by this romantic and chivalric attachment to such a degree, that, as I pondered over it during sleepless nights, I was childish enough to address myself in pathetic monologues, and even to sigh lugubriously, "Seraphina! O Seraphina!" till at last my old uncle woke up and cried, "Cousin, cousin! I believe you are dreaming aloud. Do it by daytime, if you can possibly contrive it, but at night have the goodness to let me sleep." I was very much afraid that the old gentleman, who had not failed to remark my excitement on the Baroness's arrival, had heard the name, and would overwhelm me with his sarcastic wit. But next morning all he said, as we went into the justice-hall, was, "God grant every man the proper amount of common sense, and sufficient watchfulness to keep it well under hand. It's a bad look-out when a man becomes converted into a fantastic coxcomb without so much as a word of warning." Then he took his seat at the great table and added, "Write neatly and distinctly, good cousin, that I may be able to read it without any trouble."

The respect, nay, the almost filial veneration which the Baron entertained towards my uncle, was manifested on all occasions. Thus, at the dinner-table he had to occupy the seat — which many envied him — beside the Baroness; as for me, chance threw me first in one place and then in another; but for the most part, two or three officers from the neighboring capital were wont to attach me to them, in order that they might empty to their own satisfaction their budget of news and amusing anecdotes, whilst diligently passing the wine about. Thus it happened that for several days in succession I sat at the bottom of the table at a great distance from the Baroness. At length, however, chance brought me nearer to her. Just as the doors of the dining-hall were thrown open for the assembled company, I happened to be in the midst of a conversation with the Baroness's companion and confidante, — a lady no longer in the bloom of youth, but by no means ill-looking, and not without intelligence, — and she seemed to take some interest in my remarks. According to etiquette, it was my duty to offer her my arm, and I was not a little pleased when she took her place quite close to the Baroness, who gave her a friendly nod. It may be readily imagined that all that I now said was intended not only for my fair neighbor, but also mainly for the Baroness. Whether it was that the inward tension of my feelings imparted an especial animation to all I said, at any rate my companion's attention became more riveted with every succeeding moment; in fact, she was at last entirely absorbed in the visions of the kaleidoscopic world which I unfolded to her gaze. As remarked, she was not without intelligence, and it soon came to pass that our conversation, completely independent of the multitude of words spoken by the other guests (which rambled about first to this subject and then to that), maintained its own free course, launching an effective word now and again whither I wanted it. For I did not fail to observe that my companion shot a significant glance or two across to the Baroness, and that the latter took pains to listen to us. And this was particularly the case when the conversation turned upon music and I began to speak with enthusiasm of this glorious and sacred art; nor did I conceal that, despite the fact of my having devoted myself to the dry tedious study of the law, I possessed tolerable skill on the harpsichord, could sing, and had even set several songs to music.

The majority of the company had gone into another room to take coffee and liqueurs; but, unawares, without knowing how it came about, I found myself near the Baroness, who was talking with her confidante. She at once addressed me, repeating in a still more cordial manner and in the tone in which one talks to an acquaintance, her inquiries as to how I liked living in the castle, &c. I assured her that for the first few days, not only the dreary desolation of the situation, but the ancient castle itself had affected me strangely, but even in this mood I had found much of deep interest, and that now my only wish was to be excused from the stirring scenes of the hunt, for I had not been accustomed to them. The Baroness smiled and said, "I can readily believe that this wild life in our fir forests cannot be very congenial to you. You are a musician, and, unless I am utterly mistaken, a poet as well. I am passionately fond of both arts. I can also play the harp a little, but I have to do without it here in R–sitten, for my husband does not like me to bring it with me. Its soft strains would harmonize but ill with the wild shouts of the hunters and the ringing blare of their bugles, which are the only sounds that ought to be heard here. And O heaven! how I should like to hear a little music!" I protested that I would exert all the skill I had at my command to fulfil her wish, for there must surely without doubt be an instrument of some kind in the castle, even though it were only an old harpsichord. Then the Lady Adelheid (the Baroness's confidante) burst out into a silvery laugh and asked, did I not know that within the memory of man no other instrument had ever been heard in the castle except cracked trumpets, and hunting-horns which in the midst of joy would only sound lugubrious notes, and the twanging fiddles, untuned violoncellos, and braying oboes of itinerant musicians. The Baroness reiterated her wish that she should like to have some music, and especially should like to hear me; and both she and Adelheid racked their brains all to no purpose to devise some scheme by which they could get a decent pianoforte brought to the Castle. At this moment old Francis crossed the room. "Here's the man who always can give the best advice, and can procure everything, even things before unheard of and unseen." With these words the Lady Adelheid called him to her, and as she endeavored to make him comprehend what it was that was wanted, the Baroness listened with her hands clasped and her head bent forward, looking upon the old man's face with a gentle smile. She made a most attractive picture, like some lovely, winsome child that is all eagerness to have a wished-for toy in its hands. Francis, after having adduced in his prolix manner several reasons why it would be downright impossible to procure such a wonderful instrument in such a big hurry, finally stroked his beard with an air of self-flattery and said, "But the land-steward's lady up at the village performs on the manichord, or whatever is the outlandish name they now call it, with uncommon skill, and sings to it so fine and mournfullike that it makes your eyes red, just like onions do, and makes you feel as if you would like to dance with both legs at once." "And you say she has a pianoforte?" interposed Lady Adelheid. "Aye, to be sure," continued the old man; "it comed straight from Dresden; a" — ("Oh, that's fine!" interrupted the Baroness) — "a beautiful instrument," went on the old man, "but a little weakly; for not long ago, when the organist began to play on it the hymn 'In all Thy works,'* he broke it all to pieces, so that" — ("Good gracious!" exclaimed both the Baroness and Lady Adelheid) — "so that," went on the old man again, "it had to be taken to R—— to be mended, and cost a lot of money."

"But has it come back again?" asked Lady Adelheid impatiently. "Aye, to be sure, my lady, and the steward's lady will reckon it a high honor —" At this moment the Baron chanced to pass. He looked across at our group rather astonished, and whispered with a sarcastic smile to the Baroness, "So you have to take counsel of Francis again, I see?" The Baroness cast down her eyes blushing, whilst old Francis breaking off

---

* By Paul Fleming (1609-1640); one of the pious but gloomy religious songs of this leading spirit of the "first Silesian school."

terrified, suddenly threw himself into military posture, his head erect, and his arms close and straight down his side. The old aunts came sailing down upon us in their stuff gowns and carried off the Baroness. Lady Adelheid followed her, and I was left alone as if spellbound. A struggle began to rage within me between my rapturous anticipations of now being able to be near her whom I adored, who completely swayed all my thoughts and feelings, and my sulky ill-humor and annoyance at the Baron, whom I regarded as a barbarous tyrant. If he were not, would the grey-haired old servant have assumed such a slavish attitude?

"Do you hear? Can you see, I say?" cried my great-uncle, tapping me on the shoulder; — we were going upstairs to our own apartments. "Don't force yourself so on the Baroness's attention," he said when we reached the room. "What good can come of it? Leave that to the young fops who like to pay court to ladies; there are plenty of them to do it." I related how it had all come about, and challenged him to say if I had deserved his reproof. His only reply to this, however, was, "Humph! humph!" as he drew on his dressing gown. Then, having lit his pipe, he took his seat in his easy chair and began to talk about the adventures of the hunt on the preceding day, bantering me on my bad shots. All was quiet in the castle; all the visitors, both gentlemen and ladies, were busy in their own rooms dressing for the evening. For the musicians with the twanging fiddles, untuned violoncellos, and braying oboes, of whom Lady Adelheid had spoken, were come, and a merrymaking of no less importance than a ball, to be given in the best possible style, was in anticipation. My old uncle, preferring a quiet sleep to such foolish pastimes, stayed in his chamber. I, however, had just finished dressing when there came a light tap at our door, and Francis entered. Smiling in his self-satisfied way, he announced to me that the manichord had just arrived from the land-steward's lady in a sledge, and had been carried into the Baroness's apartments. Lady Adelheid sent her compliments and would I go over at once. It may be conceived how my pulse beat, and also with what a delicious tremor at heart I opened the door of the room in which I was to find *her.* Lady Adelheid came to meet me with a joyful smile. The Baroness, already in full dress for the ball, was sitting in a meditative attitude beside the mysterious case or box, in which slumbered the music that I was called upon to awaken. When she rose, her beauty shone upon me with such glorious splendor that I stood staring at her unable to utter a word. "Come, Theodore" — (for, according to the kindly custom of the North, which is found again farther south, she addressed everybody by his or her Christian name) — "Come, Theodore," she said pleasantly, "here's the instrument come. Heaven grant it be not altogether unworthy of your skill!" As I opened the lid I was greeted by the rattling of a score of broken strings, and when I attempted to strike a chord, the effect was hideous and abominable, for all the strings which were not broken were completely out of tune. "I doubt not our friend the organist has been putting his delicate little hands upon it again," said Lady Adelheid laughing; but the Baroness was very much annoyed and said, "Oh, it really is a slice of bad luck! I am doomed, I see, never to have any pleasure here." I searched in the case of the instrument, and fortunately found some coils of strings, but no tuning-key anywhere. Hence fresh laments. "Any key will do if the ward will fit on the pegs," I explained; then both Lady Adelheid and the Baroness ran backwards and forwards in gay spirits, and before long a whole magazine of bright keys lay before me on the sounding-board.

Then I set to work diligently, and both the ladies assisted me all they could, trying first one peg and then another. At length one of the tiresome keys fitted, and they exclaimed joyfully, "This will do! it will do!" But when I had drawn the first creaking string up to just proper pitch, it suddenly snapped, and the ladies recoiled in alarm. The Baroness, handling the brittle wires with her delicate little fingers, gave me the numbers as I wanted them, and carefully held the coil whilst I unrolled it. Suddenly one of them coiled itself up again with a whirr, making the Baroness utter an impatient "Oh!" Lady Adelheid enjoyed a hearty laugh, whilst I pursued the tangled coil to the corner of the room. After we had all united our efforts to extract a perfectly straight string from it, and had tried it again, to our mortification it again broke; but at last — at last we found some good coils; the strings began to hold, and gradually the discordant jangling gave place to pure melodious chords. "Ha! it will go! it will go! The instrument is getting in tune!" exclaimed the Baroness, looking at me with her lovely smile. How quickly did this common interest banish all the strangeness and shyness which the artificial manners of social intercourse impose. A kind of confidential familiarity arose between us, which, burning through me like an electric current, consumed the timorous nervousness and constraint which had lain like ice upon my heart. That peculiar mood of diffused melting sadness which is engendered of such love as mine was had quite left me; and accordingly, when the pianoforte was brought into something like tune, instead of interpreting my deeper feelings in dreamy improvisations, as I had intended, I began with those sweet and charming canzonets which have reached us from the South. During this or the other *Senza di te* (Without thee), or *Sentimi idol mio* (Hear me, my darling), or *Almen se nonpos'io* (At least if I cannot), with numberless *Morir mi sentos* (I feel I am dying), and *Addios* (Farewell), and *O dios!* (O Heaven!), a brighter and brighter brilliancy shone in Seraphina's eyes. She had seated herself close beside me at the instrument; I felt her breath fanning my cheek; and as she placed her arm behind me on the chair-back, a white ribbon, getting disengaged from her beautiful ball-dress, fell across my shoulder, where by my singing and Seraphina's soft sighs it was kept in a continual flutter backwards and forwards, like a true love-messenger. It is a wonder how I kept from losing my head.

As I was running my fingers aimlessly over the keys, thinking of a new song, Lady Adelheid, who had been sitting in one of the corners of the room, ran across to us, and, kneeling down before the Baroness, begged her, as she took both her hands and clasped them to her bosom, "Oh, dear Baroness! darling Seraphina! now you must sing too." To this she replied, "Whatever are you thinking about, Adelheid? How could I dream of letting our virtuoso friend hear such poor singing as mine?" And she looked so lovely, as, like a shy good child, she cast down her eyes and blushed, timidly contending with the desire to sing. That I too added my entreaties can easily be imagined; nor, upon her making mention of some little Courland *Volkslieder* or popular songs, did I desist from my entreaties until she stretched out her left hand towards the instrument and tried a few notes by way of introduction. I rose to make way for her at the piano, but she would not permit me to do so, asserting that she could not play a single chord, and for that reason, since she would have to sing without accompaniment, her performance would be poor and uncertain. She began in a sweet voice, pure as a bell, that came straight from her heart, and sang a song whose simple melody bore all the characteristics of those *Volkslieder* which proceed from the lips with such a lustrous brightness, so to speak, that we cannot help perceiving in the glad light which surrounds us our own higher poetic nature. There lies a mysterious charm in the insignificant words of the text which converts them into a hieroglyphic scroll representative of the unutterable emotions which throng our hearts. Who does not know that Spanish canzonet the substance of which is in words little more than, "With my maiden I embarked on the sea; a storm came on, and my timid maiden was tossed up and down: nay, I will never again embark on the sea with my maiden?" And the Baroness's little song contained nothing more than, "Lately I was dancing with my sweetheart at a wedding; a flower fell out of my hair; he picked it up and gave it me, and said, 'When, sweetheart mine, shall we go to a wedding again?'" When, on her beginning the second verse of the song, I played an *arpeggio* accompaniment, and further when, in the inspiration which now took possession of me, I at once stole from the Baroness's own lips the melodies of the other songs she sang, I doubtless appeared in her eyes, and in those of the Lady Adelheid, to be one of the greatest of masters in the art of music, for they overwhelmed me with enthusiastic praise. The lights and illuminations from the ballroom, situated in one of the wings of the castle, now shone across into the Baroness's chamber, whilst a discordant bleating of trumpets and French horns announced that it was time to gather for the ball. "Oh, now I must go," said the Baroness. I started up from the pianoforte. "You have afforded me a delightful hour; these have been the pleasantest moments I have ever spent in R–sitten," she added, offering me her hand; and as in the extreme intoxication of delight I pressed it to my lips, I felt her fingers close upon my hand with a sudden convulsive tremor. I do not know how I managed to reach my uncle's chamber, and still less how I got into the ballroom. There was a certain Gascon who was afraid to go into battle since he was all heart, and every wound would be fatal to him. I might be compared to him; and so might everybody else who is in the same mood that I was in; every touch was then fatal. The Baroness's hand — her tremulous fingers — had affected me like a poisoned arrow; my blood was burning in my veins.

On the following morning my old uncle, without asking any direct questions, had soon drawn from me a full account of the hour I had spent in the Baroness's society, and I was not a little abashed when the smile vanished from his lips and the jocular note from his words, and he grew serious all at once, saying, "Cousin, I beg you will resist this folly which is taking such a powerful hold upon you. Let me tell you that your present conduct, as harmless as it now appears, may lead to the most terrible consequences. In your thoughtless fatuity you are standing on a thin crust of ice, which may break under you ere you are aware of it, and let you in with a plunge. I shall take good care not to hold you fast by the coat-tails, for I know you will scramble out again pretty quick, and then, when you are lying sick unto death, you will say, 'I got this little bit of a cold in a dream.' But I warn you that a malignant fever will gnaw at your vitals, and years will pass before you recover yourself, and are a man again. The deuce take your music if you can put it to no better use than to cozen sentimental young women out of their quiet peace of mind." "But," I began, interrupting the old gentleman, "but have I ever thought of insinuating myself as the Baroness's lover?" "You puppy!" cried the old gentleman, "if I thought so I would pitch you out of this window." At this juncture the Baron entered, and put an end to the painful conversation; and the business to which I now had to turn my attention brought me back from my love-sick reveries, in which I saw and thought of nothing but Seraphina.

In general society the Baroness only occasionally interchanged a few friendly words with me; but hardly an evening passed in which a secret message was not brought to me from Lady Adelheid, summoning me to Seraphina. It soon came to pass that our music alternated with conversations on divers topics. Whenever I and Seraphina began to get too absorbed in sentimental dreams and vague aspirations, the Lady Adelheid, though now hardly young enough to be so naïve and droll as she once was, yet intervened with all sorts of merry and somewhat chaotic nonsense. From several hints she let fall, I soon discovered that the Baroness really had something preying upon her mind, even as I thought I had read in her eyes the very first moment I saw her; and I clearly discerned the hostile influence of the apparition of the castle. Something terrible had happened or was to happen. Although I was often strongly impelled to tell Seraphina in what way I had come in contact with the invisible enemy, and how my old uncle had banished him, undoubtedly forever, I yet felt my tongue fettered by a hesitation which was inexplicable to myself even, whenever I opened my mouth to speak.

One day the Baroness failed to appear at the dinner table; it was said that she was a little unwell, and could not leave her room. Sympathetic inquiries were addressed to the Baron as to whether her illness was of a grave nature. He smiled in a very disagreeable way, in fact, it was almost like bitter irony, and said, "Nothing more than a slight catarrh, which she has got from our blustering sea-breezes. They can't tolerate any sweet voices; the only sounds they will endure are the hoarse 'Halloos' of the chase." At these words the Baron hurled a keen searching look at me across the table, for I sat obliquely opposite to him. He had not spoken to his neighbor, but to me. Lady Adelheid, who sat beside me, blushed a scarlet red. Fixing her eyes upon the plate in front of her, and scribbling about on it with her fork, she whispered, "And yet you must see Seraphina today; your sweet songs shall today also bring soothing and comfort to her poor heart." Adelheid addressed these words to me; but at this moment it struck me that I was almost apparently entangled in a base and forbidden intrigue with the Baroness, which could only end in some terrible crime. My old uncle's warning fell heavily upon my heart. What should I do? Not see her again? That was impossible so long as I remained in the castle; and even if I might leave the castle and return to K——, I had not the will to do it Oh! I felt only too deeply that I was not strong enough to shake myself out of this dream, which was mocking one with delusive hopes of happiness. Adelheid I almost regarded in the light of a common go-between; I would despise her, and yet, upon second thoughts, I could not help being ashamed of my folly. Had anything ever happened during those blissful evening hours which could in the least degree lead to any nearer relation with Seraphina than was permissible by propriety and morality? How dare I let the thought enter my mind that the Baroness would ever entertain any warm feeling for me? And yet I was convinced of the danger of my situation.

We broke up from dinner earlier than usual, in order to go again after some wolves which had been seen in the fir-wood close by the castle. A little hunting was just the thing I wanted in the excited frame of mind in which I then was. I expressed to my uncle my resolve to accompany the party; he gave me an approving smile and said, "That's right; I am glad you are going out with them for once. I shall stay at home, so you can take my firelock with you, and buckle my whinger round your waist; in case of need it is a good and trusty weapon, if you only keep your presence of mind." That part of the wood in which the wolves were supposed to lie was surrounded by the huntsmen. It was bitterly cold; the wind howled through the firs, and drove the light snowflakes right in my face, so that when at length it came on to be dusk I could scarcely see six paces before me. Quite benumbed by the cold, I left the place that had been assigned to me and sought shelter deeper in the wood. There, leaning against a tree, with my firelock under my arm, I forgot the wolf-hunt entirely; my thoughts had traveled back to Seraphina's cozy room. After a time shots were heard in the far distance; but at the same moment there was a rustling in the reed-bank, and I saw not ten paces from me a huge wolf about to run past me. I took aim, and fired, but missed. The brute sprang towards me with glaring eyes; I should have been lost had I not had sufficient presence of mind to draw my hunting-knife, and, just as the brute was flying at me, to drive it deep into his throat, so that the blood spurted out over my hand and arm. One of the Baron's keepers, who had stood not far from me, came running up with a loud shout, and at his repeated "Halloo!" all the rest soon gathered round us. The Baron hastened up to me, saying, "For God's sake, you are bleeding — you are bleeding. Are you wounded?" I assured him that I was not Then he turned to the keeper who had stood nearest to me, and overwhelmed him with reproaches for not having shot after me when I missed. And notwithstanding that the man maintained this to have been perfectly impossible, since in the very same moment the wolf had rushed upon me, and any shot would have been at the risk of hitting me, the Baron persisted in saying that he ought to have taken especial care of me as a less experienced hunter. Meanwhile the keepers had lifted up the dead animal; it was one of the largest that had been seen for a long time; and everybody admired my courage and resolution, although to myself what I had done appeared quite natural I had not for a moment thought of the danger I had run. The Baron in particular seemed to take very great interest in the matter; I thought he would never be done asking me whether, though I was not wounded by the brute, I did not fear the ill effects that would follow from the fright As we went back to the castle, the Baron took me by the arm like a friend, and I had to give my firelock to a keeper to carry. He still continued to talk about my heroic deed, so that eventually I came to believe in my own heroism, and lost all my constraint and embarrassment, and felt that I had established myself in the Baron's eyes as a man of courage and uncommon resolution. The schoolboy had passed his examination successfully, was now no longer a schoolboy, and all the submissive nervousness of the schoolboy had left him. I now conceived I had earned a right to try and gain Scraphina's favor. Everybody knows of course what ridiculous combinations the fancy of a love-sick youth is capable of. In the castle, over the smoking punchbowl, by the fireside, I was the hero of the hour. Besides myself the Baron was the only one of the party who had killed a wolf — also a formidable one; the rest had to be content with ascribing their bad shots to the weather and the darkness, and with relating thrilling stories of their former exploits in hunting and the dangers they had escaped.

I thought, too, that I might reap an especial share of praise and admiration from my old uncle as well; and so, with a view to this end, I related to him my adventure at pretty considerable length, nor did I forget to paint the savage brute's wild and bloodthirsty appearance in very startling colors. The old gentleman, however, only laughed in my face and said, "God is powerful even in the weak."

Tired of drinking and of the company, I was going quietly along the corridor towards the justice-hall when I saw a figure with a light slip in before me. On entering the hall I saw it was Lady Adelheid. "This is the way we have to wander about like ghosts or night-walkers in order to catch you, my brave slayer of wolves," she whispered, taking my arm. The words "ghosts" and "sleep-walkers," pronounced in the place where we were, fell like lead upon my heart; they immediately brought to my recollection the ghostly apparitions of those two awful nights. As then, so now, the wind came howling in from the sea in deep organlike cadences, rattling the oriel windows again and again and whistling fearfully through them, whilst the moon cast her pale gleams exactly upon the mysterious part of the wall where the scratching had been heard. I fancied I discerned stains of blood upon it. Doubtless Lady Adelheid, who still had hold of my hand, must have felt the cold icy shiver which ran through me. "What's the matter with you?" she whispered softly; "what's the matter with you? You are as cold as marble. Come, I will call you back into life. Do you know how very impatient the Baroness is to see you? And until she does see you she will not believe that the ugly wolf has not really bitten you. She is in a terrible state of anxiety about you. Why, my friend, — oh! how have you awakened this interest in the little Seraphina? I have never seen her like this. Ah! — so now the pulse is beginning to prickle; see how quickly the dead man comes to life! Well, come along — but softly, still! Come, we must go to the little Baroness." I suffered myself to be led away in silence. The way in which Adelheid spoke of the Baroness seemed to me undignified, and the innuendo of an understanding between us positively shameful. When I entered the room along with Adelheid, Seraphina, with a low-breathed "Oh!" advanced three or four paces quickly to meet me; but then, as if recollecting herself, she stood still in the middle of the room. I ventured to take her hand and press it to my lips. Allowing it to rest in mine, she asked, "But, for Heaven's sake! is it your business to meddle with wolves? Don't you know that the fabulous days of Orpheus and Amphion are long past, and that wild beasts have quite lost all respect for even the most admirable of singers?" But this gleeful turn, by which the Baroness at once effectually guarded against all misinterpretation of her warm interest in me, I was put immediately into the proper key and the proper mood. Why I did not take my usual place at the pianoforte I cannot explain, even to myself, nor why I sat down beside the Baroness on the sofa. Her question, "And what were you doing then to get into danger?" was an indication of our tacit agreement that conversation, not music, was to engage our attention for that evening. After I had narrated my adventure in the wood, and mentioned the warm interest which the Baron had taken in it, delicately hinting that I had not thought him capable of so much feeling, the Baroness began in a tender and almost melancholy tone, "Oh! how violent and rude you must think the Baron; but I assure you it is only whilst we are living within these gloomy, ghostly walls, and during the time there is hunting going on in the dismal fir-forests, that his character completely changes, at least his outward behavior does. What principally disquiets him in this unpleasant way is the thought, which constantly haunts him, that something terrible will happen here. And that undoubtedly accounts for the fact of his being so greatly agitated by your adventure, which fortunately has had no ill consequences.

"He won't have the meanest of his servants exposed to danger, if he knows it, still less a new-won friend whom he has come to like; and I am perfectly certain that Gottlieb, whom he blames for having left you in the lurch, will be punished; even if he escapes being locked up in a dungeon, he will yet have to suffer the punishment, so mortifying to a hunter, of going out the next time there is a hunt with only a club in his hand instead of a rifle. The circumstance that hunts like those which are held here are always attended with danger, and the fact that the Baron, though always fearing some sad accident, is yet so fond of hunting that he cannot desist from provoking the demon of mischief, make his existence here a kind of conflict, the ill effects of which I also have to feel. Many queer stories are current about his ancestor who established the entail; and I know myself that there is some dark family secret locked within these walls like a horrible ghost which drives away the owners, and makes it impossible for them to bear with it longer than a few weeks at a time — and that only amid a tumult of jovial guests. But I — Oh! how lonely I am in the midst of this noisy, merry company! And how the ghostly influences which breathe upon me from the walls stir and excite my very heart! You, my dear friend, have given me, through your musical skill, the first cheerful moments I have spent here. How can I thank you sufficiently for your kindness!" I kissed the hand she offered to me, saying, that even on the very first day, or rather during the very first night, I had experienced the ghostliness of the place in all its horrors. The Baroness fixed her staring eyes upon my face, as I went on to describe the ghostly character of the building, discernible everywhere throughout the castle, particularly in the decorations of the justice-hall, and to speak of the roaring of the wind from the sea, &c. Possibly my voice and my expressions indicated that I had something more in my mind than what I said; at any rate when I concluded, the Baroness cried vehemently, "No, no; something dreadful has happened to you in that hall, which I never enter without shuddering. I beg you — pray, pray, tell me all."

Seraphina's face had grown deadly pale; and I saw plainly that it would be more advisable to give her a faithful account of all that I had experienced than to leave her excited imagination to conjure up some apparition that might perhaps, in a way I could not foresee, be far more horrible than what I had actually encountered. As she listened to me her fear and strained anxiety increased from moment to moment; and when I mentioned the scratching on the wall she screamed, "It's horrible! Yes, yes, it's in that wall that the awful secret is concealed!" But as I went on to describe with what spiritual power and superiority of will my old uncle had banished the ghost, she sighed deeply, as though she had shaken off a heavy burden that had weighed oppressively upon her. She leaned back in the sofa and held her hands before her face. Now I first noticed that Adelheid had left us. A considerable pause ensued, and as Seraphina still continued silent, I softly rose, and going to the pianoforte, endeavored in swelling chords to invoke the bright spirits of consolation to come and deliver Seraphina from the dark influence to which my narration had subjected her. Then I soon began to sing as softly as I was able one of the Abbé Steffani's* canzonas. The melancholy strains of the *Ochi, perchè piangete* (O eyes, why weep you?) roused Seraphina out of her reverie, and she listened to me with a gentle smile upon her face, and bright pearllike tears in her eyes. How am I to account for it that I kneeled down before her, that she bent over towards me, that I threw my arms about her, that a long ardent kiss was imprinted on my lips? How am I to account for it that I did not lose my senses when she drew me softly towards her, how that I tore myself from her arms, and, quickly rising to my feet, hurried to the pianoforte? Turning from me, the Baroness took a few steps towards the window, then she turned round again and approached me with an air of almost proud dignity, which was not at all usual with her. Looking me straight in the face, she said, "Your uncle is the most worthy old man I know; he is the guardian-angel of our family. May he include me in his pious prayers!" I was unable to utter a word; the subtle poison that I had imbibed with her kiss burned and boiled in every pulse and nerve. Lady Adelheid came in. The violence of my inward conflict burst out at length in a passionate flood of tears, which I was unable to repress. Adelheid looked at me with wonder and smiled dubiously; — I could have murdered her. The Baroness gave me her hand, and said with inexpressible gentleness, "Farewell, my dear friend. Fare you right well; and remember that nobody perhaps has ever understood your music better than I have. Oh! these notes! they will echo long, long in my heart." I forced myself to utter a few stupid, disconnected words, and hurried up to my uncle's room. The old gentleman had already gone to bed. I stayed in the hall, and falling upon my knees, I wept aloud; I called upon my beloved by name, I gave myself up completely and regardlessly to all the absurd folly of a love-sick lunatic, until at last the extravagant noise I made

---

* See note, p. 40.

awoke my uncle. But his loud call, "Cousin, I believe you have gone cranky, or else you're having another tussle with a wolf. Be off to bed with you if you will be so very kind" — these words compelled me to enter his room, where I got into bed with the fixed resolve to dream only of Seraphina.

It would be somewhere past midnight when I thought I heard distant voices, a running backwards and forwards, and an opening and banging of doors — for I had not yet fallen asleep. I listened attentively; I heard footsteps approaching the corridor; the hall door was opened, and soon there came a knock at our door. "Who is there?" I cried. A voice from without answered, "Herr Justitiarius, Herr Justitiarius, wake up, wake up!" I recognized Francis's voice, and as I asked, "Is the castle on fire?" the old gentleman woke up in his turn and asked, "Where — where is there a fire? Is it that cursed apparition again? where is it?" "Oh! please get up, Herr Justitiarius," said Francis, "Please get up; the Baron wants you." "What does the Baron want me for?" inquired my uncle further; "what does he want me for at this time of night? does he not know that all law business goes to bed along with the lawyer, and sleeps as soundly as he does?" "Oh!" cried Francis, now anxiously; "please, Herr Justitiarius, good sir, please get up. My lady the Baroness is dying." I started up with a cry of dismay. "Open the door for Francis," said the old gentleman to me. I stumbled about the room almost distracted, and could find neither door nor lock; my uncle had to come and help me. Francis came in, his face pale and troubled, and lit the candles. We had scarcely thrown on our clothes when we heard the Baron calling in the hall, "Can I speak to you, good V——?" "But what have you dressed for, cousin? the Baron only wanted me," asked the old gentleman, on the point of going out. "I must go down — I must see her and then die," I replied tragically, and as if my heart were rent by hopeless grief. "Aye, just so; you are right, cousin," he said, banging the door to in my face, so that the hinges creaked, and locking it on the outside. At the first moment, deeply incensed at this restraint, I thought of bursting the door open; but quickly reflecting that this would entail the disagreeable consequences of a piece of outrageous insanity, I resolved to await the old gentleman's return; then however, let the cost be what it might, I would escape his watchfulness. I heard him talking vehemently with the Baron, and several times distinguished my own name, but could not make out anything further. Every moment my position grew more intolerable. At length I heard that someone brought a message to the Baron, who immediately hurried off. My old uncle entered the room again. "She is dead!" I cried, running towards him, "And you are a stupid fool," he interrupted coolly; then he laid hold upon me and forced me into a chair. "I must go down," I cried, "I must go down and see her, even though it cost me my life." "Do so, good cousin," said he, locking the door, taking out the key, and putting it in his pocket. I now flew into a perfectly frantic rage; stretching out my hand towards the rifle, I screamed, "If you don't instantly open the door I will send this bullet through my brains." Then the old gentleman planted himself immediately in front of me, and fixing his keen piercing eyes upon me said, "Boy, do you think you can frighten me with your idle threats? Do you think I should set much value on your life if you can go and throw it away in childish folly like a broken plaything? What have you to do with the Baron's wife? who has given you the right to insinuate yourself, like a tiresome puppy, where you have no claim to be, and where you are not wanted? do you wish to go and act the love-sick swain at the solemn hour of death?" I sank back in my chair utterly confounded After a while the old gentleman went on more gently, "And now let me tell you that this pretended illness of the Baroness is in all probability nothing. Lady Adelheid always loses her head at the least little thing. If a rain-drop falls upon her nose, she screams, 'What fearful weather it is!'

"Unfortunately the noise penetrated to the old aunts, and they, in the midst of unseasonable floods of tears, put in an appearance armed with an entire arsenal of strengthening drops, elixirs of life, and the deuce knows what. A sharp fainting-fit" — The old gentleman checked himself; doubtless he observed the struggle that was going on within me. He took a few turns through the room; then again planting himself in front of me, he had a good hearty laugh and said, "Cousin, cousin, what nonsensical folly have you now got in your head? Ah well! I suppose it can't be helped; the devil is to play his pretty games here in divers sorts of ways. You have tumbled very nicely into his clutches, and now he's making you dance to a sweet tune," He again took a few turns up and down, and again went on, "It's no use to think of sleep now; and it occurred to me that we might have a pipe, and so spend the few hours that are left of the darkness and the night." With these words he took a clay pipe from the cupboard, and proceeded to fill it slowly and carefully, humming a song to himself; then he rummaged about amongst a heap of papers, until he found a sheet, which he picked out and rolled into a spill and lighted. Blowing the tobacco smoke from him in thick clouds, he said, speaking between his teeth, "Well, cousin, what was that story about the wolf?"

I know not how it was, but this calm, quiet behavior of the old gentleman operated strangely upon me. I seemed to be no longer in R–sitten, and the Baroness was so far, far distant from me that I could only reach her on the wings of thought. The old gentleman's last question, however, annoyed me. "But do you find my hunting exploit so amusing?" I broke in, — "so well fitted for banter?" "By no means," he rejoined, "by no means, cousin mine; but you've no idea what a comical face such a whipper-snapper as you cuts, and how ludicrously he acts as well, when Providence for once in a while honors him by putting him in the way to meet with something out of the usual run of things. I once had a college friend who was a quiet, sober fellow, and always on good terms with himself. By accident he became entangled in an affair of honor, — I say by accident, because he himself was never in any way aggressive; and although most of the fellows looked upon him as a poor thing, as a poltroon, he yet showed so much firm and resolute courage in this affair as greatly to excite everybody's admiration. But from that time onwards he was also completely changed. The sober and industrious youth became a bragging, insufferable bully. He was always drinking and rioting, and fighting about all sorts of childish trifles, until he was run through in a duel by the Senior* of

---

* The reference is to a *Landsmannschaft*. These were associations, at a university, of students from the same state or country, bound to the observance of certain traditional customs, &c, and under the control of certain self-elected officers (the *Senior* being one).

an exclusive corps. I merely tell you the story, cousin; you are at liberty to think what you please about it But to return to the Baroness and her illness" — At this moment light footsteps were heard in the hall; I fancied, too, there was an unearthly moaning in the air. "She is dead!" the thought shot through me like a fatal flash of lightning. The old gentleman quickly rose to his feet and called out, "Francis, Francis!" "Yes, my good Herr Justitiarius," he replied from without. "Francis," went on my uncle, "rake the fire together a bit in the grate, and if you can manage it, you had better make us a good cup or two of tea." "It is devilish cold," and he turned to me, "and I think we had better go and sit round the fire and talk a little." He opened the door, and I followed him mechanically. "How are things going on below?" he asked. "Oh!" replied Francis; "there was not much the matter. The Lady Baroness is all right again, and ascribes her bit of a fainting-fit to a bad dream." I was going to break out into an extravagant manifestation of joy and gladness, but a stern glance from my uncle kept me quiet "And yet, after all, I think it would be better if we lay down for an hour or two. You need not mind about the tea, Francis." "As you think well, Herr Justitiarius," replied Francis, and he left the room with the wish that we might have a good night's rest, albeit the cocks were already crowing. "See here, cousin," said the old gentleman, knocking the ashes out of his pipe on the grate, "I think, cousin, that it's a very good thing no harm has happened to you either from wolves or from loaded rifles." I now saw things in the right light, and was ashamed at myself to have thus given the old gentleman good grounds for treating me like a spoiled child.

Next morning he said to me, "Be so good as to step down, good cousin, and inquire how the Baroness is. You need only ask for Lady Adelheid; she will supply you with a full budget, I have no doubt" You may imagine how eagerly I hastened downstairs. But just as I was about to give a gentle knock at the door of the Baroness's anteroom, the Baron came hurriedly out of the same. He stood still in astonishment, and scrutinised me with a gloomy searching look. "What do you want here?" burst from his lips. Notwithstanding that my heart beat, I controlled myself and replied in a firm tone, "To

inquire on my uncle's behalf how my lady, the Baroness, is?"
"Oh! it was nothing — one of her usual nervous attacks. She
is now having a quiet sleep, and will, I am sure, make her
appearance at the dinner-table quite well and cheerful. Tell
him that — tell him that." This the Baron said with a certain
degree of passionate vehemence, which seemed to me to
imply that he was more concerned about the Baroness than
he was willing to show. I turned to go back to my uncle, when
the Baron suddenly seized my arm and said, whilst his eyes
flashed fire, "I have a word or two to say to you, young man."
Here I saw the deeply injured husband before me, and feared
there would be a scene which would perhaps end ignomini-
ously for me. I was unarmed; but at that moment I remembered I had in my pocket the ingeniously-made hunting-knife
which my uncle had presented to me after we got to R–sitten.
I now followed the Baron, who led the way rapidly, with the
determination not even to spare his life if I ran any risk of
being treated dishonorably.

We entered the Baron's own room, the door of which he
locked behind him. Now he began to pace restlessly backwards and forwards, with his arms folded one over the other;
then he stopped in front of me and repeated, "I have a word
or two to say to you, young man." I had wound myself up to
a pitch of most daring courage, and I replied, raising my
voice, "I hope they will be words which I may hear without
resentment." He stared hard at me in astonishment, as though
he had failed to understand me. Then, fixing his eyes gloomily upon the floor, he threw his arms behind his back, and
again began to stride up and down the room. He took down
a rifle and put the ramrod down the barrel to see whether it
were loaded or not. My blood boiled in my veins; grasping
my knife, I stepped close up to him, so as to make it impossible for him to take aim at me. "That's a handsome weapon,"
he said, replacing the rifle in the corner. I retired a few paces,
the Baron following me. Slapping me on the shoulder, perhaps a little more violently than was necessary, he said, "I
daresay I seem to you, Theodore, to be excited and irritable;
and I really am so, owing to the anxieties of a sleepless night.
My wife's nervous attack was not in the least dangerous; that
I now see plainly. But here — here in this castle, which is

haunted by an evil spirit, I always dread something terrible happening; and then it's the first time she has been ill here. And you — you alone were to blame for it." "How that can possibly be I have not the slightest conception," I replied calmly. "I wish," continued the Baron, "I wish that damned piece of mischief, my steward's wife's instrument, were chopped up into a thousand pieces, and that you — but no, no; it was to be so, it was inevitably to be so, and I alone am to blame for all. I ought to have told you, the moment you began to play music in my wife's room, of the whole state of the case, and to have informed you of my wife's temper of mind." I was about to speak; "Let me go on," said the Baron, "I must prevent your forming any rash judgment. You probably regard me as an uncultivated fellow, averse to the arts; but I am not so by any means. There is a particular consideration, however, based upon deep conviction, which constrains me to forbid the introduction here as far as possible of such music as can powerfully affect any person's mind, and to this I of course am no exception. Know that my wife suffers from a morbid excitability, which will finally destroy all the happiness of her life. Within these strange walls she is never quit of that strained overexcited condition, which at other times occurs but temporarily, and then generally as the forerunner of a serious illness. You will ask me, and quite reasonably too, why I do not spare my delicate wife the necessity of coming to live in this weird castle, and mix amongst the wild confusion of a hunting-party. Well, call it weakness — be it so; in a word, I cannot bring myself to leave her behind. I should be tortured by a thousand fears, and quite incapable of any serious business, for I am perfectly sure that I should be haunted everywhere, in the justice-hall as well as in the forest, by the most horrid ideas of all kinds of fatal mischief happening to her. And, on the other hand, I believe that the sort of life led here cannot fail to operate upon the weakly woman like strengthening chalybeate waters. By my soul, the sea-breezes, sweeping keenly after their peculiar fashion through the fir trees, and the deep baying of the hounds, and the merry ringing notes of our hunting-horns *must* get the better of all your sickly languishing sentimentalisings at the piano, which no man ought play in *that way*. I

tell you, you are deliberately torturing my wife to death."
These words he uttered with great emphasis, whilst his eyes
flashed with a restless fire. The blood mounted to my head;
I made a violent gesture against the Baron with my hand; I
was about to speak, but he cut me short.

"I know what you are going to say," he began, "I know
what you are going to say, and I repeat that you are going the
right road to kill my wife. But that you intended this I cannot
of course for a moment maintain; and yet you will understand that I must put a stop to the thing. In short, by your
playing and singing you work her up to a high pitch of
excitement, and then, when she drifts without anchor and
rudder on the boundless sea of dreams and visions and vague
aspirations which your music, like some vile charm, has
summoned into existence, you plunge her down into the
depths of horror with a tale about a fearful apparition which
you say came and played pranks with you up in the justice-
hall. Your great-uncle has told me everything; but, pray, repeat
to me all you saw, or did not see, heard, felt, divined by
instinct."

I braced myself up and narrated calmly how everything
had happened from beginning to end, the Baron merely
interposing at intervals a few words expressive of his
astonishment. When I came to the part where my old uncle
had met the ghost with trustful courage and had exorcised
him with a few powerful words, the Baron clasped his hands,
raised them folded towards Heaven, and said with deep
emotion, "Yes, he is the guardian-angel of the family. His
mortal remains shall rest in the vault of my ancestors." When
I finished my narration, the Baron murmured to himself,
"Daniel, Daniel, what are you doing here at this hour?" as he
folded his arms and strode up and down the room. "And was
that all, Herr Baron?" I asked, making a movement as though
I would retire. Starting up as if out of a dream, the Baron
took me kindly by the hand and said, "Yes, my good friend,
my wife, whom you have dealt so hardly by without intending
it — you must cure her again; you alone can do so." I felt I
was blushing, and had I stood opposite a mirror should
undoubtedly have seen in it a very blank and absurd face. The
Baron seemed to exult in my embarrassment; he kept his eyes

fixed intently upon my face, smiling with perfectly galling irony. "How in the world can I cure her?" I managed to stammer out at length with an effort "Well," he said, interrupting me, "you have no dangerous patient to deal with at any rate. I now make an express claim upon your skill. Since the Baroness has been drawn into the enchanted circle of your music, it would be both foolish and cruel to drag her out of it all of a sudden. Go on with your music therefore. You will always be welcome during the evening hours in my wife's apartments. But gradually select a more energetic kind of music, and effect a clever alternation of the cheerful sort with the serious; and above all things, repeat your story of the fearful ghost very very often. The Baroness will grow familiar with it; she will forget that a ghost haunts this castle; and the story will have no stronger effect upon her than any other tale of enchantment which is put before her in a romance or a ghost-story book. Pray, do this, my good friend." With these words the Baron left me. I went away. I felt as if I were annihilated, to be thus humiliated to the level of a foolish and insignificant child. Fool that I was to suppose that jealousy was stirring his heart! He himself sends me to Seraphina; he sees in me only the blind instrument which, after he has made use of it, he can throw away if he thinks well. A few minutes previously I had really feared the Baron; deep down within my heart lurked the consciousness of guilt; but it was a consciousness which allowed me to feel distinctly the beauty of the higher life for which I was ripe. Now all had disappeared in the blackness of night; and I saw only the stupid boy who in childish obstinacy had persisted in taking the paper crown which he had put on his hot temples for a real golden one. I hurried away to my uncle, who was waiting for me. "Well, cousin, why have you been so long? Where have you been staying?" he cried as soon as he saw me. "I have been having some words with the Baron!" I quickly replied, carelessly and in a low voice, without being able to look at the old gentleman. "God damn it all," said he, feigning astonishment "Good gracious, boy! that's just what I thought. I suppose the Baron has challenged you, cousin?" The ringing peal of laughter which the old gentleman immediately afterwards broke out into taught me that this time too, as always, he had seen me through and through. I bit my lip, and durst not speak a word, for I knew very well that it would only be the signal for the old gentleman to overwhelm me beneath the torrent of teasing which was already hovering on the tip of his tongue.

The Baroness appeared at the dinner-table in an elegant morning-robe, the dazzling whiteness of which exceeded that of fresh-fallen snow. She looked worn and low-spirited; but she began to speak in her soft and melodious accents, and on raising her dark eyes there shone a sweet and yearning look full of aspiration in their voluptuous glow, and a fugitive blush flitted across her lily-white cheeks. She was more beautiful than ever. But who can fathom the follies of a young man who has got too hot blood in his head and heart? The bitter pique which the Baron had stirred up within me I transferred to the Baroness. The entire business seemed to me like a foul mystification; and I would now show that I was possessed of alarmingly good common-sense and also of extraordinary sagacity. Like a petulant child, I shunned the Baroness and escaped Adelheid when she pursued me, and found a place where I wished, right at the bottom end of the table between the two officers, with whom I began to carouse right merrily. We kept our glasses going gaily during dessert, and I was, as so frequently is the case in moods like mine, extremely noisy and loud in my joviality. A servant brought me a plate with some bonbons on it, with the words, "From Lady Adelheid." I took them; and observed on one of them, scribbled in pencil, "and Seraphina." My blood coursed tumultuously in my veins. I sent a glance in Adelheid's direction, which she met with a most sly and archly cunning look; and taking her glass in her hand, she gave me a slight nod. Almost mechanically I murmured to myself, "Seraphina!" then taking up my glass in my turn, I drained it at a single draft. My glance fell across in *her* direction; I perceived that she also had drunk at the very same moment and was setting down her glass. Our eyes met, and a malignant demon whispered in my ear, "Unhappy wretch, she does love you!" One of the guests now rose, and, in conformity with the custom of the North, proposed the health of the lady of the house. Our glasses rang in the midst of a tumult of joy. My heart was torn with rapture and despair; the wine burned like fire within me; everything spun round in circles; I felt as if I must hasten and throw myself at her feet and there sigh out my life. "What's the matter with you, my friend?" asked my neighbor, thus recalling me to myself; but Seraphina had left the hall. We rose from the table. I was making for the door, but Adelheid held me fast, and began to talk about divers matters; I neither heard nor understood a single word. She grasped both my hands and, laughing, shouted something in my ear. I remained dumb and motionless, as though affected by catalepsy. All I remember is that I finally took a glass of liqueur out of Adelheid's hand in a mechanical way and drank it off, and then I recollect being alone in a window, and after that I rushed out of the hall, down the stairs, and ran out into the wood. The snow was falling in thick flakes; the fir trees were moaning as they waved to and fro in the wind. Like a maniac I ran round and round in wide circles, laughing and screaming loudly, "Look, look and see. Aha! Aha! The devil is having a fine dance with the boy who thought he would taste of strictly forbidden fruit!" Who can tell what would have been the end of my mad prank if I had not heard my name called loudly from the outside of the wood? The storm had abated; the moon shone out brightly through the broken clouds; I heard dogs barking, and perceived a dark figure approaching me. It was the old man Francis. "Why, why, my good Herr Theodore," he began, "you have quite lost your way in the rough snowstorm. The Herr Justitiarius is awaiting you with much impatience." I followed the old man in silence. I found my great-uncle working in the justice-hall. "You have done well," he cried, on seeing me, "you have done a very wise thing to go out in the open air a little and get cool. But don't drink quite so much wine; you are far too young, and it's not good for you."

I did not utter a word in reply, and also took my place at the table in silence. "But now tell me, good cousin, what it was the Baron really wanted you for?" I told him all, and concluded by stating that I would not lend myself for the doubtful cure which the Baron had proposed. "And it would not be practicable," the old gentleman interrupted, "for tomorrow morning early we set off home, cousin." And so it was that I never saw Seraphina again.

As soon as we arrived in K—— my old uncle complained that he felt the effects of the wearying journey this time more than ever. His moody silence, broken only by violent outbreaks of the worst possible ill-humor, announced the return of his attacks of gout. One day I was suddenly called in; I found the old gentleman confined to his bed and unable to speak, suffering from a paralytic stroke. He held a letter in his hand, which he had crumpled up tightly in a spasmodic fit. I recognized the hand-writing of the land-steward of R–sitten; but, quite upset by my trouble, I did not venture to take the letter out of the old gentleman's hand. I did not doubt that his end was near. But his pulse began to beat again, even before the physician arrived; the old gentleman's remarkably tough constitution resisted the mortal attack, although he was in his seventieth year. That selfsame day the doctor pronounced him out of danger.

We had a more severe winter than usual; this was followed by a rough and stormy spring; and hence it was more the gout — a consequence of the inclemency of the season — than his previous accident which kept him for a long time confined to his bed. During this period he made up his mind to retire altogether from all kinds of business. He transferred his office of Justitiarius to others; and so I was cut off from all hope of ever again going to R–sitten. The old gentleman would allow no one to attend him but me; and it was to me alone that he looked for all amusement and every cheerful diversion. And though, in the hours when he was free from pain, his good spirits returned, and he had no lack of broad jests, even making mention of hunting exploits, so that I fully expected every minute to hear him make a butt of my heroic deed, when I had killed the wolf with my whinger, yet never once did he allude to our visit to R–sitten, and as may well be imagined, I was very careful, from natural shyness, not to lead him directly up to the subject. My harassing anxiety and continual attendance upon the old gentleman had thrust Seraphina's image into the background. But as soon as his sickness abated somewhat, my thoughts returned with more liveliness to that moment in the Baroness's room, which I now looked upon as a star — a bright star — that had set, for me at least, forever. An occurrence which now happened, by making me shudder with an ice-cold thrill as at sight of a visitant from the world of spirits, revived all the pain I had formerly felt. One evening, as I was opening the pocketbook which I had carried whilst at R-sitten, there fell out of the papers I was unfolding a dark curl, wrapped about with a white ribbon; I immediately recognized it as Seraphina's hair. But, on examining the ribbon more closely, I distinctly perceived the mark of a spot of blood on it! Perhaps Adelheid had skillfully contrived to secrete it about me during the moments of conscious insanity by which I had been affected during the last days of our visit; but why was the spot of blood there? It excited forebodings of something terrible in my mind, and almost converted this too pastoral love-token into an awful admonition, pointing to a passion which might entail the expenditure of precious blood. It was the same white ribbon that had fluttered about me in light wanton sportiveness as it were the first time I sat near Seraphina, and which Mysterious Night had stamped as an emblem of mortal injury. Boys ought not to play with weapons with the dangerous properties of which they are not familiar.

At last the storms of spring had ceased to bluster, and summer asserted her rights; and if the cold had formerly been unbearable, so now too was the heat when July came in. The old gentleman visibly gathered strength, and following his usual custom, went out to a garden in the suburbs. One still, warm evening, as we sat in the sweet-smelling jasmine arbor, he was in unusually good spirits, and not, as was generally the case, overflowing with sarcasm and irony, but in a gentle and almost soft and melting mood. "Cousin," he began, "I don't know how it is, but I feel so nice and warm and comfortable all over today; I have not felt like it for many years. I believe it is an augury that I shall die soon." I exerted myself to drive these gloomy thoughts from his mind. "Never mind, cousin," he said, "in any case I'm not long for this world; and so I will now discharge a debt I owe you. Do you still remember our autumn in R-sitten?" This question thrilled through me like a lightning-flash, so before I was able to make any reply he continued, "It was Heaven's will that your entrance into that castle should be signalised by memorable circumstances, and that you should become involved against your own will in the deepest secrets of the house. The time has now come when you must learn all. We have often enough talked about things which you, cousin, rather dimly guessed at than really understood. In the alternation of the seasons nature represents symbolically the cycle of human life. That is a trite remark; but I interpret it differently from everybody else. The dews of spring fall, summer's vapors fade away, and it is the pure atmosphere of autumn which clearly reveals the distant landscape, and then finally earthly existence is swallowed in the night of winter. I mean that the government of the Power Inscrutable is more plainly revealed in the clear-sightedness of old age. It is granted glimpses of the promised land, the pilgrimage to which begins with the death on earth. How clearly do I see at this moment the dark destiny of that house, to which I am knit by firmer ties than blood relationship can weave! Everything lies disclosed to the eyes of my spirit. And yet the things which I now see, in the form in which I see them — the essential substance of them, that is — this I cannot tell you in words; for no man's tongue is able to do so. But listen, my son, I will tell you as well as I am able, and do you think it is some remarkable story that might really happen; and lay up carefully in your soul the knowledge that the mysterious relations into which you ventured to enter, not perhaps without being summoned, might have ended in your destruction — but — that's all over now."

The history of the R—— entail, which my old uncle told me, I retain so faithfully in my memory even now that I can almost repeat it in his own words (he spoke of himself in the third person).

One stormy night in the autumn of 1760 the servants of R-sitten were startled out of the midst of their sleep by a terrific crash, as if the whole of the spacious castle had tumbled into a thousand pieces. In a moment everybody was on his legs; lights were lit; the house-steward, his face deadly pale with fright and terror, came up panting with his keys; but as they proceeded through the passages and halls and rooms, suite after suite, and found all safe, and heard in the appalling silence nothing except the creaking rattle of the locks, which occasioned some difficulty in opening, and the ghostlike echo of their own footsteps, they began one and all to be utterly astounded. Nowhere was there the least trace of damage. The old house-steward was impressed by an ominous feeling of apprehension. He went up into the great Knight's Hall, which had a small cabinet adjoining where Freiherr Roderick von R—— used to sleep when engaged in making his astronomical observations. Between the door of this cabinet and that of a second was a postern, leading through a narrow passage immediately into the astronomical tower. But directly Daniel (that was the house-steward's name) opened this postern, the storm, blustering and howling terrifically, drove a heap of rubbish and broken pieces of stones all over him, which made him recoil in terror; and, dropping the candles, which went out with a hiss on the floor, he screamed, "O God! O God! The Baron! he's miserably dashed to pieces!" At the same moment he heard sounds of lamentation proceeding from the Freiherr's sleeping-cabinet, and on entering it he saw the servants gathered around their master's corpse. They had found him fully dressed and more magnificently than on any previous occasion, and with a calm earnest look upon his unchanged countenance, sitting in his large and richly decorated armchair as though resting after severe study. But his rest was the rest of death. When day dawned it was seen that the crowning turret of the tower had fallen in. The huge square stones had broken through the ceiling and floor of the observatory-room, and then, carrying down in front of them a powerful beam that ran across the tower, they had dashed in with redoubled impetus the lower vaulted roof, and dragged down a portion of the castle walls and of the narrow connecting-passage. Not a single step could be taken beyond the postern threshold without risk of falling at least eighty feet into a deep chasm.

The old Freiherr had foreseen the very hour of his death, and had sent intelligence of it to his sons. Hence it happened that the very next day saw the arrival of Wolfgang, Freiherr von R——, eldest son of the deceased, and now lord of the entail. Relying confidently upon the probable truth of the old man's foreboding, he had left Vienna, which city he chanced to have reached in his travels, immediately he re-

ceived the ominous letter, and hastened to R–sitten as fast as
he could travel. The house-steward had draped the great hall
in black, and had had the old Freiherr laid out in the clothes
in which he had been found, on a magnificent state-bed, and
this he had surrounded with tall silver candlesticks with
burning wax-candles. Wolfgang ascended the stairs, entered
the hall, and approached close to his father's corpse, without
speaking a word. There he stood with his arms folded on his
chest, gazing with a fixed and gloomy look and with knitted
brows, into his father's pale countenance. He was like a statue;
not a tear came from his eyes. At length, with an almost
convulsive movement of the right arm towards the corpse,
he murmured hoarsely, "Did the stars compel you to make
the son whom you loved miserable?" Throwing his hands
behind his back and stepping a short pace backwards, the
Baron raised his eyes upwards and said in a low and well-nigh
broken voice, "Poor, infatuated old man! Your carnival farce
with its shallow delusions is now over. Now you no doubt
see that the possessions which are so niggardly dealt out to
us here on earth have nothing in common with Hereafter
beyond the stars. What will — what power can reach over
beyond the grave?" The Baron was silent again for some
seconds, then he cried passionately, "No, your perversity shall
not rob me of a grain of my earthly happiness, which you
strove so hard to destroy," and therewith he took a folded
paper out of his pocket and held it up between two fingers
to one of the burning candles that stood close beside the
corpse. The paper was caught by the flame and blazed up
high; and as the reflection flickered and played upon the face
of the corpse, it was as though its muscles moved and as
though the old man uttered toneless words, so that the
servants who stood some distance off were filled with great
horror and awe. The Baron calmly finished what he was doing
by carefully stamping out with his foot the last fragment of
paper that fell on the floor blazing. Then, casting yet another
moody glance upon his father, he hurriedly left the hall.

On the following day Daniel reported to the Freiherr the
damage that had been done to the tower, and described at
great length all that had taken place on the night when their
dear dead master died; and he concluded by saying that it

would be a very wise thing to have the tower repaired at once, for, if a further fall were to take place, there would be some danger of the whole castle — well, if not tumbling down, at any rate suffering serious damage.

"Repair the tower?" the Freiherr interrupted the old servant curtly, whilst his eyes flashed with anger, "Repair the tower? Never, never! Don't you see, old man," he went on more calmly, "don't you see that the tower could not fall in this way without some special cause? How if it was my father's own wish that the place where he carried on his unhallowed astrological labors should be destroyed — how if he had himself made certain preparations by which he was enabled to bring down the turret whenever he pleased and so occasion the ruin of the interior of the tower! But be that as it may. And if the whole castle tumbles down, I shan't care; I shall be glad. Do you imagine I am going to dwell in this weird owls' nest? No; my wise ancestor who had the foundations of a new castle laid in the beautiful valley yonder — he has begun a work which I intend to finish." Daniel said crestfallen, "Then will all your faithful old servants have to take up their bundles and go?" "That I am not going to be waited upon by helpless, weak-kneed old fellows like you is quite certain; but for all that I shall turn none away. You may all enjoy the bread of charity without working for it." "And am I," cried the old man, greatly hurt, "am I, the house-steward, to be forced to lead such a life of inactivity?" Then the Freiherr, who had turned his back upon the old man and was about to leave the room, wheeled suddenly round, his face perfectly ablaze with passion, strode up to the old man as he stretched out his doubled fist towards him, and shouted in a thundering voice, "You, you hypocritical old villain, it's you who helped my old father in his unearthly practices up yonder; you lay upon his heart like a vampire; and perhaps it was you who basely took advantage of the old man's mad folly to plant in his mind those diabolical ideas which brought me to the brink of ruin. I ought, I tell you, to kick you out like a mangy cur." The old man was so terrified at these harsh terrible words that he threw himself upon his knees beside the Freiherr; but the Baron, as he spoke these last words, threw forward his right foot, perhaps quite unintentionally (as is frequently the case in anger, when the body mechanically obeys the mind, and what is in the thought is imitatively realized in action) and hit the old man so hard on the chest that he rolled over with a stifled scream. Rising painfully to his feet and uttering a most singular sound, like the howling whimper of an animal wounded to death, he looked the Freiherr through and through with a look that glared with mingled rage and despair. The purse of money which the Freiherr threw down as he went out of the room, the old man left lying on the floor where it fell.

Meanwhile all the nearest relatives of the family who lived in the neighborhood had arrived, and the old Freiherr was interred with much pomp in the family vault in the church at R–sitten; and now, after the invited guests had departed, the new lord of the entail appeared to shake off his gloomy mood, and to be prepared to duly enjoy the property that had fallen to him. Along with V——, the old Freiherr's Justitiarius, who won his full confidence in the very first interview they had, and who was at once confirmed in his office, the Baron made an exact calculation of his sources of income, and considered how large a part he could devote to making improvements and how large a part to building a new castle. V—— was of opinion that the old Freiherr could not possibly have spent all his income every year, and that there must certainly be money concealed somewhere, since he had found nothing amongst his papers except one or two bank-notes for insignificant sums, and the ready-money in the iron safe was but very little more than a thousand thalers, or about £150. Who would be so likely to know anything about it as Daniel, who in his obstinate self-willed way was perhaps only waiting to be asked about it? The Baron was now not a little concerned at the thought that Daniel, whom he had so grossly insulted, might let large sums molder somewhere sooner than discover them to him, not so much, of course, from any motives of self-interest, — for of what use could even the largest sum of money be to him, a childless old man, whose only wish was to end his days in the castle of R–sitten? — as from a desire to take vengeance for the affront put upon him. He gave V—— a circumstantial account of the entire scene with Daniel, and concluded by saying that from several items of information communicated to him he had learned that it was Daniel alone who had contrived to nourish in the old Freiherr's mind such an inexplicable aversion to ever seeing his sons in R–sitten. The Justitiarius declared that this information was perfectly false, since there was not a human creature on the face of the earth who would have been able to guide the Freiherr's thoughts in any way, far less determine them for him; and he undertook finally to draw from Daniel the secret, if he had one, as to the place in which they would be likely to find money concealed. His task proved far easier than he had anticipated, for no sooner did he begin, "But how comes it, Daniel, that your old master has left so little ready-money?" than Daniel replied, with a repulsive smile, "Do you mean the few trifling thalers, Herr Justitiarius, which you found in the little strongbox? Oh! the rest is lying in the vault beside our gracious master's sleeping-cabinet. But the best," he went on to say, whilst his smile passed over into an abominable grin, and his eyes flashed with malicious fire, "but the best of all — several thousand gold pieces — lies buried at the bottom of the chasm beneath the ruins." The Justitiarius at once summoned the Freiherr; they proceeded there, and then into the sleeping-cabinet, where Daniel pushed aside the wainscot in one of the corners, and a small lock became visible. Whilst the Freiherr was regarding the polished lock with covetous eyes, and making preparations to try and unlock it with the keys of the great bunch which he dragged with some difficulty out of his pocket, Daniel drew himself up to his full height, and looked down with almost malignant pride upon his master, who had now stooped down in order to see the lock better. Daniel's face was deadly pale, and he said, his voice trembling, "If I am a dog, my lord Freiherr, I have also at least a dog's fidelity." Therewith he held out a bright steel key to his master, who greedily snatched it out of his hand, and with it he easily succeeded in opening the door.

They stepped into a small and low-vaulted apartment, in which stood a large iron coffer with the lid open, containing many money-bags, upon which lay a strip of parchment, written in the old Freiherr's familiar handwriting, large and old-fashioned.

One hundred and fifty thousand Imperial thalers in old *Fredericks d'or*,* money saved from the revenues of the estate-tail of R–sitten; this sum has been set aside for the building of the castle. Further, the lord of the entail who succeeds me in the possession of this money shall, upon the highest hill situated eastward from the old tower of the castle (which he will find in ruins), erect a high beacon tower for the benefit of mariners, and cause a fire to be kindled on it every night. R–sitten, on Michaelmas Eve of the year 1760.

RODERICK, FREIHERR VON R.

The Freiherr lifted up the bags one after the other and let them fall again into the coffer, delighted at the ringing clink of so much gold coin; then he turned round abruptly to the old house-steward, thanked him for the fidelity he had shown, and assured him that they were only vile tattling calumnies which had induced him to treat him so harshly in the first instance. He should not only remain in the castle, but should also continue to discharge his duties, uncurtailed in any way, as house-steward, and at double the wages he was then having. "I owe you a large compensation; if you will take money, help yourself to one of these bags." As he concluded with these words, the Baron stood before the old man, with his eyes bent upon the ground, and pointed to the coffer; then, approaching it again, he once more ran his eyes over the bags. A burning flush suddenly mounted into the old house-steward's cheeks, and he uttered that awful howling whimper — a noise as of an animal wounded to death, according to the Freiherr's previous description of it to the Justitiarius. The latter shuddered, for the words which the old man murmured between his teeth sounded like, "Blood for gold." Of all this the Freiherr, absorbed in the contemplation of the treasure before him, had heard not the least. Daniel tottered in every limb, as if shaken by an ague fit; approaching the Freiherr with bowed head in a humble attitude, he kissed his hand, and

---

* Imperial thalers varied in value at different times, but estimating their value at three shillings, the sum here mentioned would be equivalent to about £22,500. A *Frederick d'or* was a gold coin worth five thalers.

drawing his handkerchief across his eyes under the pretence of wiping away his tears, said in a whining voice, "Alas! my good and gracious master, what am I, a poor childless old man, to do with money? But the doubled wages I accept with gladness, and will continue to do my duty faithfully and zealously."

The Freiherr, who had paid no particular heed to the old man's words, now let the heavy lid of the coffer fall to with a bang, so that the whole room shook and cracked, and then, locking the coffer and carefully withdrawing the key, he said carelessly, "Very well, very well, old man." But after they entered the hall he went on talking to Daniel, "But you said something about a quantity of gold pieces buried underneath the ruins of the tower?" Silently the old man stepped towards the postern, and after some difficulty unlocked it. But so soon as he threw it open the storm drove a thick mass of snowflakes into the hall; a raven was disturbed and flew in croaking and screaming and dashed with its black wings against the window, but regaining the open postern it disappeared downwards into the chasm. The Freiherr stepped out into the corridor; but one single glance downwards, and he started back trembling. "A fearful sight! – I'm giddy!" he stammered as he sank almost fainting into the Justitiarius' arms. But quickly recovering himself by an effort, he fixed a sharp look upon the old man and asked, "Down there, you say?" Meanwhile the old man had been locking the postern, and was now leaning against it with all his bodily strength, and was gasping and grunting to get the great key out of the rusty lock. This at last accomplished, he turned round to the Baron, and, changing the huge key about backwards and forwards in his hands, replied with a peculiar smile, "Yes, there are thousands and thousands down there – all my dear dead master's beautiful instruments – telescopes, quadrants, globes, dark mirrors, they all lie smashed to atoms underneath the ruins between the stones and the big balk." "But money – coined money," interrupted the Baron, "you spoke of gold pieces, old man?" "I only meant things which had cost several thousand gold pieces," he replied; and not another word could be got out of him.

The Baron appeared highly delighted to have all at once come into possession of all the means requisite for carrying out his favorite plan, namely, that of building a new and magnificent castle. The Justitiarius indeed stated it as his opinion that, according to the will of the deceased, the money could only be applied to the repair and complete finishing of the interior of the old castle, and further, any new erection would hardly succeed in equaling the commanding size and the severe and simple character of the old ancestral castle. The Freiherr, however, persisted in his intention, and maintained that in the disposal of property respecting which nothing was stated in the deeds of the entail the irregular will of the deceased could have no validity. He at the same time led V—— to understand that he should conceive it to be his duty to embellish R–sitten as far as the climate, soil, and environs would permit, for it was his intention to bring home shortly as his dearly loved wife a lady who was in every respect worthy of the greatest sacrifices.

The air of mystery with which the Freiherr spoke of this alliance, which possibly had been already consummated in secret, cut short all further questions from the side of the Justitiarius. Nevertheless he found in it to some extent a redeeming feature, for the Freiherr's eager grasping after riches now appeared to be due not so much to avarice strictly speaking as to the desire to make one dear to him forget the more beautiful country she was relinquishing for his sake. Otherwise he could not acquit the Baron of being avaricious, or at any rate insufferably close-fisted, seeing that, even though rolling in money and even when gloating over the old *Fredericks d'or,* he could not help bursting out with the peevish grumble, "I know the old rascal has concealed from us the greatest part of his wealth, but next spring I will have the ruins of the tower turned over under my own eyes."

The Freiherr had architects come, and discussed with them at great length what would be the most convenient way to proceed with his castle-building. He rejected one drawing after another; in none of them was the style of architecture sufficiently rich and grandiose. He now began to draw plans himself, and, inspirited by this employment, which constantly placed before his eyes a sunny picture of the happiest future, brought himself into such a genial humor that it often bordered on wild exuberance of spirits, and even communicated itself to all about him. His generosity and profuse hospitality belied all imputations of avarice at any rate. Daniel also seemed to have now forgotten the insult that had been put upon him. Towards the Freiherr, although often followed by him with mistrustful eyes on account of the treasure buried in the chasm, his bearing was both quiet and humble. But what struck everybody as extraordinary was that the old man appeared to grow younger from day to day. Possibly this might be, because he had begun to forget his grief for his old master, which had stricken him sore, and possibly also because he had not now, as he once had, to spend the cold nights in the tower without sleep, and got better food and good wine such as he liked; but whatever the cause might be, the old greybeard seemed to be growing into a vigorous man with red cheeks and well-nourished body, who could walk firmly and laugh loudly whenever he heard a jest to laugh at.

The pleasant tenor of life at R–sitten was disturbed by the arrival of a man whom one would have judged to be quite in his element there. This was Wolfgang's younger brother Hubert, at the sight of whom Wolfgang had screamed out, with his face as pale as a corpse's, "Unhappy wretch, what do you want here?" Hubert threw himself into his brother's arms, but Wolfgang took him and led him away up to a retired room, where he locked himself in with him. They remained closeted several hours, at the end of which time Hubert came down, greatly agitated, and called for his horses. The Justitiarius intercepted him; Hubert tried to pass him; but V——, inspired by the hope that he might perhaps stifle in the bud what might else end in a bitter life-long quarrel between the brothers, besought him to stay, at least a few hours, and at the same moment the Freiherr came down calling, "Stay here, Hubert! you will think better of it." Hubert's countenance cleared up; he assumed an air of composure, and quickly pulling off his costly fur coat, and throwing it to a servant behind him, he grasped V——'s hand and went with him into the room, saying with a scornful smile, "So the lord of the entail will tolerate my presence here, it seems." V—— thought that the unfortunate misunderstanding would assuredly be smoothed away now, for it was only separation and existence apart from each other that would, he conceived, be able to foster it. Hubert took up the steel tongs which stood near the fire-grate, and as he proceeded to break up a knotty piece of wood that would only sweal, not burn, and to rake the fire together better, he said to V——, "You see what a good-natured fellow I am, Herr Justitiarius, and that I am skillful in all domestic matters. But Wolfgang is full of the most extraordinary prejudices, and – a bit of a miser." V—— did not deem it advisable to attempt to fathom further the relations between the brothers, especially as Wolfgang's face and conduct and voice plainly showed that he was shaken to the very depths of his nature by diverse violent passions.

Late in the evening V—— had occasion to go up to the Freiherr's room in order to learn his decision about some matter or other connected with the estate-tail. He found him pacing up and down the room with long strides, his arms crossed on his back, and much perturbation in his manner. On perceiving the Justitiarius he stood still, and then, taking him by both hands and looking him gloomily in the face, he said in a broken voice, "My brother is come. I know what you are going to say," he proceeded almost before V—— had opened his mouth to put a question. "Unfortunately you know nothing. You don't know that my unfortunate brother – yes, I will not call him anything worse than unfortunate – that, like a spirit of evil, he crosses my path everywhere, ruining my peace of mind. It is not his fault that I have not been made unspeakably miserable; he did his best to make me so, but Heaven willed it otherwise. Ever since he has known of the conversion of the property into an entail, he has persecuted me with deadly hatred. He envies me this property, which in his hands would only be scattered like chaff. He is the wildest spendthrift I ever heard of. His load of debt exceeds by a long way the half of the unentailed property in Courland that fell to him, and now, pursued by his creditors, who fail not to worry him for payment, he hurries here to me to beg for money." "And you, his brother, refuse to give him any?" V—— was about to interrupt him; but the Freiherr, letting V——'s hands fall, and taking a long step backwards, went on in a loud and vehement tone. "Stop! yes; I refuse. I neither can nor will give away a single thaler of the revenues of the entail. But listen, and I will tell you what was the proposal which I made the insane fellow a few hours ago, and made in vain, and then pass judgment upon the feelings of duty by which I am actuated. Our unentailed possessions in Courland are, as you are aware, considerable; the half that falls to me I am willing to renounce, but in favor of his family. For Hubert has married, in Courland, a beautiful lady, but poor. She and the children she has borne him are starving. The estates should be put under trust; sufficient should be set aside out of the revenues to support him, and his creditors be paid by arrangement. But what does he care for a quiet life — a life free of anxiety? — what does he care for wife and child? Money, ready-money, and large quantities, is what he will have, that he may squander it in infamous folly. Some demon has made him acquainted with the secret of the hundred and fifty thousand thalers, half of which he in his mad way demands, maintaining that this money is movable property and quite apart from the entailed portion. This, however, I must and will refuse him, but the feeling haunts me that he is plotting my destruction in his heart."

No matter how great the efforts which V—— made to persuade the Freiherr out of this suspicion against his brother, in which, of course, not being initiated into the more circumstantial details of the disagreement, he could only appeal to broad and somewhat superficial moral principles, he yet could not boast of the smallest success. The Freiherr commissioned him to treat with his hostile and avaricious brother Hubert. V—— proceeded to do so with all the circumspection he was master of, and was not a little gratified when Hubert at length declared, "Be it so then; I will accept my brother's proposals, but upon condition that he will now, since I am on the point of losing both my honor and my good name forever through the severity of my creditors, make me an advance of a thousand *Fredericks d'or* in hard cash, and further grant that in time to come I may take up my residence, at least for a short time occasionally, in our beautiful R-sitten, along with my good brother." "Never, never!" exclaimed the Freiherr violently, when V—— laid his brother's amended

counter-proposals before him. "I will never consent that
Hubert stay in my house even a single minute after I have
brought home my wife. Go, my good friend, tell this mar-
peace that he shall have two thousand *Fredericks d'or,* not as
an advance, but as a gift — only, bid him go, bid him go."
V—— now learned at one and the same time that the ground
of the quarrel between the two brothers must be sought for
in this marriage. Hubert listened to the Justitiarius proudly
and calmly, and when he finished speaking replied in a hoarse
and hollow tone, "I will think it over; but for the present I
shall stay a few days in the castle." V—— exerted himself to
prove to the discontented Hubert that the Freiherr, by making
over his share of their unentailed property, was really doing
all he possibly could do to indemnify him, and that on the
whole he had no cause for complaint against his brother,
although at the same time he admitted that all institutions
of the nature of primogeniture, which vested such prepon-
derant advantages in the eldest-born to the prejudice of the
remaining children, were in many respects hateful. Hubert
tore his waistcoat open from top to bottom like a man whose
breast was cramped and he wanted to relieve it by fresh air.
Thrusting one hand into his open shirt-frill and planting the
other in his side, he spun round on one foot in a quick
pirouette and cried in a sharp voice, "Pshaw! What is hateful
is born of hatred." Then bursting out into a shrill fit of
laughter, he said, "What condescension my lord of the entail
shows in being thus willing to throw his gold pieces to the
poor beggar!" V—— saw plainly that all idea of a complete
reconciliation between the brothers was quite out of the
question.

To the Freiherr's annoyance, Hubert established himself in
the rooms that had been appointed for him in one of the
side wings of the castle as if with the view to a very long stay.
He was observed to hold frequent and long conversations
with the house-steward; nay, the latter was sometimes even
seen to accompany him when he went out wolf-hunting.
Otherwise he was very little seen, and studiously avoided
meeting his brother alone, at which the latter was very glad.
V—— felt how strained and unpleasant this state of things
was, and was obliged to confess to himself that the peculiar

uneasiness which marked all that Hubert both said and did was such as to destroy intentionally and effectually all the pleasure of the place. He now perfectly understood why the Freiherr had manifested so much alarm on seeing his brother.

One day as V—— was sitting by himself in the justice-room amongst his law-papers, Hubert came in with a grave and more composed manner than usual, and said in a voice that bordered upon melancholy, "I will accept my brother's last proposals. If you will contrive that I have the two thousand *Fredericks d'or* today, I will leave the castle this very night – on horseback – alone." "With the money?" asked V——. "You are right," replied Hubert; "I know what you would say – the weight! Give it me in bills on Isaac Lazarus of K——. For to K—— I am going this very night. Something is driving me away from this place. The old fellow has bewitched it with evil spirits." "Do you mean your father, Herr Baron?" asked V—— sternly. Hubert's lips trembled; he had to cling to the chair to keep from falling; but then suddenly recovering himself, he cried, "Today then, please, Herr Justitiarius," and staggered to the door, not, however, without some exertion. "He now sees that no deceptions are any longer of avail, that he can do nothing against my firm will," said the Freiherr whilst drawing up the bills on Isaac Lazarus in K——. A burden was lifted off his heart by the departure of his inimical brother; and for a long time he had not been in such cheerful spirits as he was at supper. Hubert had sent his excuses; and there was not one who regretted his absence.

The room which V—— occupied was somewhat retired, and its windows looked upon the castle-yard. In the night he was suddenly startled up out of his sleep, and was under the impression that he had been awakened by a distant and pitiable moan. But listen as he would, all remained still as the grave, and so he was obliged to conclude that the sound which had fallen upon his ears was the delusion of a dream. But at the same time he was seized with such a peculiar feeling of breathless anxiety and terror that he could not stay in bed. He got up and approached the window. It was not long, however, before the castle door was opened, and a figure with a blazing torch came out of the castle and went across the courtyard. V—— recognized the figure as that of old Daniel, and saw him open the stable-door and go in, and soon afterwards bring out a saddle horse. Now a second figure came into view out of the darkness, well wrapped in furs, and with a fox-skin cap on his head. V—— perceived that it was Hubert; but after he had spoken excitedly with Daniel for some minutes, he returned into the castle. Daniel led back the horse into the stable and locked the door, and also that of the castle, after he had returned across the courtyard in the same way in which he crossed it before. It was evident Hubert had intended to go away on horseback, but had suddenly changed his mind; and no less evident was it that there was a dangerous understanding of some sort between Hubert and the old house-steward. V—— looked forward to the morning with burning impatience; he would acquaint the Freiherr with the occurrences of the night. Really it was now time to take precautionary measures against the attacks of Hubert's malice, which V—— was now convinced, had been betrayed in his agitated behavior of the day before.

Next morning, at the hour when the Freiherr was in the habit of rising, V—— heard people running backwards and forwards, doors opened and slammed to, and a tumultuous confusion of voices talking and shouting. On going out of his room he met servants everywhere, who, without heeding him, ran past him with ghastly pale faces, upstairs, downstairs, in and out the rooms. At length he ascertained that the Freiherr was missing, and that they had been looking for him for hours in vain. As he had gone to bed in the presence of his personal attendant, he must have afterwards got up and gone away somewhere in his dressing gown and slippers, taking the large candlestick with him, for these articles were also missed. V——, his mind agitated with dark forebodings, ran up to the ill-fated hall, the cabinet adjoining which Wolfgang had chosen, like his father, for his own bedroom. The postern leading to the tower stood wide open, with a cry of horror V—— shouted, "There — he lies dashed to pieces at the bottom of the ravine." And it was so. There had been a fall of snow, so that all they could distinctly make out from above was the rigid arm of the unfortunate man protruding from between the stones. Many hours passed before the workmen succeeded, at great risk of life, in descending by means of ladders bound together, and drawing up the corpse by the aid of ropes. In the last agonies of death the Baron had kept a tight hold upon the silver candlestick; the hand in which it was clenched was the only uninjured part of his whole body, which had been shattered in the most hideous way by rebounding on the sharp stones.

Just as the corpse was drawn up and carried into the hall, and laid upon the very same spot on the large table where a few weeks before old Roderick had lain dead, Hubert burst in, his face distorted by the frenzy of despair. Quite overpowered by the fearful sight he wailed, "Brother! O my poor brother! No; this I never prayed for from the demons who had entered into me." This suspicious self-exculpation made V—— tremble; he felt impelled to proceed against Hubert as the murderer of his brother. Hubert, however, had fallen on the floor senseless; they carried him to bed; but on taking strong restoratives he soon recovered. Then he appeared in V——'s room, pale and sorrow-stricken, and with his eyes half clouded with grief; and unable to stand owing to his weakness, he slowly sank down into an easy chair, saying, "I have wished for my brother's death, because my father had made over to him the best part of the property through the foolish conversion of it into an entail. He has now found a fearful death. I am now lord of the estate-tail, but my heart is rent with pain – I can – I shall never be happy. I confirm you in your office; you shall be invested with the most extensive powers in respect to the management of the estate, upon which I cannot bear to live." Hubert left the room, and in two or three hours was on his way to K——.

It appeared that the unfortunate Wolfgang had got up in the night, probably with the intention of going into the other cabinet where there was a library. In the stupor of sleep he had mistaken the door, and had opened the postern, taken a step out, and plunged headlong down. But after all had been said, there was nevertheless a good deal that was strained and unlikely in this explanation. If the Baron was unable to sleep and wanted to get a book out of the library, this of itself excluded all idea of sleep-stupor; but this condition alone could account for any mistaking of the postern for the door of the cabinet. Then again, the former was fast locked, and

required a good deal of exertion to unlock it. These improb-
abilities V—— accordingly put before the domestics, who had
gathered round him, and at length the Freiherr's body-ser-
vant, Francis by name, said, "Nay, nay, my good Herr Justitiarius; it couldn't have happened in that way." "Well, how
then?" asked V—— abruptly and sharply. But Francis, a
faithful, honest fellow, who would have followed his master
into his grave, was unwilling to speak out before the rest; he
stipulated that what he had to say about the event should be
confided to the Justitiarius alone in private. V—— now
learned that the Freiherr used often to talk to Francis about
the vast treasure which he believed lay buried beneath the
ruins of the tower, and also that frequently at night, as if
goaded by some malicious fiend, he would open the postern,
the key of which Daniel had been obliged to give him, and
would gaze with longing eyes down into the chasm where the
supposed riches lay. There was now no doubt about it; on
that ill-omened night the Freiherr, after his servant had left
him, must have taken one of his usual walks to the postern,
where he had been most likely suddenly seized with dizziness,
and had fallen over. Daniel, who also seemed much upset by
the Freiherr's terrible end, thought it would be a good thing
to have the dangerous postern walled up; and this was at once
done.

Freiherr Hubert von R——, who had then succeeded to
the entail, went back to Courland without once showing
himself at R–sitten again. V—— was invested with full powers
for the absolute management of the property. The building
of the new castle was not proceeded with; but on the other
hand the old structure was put in as good a state of repair as
possible. Several years passed before Hubert came again to
R–sitten, late in the autumn, but after he had remained shut
up in his room with V—— for several days, he went back to
Courland. Passing on his way through K——, he deposited
his will with the government authorities there.

The Freiherr, whose character appeared to have undergone
a complete revolution, spoke more than once during his stay
at R–sitten of presentiments of his approaching death. And
these apprehensions were really not unfounded, for he died
in the very next year. His son, named, like the deceased Baron,

Hubert, soon came over from Courland to take possession of the rich inheritance; and was followed by his mother and his sister. The youth seemed to unite in his own person all the bad qualities of his ancestors: he proved himself to be proud, arrogant, impetuous, avaricious, in the very first moments after his arrival at R-sitten. He wanted to have several things which did not suit his notions of what was right and proper altered there and then: the cook he kicked out of doors; and he attempted to thrash the coachman, in which, however, he did not succeed, for the big brawny fellow had the impudence not to submit to it. In fact, he was on the high road to assuming the *rôle* of a harsh and severe lord of the entail, when V—— interposed in his firm earnest manner, declaring most explicitly that not a single chair should be moved, that not even a cat should leave the house if she liked to stay in it, until after the will had been opened. "You have the presumption to tell me, the lord of the entail," began the Baron. V——, however, cut short the young man, who was foaming with rage, and said, whilst he measured him with a keen searching glance, "Don't be in too great a hurry, Herr Baron. At all events, you have no right to exercise authority here until after the opening of your father's will. It is I — I alone — who am now master here; and I shall know how to meet violence with violent measures. Please to recollect that by virtue of my powers as executor of your father's will, as well as by virtue of the arrangements which have been made by the court, I am empowered to forbid your remaining in R-sitten if I think fit to do so; and so, if you wish to spare me this disagreeable step, I would advise you to go away quietly to K——." The lawyer's earnestness, and the resolute tone in which he spoke, lent the proper emphasis to his words. Hence the young Baron, who was charging with far too sharp-pointed horns, felt the weakness of his weapons against the firm bulwark, and found it convenient to cover the shame of his retreat with a burst of scornful laughter.

Three months passed and the day was come on which, in accordance with the expressed wish of the deceased, his will was to be opened at K——, where it had been deposited. In the chambers there was, besides the officers of the court, the Baron, and V——, a young man of noble appearance, whom

V—— had brought with him, and who was taken to be V——'s clerk, since he had a parchment deed sticking out from the breast of his buttoned-up coat. Him the Baron treated as he did nearly all the rest, with scornful contempt; and he demanded with noisy impetuosity that they should make haste and get done with all their tiresome needless ceremonies as quickly as possible and without over many words and scribblings. He couldn't for the life of him make out why any will should be wanted at all with respect to the inheritance, and especially in the case of entailed property; and no matter what provisions were made in the will, it would depend entirely upon his decision as to whether they should be observed or not. After casting a hasty and surly glance at the handwriting and the seal, the Baron acknowledged them to be those of his dead father. Upon the clerk of the court preparing to read the will aloud, the young Baron, throwing his right arm carelessly over the back of his chair and leaning his left on the table, whilst he drummed with his fingers on its green cover, sat staring with an air of indifference out of the window. After a short preamble the deceased Freiherr Hubert von R—— declared that he had never possessed the estate-tail as its lawful owner, but that he had only managed it in the name of the deceased Freiherr Wolfgang von R——'s only son, called Roderick after his grandfather; and he it was to whom, according to the rights of family priority, the estate had fallen on his father's death. Amongst Hubert's papers would be found an exact account of all revenues and expenditure, as well as of existing movable property, &c. The will went on to relate that Wolfgang von R—— had, during his travels, made the acquaintance of Mdlle. Julia de St. Val in Geneva, and had fallen so deeply in love with her that he resolved never to leave her side again. She was very poor; and her family, although noble and of good repute, did not, however, rank amongst the most illustrious, for which reason Wolfgang dared not expect to receive the consent of old Roderick to a union with her, for the old Freiherr's aim and ambition was to promote by all possible means the establishment of a powerful family. Nevertheless he ventured to write from Paris to his father, acquainting him with the fact that his affections were engaged. But what he had foreseen was actually realized; the old Baron declared categorically that he had himself chosen the future mistress of the entail, and therefore there could never be any mention made of any other. Wolfgang, instead of crossing the Channel into England, as he was to have done, returned into Geneva under the assumed name of Born, and married Julia, who after the lapse of a year bore him a son, and this son became on Wolfgang's death the real lord of the entail. In explanation of the facts why Hubert, though acquainted with all this, had kept silent so long and had represented himself as lord of the entail, various reasons were assigned, based upon agreements formerly made with Wolfgang, but they seemed for the most part insufficient and devoid of real foundation.

The Baron sat staring at the clerk of the court as if thunderstruck, whilst the latter went on proclaiming all this bad news in a provokingly monotonous and jarring tone. When he finished, V—— rose, and taking the young man whom he had brought with him by the hand, said, as he bowed to the assembled company, "Here I have the honor to present to you, gentlemen, Freiherr Roderick von R——, lord of the entail of R-sitten." Baron Hubert looked at the youth, who had, as it were, fallen from the clouds to deprive him of the rich inheritance together with half the unentailed Courland estates, with suppressed fury in his gleaming eyes; then, threatening him with his doubled fist, he ran out of the court without uttering a word. Baron Roderick, on being challenged by the court-officers, produced the documents by which he was to establish his identity as the person whom he represented himself to be. He handed in an attested extract from the register of the church where his father was married, which certified that on such and such a day Wolfgang Born, merchant, born in K——, had been united in marriage with the blessing of the Church to Mdlle. Julia de St. Val, in the presence of certain witnesses, who were named. Further, he produced his own baptismal certificate (he had been baptized in Geneva as the son of the merchant Born and his wife Julia, née De St. Val, begotten in lawful wedlock), and various letters from his father to his mother, who was long since dead, but they none of them had any other signature than W.

V—— looked through all these papers with a cloud upon his face; and as he put them together again, he said, somewhat troubled, "Ah well! God will help us!"

The very next morning Freiherr Hubert von R—— presented, through an advocate whose services he had succeeded in enlisting in his cause, a statement of protest to the government authorities in K——, actually calling upon them to effectuate the immediate surrender to him of the entail of R-sitten. It was incontestable, maintained the advocate, that the deceased Freiherr Hubert Von R—— had not had the power to dispose of entailed property either by testament or in any other way. The testament in question, therefore, was nothing more than an evidential statement, written down and deposited with the court, to the effect that Freiherr Wolfgang von R—— had bequeathed the estate-tail to a son who was at that time still living; and accordingly it had as evidence no greater weight than that of any other witness, and so could not by any possibility legitimately establish the claims of the person who had announced himself to be Freiherr Roderick von R——. Hence it was rather the duty of this new claimant to prove by action at law his alleged rights of inheritance, which were hereby expressly disputed and denied, and so also to take proper steps to maintain his claim to the estate-tail, which now, according to the laws of succession, fell to Baron Hubert von R——. By the father's death the property came at once immediately into the hands of the son. There was no need for any formal declaration to be made of his entering into possession of the inheritance, since the succession could not be alienated; at any rate, the present owner of the estate was not going to be disturbed in his possession by claims which were perfectly groundless. Whatever reasons the deceased might have had for bringing forward another heir of entail were quite irrelevant. And it might be remarked that he had himself had an intrigue in Switzerland, as could be proved if necessary from the papers he had left behind him; and it was quite possible that the person whom he alleged to be his brother's son was his own son, the fruit of an unlawful love, for whom in a momentary fit of remorse he had wished to secure the entail.

However great was the balance of probability in favor of the truth of the circumstances as stated in the will, and however revolted the judges were, particularly by the last clauses of the protest, in which the son felt no compunction at accusing his dead father of a crime, yet the views of the case there stated were after all the right ones; and it was only due to V——'s restless exertions, and his explicit and solemn assurance that the proofs which were necessary to establish legitimately the identity of Freiherr Roderick von R—— should be produced in a very short time, that the surrender of the estate to the young Baron was deferred, and the contrivance of the administration of it in trust agreed to, until after the case should be settled.

V—— was only too well aware how difficult it would be for him to keep his promise. He had turned over all old Roderick's papers without finding the slightest trace of a letter or any kind of a statement bearing upon Wolfgang's relation to Mdlle. de St. Val. He was sitting wrapt in thought in old Roderick's sleeping-cabinet, every hole and corner of which he had searched, and was working at a long statement of the case that he intended dispatching to a certain notary in Geneva, who had been recommended to him as a shrewd and energetic man, to request him to procure and forward certain documents which would establish the young Freiherr's cause on firm ground. It was midnight; the full moon shone in through the windows of the adjoining hall, the door of which stood open. Then V—— fancied he heard a noise as of someone coming slowly and heavily up the stairs, and also at the same time a jingling and rattling of keys. His attention was arrested; he rose to his feet and went into the hall, where he plainly made out that there was someone crossing the anteroom and approaching the door of the hall where he was. Soon afterwards the door was opened and a man came slowly in, dressed in night-clothes, his face ghastly pale and distorted; in the one hand he bore a candlestick with the candles burning, and in the other a huge bunch of keys. V—— at once recognized the house-steward, and was on the point of addressing him and inquiring what he wanted so late at night, when he was arrested by an icy shiver; there was something so unearthly and ghostlike in the old man's manner and bearing as well as in his set, pallid face. He perceived that he was in presence of a somnambulist. Crossing the hall obliquely with measured strides, the old man went straight to the walled-up postern that had formerly led to the tower. He came to a halt immediately in front of it, and uttered a wailing sound that seemed to come from the bottom of his heart, and was so awful and so loud that the whole apartment rang again, making V—— tremble with dread. Then, setting the candlestick down on the floor and hanging the keys on his belt, Daniel began to scratch at the wall with both hands, so that the blood soon burst out from beneath his fingernails, and all the while he was moaning and groaning as if tortured by nameless agony. After placing his ear against the wall in a listening attitude, he waved his hand as if hushing someone, stooped down and picked up the candlestick, and finally stole back to the door with soft measured footsteps. V—— took his own candle in his hand and cautiously followed him. They both went downstairs; the old man unlocked the great main door of the castle, V—— slipped cleverly through. Then they went to the stable, where old Daniel, to V——'s perfect astonishment, placed his candlestick so skillfully that the entire interior of the building was sufficiently lighted without the least danger. Having fetched a saddle and bridle, he put them on one of the horses which he had loosed from the manger, carefully tightening the girth and taking up the stirrup-straps. Pulling the tuft of hair on the horse's forehead outside the front strap, he took him by the bridle and led him out of the stable, clicking with his tongue and patting his neck with one hand. On getting outside in the courtyard he stood several seconds in the attitude of one receiving commands, which he promised by sundry nods to carry out. Then he led the horse back into the stable, unsaddled him, and tied him to the manger. This done, he took his candle-stick, locked the stable, and returned to the castle, finally disappearing in his own room, the door of which he carefully bolted. V—— was deeply agitated by this scene; the presentiment of some fearful deed rose up before him like a black and fiendish specter, and refused to leave him.

Being so keenly alive as he was to the precarious position of his *protégé,* he felt that it would at least be his duty to turn what he had seen to his account.

Next day, just as it was beginning to be dusk, Daniel came into the Justitiarius's room to receive some instructions relating to his department of the household. V—— took him by the arms, and forcing him into a chair, in a confidential way began, "See you here, my old friend Daniel, I have long been wishing to ask you what you think of all this confused mess into which Hubert's peculiar will has tumbled us. Do you really think that the young man is Wolfgang's son, begotten in lawful marriage?" The old man, leaning over the arm of his chair, and avoiding V——'s eyes, for V—— was watching him most intently, replied doggedly, "Bah! Maybe he is; maybe he is not. What does it matter to me? It's all the same to me who's master here now." "But I believe," went on V——, moving nearer to the old man and placing his hand on his shoulder, "but I believed you possessed the old Freiherr's full confidence, and in that case he assuredly would not conceal from you the real state of affairs with regard to his sons. He told you, I dare say, about the marriage which Wolfgang had made against his will, did he not?" "I don't remember to have ever heard him say anything of that sort," replied the old man, yawning with the most ill-mannered loudness. "You are sleepy, old man," said V——; "perhaps you have had a restless night?" "Not that I am aware," he rejoined coldly; "but I must go and order supper." Whereupon he rose heavily from his chair and rubbed his bent back, yawning again, and that still more loudly than before. "Stay a little while, old man," cried V——, taking hold of his hand and endeavoring to force him to resume his seat; but Daniel preferred to stand in front of the study-table; propping himself upon it with both hands, and leaning across towards V——, he asked sullenly, "Well, what do you want? What have I to do with the will? What do I care about the quarrel over the estate?" "Well, well," interposed V——, "we'll say no more about that now. Let us turn to some other topic, Daniel. You are out of humor and yawning, and all that is a sign of great weariness, and I am almost inclined to believe that it really was *you* last night, who" — "Well, what did I do last night?"

asked the old man without changing his position. V—— went on, "Last night, when I was sitting up above in your old master's sleeping-cabinet next the great hall, you came in at the door, your face pale and rigid; and you went across to the bricked-up postern and scratched at the wall with both your hands, groaning as if in very great pain. Do you walk in your sleep, Daniel?" The old man dropped back into the chair which V—— quickly managed to place for him; but not a sound escaped his lips. His face could not be seen, owing to the gathering dusk of the evening; V—— only noticed that he took his breath short and that his teeth were rattling together. "Yes," continued V—— after a short pause, "there is one thing that is very strange about sleep-walkers. On the day after they have been in this peculiar state in which they have acted as if they were perfectly wide awake, they don't remember the least thing, that they did." Daniel did not move. "I have come across something like what your condition was yesterday once before in the course of my experience," proceeded V——.

"I had a friend who regularly began to wander about at night as you do whenever it was full moon, — nay, he often sat down and wrote letters. But what was most extraordinary was that if I began to whisper softly in his ear I could soon manage to make him speak; and he would answer correctly all the questions I put to him; and even things that he would most jealously have concealed when awake now fell from his lips unbidden, as though he were unable to offer any resistance to the power that was exerting its influence over him. Deuce take it! I really believe that, if a man who's given to walking in his sleep had ever committed any crime, and hoarded it up as a secret ever so long, it could be extracted from him by questioning when he was in this peculiar state. Happy are they who have a clean conscience like you and me, Daniel! We may walk as much as we like in our sleep; there's no fear of anybody extorting the confession of a crime from us. But come now, Daniel! when you scratch so hideously at the bricked-up postern, you want, I dare say, to go up the astronomical tower, don't you? I suppose you want to go and experiment like old Roderick – eh? Well, next time you come, I shall ask you what you want to do." Whilst V—— was speaking, the old man was shaken with continually increasing agitation; but now his whole frame seemed to heave and rock convulsively past all hope of cure, and in a shrill voice he began to utter a string of unmeaning gibberish. V—— rang for the servants. They brought lights; but as the old man's fit did not abate, they lifted him up as though he had been a mere automaton, not possessed of the power of voluntary movement, and carried him to bed. After continuing in this frightful state for about an hour, he fell into a profound sleep resembling a dead faint When he awoke he asked for wine; and, after he had got what he wanted, he sent away the man who was going to sit with him, and locked himself in his room as usual.

V—— had indeed really resolved to make the attempt he spoke of to Daniel, although at the same time he could not forget two facts. In the first place, Daniel, having now been made aware of his propensity to walk in his sleep, would probably adopt every measure of precaution to avoid him; and on the other hand, confessions made whilst in this condition would not be exactly fitted to serve as a basis for further proceedings. In spite of this, however, he repaired to the hall on the approach of midnight, hoping that Daniel, as frequently happens to those afflicted in this way, would be constrained to act involuntarily. About midnight there arose a great noise in the courtyard. V—— plainly heard a window broken in; then he went downstairs, and as he traversed the passages he was met by rolling clouds of suffocating smoke, which, he soon perceived were pouring out of the open door of the house-steward's room. The steward himself was just being carried out, to all appearance dead, in order to be taken and put to bed in another room. The servants related that about midnight one of the under-grooms had been awakened by a strange hollow knocking; he thought something had befallen the old man, and was preparing to get up and go and see if he could help him, when the night watchman in the court shouted, "Fire! Fire! The Herr House-Steward's room is all of a bright blaze!" At this outcry several servants at once appeared on the scene; but all their efforts to burst open the room door were unavailing. Whereupon they hurried out into the court, but the resolute watchman had already broken in the window, for the room was low and on the basement story, had torn down the burning curtains, and by pouring a few buckets of water on them had at once extinguished the fire. The house-steward they found lying on the floor in the middle of the room in a swoon. In his hand he still held the candlestick tightly clenched, the burning candles of which had caught the curtains, and so occasioned the fire. Some of the blazing rags had fallen upon the old man, burning his eyebrows and a large portion of the hair of his head. If the watchman had not seen the fire the old man must have been helplessly burned to death. The servants, moreover, to their no little astonishment found the room door secured on the inside by two quite new bolts, which had been fastened on since the previous evening, for they had not been there then. V—— perceived that the old man had wished to make it impossible for him to get out of his room; for the blind impulse which urged him to wander in his sleep he could not resist. The old man became seriously ill; he did not speak; he took but little nourishment; and lay staring before him with the reflection of death in his set eyes, just as if he were clasped in the vicelike grip of some hideous thought. V—— believed he would never rise from his bed again.

V—— had done all that could be done for his client; and he could now only await the result in patience; and so he resolved to return to K——. His departure was fixed for the following morning. As he was packing his papers together late at night, he happened to lay his hand upon a little sealed packet which Freiherr Hubert von R—— had given him, bearing the inscription, "To be read after my will has been opened," and which by some unaccountable means had hitherto escaped his notice. He was on the point of breaking the seal when the door opened and Daniel came in with still, ghostlike step. Placing upon the table a black portfolio which he carried under his arm, he sank upon his knees with a deep groan, and grasping V——'s hands with a convulsive clutch he said, in a voice so hollow and hoarse that it seemed to come from the bottom of a grave, "I should not like to die on the scaffold! There is One above who judges!" Then, rising with some trouble and with many painful gasps, he left the room as he had come.

V—— spent the whole of the night in reading what the black portfolio and Hubert's packet contained. Both agreed in all circumstantial particulars, and suggested naturally what further steps were to be taken. On arriving at K——, V—— immediately repaired to Freiherr Hubert von R——, who received him with ill-mannered pride. But the remarkable result of the interview, which began at noon and lasted on without interruption until late at night, was that the next day the Freiherr made a declaration before the court to the effect that he acknowledged the claimant to be, agreeably to his father's will, the son of Wolfgang von R——, eldest son of Freiherr Roderick von R——, and begotten in lawful wedlock with Mdlle. Julia de St. Val, and furthermore acknowledged him as rightful and legitimate heir to the entail. On leaving the court he found his carriage, with post-horses, standing before the door; he stepped in and was driven off at a rapid rate, leaving his mother and his sister behind him. They would perhaps never see him again, he wrote, along with other perplexing statements. Roderick's astonishment at this unexpected turn which the case had taken was very great; he pressed V—— to explain to him how this wonder had been brought about, what mysterious power was at work in the matter. V——, however, evaded his questions by giving him hopes of telling him all at some future time, and when he should have come into possession of the estate. For the surrender of the entail to him could not be effected immediately, since the court, not content with Hubert's declaration, required that Roderick should also first prove his own identity to their satisfaction. V—— proposed to the Baron that he should go and live at R-sitten, adding that Hubert's mother and sister, momentarily embarrassed by his sudden departure, would prefer to go and live quietly on the ancestral property rather than stay in the dear and noisy town. The glad delight with which Roderick welcomed the prospect of dwelling, at least for a time, under the same roof with the Baroness and her daughter, betrayed the deep impression which the lovely and graceful Seraphina had made upon him. In fact, the Freiherr made such good use of his time in R-sitten that, at the end of a few weeks, he had won Seraphina's love as well as her mother's cordial approval of her marriage with him. All this was for V—— rather too quick work, since Roderick's claims to be lord of the entail still continued to be rather doubtful. The life of idyllic happiness at the castle was interrupted by letters from Courland. Hubert had not shown himself at all at the estates, but had traveled direct to St Petersburg, where he had taken military service and was now in the field against the Persians, with whom Russia happened to be just then waging war. This obliged the Baroness and her daughter to set off immediately for their Courland estates, where everything was in confusion and disorder. Roderick, who regarded himself in the light of an accepted son-in-law, insisted upon accompanying his beloved; and hence, since V—— likewise returned to K——, the castle was left in its previous loneliness. The house-steward's malignant complaint grew worse and worse, so that he gave up all hopes of ever getting about again; and his office was conferred upon an old *chasseur,* Francis by name, Wolfgang's faithful servant.

At last, after long waiting, V—— received from Switzerland information of the most favorable character. The priest who had married Roderick was long since dead; but there was found in the church register a memorandum in his hand writing, to the effect that the man of the name of Born, whom he had joined in the bonds of wedlock with Mdlle. Julia de St. Val, had established completely to his satisfaction his identity as Freiherr Wolfgang von R——, eldest son of Freiherr Roderick von R—— of R-sitten. Besides this, two witnesses of the marriage had been discovered, a merchant of Geneva and an old French captain, who had moved to Lyons; to them also Wolfgang had in confidence stated his real name; and their affidavits confirmed the priest's notice in the church register. With these memoranda in his hands, drawn up with proper legal formalities, V—— now succeeded in securing his client in the complete possession of his rights; and as there was now no longer any hindrance to the surrender to him of the entail, it was to be put into his hands in the ensuing autumn. Hubert had fallen in his very first engagement, thus sharing the fate of his younger brother, who had likewise been slain in battle a year before his father's death. Thus the Courland estates fell to Baroness Seraphina von R——, and made a handsome dowry for her to take to the too happy Roderick.

November had already come in when the Baroness, along with Roderick and his betrothed, arrived at R–sitten. The formal surrender of the estate-tail to the young Baron took place, and then his marriage with Seraphina was solemnised. Many weeks passed amid a continual whirl of pleasure; but at length the wearied guests began gradually to depart from the castle, to V——'s great satisfaction, for he had made up his mind not to take his leave of R–sitten until he had initiated the young lord of the entail in all the relations and duties connected with his new position down to the minutest particulars. Roderick's uncle had kept an account of all revenues and disbursements with the most detailed accuracy; hence, since Hubert had only retained a small sum annually for his own support, the surplus revenues had all gone to swell the capital left by the old Freiherr, till the total now amounted to a considerable sum. Hubert had only employed the income of the entail for his own purposes during the first three years, but to cover this he had given a mortgage on the security of his share of the Courland property.

From the time when old Daniel had revealed himself to V—— as a somnambulist, V—— had chosen old Roderick's bedroom for his own sitting room, in order that he might the more securely gather from the old man what he afterwards voluntarily disclosed. Hence it was in this room and in the adjoining great hall that the Freiherr transacted business with V——. Once they were both sitting at the great table by the bright blazing fire; V—— had his pen in his hand, and was noting down various totals and calculating the riches of the lord of the entail, whilst the latter, leaning his head on his hand, was blinking at the open account-books and formidable-looking documents. Neither of them heard the hollow roar of the sea, nor the anxious cries of the sea-gulls as they dashed against the windowpanes, flapping their wings and flying backwards and forwards, announcing the oncoming storm. Neither of them heeded the storm, which arose about midnight, and was now roaring and raging with wild fury round the castle walls, so that all the sounds of ill omen in the fire-grates and narrow passages awoke, and began to

whistle and shriek in a weird, unearthly way. At length, after
a terrific blast, which made the whole castle shake, the hall
was completely lit up by the murky glare of the full moon,
and V—— exclaimed, "Awful weather!" The Freiherr, quite
absorbed in the consideration of the wealth which had fallen
to him, replied indifferently, as he turned over a page of the
receipt-book with a satisfied smile, "It is indeed; very stormy!"
But, as if clutched by the icy hand of Dread, he started to his
feet as the door of the hall flew open and a pale spectral figure
became visible, striding in with the stamp of death upon its
face. It was Daniel, who, lying helpless under the power of
disease, was deemed in the opinion of V—— as of everybody
else incapable of the ability to move a single limb; but, again
coming under the influence of his propensity to wander in
his sleep at full moon, he had, it appeared, been unable to
resist it. The Freiherr stared at the old man without uttering
a sound; and when Daniel began to scratch at the wall, and
moan as though in the painful agonies of death, Roderick's
heart was filled with horrible dread. With his face ashy pale
and his hair standing straight on end, he leapt to his feet and
strode towards the old man in a threatening attitude and cried
in a loud firm voice, so that the hall rang again, "Daniel,
Daniel, what are you doing here at this hour?" Then the old
man uttered that same unearthly howling whimper, like the
death-cry of a wounded animal, which he had uttered when
Wolfgang had offered to reward his fidelity with gold; and he
fell down on the floor. V—— summoned the servants; they
raised the old man up; but all attempts to restore animation
proved fruitless. Then the Freiherr cried, almost beside himself, "Good God! Good God! Now I remember to have heard
that a sleepwalker may die on the spot if anybody calls him
by his name. Oh! oh! unfortunate wretch that I am! I have
killed the poor old man! I shall never more have a peaceful
moment so long as I live." When the servants had carried the
corpse away and the hall was again empty, V—— took the
Freiherr, who was still continuing his self-reproaches, by the
hand and led him in impressive silence to the walled-up
postern, and said, "The man who fell down dead at your feet,
Freiherr Roderick, was the atrocious murderer of your father."
The Freiherr fixed his staring eyes upon V—— as though he

saw the foul fiends of hell. But V—— went on, "The time has come now for me to reveal to you the hideous secret which, weighing upon the conscience of this monster and burdening him with curses, compelled him to roam abroad in his sleep. The Eternal Power has seen fit to make the son take vengeance upon the murderer of his father.

"The words which you thundered in the ears of that fearful night-walker were the last words which your unhappy father spoke." V—— sat down in front of the fire, and the Freiherr, trembling and unable to utter a word, took his seat beside him. V—— began to tell him the contents of the document which Hubert had left behind him, and the seal of which he (V——) was not to break until after the opening of the will Hubert lamented, in expressions testifying to the deepest remorse, the implacable hatred against his elder brother which took root in him from the moment that old Roderick established the entail. He was deprived of all weapons; for, even if he succeeded in maliciously setting the son at variance with the father, it would serve no purpose, since even Roderick himself had not the power to deprive his eldest son of his birth-right, nor would he on principle have ever done so, no matter how his affections had been alienated from him. It was only when Wolfgang formed his connection with Julia de St. Val in Geneva that Hubert saw his way to effecting his brother's ruin. And that was the time when he came to an understanding with Daniel, to provoke the old man by villainous devices to take measures which should drive his son to despair.

He was well aware of old Roderick's opinion that the only way to ensure an illustrious future for the family to all subsequent time was by means of an alliance with one of the oldest families in the country. The old man had read this alliance in the stars, and any pernicious derangement of the constellation would only entail destruction upon the family he had founded. In this way it was that Wolfgang's union with Julia seemed to the old man like a sinful crime, committed against the ordinances of the Power which had stood by him in all his worldly undertakings; and any means that might be employed for Julia's ruin he would have regarded as justified for the same reason, for Julia had, he conceived, ranged herself against him like some demoniacal principle. Hubert knew that his brother loved Julia passionately, almost to madness in fact, and that the loss of her would infallibly make him miserable, perhaps kill him. And Hubert was all the more ready to assist the old man in his plans as he had himself conceived an unlawful affection for Julia, and hoped to win her for himself. It was, however, determined by a special dispensation of Providence that all attacks, even the most virulent, were to be thwarted by Wolfgang's resoluteness; nay, that he should contrive to deceive his brother: the fact that his marriage was actually solemnised and that of the birth of a son were kept secret from Hubert In Roderick's mind also there occurred, along with the presentiment of his approaching death, the idea that Wolfgang had really married the Julia who was so hostile to him. In the letter which commanded his son to appear at R-sitten on a given day to take possession of the entail, he cursed him if he did not sever his connection with her. This was the letter that Wolfgang burned beside his father's corpse. To Hubert the old man wrote, saying that Wolfgang had married Julia, but that he would part from her. This Hubert took to be a fancy of his visionary father's; accordingly he was not a little dismayed when on reaching R-sitten Wolfgang with perfect frankness not only confirmed the old man's supposition, but also went on to add that Julia had borne him a son, and that he hoped in a short time to surprise her with the pleasant intelligence of his high rank and great wealth, for she had hitherto taken him for Born, a merchant from M——. He intended going to Geneva himself to fetch his beloved wife. But before he could carry out this plan he was overtaken by death. Hubert carefully concealed what he knew about the existence of a son born to Wolfgang in lawful wedlock with Julia, and so usurped the property that really belonged to his nephew. But only a few years passed before he became a prey to bitter remorse. He was reminded of his guilt in terrible wise by destiny, in the hatred which grew up and developed more and more between his two sons. "You are a poor starving beggar!" said the elder, a boy of twelve, to the younger, "but I shall be lord of R-sitten when father dies, and then you will have to be humble and kiss my hand when you want me to give you money to buy a new coat." The younger, goaded to ungovernable fury by his brother's proud and scornful words, threw the knife at him which he happened to have in his hand, and almost killed him. Hubert, for fear of some dire misfortune, sent the younger away to St. Petersburg; and he served afterwards as officer under Suwaroff, and fell fighting against the French. Hubert was prevented revealing to the world the dishonest and deceitful way in which he had acquired possession of the estate-tail by the shame and disgrace which would have come upon him; but he would not rob the rightful owner of a single penny more. He caused inquiries to be set on foot in Geneva, and learned that Madame Born had died of grief at the incomprehensible disappearance of her husband, but that young Roderick Born was being brought up by a worthy man who had adopted him.

"Hubert then caused himself to be introduced under an assumed name as a relative of Born the merchant, who had perished at sea, and he forwarded at given times sufficient sums of money to give the young heir of entail a good and respectable education. How he carefully treasured up the surplus revenues from the estate, and how he drew up the terms of his will, we already know. Respecting his brother's death, Hubert spoke in strangely obscure terms, but they allowed this much to be inferred, that there must be some mystery about it, and that he had taken part, indirectly, at least, in some heinous crime.

The contents of the black portfolio made everything clear. Along with Hubert's traitorous correspondence with Daniel was a sheet of paper written and signed by Daniel. V—— read a confession at which his very soul trembled, appalled. It was at Daniel's instigation that Hubert had come to R–sitten; and it was Daniel again who had written and told him about the one hundred and fifty thousand thalers that had been found. It has been already described how Hubert was received by his brother, and how, deceived in all his hopes and wishes, he was about to go off when he was prevented by V——, Daniel's heart was tortured by an insatiable thirst for vengeance, which he was determined to take on the young man who had proposed to kick him out like a mangy cur. He it was who relentlessly and incessantly fanned the flame of passion by which Hubert's desperate heart was consumed. Whilst in the fir forests hunting wolves, out in the midst of a blinding snowstorm, they agreed to effect his destruction. "Make away with him!" murmured Hubert, looking askance and taking aim with his rifle. "Yes, make away with him," snarled Daniel, "but not in *that way,* not in *that way!*" And he made the most solemn asseverations that he would murder the Freiherr and not a soul in the world should be the wiser. When, however, Hubert had got his money, he repented of the plot; he determined to go away in order to shun all further temptation. Daniel himself saddled his horse and brought it out of the stable; but as the Baron was about to mount, Daniel said to him in a sharp, strained voice, "I thought you would stay on the entail, Freiherr Hubert, now that it has just fallen to you, for the proud lord of the entail lies dashed to pieces at the bottom of the ravine, below the tower." The steward had observed that Wolfgang, tormented by his thirst for gold, often used to rise in the night, go to the postern which formerly led to the tower, and stand gazing with longing eyes down into the chasm, where, according to his (Daniel's) testimony, vast treasures lay buried. Relying upon this habit, Daniel waited near the hall-door on that ill-omened night; and as soon as he heard the Freiherr open the postern leading to the tower, he entered the hall and proceeded to where the Freiherr was standing, close by the brink of the chasm. On becoming aware of the presence of his villainous servant, in whose eyes the gleam of murder shone, the Freiherr turned round and said with a cry of terror, "Daniel, Daniel, what are you doing here at this hour?" But then Daniel shrieked wildly, "Down with you, you mangy cur!" and with a powerful push of his foot he hurled the unhappy man over into the deep chasm.

Terribly agitated by this awful deed, Freiherr Roderick found no peace in the castle where his father had been murdered. He went to his Courland estates, and only visited R-sitten once a year, in autumn. Francis — old Francis — who had strong suspicions as to Daniel's guilt, maintained that he often haunted the place at full moon, and described the nature of the apparition much as V—— afterwards experienced it for himself when he exorcised it. It was the disclosure of these circumstances, also, which stamped his father's memory with dishonor, that had driven young Freiherr Hubert out into the world.

This was my old great-uncle's story. Now he took my hand, and whilst his eyes filled with tears, he said, in a broken voice, "Cousin, cousin! And she too — the beautiful lady — has fallen a victim to the dark destiny, the grim, mysterious power which has established itself in that old ancestral castle. Two days after we left R-sitten the Freiherr arranged an excursion on sledges as the concluding event of the visit. He drove his wife himself; but as they were going down the valley the horses, for some unexplained reason, suddenly taking fright, began to snort and kick and plunge most savagely. 'The old man! The old man is after us!' screamed the Baroness in a shrill, terrified voice. At this same moment the sledge was overturned with a violent jerk, and the Baroness was hurled to a considerable distance. They picked her up lifeless — she was quite dead. The Freiherr is perfectly inconsolable, and has settled down into a state of passivity that will kill him. We shall never go to R-sitten again, cousin!"

Here my uncle paused. As I left him my heart was rent by emotion; and nothing but the all-soothing hand of Time could assuage the deep pain which I feared would cost me my life.

Years passed. V—— was resting in his grave, and I had left my native country. Then I was driven northwards, as far as St. Petersburg, by the devastating war which was sweeping over all Germany. On my return journey, not far from K——, I was driving one dark summer night along the shore of the Baltic, when I perceived in the sky before me a remarkably large bright star. On coming nearer I saw by the red flickering flame that what I had taken for a star must be a large fire, but could not understand how it could be so high up in the air. "Postilion, what fire is that before us yonder?" I asked the man who was driving me. "Oh! why, that's not a fire; it's the beacon tower of R-sitten." "R-sitten!" Directly the postilion mentioned the name all the experiences of the eventful autumn days which I had spent there recurred to my mind with lifelike reality. I saw the Baron — Seraphina — and also the remarkably eccentric old aunts — myself as well, with my bare milk-white face, my hair elegantly curled and powdered, and wearing a delicate sky-blue coat — nay, I saw myself in my love-sick folly, sighing like a furnace, and making lugubrious odes on my mistress's eyebrows. The somber, melancholy mood into which these memories plunged me was relieved by the bright recollection of V——'s genial jokes, shooting up like flashes of colored light, and I found them now still more entertaining than they had been so long ago. Thus agitated by pain mingled with much peculiar pleasure, I reached R–sitten early in the morning and got out of the coach in front of the post-house, where it had stopped I recognized the house as that of the land-steward; I inquired after him. "Begging your pardon," said the clerk of the post-house, taking his pipe from his mouth and giving his nightcap a tilt, "begging your pardon; there is no land-steward here; this is a Royal Government office, and the Herr Administrator is still asleep." On making further inquiries I learnt that Freiherr Roderick von R——, the last lord of the entail, had died sixteen years before without descendants, and that the entail in accordance with the terms of the original deeds had now escheated to the state. I went up to the castle; it was a mere heap of ruins. I was informed by an old peasant, who came out of the fir-forest, and with whom I entered into conversation, that a large portion of the stones had been employed in the construction of the beacon-tower. He also could tell the story of the ghost which was said to have haunted the castle, and he affirmed that people often heard unearthly cries and lamentations amongst the stones, especially at full moon.

Poor short-sighted old Roderick! What a malignant destiny did you conjure up to destroy with the breath of poison, in the first moments of its growth, that race which you intended to plant with firm roots to last on till eternity!

Arthur's Hall*

*Y*ou must of course, indulgent reader, have heard a good deal about the remarkable old commercial town of Dantzic. Perhaps you may be acquainted from abundant descriptions with all the sights to be seen there; but I should like it best of all if you have ever been there yourself in former times, and seen with your own eyes the wonderful hall into which I will now take you — I mean Arthur's Hall.†

At the hour of noon the hall was crammed full of men of the most diverse nations, all pushing about and immersed to the eyes in business, so that the ears were deafened by the confused din. But when the exchange hours were over, and the merchants had gone to dinner, and only a few odd individuals hurried through the hall on business (for it served as a means of communication between two streets), that I dare say was the time when you, gracious reader, liked to visit Arthur's Hall best, whenever you were in Dantzic. For then a kind of magical twilight fell through the dim windows, and all the strange reliefs and carvings, with which the wall was too profusely decorated, became instinct with life and mo-

---

* Written for the *Urania* for 1817.

† The *Artushof* or *Junkerhof* derives its names from its connection with the Arthurian cycle of legends, and from the fact that there the *Stadtjunker,* or wealthy merchants of Dantzic, used formerly to meet both to transact business and for the celebration of festive occasions. It has been used as an exchange since 1742. The site of the present building was occupied by a still older one down to 1552, and to this the hall, which is vaulted and supported on four slender pillars of granite, belongs architecturally. It was very quaintly decorated with pictures, statues, reliefs, &&, both of Christian and Pagan traditions.

tion. Stags with immense antlers, together with other wonderful animals, gazed down upon you with their fiery eyes till you could hardly look at them; and the marble statue of the king, also in the midst of the hall, caused you to shiver more in proportion as the dusk of evening deepened. The great picture representing an assemblage of all the Virtues and Vices, with their respective names attached, lost perceptibly in moral effect; for the Virtues, being high up, were blended unrecognizably in a grey mist, whilst the Vices — wondrously beautiful ladies in gay and brilliant costumes — stood out prominently and very seductively, threatening to enchant you with their sweet soft words. You preferred to turn your eyes upon the narrow border which went almost all round the hall, and on which were represented in pleasing style long processions of gay-uniformed militia of the olden time, when Dantzic was an Imperial town. Honest burgomasters, their features stamped with shrewdness and importance, ride at the head on spirited horses with handsome trappings, whilst the drummers, pipers, and halberdiers march along so jauntily and lifelike, that you soon begin to hear the merry music they play, and look to see them all defile out of that great window up there into the Langemarkt.*

While, then, they are marching off, you, indulgent reader, — if you were, that is, a tolerable sketcher, — would not be able to do otherwise than copy with pen and ink yon magnificent burgomaster with his remarkably handsome page. Pen and ink and paper, provided at public cost, were always to be found lying about on the tables; accordingly the material would be all ready at hand, and you would have felt the temptation irresistible. This you would have been permitted to do, but not so the young merchant Traugott, who, on beginning to do anything of this kind, encountered a thousand difficulties and vexations. "Advise our friend in Hamburg at once that that business has been settled, my good Herr Traugott," said the wholesale and retail merchant, Elias Roos, with whom Traugott was about to enter upon an immediate partnership, besides marrying his only daughter, Christina. After a little trouble, Traugott found a place at one

---

* A broad street crossing Dantzic in an east-to-west direction.

of the crowded tables; he took a sheet of paper, dipped his pen in the ink, and was about to begin with a free caligraphic flourish, when, running over once more in his mind what he wished to say, he cast his eyes upwards. Now it happened that he sat directly opposite a procession of figures, at the sight of which he was always, strangely enough, affected with an inexplicable sadness. A grave man, with something of dark melancholy in his face, and with a black curly beard and dressed in sumptuous clothing, was riding a black horse, which was led by the bridle by a marvelous youth: his rich abundance of hair and his gay and graceful costume gave him almost a feminine appearance. The face and form of the man made Traugott shudder inwardly, but a whole world of sweet vague aspirations beamed upon him from the youth's coun- tenance. He could never tear himself away from looking at these two; and hence, on the present occasion, instead of writing Herr Elias Roos's letter of advice to Hamburg, he sat gazing at the wonderful picture, absently scribbling all over his paper. After this had lasted some time, a hand clapped him on the shoulder from behind, and a gruff voice said, "Nice — very nice; that's what I like; something maybe made of that." Traugott, awakening out of his dreamy reverie, whisked himself round; but, as if struck by a lightning flash, he remained speechless with amazement and fright, for he was staring up into the face of the dark melancholy man who was depicted on the wall before him. He it was who uttered the words stated above; at his side stood the delicate and wonderfully beautiful youth, smiling upon him with inde- scribable affection. "Yes, it is they — the very same!" was the thought that flashed across Traugott's mind. "I expect they will at once throw off their unsightly mantles and stand forth in all the splendors of their antique costume." The members of the crowd pushed backwards and forwards amongst each other, and the strangers had soon disappeared in the crush; but even after the hours of 'Change were long over, and only a few odd individuals crossed the hall, Traugott still remained in the self-same place with the letter of advice in his hand, as though he were converted into a solid stone statue.

At length he perceived Herr Elias Roos coming towards him with two strangers. "What are you about, cogitating here so long after noon, my respected Herr Traugott?" asked Elias Roos; "have you sent off the letter all right?" Mechanically Traugott handed him the paper; but Herr Elias Roos struck his hands together above his head, stamping at first gently, but then violently, with his right foot, as he cried, making the hall ring again, "Good God! Good God! what childish tricks are these? Nothing but sheer childishness, my respected Traugott, — my good-for-nothing son-in-law — my imprudent partner. Why, the devil must be in your honor! The letter — the letter! O God! the post!" Herr Elias Roos was almost choking with vexation, whilst the two strangers were laughing at the singular letter of advice, which could hardly be said to be of much use. For, immediately after the words, "In reply to yours of the 20th inst. respecting —" Traugott had sketched the two extraordinary figures of the old man and the youth in neat bold outlines. The two strangers sought to pacify Herr Elias Roos by addressing him in the most affectionate manner; but Herr Elias Roos tugged his round wig now on this side and now on that, struck his cane against the floor, and cried, "The young devil! — was to write letter of advice — makes drawings — ten thousand marks gone — dam!" He blew through his fingers and then went on lamenting, "Ten thousand marks!" "Don't make a trouble of it, my dear Herr Roos," said at length the elder of the two strangers. "The post is of course gone; but I am sending off a courier to Hamburg in an hour. Let me give him your letter, and it will then reach its destination earlier than it would have done by the post" "You incomparable man!" exclaimed Herr Elias, his face a perfect blaze of sunshine. Traugott had recovered from his awkward embarrassment; he was hastening to the table to write the letter, but Herr Elias pushed him away, casting a right malicious look upon him, and murmuring between his teeth, "No need for you, my good son!"

Whilst Herr Elias was studiously busy writing, the elder gentleman approached young Traugott, who was standing silent with shame, and said to him, "You don't seem to be exactly in your place, my good sir. It would never have come into a true merchant's head to make drawings instead of writing a business letter as he ought" Traugott could not help feeling that this reproach was only too well founded. Much embarrassed, he replied, "By my soul, this hand has already written many admirable letters of advice; it is only, occasionally that such confoundedly odd ideas come into my mind." "But, my good sir," continued the stranger smiling, "these are not confoundedly odd ideas at all. I can really hardly believe that all your business letters taken together have been so admirable as these sketches, outlined so neatly and boldly and firmly. There is, I am sure, true genius in them." With these words the stranger took out of Traugott's hand the letter — or rather what was begun as a letter but had ended in sketches — carefully folded it together, and put it in his pocket. This awakened in Traugott's mind the firm conviction that he had done something far more excellent than write a business letter. A strange spirit took possession of him; so that, when Herr Elias Roos, who had now finished writing, addressed him in an angry tone, "Your childish folly might have cost me ten thousand marks," he replied louder and with more decision than was his habit, "Will your worship please not to behave in such an extraordinary way, else I will never write you another letter of advice so long as I live, and we will separate." Herr Elias pushed his wig right with both hands and stammered, as he stared hard at Traugott, "My estimable colleague, my dear, dear son, what proud words you are using!" The old gentleman again interposed, and a few words sufficed to restore perfect peace; and so they all went to Herr Elias's house to dinner, for he had invited the strangers home with him. Fair Christina received them in holiday attire, all clean and prim and proper; and soon she was wielding the excessively heavy silver soup-ladle with a practiced hand.

Whilst these five persons are sitting at table, I could, gracious reader, bring them pictorially before your eyes; but I shall only manage to give a few general outlines, and those certainly worse than the sketches which Traugott had the audacity to scribble in the inauspicious letter; for the meal will soon be over; and besides, I am urged by an impulse I cannot resist to go on with the remarkable history of the excellent Traugott, which I have undertaken to relate to you.

That Herr Elias Roos wears a round wig you already know from what has been stated above; and I have no need to add anything more; for after what he has said, you can now see the round little man with his liver-colored coat, waistcoat, and trousers, with gilt buttons, quite plainly before your eyes. Of Traugott I have a very great deal to say, because this is his history which I am telling, and so of course he occurs in it. If now it be true that a man's thoughts and feelings and actions, making their influence felt from within him outwards, so model and shape his bodily form as to give rise to that wonderful harmony of the whole man, that is not to be explained but only felt, which we call character, then my words will of themselves have already shown you Traugott himself in the flesh. If this is not the case, then all my gossip is wasted, and you may forthwith regard my story as unread. The two strangers are uncle and nephew, formerly retail dealers, but now merchants trading on their gains, and friends of Herr Elias Roos, that is to say, they had a good many business transactions together. They live at Königsberg, dress entirely in the English fashion, carry about with them a mahogany boot-jack which has come from London, possess considerable taste for art, and are, in a word, experienced, well-educated people. The uncle has a gallery of art objects and collects hand-sketches (witness the pilfered letter of advice).

But properly my chief business was to give you, kindly reader, a true and lifelike description of Christina; for her nimble person will, I observe, soon disappear; and it will be as well for me to get a few traits jotted down at once. Then she may willingly go! Picture to yourself a medium-sized stoutish female of from two to three and twenty years of age, with a round face, a short and rather turned-up nose, and friendly light-blue eyes, which smile most prettily upon everybody, saying, "I shall soon be married now." Her skin is dazzling white, her hair is not altogether of a too reddish tinge; she has lips which were certainly made to be kissed, and a mouth which, though indeed rather wide, she yet screws up small in some extraordinary way, but so as to display then two rows of pearly teeth. If we were to suppose that the flames from the next-door neighbor's burning house were to dart in at her chamber-window, she would make haste to feed the canary and lock up the clean linen from the wash, and then assuredly hasten down into the office and inform Herr Elias Roos that by that time his house also was on fire. She has never had an almond-cake spoilt, and her melted-butter always thickens properly, owing to the fact that she never stirs the spoon round towards the left, but always towards the right. But since Herr Elias Roos has poured out the last bumper of old French wine, I will only hasten to add that pretty Christina is uncommonly fond of Traugott because he is going to marry her; for what in the name of wonder should she do if she did not get married?

After dinner Herr Elias Roos proposed to his friends to take a walk on the ramparts. Although Traugott, whose mind had never been stirred by so many wonderful and extraordinary things as today, would very much have liked to escape the company, he could not contrive it; for, just as he was going out of the door, without having even kissed his betrothed's hand, Herr Elias caught him by the coat-tails, crying, "My honored son-in-law, my good colleague, but you're not going to leave us?" And so he had to stay.

A certain professor of physics once stated the theory that the *Anima Mundi*, or Spirit of the World, had, as a skillful experimentalist, constructed somewhere an excellent electric machine, and from it proceed certain very mysterious wires, which pass through the lives of us all; these we do our best to creep round and avoid, but at some moment or other we must tread upon them, and then there passes a flash and a shock through our souls, suddenly altering the forms of everything within them. Upon this thread Traugott must surely have trod in the moment that he was unconsciously sketching the two persons who stood in living shape behind him, for the singular appearance of the strangers had struck him with all the violence of a lightning-flash; and he now felt as if he had very clear conceptions of all those things which he had hitherto only dimly guessed at and dreamt about. The shyness which at other times had always fettered his tongue so soon as the conversation turned upon things which lay concealed like holy secrets at the bottom of his heart had now left him; and hence it was that, when the uncle attacked the curious half-painted, half-carved pictures in Arthur's Hall as wanting in taste, and then proceeded more particularly to

condemn the little pictures representing the soldiers as being
whimsical, Traugott boldly maintained that, although it was
very likely true that all these things did not harmonize with
the rules of good taste, nevertheless he had experienced, what
indeed several others had also experienced, viz., a wonderful
and fantastic world had been unfolded to him in Arthur's
Hall, and some few of the figures had reminded him in even
lifelike looks, nay, even in plain distinct words, that he also
was a great master, and could paint and wield the chisel as
well as the man out of whose unknown studio they themselves
had proceeded Herr Elias certainly looked more stupid than
usual whilst the young fellow was saying such grand things,
but the uncle made answer in a very malicious manner, "I
repeat once more, I do not comprehend why you want to be
a merchant, why you haven't rather devoted yourself altogether to art."

Traugott conceived an extreme repugnance to the man, and
accordingly he joined the nephew for the walk, and found
his manner very friendly and confidential. "O Heaven!" said
the latter, "how I envy you your beautiful and glorious talent!
I wish I could only sketch like you! I am not at all wanting
in genius; I have already sketched some deucedly pretty eyes
and noses and ears, aye, and even three or four entire heads;
— but, dash it all! the business, you know! the business!" "I
always thought," said Traugott, "that as soon as a man detected the spark of true genius — of a genuine love for art —
within him, he ought not to know anything about any other
business." "You mean he ought to be an artist!" rejoined the
nephew. "Ah! how can you say so? See you here, my estimable
friend! I have, I believe, reflected more upon these things than
many others; in fact, I am such a decided admirer of art, and
have gone into the real essential nature of the thing far deeper
than I am even able to express, and so I can only make use
of hints and suggestions." The nephew, as he expressed these
opinions, looked so learned and so profound that Traugott
really began to feel in awe of him. "You will agree with me,"
continued the nephew, after he had taken a pinch of snuff
and had sneezed twice, "you will agree with me that art
embroiders our life with flowers; amusement, recreation after
serious business — that is the praiseworthy end of all effort

in art; and the attainment of this end is the more perfect in proportion as the art products assume a nearer approach to excellence. This end is very clearly seen in life; for it is only the man who pursues art in the spirit I have just mentioned who enjoys comfort and ease; whilst these forever and eternally flee away from the man who, directly contrary to the nature of the case, regards art as a true end in itself — as the highest aim in life. And so, my good friend, don't take to heart what my uncle said to try and persuade you to turn aside from the serious business of life, and rely upon a way of employing your energies which, if without support, will only make you stagger about like a helpless child." Here the nephew paused as if expecting Traugott's reply; but Traugott did not know for the life of him what he ought to say. All that the nephew had said struck him as indescribably stupid talk. He contented himself with asking, "But what do you really mean by the serious business of life?" The nephew looked at him somewhat taken aback. "Well, by my soul, you can't help conceding to me that a man who is alive must live, and that's what your artist by profession hardly ever succeeds in doing, for he's always hard up." And he went on with a long rigmarole of bosh, which he clothed in fine words and stereotyped phrases. The end of it all appeared to be pretty much this — that by living he meant little else than having no debts but plenty of money, plenty to eat and drink, a beautiful wife, and also well-behaved children, who never got any grease-stains on their nice Sunday-clothes, and so on. This made Traugott feel a tightness in his throat, and he was glad when the clever nephew left him, and he found himself alone in his own room.

"What a wretched miserable life I lead, to be sure!" he soliloquised. "On beautiful mornings in the glorious golden spring-time, when into even the obscure streets of the town the warm west wind finds its way, and its faint murmurings and rustlings seem to be telling of all the wonders which are to be seen blooming in the woods and fields, then I have to crawl down sluggishly and in an ill-temper into Herr Elias Roos's smoke-begrimed office. And there sit pale faces before huge ugly-shaped desks; all are working on amidst gloomy silence, which is only broken by the rustle of leaves turned over in the big books, by the chink of money that is being counted, and by unintelligible sounds at odd intervals. And then again what work it is! What is the good of all this thinking and all this writing? Merely that the pile of gold pieces may increase in the coffers, and that the Fafnir's* treasure, which always brings mischief, may glitter and sparkle more and more! Oh, how gladly a painter or a sculptor must go out into the air, and with head erect imbibe all the refreshing influences of spring, until they people the inner world of his mind with beautiful images pulsing with glad and energetic life! Then from the dark bushes step forth wonderful figures, which his own mind has created, and which continue to be his own, for within him dwells the mysterious wizard power of light, of color, of form; hence he is able to give abiding shape to what he has seen with the eye of his mind, in that he represents it in a material substitute. What is there to prevent me tearing myself loose from this hated mode of life? That remarkable old man assured me that I am called to be an artist, and still more so did the nice handsome youth. For although he did not speak a word, it yet somehow struck me that his glance said plainly what I had for such a long time felt like a vague emotional pulsation within me, and what, oppressed by a multitude of doubts, has hitherto been unable to rise to the level of consciousness. Instead of going on in this miserable way, could I not make myself a good painter?"

Traugott took out all the things that he had ever drawn and examined them with critical eyes. Several things looked quite different today from what they had ever done before, and that not worse, but better. His attention was especially attracted by one of his childish attempts, of the time when he was quite a boy; it was a sketch of the old burgomaster and the handsome page, the outlines very much wanting in

---

* In Scandinavian mythology, Fafnir, the worm, became the owner of the treasure which his father, Hreidmar, had exacted as blood-money from Loki, because he had slain Hreidmar's son Otur, the sea-otter. This treasure Loki had taken by violence from its rightful owner, a dwarf, who in revenge prophesied that the possession of the treasure should henceforward be fraught with dire mischief to every successive owner of it.

firmness, of course, but nevertheless recognizable. And he remembered quite well that these figures had made a strange impression upon him even at that time, and how one evening at dusk they enticed him with such an irresistible power of attraction, that he had to leave his playmates and go into Arthur's Hall, where he took almost endless pains to copy the picture. The contemplation of this drawing filled him with a feeling of very deep yearning sadness. According to his usual habit, he ought to go and work a few hours in the office; but he could not do it; he went out to the Carlsberg* instead. There he stood and gazed out over the heaving sea, striving to decipher in the waves and in the grey misty clouds which had gathered in wonderful shapes over Hela,† as in a magic mirror, his own destiny in days to come.

Don't you too believe, kindly reader, that the sparks which fall into our hearts from the higher regions of Love are first made visible to us in the hours of hopeless pain? And so it is with the doubts that storm the artist's mind. He sees the Ideal and feels how impotent are his efforts to reach it; it will flee before him, he thinks, always unattainable. But then again he is once more animated by a divine courage; he strives and struggles, and his despair is dissolved into a sweet yearning, which both strengthens him and spurs him on to strain after his beloved idol, so that he begins to see it continually nearer and nearer, but never reaches it.

Traugott was now tortured to excess by this state of hopeless pain. Early next morning, on again looking over his drawings, which he had left lying on the table he thought them all paltry and foolish, and he now called to mind the oft-repeated words of one of his artistic friends, "A great deal of the mischief done by dabblers in art of moderate abilities arises from the fact that so many people take a somewhat keen superficial excitement for a real essential vocation to pursue art." Traugott felt strongly urged to look upon Arthur's Hall and his adventure with the two mysterious personages, the old man and the young one, for one of these states of superficial

---

*   A hill to the northwest of Dantzic, affording a splendid view of the Gulf of Dantzic.

†   A long narrow spit of land projecting from the coast at a point north of Dantzic in a south-southeast direction into the Gulf of Dantzic.

excitement; so he condemned himself to go back to the office again; and he worked so assiduously at Herr Elias Roos's, without heeding the disgust which frequently so far overcame him that he had to break off suddenly and rush off out into the open air. With sympathetic concern, Herr Elias Roos set this down to the indisposition which, according to his opinion, the fearfully pale young man must be suffering from.

Some time passed; Dominic's Fair* came, after which Traugott was to marry Christina and be introduced to the mercantile world as Herr Elias Roos's partner. This period he regarded as that of a sad leave-taking from all his high hopes and aspirations; and his heart grew heavy whenever he saw dear Christina as busy as a bee superintending the scrubbing and polishing that was going on everywhere in the middle story, folding curtains with her own hands, and giving the final polish to the brass pots and pans, &c.

One day, in the thick of the surging crowd of strangers in Arthur's Hall, Traugott heard close behind him a voice whose well-known tones made his heart jump. "And do you really mean to say that this stock stands at such a low figure?" Traugott whisked himself quickly round, and saw, as he had expected, the remarkable old man, who had appealed to a broker to get him to buy some stock, the price of which had at that moment fallen to an extremely low figure. Behind the old man stood the youth, who greeted Traugott with a friendly but melancholy smile. Then Traugott hastened to address the old man. "Excuse me, sir; the price of the stock which you are desirous of selling is really no higher than what you have been told; nevertheless, it may with confidence be anticipated that in a few days the price will rise considerably. If, therefore, you take my advice, you will postpone the conversion of your stock for a little time longer." "Eh! sir?" replied the old man rather coldly and roughly, "what have you to do with my business? How do you know that just now a silly bit of paper like this is of no use at all to me, whilst ready money is what I have great need of?" Traugott, not a little abashed because the old man had taken his well-meant intention in such ill part, was on the point of retiring, when

---

* August 4th.

the youth looked at him with tears in his eyes, as if in entreaty. "My advice was well meant, sir," he replied quickly; "I cannot suffer you to inflict upon yourself an important loss. Let me have your stock, but on the condition that I afterwards pay for it the higher price which it will be worth in a few day's time." "Well, you are an extraordinary man," said the old man. "Be it so then; although I can't understand what induces you to want to enrich me." So saying, he shot a keen flashing glance at the youth, who cast down his beautiful blue eyes in shy confusion. They both followed Traugott to the office, where the money was paid over to the old man, whose face was dark and sullen as he put it in his purse. Whilst he was doing so, the youth whispered softly to Traugott, "Are you not the gentleman who was sketching such pretty figures several weeks ago in Arthur's Hall?" "Certainly I am," replied Traugott, and he felt how the remembrance of the ridiculous episode of the letter of advice drove the hot blood into his face. "Oh then, I don't at all wonder," the youth was continuing, when the old man gave him an angry look, which at once made him silent. In the presence of these strangers Traugott could not get rid of a certain feeling of awkward constraint; and so they went away before he could muster courage enough to inquire further into their circumstances and mode of life.

In fact there was something so quite out of the ordinary in the appearance of these two persons that even the clerks and others in the office were struck by it. The surly book-keeper had stuck his pen behind his ear, and leaning on his arms, which he clasped behind his head, he sat watching the old man with keen glittering eyes. "God forgive me," he said when the strangers had left the office, "if he didn't look like an old picture of the year 1400 in St. John's parish church, with his curly beard and black mantle." Herr Elias set him down without more ado as a Polish Jew, notwithstanding his noble bearing and his extremely grave old-German face, and cried with a simper, "Silly fellow! sells his stock now; might make at least ten percent, more in a week." Of course he knew nothing about the additional price which had been agreed upon, and which Traugott intended to pay out of his own pocket. And this he really did do when some days later he again met the old man and the youth in Arthur's Hall.

The old man said, "My son has reminded me that you are an artist also, and so I will accept what I should have otherwise refused." They were standing close beside one of the four granite pillars which support the vaulted roof of the hall, and immediately in front of the two painted figures which Traugott had formerly sketched in the letter of advice. Without reserve he spoke of the great resemblance between these figures and the old man himself and the youth. The old man smiled a peculiar smile, and laying his hand on Traugott's shoulder, said in a low and deliberate tone, "Then you didn't know that I am the German painter Godofredus Berklinger, and that it was I who painted the pictures which seem to give you so much pleasure, a long time ago, whilst still a learner in art. That burgomaster I copied in commemoration of myself, and that the page who is leading the horse is my son you can of course very easily see by comparing the faces and figures of the two." Traugott was struck dumb with astonishment. But he very soon came to the conclusion that the old man, who took himself to be the artist of a picture more than two hundred years old must be laboring under some peculiar delusion. The old man went on, lifting up his head and looking proudly about him, "Aye, that was an artistic age if you like — glorious, vigorous, flourishing, when I decorated this hall with all these gay pictures in honor of the wise King Arthur and his Round Table. I verily believe that the tall stately figure who once came to me as I was working here, and exhorted me to go on and gain my mastership — for at that time I had not reached that dignity, — was King Arthur himself." Here the young man interposed, "My father is an artist, sir, who has few equals; and you would have no cause to be sorry if he would allow you to inspect his works." Meanwhile the old man was taking a turn through the hall, which had now become empty; he now called to the youth to go, and then Traugott begged him to show him his pictures. The old man fixed his eyes upon him and regarded him for some time with a keen and searching glance, and at length said with much gravity, "You are, I must say, rather audacious to be wanting to enter the inner shrine before you have begun your probationary years. But — be it so! If your eyes are still too dull to see, you may at least dimly feel. Come and see me early tomorrow morning," and he indicated where he lived. Next morning Traugott did not fail to get away from business early and hasten to the retired street where the remarkable old man lived. The youth, dressed in old-German style, opened the door to receive him and led him into a spacious room, in the center of which he found the old man sitting on a little stool in front of a large piece of outstretched grey primed canvas. "You have come exactly at the right time, sir," the old man cried by way of greeting, "for I have just put the finishing-touch to yon large picture, which has occupied me more than a year and cost me no small amount of trouble. It is the fellow of a picture of the same size, representing 'Paradise Lost,' which I completed last year and which I can also show you here. This, as you will observe, is 'Paradise Regained,' and I should be very sorry for you if you begin to put on critical airs and try to get some allegory out of it Allegorical pictures are only painted by duffers and bunglers; my picture is not to *signify* but to *be.* You perceive how all these varied groups of men and animals and fruits and flowers and stones unite to form one harmonic whole, whose loud and excellent music is the divinely pure chord of glorification."

And the old man began to dwell more especially upon the individual groups; he called Traugott's attention to the secrets of the division of light and shade, to the glitter of the flowers and the metals, to the singular shapes which, rising up out of the calyx of the lilies, entwined themselves about the forms of the divinely beautiful youths and maidens who were dancing to the strains of music, and he called his attention to the bearded men who, with all the strong pride of youth in their eyes and movements, were apparently talking to various kinds of curious animals. The old man's words, whilst they grew continually more emphatic, grew also continually more incomprehensible and confused. "That's right, old greybeard, let thy diamond crown flash and sparkle," he cried at last, riveting a fixed but fiery glance upon the canvas. "Throw off the Isis veil which thou didst put over thy head when the profane approached thee. What art thou folding thy dark robe so carefully over thy breast for? I want to see thy heart; that is the philosopher's stone through which the mystery is revealed. Art thou not I? Why dost thou put on such a bold and mighty air before me? Wilt thou contend with thy master? Thinkest thou that the ruby, thy heart, which sparkles so, can crush my breast? Up then — step forward — come here! I have created thee, for I am" — Here the old man suddenly fell on the floor like one struck by lightning. Whilst Traugott lifted him up, the youth quickly wheeled up a small armchair, into which they placed the old man, who soon appeared to have fallen into a gentle sleep.

"Now you know, my kind sir, what is the matter with my good old father," said the youth softly and gently. "A cruel destiny has stripped off all the blossoms of his life; and for several years past he has been insensible to the art for which he once lived. He spends days and days sitting in front of a piece of outstretched primed canvas, with his eyes fixed upon it in a stare; that he calls painting. Into what an overwrought condition the description of such a picture brings him, you have just seen for yourself. Besides this he is haunted by another unhappy thought, which makes my life to be a sad and agitated one; but I regard it as a fatality by which I am swept along in the same stream that has caught him. You would like something to help you to recover from this extraordinary scene; please follow me then into the adjoining room, where you will find several pictures of my father's early days, when he was still a productive artist."

And great was Traugott's astonishment to find a row of pictures apparently painted by the most illustrious masters of the Netherlands School. For the most part they represented scenes taken from real life; for example, a company returning from hunting, another amusing themselves with singing and playing, and such like subjects. They bore evidences of great thought, and particularly the expression of the heads, which were realized with especially vigorous lifelike power. Just as Traugott was about to return into the former room, he noticed another picture close beside the door, which held him fascinated to the spot. It was a remarkably pretty maiden dressed in old-German style, but her face was exactly like the youth's, only fuller and with a little more color in it, and she seemed to be somewhat taller too. A tremor of nameless delight ran through Traugott at the sight of this beautiful girl. In strength and vitality the picture was quite equal to anything by Van Dyk. The dark eyes were looking down upon Traugott with a soft yearning look, whilst her sweet lips appeared to be half opened ready to whisper loving words. "O heaven! Good heaven!" sighed Traugott with a sigh that came from the very bottom of his heart; "where — oh! where can I find her?" "Let us go," said the youth. Then Traugott cried in a sort of rapturous frenzy, "Oh! it is indeed she! — the beloved of my soul, whom I have so long carried about in my heart, but whom I only knew in vague stirrings of emotion. Where — oh! where is she?" The tears started from young Berklinger's eyes; he appeared to be shaken by a convulsive and sudden attack of pain, and to control himself with difficulty. "Come along," he at length said, in a firm voice, "that is a portrait of my unhappy sister Felicia.* She has gone forever. You will never see her."

Like one in a dream, Traugott suffered himself to be led into the other room. The old man was still sleeping; but all at once he started up, and staring at Traugott with eyes flashing with anger, he cried, "What do you want? What do you want, sir?" Then the youth stepped forward and reminded him that he had just been showing his new picture to Traugott, had he forgotten? At this Berklinger appeared to recollect all that had passed; it was evident that he was much affected; and he replied in an undertone, "Pardon an old man's forgetfulness, my good sir." "Your new piece is an admirable — an excellent work. Master Berklinger," Traugott proceeded; "I have never seen anything equal to it. I am sure it must cost a great deal of study and an immense amount of labor before a man can advance so far as to turn out a work like that. I discern that I have an inextinguishable propensity for art, and I earnestly entreat you, my good old master, to accept me as your pupil; you will find me industrious." The old man grew quite cheerful and amiable; and embracing

---

* The name in the text is *Felizitas* — Felicity; Felicia has been adopted in the translation as being the nearest approach to it. Felicity would in all probability be extremely strange to English ears, besides being liable to lead to ambiguities.

Traugott, he promised that he would be a faithful master to him.

Thus it came to pass that Traugott visited the old painter every day that came, and made very rapid progress in his studies. He now conceived an unconquerable disgust of business, and was so careless that Herr Elias Roos had to speak out and openly find fault with him; and finally he was very glad when Traugott kept away from the office altogether, on the pretext that he was suffering from a lingering illness. For this same reason the wedding, to Christina's no little annoyance, was indefinitely postponed. "Your Herr Traugott seems to be suffering from some secret trouble," said one of Herr Elias Roos's merchant-friends to him one day; "perhaps it's the balance of some old love-affair that he's anxious to settle before the wedding-day. He looks very pale and distracted." "And why shouldn't he then?" rejoined Herr Elias. "I wonder now," he continued after a pause, — "I wonder now if that little rogue Christina has been having words with him? My book-keeper — the love-smitten old ass — he is always kissing and squeezing her hand. Traugott's devilishly in love with my little girl, I know. Can there be any jealousy? Well, I'll sound my young gentleman."

But however carefully he sounded he could find no satisfactory bottom, and he said to his merchant-friend, "That Traugott is a most peculiar fellow; well, I must just let him go his own way; though if he had not fifty thousand thalers in my business I know what I should do, since now he never does a stroke of anything."

Traugott, absorbed in art, would now have led a real bright sunshiny life, had his heart not been torn with passionate love for the beautiful Felicia, whom he often saw in wonderful dreams. The picture had disappeared; the old man had taken it away; and Traugott durst not ask him about it without risk of seriously offending him. On the whole, old Berklinger continued to grow more confidential; and instead of taking any honorarium for his instruction, he permitted Traugott to help out his narrow house-keeping in many ways. From young Berklinger Traugott learned that the old man had been obviously taken in in the sale of a little cabinet, and that the stock which Traugott had realized for them was all that they had left of the price received for it, as well as all the money they possessed. But it was only seldom that Traugott was allowed to have any confidential conversation with the youth; the old man watched over him with the most singular jealousy, and at once scolded him sharply if he began to converse freely and cheerfully with their friend. This Traugott felt all the more painfully since he had conceived a deep and heartfelt affection for the youth, owing to his striking likeness to Felicia. Indeed he often fancied, when he stood near the young man, that he was standing beside the picture he loved so much, now alive and breathing, and that he could feel her soft breath on his cheek; and then he would like to have drawn the youth, as if he really were his darling Felicia herself, to his swelling heart.

Winter was past; beautiful spring was filling the woods and fields with brightness and blossoms. Herr Elias Roos advised Traugott either to drink whey for his health's sake or to go somewhere to take the baths. Fair Christina was again looking forward with joy to the wedding, although Traugott seldom showed himself — and thought still less of his relations with her.

Once Traugott was confined to the office the whole day long, making a requisite squaring up of his accounts, &c.; he had been obliged to neglect his meals, and it was beginning to get very dark when he reached Berklinger's remote dwelling. He found nobody in the first room, but from the one adjoining he heard the music of a lute. He had never heard the instrument there before. He listened; a song, from time to time interrupted, accompanied the music like a low soft sigh. He opened the door. O Heaven! with her back towards him sat a female figure, dressed in old-German style with a high lace ruff, exactly like the picture. At the noise which Traugott unavoidably made on entering, the figure rose, laid the lute on the table, and turned round. It was she, Felicia herself! "Felicia!" cried Traugott enraptured; and he was about to throw himself at the feet of his beloved divinity when he felt a powerful hand laid upon his collar behind, and himself dragged out of the room by someone with the strength of a giant. "You abandoned wretch! you incomparable villain!" screamed old Berklinger, pushing him on before him, "so that was your love for art? Do you mean to murder me?" And therewith he hurled him out at the door, whilst a knife glittered in his hand. Traugott flew downstairs and hurried back home stupefied; nay, half crazy with mingled delight and terror.

He tossed restlessly on his couch, unable to sleep. "Felicia! Felicia!" he exclaimed time after time, distracted with pain and the pangs of love. "You are there, you are there, and I may not see you, may not clasp you in my arms! You love me, oh yes! that I know. From the pain which pierces my breast so savagely I feel that you love me."

The morning sun shone brightly into Traugott's chamber; then he got up, and determined, let the cost be what it might, that he would solve the mystery of Berklinger's house. He hurried off to the old man's, but his feelings may not be described when he saw all the windows wide open and the maid-servants busy sweeping out the rooms. He was struck with a presentiment of what had happened. Berklinger had left the house late on the night before along with his son, and was gone nobody knew where. A carriage drawn by two horses had fetched away the box of paintings and the two little trunks which contained all Berklinger's scanty property. He and his son had followed half an hour later. All inquiries as to where they had gone remained fruitless: no livery-stable keeper had let out horses and carriage to persons such as Traugott described, and even at the town gates he could learn nothing for certain; — in short, Berklinger had disappeared as if he had flown away on the mantle* of Mephistopheles.

Traugott went back home prostrated by despair. "She is gone! She is gone! The beloved of my soul! All — all is lost!" Thus he cried as he rushed past Herr Elias Roos (for he happened to be just at that moment in the entrance hall) towards his own room. "God bless my soul!" cried Herr Elias, pulling and tugging at his wig. "Christina! Christina!" he shouted, till the whole house echoed. "Christina! You disgraceful girl! My good-for-nothing daughter!" The clerks and others in the office rushed out with terrified faces; the book-

---

* A mode of aërial conveyance made use of on occasion by the personage named, in the popular Faust legend.

keeper asked amazed, "But Herr Roos?" Herr Roos, however, continued to scream without stopping, "Christina! Christina!" At this point Miss Christina stepped in through the house-door, and raising her broad-brimmed straw-hat just a little and smiling, asked what her good father was bawling in this outrageous way for. "I strictly beg you will let such unnecessary running away alone," Herr Elias began to storm at her. "My son-in-law is a melancholy fellow and as jealous as a Turk. You'd better stay quietly at home, or else there'll be some mischief done. My partner is in there screaming and crying about his betrothed, because she will gad about so." Christina looked at the book-keeper astounded; but he gave a significant glance in the direction of the cupboard in the office where Herr Roos was in the habit of keeping his cinnamon water. "You'd better go in and console your betrothed," he said as he strode away. Christina went up to her own room, only to make a slight change in her dress, and give out the clean linen, and discuss with the cook what would have to be done about the Sunday roast-joint, and at the same time pick up a few items of town-gossip, then she would go at once and see what really was the matter with her betrothed.

You know, kindly, reader, that we all of us, when in Traugott's case, have to go through our appointed stages; we can't help ourselves. Despair is succeeded by a dull dazed sort of moody reverie, in which the crisis is wont to occur; and this then passes over into a milder pain, in which Nature is able to apply her remedies with effect.

It was in this stage of sad but beneficial pain that, some days later, Traugott again sat on the Carlsberg, gazing out as before upon the sea-waves and the grey misty clouds which had gathered over Hela; but he was not seeking as before to discover the destiny reserved for him in days to come; no, for all that he had hoped for, all that he had dimly dreamt of, had vanished. "Oh!" said he, "my call to art was a bitter, bitter deception. Felicia was the phantom who deluded me into the belief in that which never had any other existence but in the insane fancy of a fever-stricken mind. It's all over. I will give it all up, and go back — into my dungeon. I have made up my mind; I will go back." Traugott again went back to his work in the office, whilst the wedding-day with Christina was once more fixed. On the day before the wedding was to come off, Traugott was standing in Arthur's Hall, looking, not without a good deal of heart-rending sadness, at the fateful figures of the old burgomaster and his page, when his eye fell upon the broker to whom Berklinger was trying to sell his stock. Without pausing to think, almost mechanically in fact, he walked up to him and asked, "Did you happen to know the strikingly curious old man with the black curly beard who some time ago frequently used to be seen here along with a handsome youth?" "Why, to be sure I did," answered the broker; "that was the crack-brained old painter Gottfried Berklinger." "Then don't you know where he has gone to and where he is now living?" asked Traugott again. "Aye, that I do," replied the broker; "he has now for a long time been living quietly at Sorrento along with his daughter." "With his daughter Felicia?" asked Traugott so vehemently and so loudly that everybody turned round to look at him. "Why, yes," went on the broker calmly, "that was, you know, the pretty youth who always followed the old man about everywhere. Half Dantzic knew that he was a girl, notwithstanding that the crazy old fellow thought there was not a single soul could guess it. It had been prophesied to him that if his daughter were ever to get married he would die a shameful death; and accordingly he determined never to let anybody know anything about her, and so he passed her off everywhere as his son." Traugott stood like a statue; then he ran off through the streets — away out of the town-gates — into the open country, into the woods, loudly lamenting, "Oh! miserable wretch that I am! It was she — she, herself; I have sat beside her scores and hundreds of times — have breathed her breath — pressed her delicate hands — looked into her beautiful eyes — heard her sweet words — and now I have lost her! No; not lost I will follow her into the land of art. I acknowledge the finger of destiny. Away — away to Sorrento."

He hurried back home. Herr Elias Roos got in his way; Traugott laid hold of him and carried him along with him into the room. "I shall never marry Christina, never!" he screamed. "She looks like *Voluptas* (Pleasure) and *Luxuries* (Wantonness), and her hair is like that of *Ira* (Wrath), in the picture in Arthur's Hall. O Felicia! Felicia! My beautiful darling! Why do you stretch out your arms so longingly towards me? I am coming, I am coming. And now let me tell you, Herr Elias," he continued, again laying hold of the pale merchant, "you will never see me in your damned office again. What do I care for your cursed ledgers and day-books? I am a painter, aye, and a good painter too. Berklinger is my master, my father, my all, and you are nothing — nothing at all." And therewith he gave Herr Elias a good shaking. Herr Elias, however, began to shout at the top of his voice, "Help! help! Come here, folks! Help! My son-in-law's gone mad. My partner's in a raging fit Help! help!" Everybody came running out of the office. Traugott had released his hold upon Elias and now sank down exhausted in a chair. They all gathered round him; but when he suddenly leapt to his feet and cried with a wild look, "What do you all want?" they all hurried off out of the room in a string, Herr Elias in the middle.

Soon afterwards there was a rustling of a silk dress, and a voice asked, "Have you really gone crazed, my dear Herr Traugott, or are you only jesting?" It was Christina. "I am not the least bit crazed, my angel," replied Traugott, "nor is it one whit truer that I am jesting. Pray compose yourself, my dear, but our wedding won't come off tomorrow; I shall never marry you, neither tomorrow, nor at any other time." "There is not the least need of it," said Christina very calmly. "I have not been particularly pleased with you for some time, and someone I know will value it far differently if he may only lead home as his bride the rich and pretty Miss Christina Roos. Adieu!" Therewith she rustled off. "She means the book-keeper," thought Traugott. As soon as he had calmed down somewhat he went to Herr Elias and explained to him in convincing terms that he need not expect to have him either as his son-in-law or as his partner in the business. Herr Elias reconciled himself to the inevitable; and repeated with downright honest joy in the office again and again that he thanked God to have got rid of that crazy-headed Traugott — even after the latter was a long, long way distant from Dantzic.

On at length arriving at the longed-for country, Traugott found a new life awaiting him, bright and brilliant. At Rome he was introduced to the circle of the German colony of painters and shared in their studies. Thus it came to pass that he stayed there longer than would seem to have been permissible in the face of his longing to find Felicia again, by which he had hitherto been so restlessly urged onwards. But his longing was now grown weaker; it shaped itself in his heart like a fascinating dream, whose misty shimmer enveloped his life on all sides, so that he believed that all he did and thought, and all his artistic practice, were turned towards the higher supernatural regions of blissful intuitions. All the female figures which his now experienced artistic skill enabled him to create bore lovely Felicia's features. The young painters were greatly struck by the exquisitely beautiful face, the original of which they in vain sought to find in Rome; they overwhelmed Traugott with multitudes of questions as to where he had seen the beauty. Traugott however was very shy of telling of his singular adventure in Dantzic, until at last, after the lapse of several months, an old Königsberg friend, Matuszewski by name, who had come to Rome to devote himself entirely to art, declared joyfully that he had seen there — in Rome, the girl whom Traugott copied in all his pictures. Traugott's wild delight may be imagined. He no longer concealed what it was that had attracted him so strongly to art, and urged him on with such irresistible power into Italy; and his Dantzic adventure proved so singular and so attractive that they all promised to search eagerly for the lost loved one.

Matuszewski's efforts were the most successful. He had soon found out where the girl lived, and discovered moreover that she really was the daughter of a poor old painter, who just at that period was busy putting a new coat on the walls of the church Trinita del Monte. All these things agreed nicely. Traugott at once hastened to the church in question along with Matuszewski; and in the painter, whom he saw working up on a very high scaffolding, he really thought he recognized old Berklinger. Thence the two friends hurried off to the old man's dwelling, without having been noticed by him. "It is she," cried Traugott, when he saw the painter's daughter standing on the balcony, occupied with some sort of feminine work. "Felicia, my Felicia!" he exclaimed aloud in his joy, as he burst into the room. The girl looked up very much alarmed. She had Felicia's features; but it was not Felicia. In his bitter disappointment poor Traugott's wounded heart was rent as if from innumerable dagger-thrusts. In a few words Matuszewski explained all to the girl. In her pretty shy confusion, with her cheeks deep crimson, and her eyes cast down upon the ground, she made a marvelously attractive picture to look at; and Traugott, whose first impulse had been quickly to retire, nevertheless, after casting but a single pained glance at her, remained standing where he was, as though held fast by silken bonds. His friend was not backward in saying all sorts of complimentary things to pretty Dorina, and so helped her to recover from the constraint and embarrassment into which she had been thrown by the extraordinary manner of their entrance. Dorina raised the "dark fringed curtains of her eyes" and regarded the stranger with a sweet smile, and said that her father would soon come home from his work, and would be very pleased to see some German painters, for he esteemed them very highly. Traugott was obliged to confess that, exclusive of Felicia, no girl had ever excited such a warm interest in him as Dorina did. She was in fact almost a second Felicia; the only differences were that Dorina's features seemed to him less delicate and more sharply cut, and her hair was darker. It was the same picture, only painted by Raphael instead of by Rubens.

It was not long before the old gentleman came in; and Traugott now plainly saw that he had been greatly misled by the height of the scaffolding in the church, on which the old man had stood. Instead of his being the strong Berklinger, he was a thin, mean-looking little old man, timid and crushed by poverty. A deceptive accidental light in the church had given his clean-shaved chin an appearance similar to Berklinger's black curly beard. In conversing about art matters the old man unfolded considerable ripe practical knowledge; and Traugott made up his mind to cultivate his acquaintance; for though his introduction to the family had been so painful, their society now began to exercise a more and more agreeable influence upon him.

Dorina, the incarnation of grace and childlike ingenuousness, plainly allowed her preference for the young German painter to be seen. And Traugott warmly returned her affection. He grew so accustomed to the society of the pretty child (she was but fifteen), that he often spent the whole day with the little family; his studio he transferred to the spacious apartment which stood empty next their rooms; and finally he established himself in the family itself. Hence he was able of his prosperity to do much in a delicate way to relieve their straitened circumstances; and the old man could not very well think otherwise than that Traugott would marry Dorina; and he even said so to him without reservation. This put Traugott in no little consternation: for he now distinctly recollected the object of his journey, and perceived where it seemed likely to end. Felicia again stood before his eyes instinct with life; but, on the other hand, he felt that he could not leave Dorina. His vanished darling he could not, for some extraordinary reason, conceive of as being his wife. She was pictured in his imagination as an intellectual vision, that he could neither lose nor win. Oh! to be immanent in his beloved intellectually forever! never to have her and own her physically! But Dorina was often in his thoughts as his dearly loved wife; and as often as he contemplated the idea of again binding himself in the indissoluble bonds of betrothal,* he felt a delicious tremor run through him and a gentle warmth pervade his veins; and yet he regarded it as unfaithfulness to his first love. Thus Traugott's heart was the scene of contest between the most contradictory feelings; he could not make up his mind what to do. He avoided the old painter; and *he* accordingly feared Traugott intended to receive his dear child. He had moreover already spoken of Traugott's wedding as a settled thing; and it was only under this impression that he had tolerated Dorina's familiar intimacy with Traugott, which otherwise would have given the girl an ill name. The blood of the Italian boiled within him, and one day he roundly declared to Traugott that he must either marry Dorina or leave him, for he would not tolerate this familiar intercourse an hour longer. Traugott was tormented by the keenest annoyance as well as by the bitterest vexation. The old man he viewed in the light of a vile matchmaker; his own actions and behavior were contemptible; and that he had ever deserted Felicia he

---

* In Germany the betrothal is a more significant act than in England, and by some regarded as more sacred and binding than the actual marriage ceremony.

now judged to be sinful and abominable. His heart was sore wounded at parting from Dorina; but with a violent effort he tore himself free from the sweet bonds. He hastened away to Naples, to Sorrento.

He spent a whole year in making the strictest inquiries after Berklinger and Felicia; but all was in vain; nobody knew anything about them. The sole gleam of intelligence that he could find was a vague sort of presumption, which was founded merely upon the tradition that an old German painter had been seen in Sorrento several years before — and that was all. After being driven backwards and forwards like a boat on the restless sea, Traugott at length came to a stand in Naples; and in proportion as his industry in art pursuits again awakened, the longing for Felicia which he cherished in his bosom grew softer and milder. But he never saw any pretty girl, if she was the least like Dorina in figure, movement, or bearing, without feeling most bitterly the loss of the dear sweet child. Yet when he was painting he never thought of Dorina, but always of Felicia; she continued to be his constant ideal.

At length he received letters from his native town. Herr Elias Roos had departed this life, his business agent wrote, and Traugott's presence was required in order to settle matters with the book-keeper, who had married Miss Christina and undertaken the business. Traugott hurried back to Dantzic by the shortest route.

Again he was standing in Arthur's Hall, leaning against the granite pillar, opposite the burgomaster and the page; he dwelt upon the wonderful adventure which had had such a painful influence upon his life; and, a prey to deep and hopeless sadness, he stood and looked with a set fixed gaze upon the youth, who greeted him with living eyes, as it were, and whispered in a sweet and charming voice, "And so you could not desert me then after all?"

"Can I believe my eyes? Is it really your own respected self come back again safe and sound, and quite cured of your unpleasant melancholy?" croaked a voice near Traugott. It was the well-known broker. "I have not found her," escaped Traugott involuntarily. "Whom do you mean? Whom has your honor not found?" asked the broker. "The painter

Godofredus Berklinger and his daughter Felicia," rejoined Traugott. "I have searched all Italy for them; not a soul knew anything about them in Sorrento." This made the broker open his eyes and stare at him, and he stammered, "Where do you say you have searched for Berklinger and Felicia? In Italy? in Naples? in Sorrento?" "Why, yes; to be sure," replied Traugott, very testily. Whereupon the broker struck his hands together several times in succession, crying as he did so, "Did you ever now? Did you ever hear tell of such a thing? But Herr Traugott! Herr Traugott!" "Well, what is there to be so much astonished at?" rejoined Traugott, "don't behave in such a foolish fashion, pray. Of course a man will travel as far as Sorrento for his sweetheart's sake. Yes, yes; I loved Felicia and followed her." But the broker skipped about on one foot, and continued to say, "Well, now, did you ever? did you ever?" until Traugott placed his hand earnestly upon his arm and asked, "Come, tell me then, in heaven's name! what is it that you find so extraordinary?" The broker began, "But, my good Herr Traugott, do you mean to say you don't know that Herr Aloysius Brandstetter, our respected town-councilor and the senior of our guild, calls his little villa, in that small fir-wood at the foot of Carlsberg, in the direction of Conrad's Hammer, by the name of Sorrento? He bought Berklinger's pictures of him and took the old man and his daughter into his house, that is, out to Sorrento. And there they lived for several years; and if you, my respected Herr Traugott, had only gone and planted your own two feet on the middle of the Carlsberg, you could have had a view right into the garden, and could have seen Miss Felicia walking about there dressed in curious old-German style, like the women in those pictures — there was no need for you to go to Italy. Afterwards the old man — but that is a sad story" "Never mind; go on," said Traugott, hoarsely. "Yes," continued the broker. "Young Brandstetter came back from England, saw Miss Felicia, and fell in love with her. Coming unexpectedly upon the young lady in the garden, he fell upon his knees before her in romantic fashion, and swore that he would wed her and deliver her from the tyrannical slavery in which her father kept her. Close behind the young people, without their having observed it, stood the old man; and the very self-same moment in which Felicia said, 'I will be yours,' he fell down with a stifled scream, and was dead as a door nail. It's said he looked very very hideous — all blue and bloody, because he had by some inexplicable means burst an artery. After that Miss Felicia could not bear young Brandstetter at all, and at last she married Mathesius, criminal and aulic counselor, of Marienwerder. Your honor, as an old flame, should go and see the *Frau Kriminalräthin*. Marienwerder is not so far, you know, as your real Italian Sorrento. The good lady is said to be very comfortable and to have enriched the world with divers children."

Silent and crushed, Traugott hastened from the Hall. This issue of his adventure filled him with awe and dread. "No, it is not she — it is not she!" he cried. "It is not Felicia, that divine image which enkindled an infinite longing in my bosom, whom I followed into yon distant land, seeing her before me everywhere where I went like my star of fortune, twinkling and glittering with sweet hopes. Felicia — *Kriminalräthin* Mathesius! Ha! Ha! Ha! — *Kriminalräthin* Mathesius!" Traugott, shaken by extreme sensations of misery, laughed aloud and hastened in his usual way through the Oliva Gate along the Langfuhr* to the Carlsberg. He looked down into Sorrento, and the tears gushed from his eyes. "Oh!" he cried, "Oh! how deep, how incurably deep an injury, O thou eternal ruling Power, does thy bitter irony inflict upon poor man's soft heart! But no, no! But why should the child cry over the incurable pain when instead of enjoying the light and warmth he thrusts his hand into the flames? Destiny visibly laid its hand upon me, but my dimmed vision did not recognize the higher nature at work; and I had the presumption to delude myself with the idea that the forms, created by the old master and mysteriously awakened to life, which stepped down to meet me, were my own equals, and that I could draw them down into the miserable transitoriness of earthly existence. No, no, Felicia, I have never lost you; you are and will be mine forever, for you yourself are the creative artistic power dwelling within me. Now, — and only now have I first come

---

* A suburb of Dantzic, on the N.W., 3½ miles nearer than Carlsberg; it is connected with the city by a double avenue of fine limes.

to know you. What have you — what have I to do with the *Kriminalräthin* Mathesius? I fancy, nothing at all."

"Neither did I know what you should have to do with her, my respected Herr Traugott," a voice broke in. Traugott awakened out of his dream. Strange to say, he found himself, without knowing how he got there, again leaning against the granite pillar in Arthur's Hall. The person who had spoken the abovementioned words was Christina's husband. He handed to Traugott a letter that had just arrived from Rome. Matuszewski wrote: —

"Dorina is prettier and more charming than ever, only pale with longing for you, my dear friend. She is expecting you every hour, for she is most firmly convinced that you could never be untrue to her. She loves you with all her heart. When shall we see you again?"

"I am very pleased that we settled all our business this morning," said Traugott to Christina's husband after he had read this, "for tomorrow I set out for Rome, where my bride is most anxiously longing for me."

END OF VOLUME I

www.ingramcontent.com/pod-product-compliance
Lightning Source LLC
Chambersburg PA
CBHW030351020726
47493CB00003B/776